FIRE

(Book 2 of the Kalima Chronicles)

By Aiki Flinthart

2019

Thank you to the readers who have enjoyed my other books enough to leave nice reviews and to let me know. Because of you, I keep writing.

To Rob Porteous for spotting the plot hole before this was published. Thankyou!

And...as always...thanks to my husband for his patience and encouragement. Seriously. Patient. Unbelievably patient.

FIRE

Cover artwork by Croco Design
Copyright © 2019 Aiki Flinthart

A Cataloging-in-Publications entry for this title is available from the National Library of Australia.

ISBN-13: 978-0-6482878-8-9 (Trade Paperback)
ISBN-13: 978-0-6482878-7-2 (e-book)
Computing Advantages & Training P/L
PO Box 3388, Darra
QLD 4076, Australia

Discover other titles by Aiki Flinthart
at: **www.aikiflinthart.com**
Including:

The Ruadhan Sidhe Novels (YA Urban Fantasy)
Shadows Wake (#1)
Shadows Bane (#2)
Shadows Fate (#3)

The 80AD series (YA Adventure/Fantasy)
80AD Book 1: *The Jewel of Asgard*
80AD Book 2: *The Hammer of Thor*
80AD Book 3: *The Tekhen of Anuket*
80AD Book 4: *The Sudarshana*
80AD Book 5: *The Yu Dragon*

The Kalima Chronicles (YA Adventure/Fantasy)
IRON (#1)
FIRE (#2)
STEEL (#3)

Sold! (Contemporary Romance/Adventure)

Short Story Anthologies
Return
Like a Woman

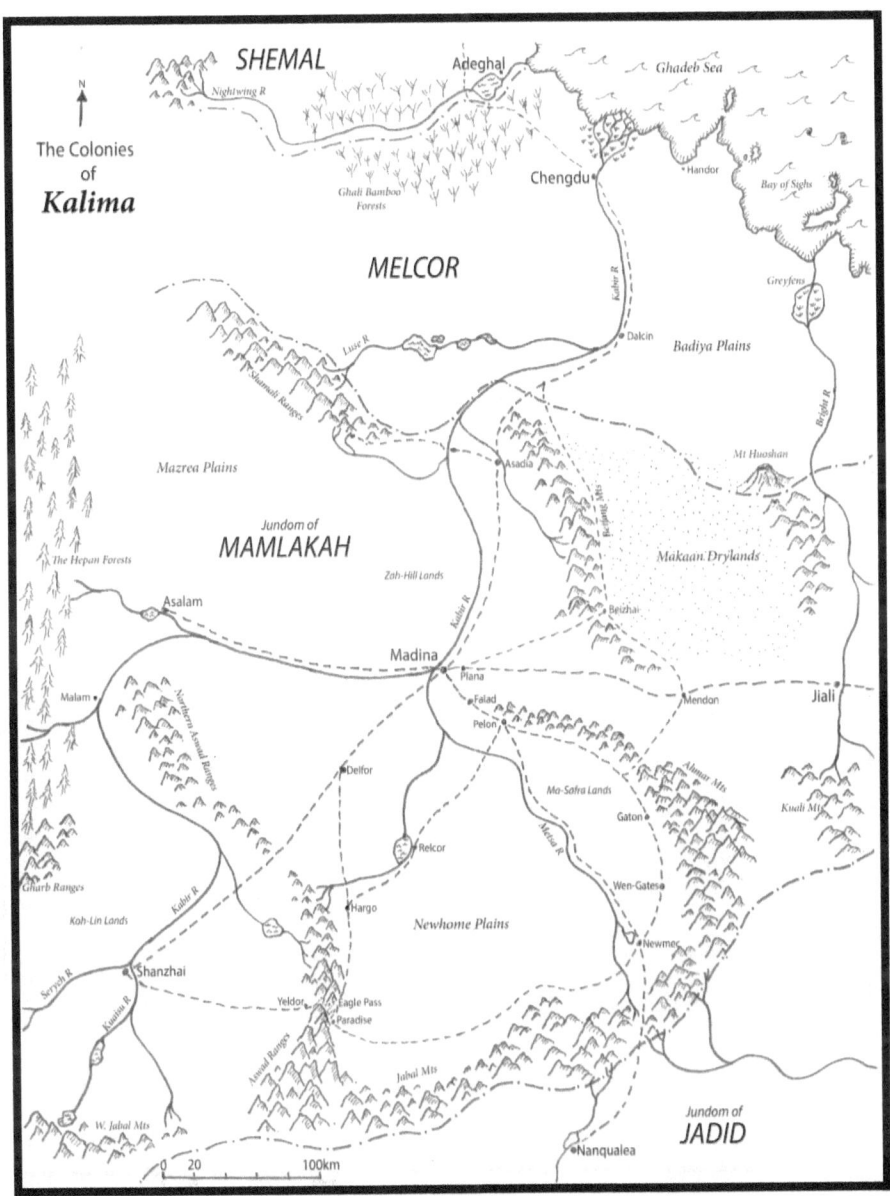

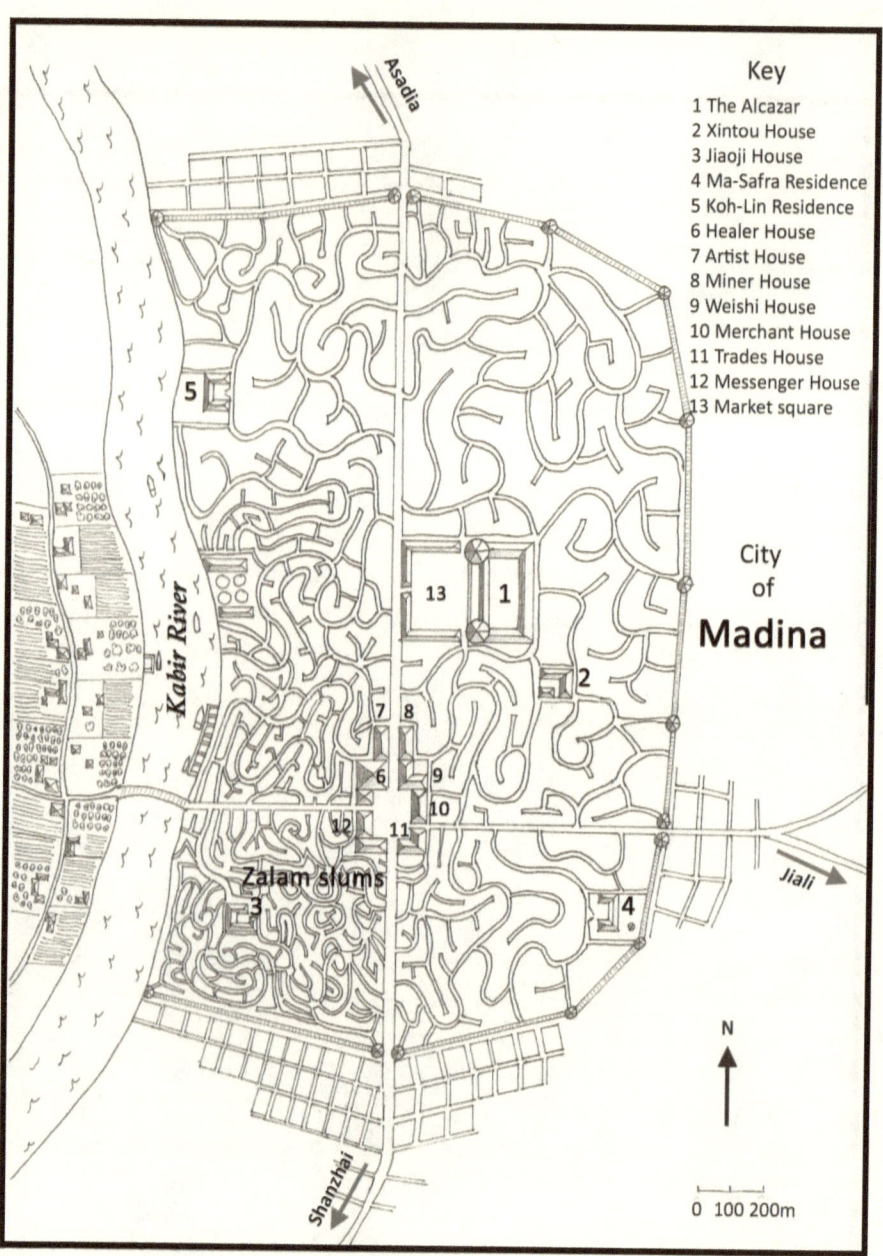

Key

1 The Alcazar
2 Xintou House
3 Jiaoji House
4 Ma-Safra Residence
5 Koh-Lin Residence
6 Healer House
7 Artist House
8 Miner House
9 Weishi House
10 Merchant House
11 Trades House
12 Messenger House
13 Market square

City
of
Madina

Asadia

Kabir River

Zalam slums

Shanzhai

Jiali

N

0 100 200m

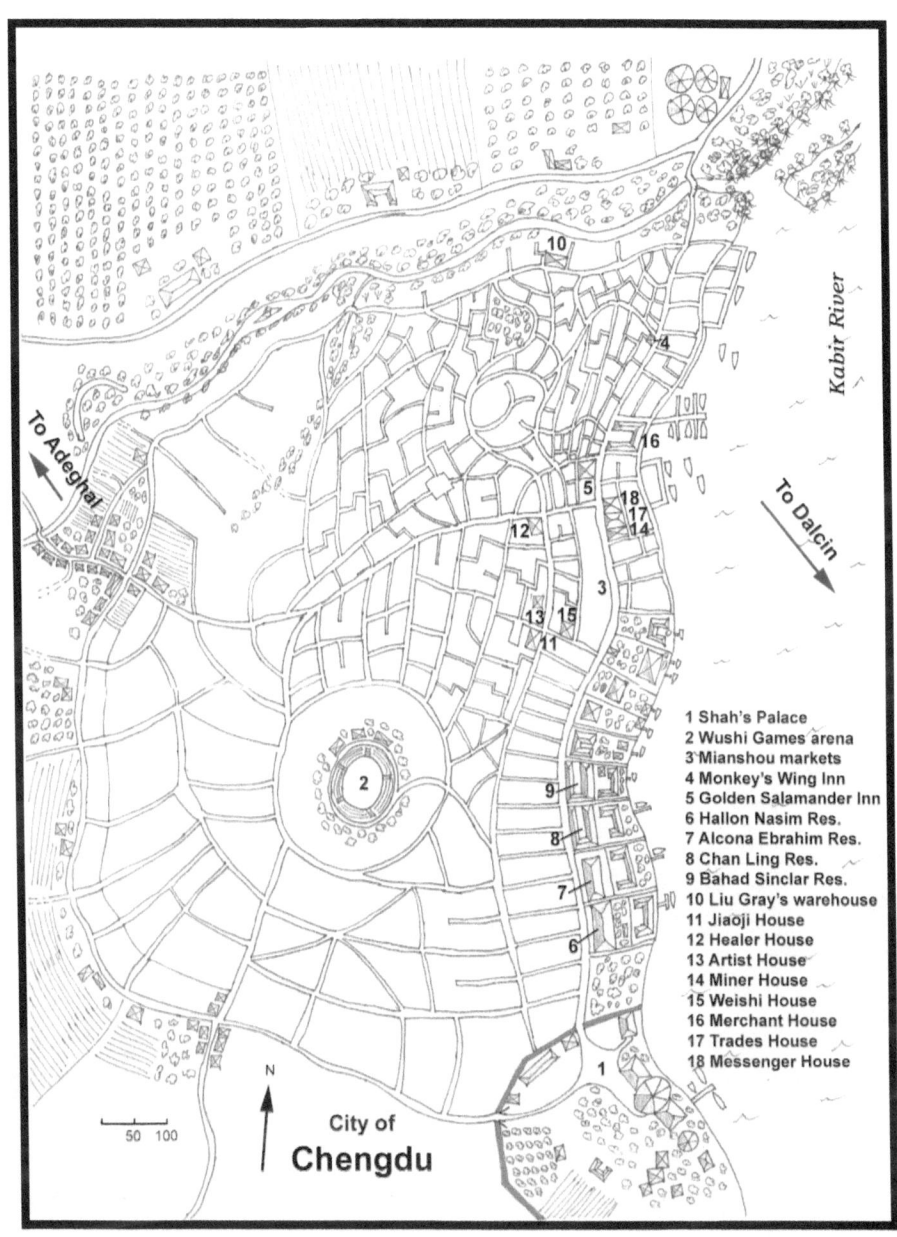

1 Shah's Palace
2 Wushi Games arena
3 Mianshou markets
4 Monkey's Wing Inn
5 Golden Salamander Inn
6 Hallon Nasim Res.
7 Alcona Ebrahim Res.
8 Chan Ling Res.
9 Bahad Sinclar Res.
10 Liu Gray's warehouse
11 Jiaoji House
12 Healer House
13 Artist House
14 Miner House
15 Weishi House
16 Merchant House
17 Trades House
18 Messenger House

City of
Chengdu

FIRE

Aiki Flinthart 2019

Part I

CHAPTER ONE

ALERE

Freedom was a state of mind, as much as a state of being.

Alere leaned on the *Kuailong*'s gunwale and raised her face to the star-spattered sky, welcoming the night's ice-sharp emptiness; revelling in a moment of respite after the last week of war and destruction.

The calm solitude wouldn't last. The liberty she had hoped for when she left Madina had been a rebellious child's dream. She was bound, now, by the iron chains of privilege to an inescapable path. She smiled wryly and straightened. Only a shazi would complain about choosing to live a life of luxury as Jun-Heir to the second-most powerful man in Mamlakah.

Alere glanced south, towards Shanzhai city, but there was little to be seen. Around the anchored chuan, the deep river gorge lay shadowed and silent, hoary with frost.

Overhead, Luna-Yi's red crescent washed watered-blood light over pale pockets of snow that clung to rocks and branches. Bare twigs of winter-stripped trees scratched at the sky's black-sapphire expanse. Night-shadows slipped across the deck, dancing to the wind's whistling and the chuan's gentle creaking.

This… Alere sucked a deep breath. The clean scent of snow and ice cleared her nose and honed her wits. Her eyes watered in the thin air. She sighed and her breath billowed, cloaking the world in the fog of her resignation.

The adventure, the freedom…this she would miss.

But the iron ties that chained her to Shanzhai were her choice.

Most of them. Alere stared down at the Kabir River's black-silk waters and ran her thumb over the faintly-glimmering yanstone embedded in her steel dagger's pommel. As always, the silver-gilt lure of her twin sister's mind pulled at her. Mina had left Shanzhai because of Alere's choices.

She shook her head and pushed uncertainty aside. She had done the right thing. The important thing. Her conscience should be clear. When this was all over, she would find a way to live her own life. Come to terms with the deaths she'd caused.

No, the murders.

But, for now, it was more important to focus on catching up with Mina – and Rohne Marin-Kin.

Regret was the killer of confidence and imagining what-might-have-been was time wasted.

The danger to Mina was real; here and now.

She smoothed her thumb over the yanstones again. Warm reassurance oozed into her body, easing the tension that was her constant companion since Mina had left Shanzhai city four days before. There was nothing she could do to find her twin right now. In the east, the weak orange winter-sun was merely a glow behind the Aswad Ranges' sharp teeth. Perhaps, as the old saying went, morning would bring light into darkness.

Dawn wasn't far off and they would get underway soon. The chuanzhu, Dalor Khan, had ordered the *Kuailong* tied for the night, close to shore, in a quiet section of the Kabir River. Even by day, the tumbling white-jade waters were winter-shallow and treacherous with exposed rocks. Night travel was impossible, which meant frustrating delays in catching up with the chuan carrying Mina and Rohne.

If Mina was caught and recognised before the new rulings legalising kin-children were made public, she would be executed. Or held hostage as proof that Alere was not who she pretended to be. That her Jun Second father, Rafi Koh-Lin, had lied to the twenty other Juns who ruled Mamlakah. And that could plunge Mamlakah into the very war Alere had fought so hard to prevent.

So why had Rohne taken Mina away from Shanzhai? He must have understood the danger. What made him leave on the eve of the battle against Hanna Zah-Hill?

There were too many unanswered questions.

They kept Alere awake at night. Those and the nightmares. Even the rhythmic sloshing of water against the chuan's magnal alloy hull wasn't enough to dampen the dreams of fire and death.

Had she freed the whole Jundom of Mamlakah only to imprison herself in regrets? And a life of servitude as Jun-Heir to her Jun Second father, Rafi? Was that the result Mistress Li of Xintou House had intended when she advised choosing the important over personal desires? She had set Alere's feet on the path to prevent war. But had she truly wanted Alere to kill Ven Zah-Hill – Jun First of Mamlakah – and his Bonded Xintou-telepath?

With a growl, Alere sheathed the yanstone-and-steel dagger. Who knew what Mistress Li thought or intended? She had been leader of Xintou House and the power behind the Jun First throne forever, espousing stability at all costs.

At any cost, apparently.

Only time would dull the memory of Jun First Ven Zah-Hill's death at Alere's hand; by her blade. Until then, she'd have to bear with the nightmares – like those that had driven her from her warm bed tonight.

Cold prickled across her skin. She was a shazi for leaving her cloak and boots in her cabin. She shoved unruly dark hair back from her face and rubbed briskly at her arms.

She touched the yanstones again. Warmth slipped under skin, through muscles, and she relaxed. But a familiar compulsion to find Mina surged immediately after, stronger than before, leaving the taste of iron and smoke on her tongue. Alere paced the small upper deck. She tried to reach Mina's thoughts, but her twin sister was too far away, and too deeply asleep.

A buzz of insect wings made her duck and cover her ears. Nightwings. Three, each with a wingspan as wide as her arms, circling the chuan in an intricate tri-gender mating dance. It wasn't yet egg-laying season, but they were still capable of delivering a nasty sting. They buzzed past again, only visible by the faint silver luminescence streaking their undersides. She watched warily, dagger drawn.

They darted downstream, chasing each other in a dizzying display of aerobatics.

Past another chuan.

Alere straightened, squinting in the half-light, trying to make out any identifying marks. What was another chuan doing on this part of the river? It lay, dark and silent, only a hundred or so paces downriver. Was it a wreck? Should she rouse the crew to give aid?

Rafi had spent two days and a staggering number of iron coins convincing Chuanzhu Dalor Khan to risk his new vessel, the *Kuailong,* on the Kabir in winter. With the low water levels, floating ice and winter storms, Dalor's shallow-drafted chuan with its tough, light magnal hull was the only one left in Shanzhai that could make the trip to Madina.

Could the vessel ahead be Rohne and Mina's? No. They'd left four days before on a chuan marked with Shanzhai's green dragon. The same one that carried Jarran Zah-Hill, the new Jun First, to Madina. This one seemed to have a salamander emblem. The symbol for the Jundom of Melcor, to the north. The name was difficult to make out in the gloom. The *Nasir.* A type of scavenger bird. What was a Melcori vessel doing so far upriver? A few portaged overland from Madina to Shanzhai each year and sailed back to Melcor with trade goods, but Dalor said they'd all left two weeks before.

Alere frowned. Where was Dalor's watchman? He should have sounded the alert with a vessel that close. It must have been there a while, so perhaps he hadn't seen it in the dark. She checked the lower deck and swore softly.

A body lay crumpled on the pale bamboo surface. Eight figures prowled the lower deck. They moved with smooth stealth and carried long, sinuous daggers that gleamed in the half-light. Headed for the door leading to the sleeping quarters. Too many to take on by herself. Her fingers and bare toes were numb with cold. Her limbs stiff. And she had stupidly left her alzin armour stored under the bunk in her cabin, along with her bow and throwing knives.

'Jiche!' Alere crouched out of sight. She laid her hands on the yanstones in her weapons. The stones' silver-gilt warmth engulfed her mind. The taste of iron and smoke filled her mouth. She stretched her thoughts out, seeking her companions belowdecks.

Kett slept. Trained in Weishi House and in Xintou House, her former weishi-bodyguard's mind was too well-warded to breach. Rafi, and Corin Johnston, were the same. Hardly surprising as her father and her father's spymaster had also been trained by xintou-telepaths to ward their thoughts.

Only Gavon Abdul-kin, yongbing-mercenary, was unwarded.

She swore again. He would hate the intrusion but there was no helping it.

Gavon! Wake up. We're boarded.

He snapped awake like the experienced warrior he was. She repeated the warning. Without wasting time on questions, he roused the others.

Corin was then simple to find: an intensity of energy, intelligence, and life-joy. He was still drowsy, his waking-wards not yet complete.

Cor?

His Outer wards slammed into place, shielding his mind and sending her reeling. She blinked and tried again. He relaxed and let her in.

Alere? Gaisi! You scared me, woman. Voices in your head is a sign of insanity.

Then keep your wards up. She was acerbic, shaken by the force of his rejection. *I'm on the upper deck. There's a chuan downstream. Melcori markings. There are eight men on the lower deck. Not sure how many more. Take Gavon through the access hatch in the cabin, down to crewquarters. Wake them. Send Kett and Rafi to Dalor's cabin. They can climb out through his windows and stand with me. Tell Kett to bring my bow.*

Done. His reply was unhesitating. *Stay hidden until we get there.*

She basked in the mental equivalent of a blown kiss as they parted.

There was nowhere to hide, though. Any moment the dawnlight would be bright enough to reveal her position. She was better off taking a stand at the top of the stairs. Hopefully they didn't have bows.

Holding the sword sheath so it wouldn't clatter against the deck, she half-crawled alongside the gunwale and put her back against the solid railing close to the stairs.

The first head appeared. She waited until his foot was on the deck.

She rose, drew her steel and drove it to the hilt through his alzin vest. A scream burst from his lips. She swore and thrust him ungracefully backward, into his companions. His shout echoed off the river gorge's high, black-rock walls and spawned copies from the mouths of the other boarders.

Trapdoors flew open on the lower deck. Corin, Gavon, and Dalor's crew spilled from every possible opening at once. The clash of steel, ceramic, and bronze ricocheted. A clamour of voices rose, filling the narrow valley with unintelligible sound. An arrow arced over from the Melcori chuan. It scythed through the brightening sky to land less than a pace from Corin's feet, where he fought on the lower deck.

Another landed in the timber at Alere's feet. More. Each one closer as the archers found their range. A shaft brushed her shoulder. They were good. She skipped backward and four men swarmed up the stairs. They advanced on her in a semi-circle.

Jiche! Where was Kett?

A ceramic blade swept in from her left. She stepped back. The tip skimmed her throat. She moved in and sliced low. Her edge bit through a leather leg guard, into flesh. Not deeply, but enough to make the man pause. She wrenched the blade free and struck aside his half-raised sword. Her dagger sliced backhand across his exposed throat.

'Take 'em alive!' A huge body slammed into her. And a second. She staggered, driven back against the railing. Her attacker's rank breath gusted from a mouth full of blackened, broken teeth. Alere jabbed the sword-pommel at his jaw. He struck the inside of her wrist, numbing her hand. The sword clattered to the deck. She drove a knee into his groin. He grunted and fell back a step. The other boarder grabbed her dagger-hand. She twisted free and plunged the blade into his neck. Blood spurted, making the hilt slippery.

The first recovered and smashed her dagger-hand into the railing, jarring the blade loose. The fourth man leapt in.

Alere kicked at his knee and it crunched beneath her heel. He screamed and collapsed. Only one holding her now. The biggest. Twice her weight, and all muscle. His thick hand still held her wrist. She jabbed with stiffened fingers at his throat. He blocked and his fist struck her temple. Light burst behind her eyes, blinding. Darkness roared. Pressed against the railing, she couldn't make space to recover. Huge hands shoved at her chest. She toppled backwards, scrabbling at the gunwale as she went over.

'Alli!'

Something latched onto her wrist and she jerked to a halt, wrenching her shoulder. A large body flew past and splashed into the water. Her heels hit the side of the chuan, jarring pain through her legs. She squinted up. Kett half-lay over the gunwale, one hand wrapped around her wrist, the other gripping the railing.

Icy water splashed Alere's feet and she glanced down. The river's cold, black depth swirled and rippled just a bodylength below. Her heart thudded blood in her ears.

'Alli, I can't...pull you up.' Kett bared his teeth in a grimace. His arms and shoulders shook.

Alere looked up at him, then back down at the river; at its seductive, dark draw. The water held a kind of peace in the midst of the chaos.

'Alli?' Kett's call held urgency, fear. The chuan rocked as a surge of water eddied against it. Kett's grip on her arm slipped and he swore. 'Alli!' His grey eyes caught hers. 'I can't...you have to help. You have to climb. If you don't, you'll die. The river's too cold and deep here. And there are shaytan-salamanders.'

She glanced once more at the blackness below.

Something, deep in her mind, urged her to let go.

'Alli...please?'

CHAPTER TWO

ALERE

Alere frowned and shook her head. Letting go? Where had that thought come from?

She gripped Kett's wrist and he gave a breathless half-laugh.

'Hold on,' he said. 'I'm going to swing you. Grab the rail.'

She pushed along the slippery magnal metal hull with her bare feet. Kett grunted, his neck and arms cording as he swung her. She stretched out. Her fingertips caught the top of the rail and she clung to the smooth timber. Kett edged along, lifting her a fraction higher. Alere shifted her grip and got better purchase. Together, they dragged her up the side of the chuan and back onto the deck.

Alere collapsed, trembling, her shoulder aching and fingers bloodless.

Kett knelt beside her, panting. 'You alright?'

She rotated her shoulder and winced. 'I think so. Thanks.'

'You scared me. Don't do that again.'

'I—'

'Here.' He thrust her bow and quiver into her hands. 'Get onto the storage locker by the midship rail and use that.' He gripped his sword. 'I'll guard your back.'

Grateful for his steady, enduring presence, she touched his arm. 'You always do. Thank you.'

Kett stared impassively at her for a moment, then nodded.

Heavy steps thudded across the deck. A Melcori-crewman ran towards them, a bronze blade in each hand, his long, dark hair flying.

Kett rose and drew his steel sword. 'Leave this to me. Your father needs help. Go.' He nodded towards the other side of the deck. Rafi Koh-Lin was beset by four men who fought like wild xiao-cats: without a great deal of style, but with unmatched ferocity.

Alere scrabbled across the deck and grabbed her lost sword and dagger, resheathing them as she ran. A quick leap landed her on the flat storage locker roof. The chuan pitched and she steadied herself. She nocked an arrow to her horsebow. Thumb-ring and arrow both in place, she scanned the deck. A few slow breaths helped control the the rush of adrenalin that soaked her blood and shook her hands.

One man lay bleeding at Rafi's feet. Alere flexed her injured shoulder and sighted. The three remaining boarders weren't trying to kill her father, just corner him. Though more skilled, Rafi was older and a little slower. In a moment he would be trapped against the railing. Alere loosed an arrow, redrew and loosed the next. Then the third. All three men fell. One arrow through a neck, one through the meat of his belly, one through the chest. Rafi finished the second and saluted her.

A whistling sound made her turn. From the other chuan, tiny glowing balls of flame arced through the air, leaving green trails on her retinas when she blinked. Flaming arrows? Three archers stood at the rail. They were prepared to burn Dalor's vessel to the waterline? What happened to taking her alive?

An arrow thunked into the timber two paces away, its cloth-wrapped shaft still alight. She yanked it free, nocked the flaming shaft and raised her sights to the other chuan. With her knees soft against the motion of the vessel, she relaxed. There was a slight breeze at her back. She allowed for it and released.

The arrow flew true, landing at the base of the red sail furled to the Melcori vessel's single mast. The sailors spotted the flame licking at their canvas and cries of alarm rose with the smoke. The crew dashed for buckets. That distracted the enemy archers, giving her time to line them up.

Her first arrow rose high, with perfect line and distance. But her target saw it coming and leapt aside. Alere followed immediately with a second shaft, aimed at where he would be. That one hit. The archer dropped his bow into the foaming water and clutched the slender timber skewer protruding from his chest. He toppled overboard.

'Alli! On your left.' Kett's warning caught her mid-draw. She spun and released. The man attempting to climb onto the storage locker behind her screamed. He fell backward with an arrow through his eye.

Another flaming arrow landed on the deck below. Corin paused long enough to yank it free and toss it overboard before the fire could take hold. He caught her gaze and smiled broadly. Three upraised fingers and a wave at the dead strewn across the deck must indicate his count. She held up six fingers. He threw back his head, his laugh carrying in the cold air.

There were no more boarders standing. The Melcori crew lay decimated. Alere turned her attention back to the *Nasir*. The Melcori crew slashed the line mooring their vessel to shore. They'd put out the fire and now unfurled the sail. A long, charred hole divided the sail almost in two. But it held together, billowing out in the sharp breeze.

Alere nocked another arrow and studied the men visible on the *Nasir*'s deck. There. Standing by the wheel. One man shouted orders that the remaining crew scurried to obey. Their chuanzhu.

The screams of the wounded and dying, and the smell of blood wafted from the carnage on Dalor's chuan. Alere blotted them out. She stretched her neck and shoulder. The *Nasir* slid into the Kabir's fast-flowing current. Alere set her feet, drawing the string and a deep breath.

The chuan slipped further away. The *Nasir*'s chuanzhu glanced over his shoulder. He caught her eye and extended his fist, little pointing finger down, in a rude hand signal. He turned his back. Alere relaxed the bowstring.

'Take the shot,' Ket called from across the deck, watching the *Nasir*.

'It's too far!'

'Only if you think it is,' he said. 'Don't let him intimidate you. Take the shot.'

Quashing a tremor of self-doubt, she drew again and leaned back to raise the tip of the arrow. Tightening the muscles between her shoulderblades lengthened the draw. She released. The arrow flew along with the breath from her lips. She held her position until the shaft was well clear and soaring serenely through the brightening peridot sky.

On the *Kuailong*, movement ceased as all eyes followed the arrow's perfect arc. Silence held sway: a frozen moment stolen from madness.

The chuanzhu on the *Nasir* continued to shout orders to his frantic crew.

The broadhead buried itself into the back of his skull.

He fell forward, dead before he even hit the deck.

The moment broke. A ragged cheer arose from Dalor's men. The Melcori chuan wove and pitched into the main current, its hands confused and chaotic. A crewman with unusual, bright red hair leapt to the wheel and took control of the *Nasir*.

After a speculative look at Alere, Dalor shouted his crew down and set them to work dousing pockets of fire and cleaning the decks. Corin bounded up the ladder from the lower deck, his blond hair flying in the rising breeze, escaping its mawei tie, as it always did. Gavon, stocky and dark-bearded, with his hair so short as to be almost shaven, followed more slowly. Blood glistened on his ceramic blade. He gave her a grave nod of acknowledgement. His expertise had refined her ability to hit distant, moving targets and she was grateful for it, now. She slung the bow across her back.

The winter breeze cut through her thin, bamboo-cloth shirt. Shivering, she wrapped her arms around herself as the fire of adrenalin ebbed. A dull mind and stiff muscles replaced it.

Corin paused below her position, squinting against the rising sun. He swept her a deep, flourishing bow, more suited to the grand ballroom in her father's Shanzhai castle than the shifting deck of this small chuan. He brought his hands together in slow applause. It was often hard to tell if he was being serious or ironic.

'Wasai.' He shook his head. 'That was the most impressive feat of marksmanship I've seen...well, ever.'

The genuine warmth in his green eyes said he was serious. And his smile held more than simple admiration. Alere flushed. Corin's hands slid around her waist and he lifted her off the storage locker. Not that she needed help. Her heart fluttered. He lowered her slowly, holding her gaze. His mouth curved in a sensual smile for her alone and the rest of the world faded for a moment.

'I'm glad you're alright,' he murmured. 'Have I told you recently how incredible you are?' He hesitated, leaned down, and brushed his lips across hers.

'You do remember that I trained in Jiaoji House for three years, don't you?' she said.

He paused, quirking a grin. 'And?'

'And I know what you're doing.' Her heart thudded. She might have learned every method of seduction, but that didn't make her immune to its lure. Especially from Corin.

He chuckled. 'Good. I'd be more worried if you didn't know.'

Laughter bubbled up and she pushed free of his tempting warmth. She eyed the curious crew meaningfully. 'Well, you have terrible timing. Again.'

'True. It's a conspiracy against us.' He sighed, kissed her forehead, and released her.

Kett approached, cleaning his blade and sliding the steel carefully into its sheath. With his dark hair neatly tied and any bloodstains invisible on his black weishi's tunic and trous, he looked more like he'd wandered onto the deck for a stroll than had just killed men in hand-to-hand combat.

'Well shot, Alli.' He passed her the oiled cloth and she cleaned her blades.

'A lot of luck.' She lifted one shoulder.

He smiled faintly, grey eyes alight. 'Only if you count ten years of training as luck. Perhaps,' he added as she opened her mouth to protest, 'we'll call it a lot of skill and a reasonable amount of luck.'

Rafi strode over, his clear blue gaze on the Melcori ship as it vanished around a bend. He sheathed his weapon. Absently, he flexed his fingers and shook his wrist. 'I'm out of practice. Good thing they weren't trying to kill me.'

Of a height with Kett and fractionally taller than Corin, Rafi Koh-Lin dominated the company. His plain brown bamboo-cloth shirt and grey trous gave no indication he was Jun Second and arguably the most powerful man in Mamlakah. But his intense charisma and confidence was almost overwhelming. Alere kept silent.

He grimaced. 'It's a pity they've escaped and we've none left alive to question. This act is unusual for the Melcori and I'd like to know what prompted it. However, they're not our mission. I've ordered Dalor to let them go. We must focus on catching up with Jarran.'

Alere hunched a shoulder, trying to hold onto the moment of buoyancy, the thrill of success. What did she have to do to impress him? She frowned. Why was she trying to impress him, anyway? She'd known her father for a week. For twenty years she'd managed without his approval.

Rafi's eyes were still on the river north. 'Jarran's chuan left four days ago. By river it's less than a week to Madina. I should have received two flitters from my men with progress reports. I've received one this morning from my wife, Yasmin, in Shanzhai. She's heard nothing from Jarran or my weishi on his chuan.'

'And you're worried Rohne Marin-kin may have something to do with it,' Kett added, 'since he left on the same vessel, and took Mina with him.'

Rafi nodded, shading his face with a hand as the sun finally cleared the mountains and poured its light and feeble warmth into the valley. 'Jarran Zah-Hill, as new Jun First, is the best hope Mamlakah has of coming through the economic crisis Hanna Zah-Hill and her son, Ven, brought on us. He runs a successful chain of businesses.' He smiled wryly. 'And that's not unlike running a successful Jundom. But it's my duty as Jun Second to make sure he's safe and to help him settle in. I thought I was doing the right thing by sending him to Madina without me. So he could begin his reign visibly independent, but...'

'But what?' Alere asked.

He scanned their path downriver. 'If Rohne has betrayed us somehow, then he has both the new Jun First and my kin-daughter as hostage. And, even if Rohne has done nothing, his existence as a male xintou puts all of them in danger. And Jarran also has his young daughters with him.'

'I know we're all conditioned by Xintou House to fear male telepaths,' Alere said, 'but Rohne's done nothing wrong that I know of.'

Rafi's lips tightened. 'True, but the political situation is too volatile to risk Jarran's safety at the moment. Jarran's seat on the throne depends on his being accepted by the other twenty ruling Juns. If they think he's under the control of a male xintou – or even associated with one...' He shook his head. 'The jundom could easily descend into a bloodbath if the other Juns start fighting for the Jun First position. The lands controlled by the Zah-Hill Jun First family are the richest in Mamlakah.'

'Shenshi?' Corin's urgent hail brought them to his side.

He knelt by one of the fallen raiders and his expression lacked its usual glint of humour. Lifting the man's bare foot, Corin angled it towards Rafi, who ran a hand over his short, greying hair and gave a heavy sigh. Beside him, Gavon made a noise suspiciously like a growl. Something akin to black hatred flared in his dark eyes.

Alere inspected the bared skin. An old burn-scar puckered the sole. So, the dead man had been a Melcori slave at some point. Gavon pulled out his dagger and sliced at the sleeve covering the body's left arm. He revealed a tattooed N on the flaccid bicep.

'Mhareb-slave.' Gavon dropped the sleeve and brushed his fingers off fastidiously.

The words translated to 'warrior-slave', which meant nothing to Alere beyond the literal. She was reluctant to ask Gavon to explain, for he had once been a slave, himself. Kett showed nothing of his thoughts, only cool understanding and faint curiosity, not alarm. Corin, in his role as spy for Rafi, was a master of hiding his feelings behind a flippant front. So, it was a surprise to see the faintest flicker of revulsion as he inspected the branded skin.

Rafi's mouth twisted. 'A slaver-ship. Dalor suspected as much when we woke him. They grow bolder each year.' He waved the chuanzhu over.

Dalor studied the body and folded sinewy arms across his chest. His bronze dagger, small in fingers gnarled and thickened by years on the ropes, glinted in the dawn's pink light. He tapped one bare foot restlessly on the bamboo boards. His thick, black hair was braided into a waist-length mawei, held back from a face crevassed by time and exposure.

'Gouri slavers on the *Kuailong*, Shenshi Rafi.' His sneering tone made the Jun Second's title into an insult. 'They shouldn't be here. I have an arrangement with Jahil, the Shah of Melcor. My vessels are off limits and his Slavemasters are meant to stay north of Madina. He'll hear from me when I'm next in Chengdu.' He glared downriver then back at Rafi. 'They were after you. I saw that much.' He pointed the dagger-tip at Rafi, sharp black eyes fixed in a scowl. 'They come back and I'm holding you responsible, shehnsi. You threatened my livelihood if I didn't agree to this trip.'

Rafi gazed coolly down his nose. Dalor stared right back, as though he would happily slit his Jun Second's throat and throw him overboard.

'Understood, chuanzhu.' Rafi lifted his chin. Every inch the Jun, he towered a good head over Dalor. 'Now, get us underway.'

Dalor turned on his heel and stalked away, shouting orders. Rafi followed.

Kett helped Corin throw the slaver overboard. Alere watched, troubled. Should they be taken ashore and buried with the proper rites? Someone should at least sing the *Song of Passing* and ring the *Kuailong*'s watchbell four times. Then again, there was little time for niceties and digging was impossible in the winter-frozen ground, anyway.

Seeing Gavon staring blindly after the first drifting corpse, Alere raised a brow at him. 'Is Dalor right? Is it unusual for them to come this far?'

He watched another body splash into the Kabir River and spat after it, satisfaction replacing anger in his expression. 'Aye, boyo. They don't normally come south of the border between Mamlakah and Melcor.' He frowned. 'But I've been hearing stories. People being snatched from well inside Mamlakah.'

'But why?' Alere said.

'Melcor's economy works on the backs of its slaves.' Gavon's eyes narrowed. 'The trade deals Hanna Zah-Hill and her son, Ven, made for Mamlakah were all in Jahil's favour. So Melcor has grown arrogant. Thinking Mamlakah's weak.' He pointed at the corpse in the water. 'These belonged to Shah Jahil's kin-brother, Hallon Nasim. The Slavemaster with the most power in the land. But I don't think even Jahil knows how farspread Hallon and the other three Slavemasters cast their nets now.'

Gavon spat again, his eyes hardening to obsidian. 'At least we've killed enough of the *Nasir*'s crew that they shouldn't be able to attack yer sister's chuan. For just know, boyo, that if the slavers get their claws into ye or yer kin, ye can kiss yer life or theirs goodbye.' He rotated the leather-and-bronze guards he wore on his forearms and swore.

'I'm sorry,' she said, not really knowing what else to say.

'Ye've nothing to be sorry for, boyo. Ye did yer training proud today. When we first met ye were still a loose-haired child.' He clapped her on the shoulder. 'Now yer a warrior worthy of that mawei ye tie yer hair in. Especially with those steel blades.' He pointed at her weapons. 'Can I see them?'

She drew forth her sword and dagger. The steel appeared undamaged. She caressed the sword's smooth length before giving both blades to Gavon.

He held them up to the rising sun so the fire-orange light gleamed along their lengths. The matched pair was a gift from Corin and Rafi. Steel, the rarest metal on the planet, set with even rarer yanstones. Exquisite death. She normally kept the pommels covered with thin suede to hide their value and protect the stones.

'They are beauties.' Gavon hefted the sword, twirling it with easy expertise. He returned them. 'A little light and short for me, but perfect for ye.'

'Yes,' she said. 'They're perfect, but...' She didn't know how to voice her unease. Every time she used them, she inflicted death. Messy, complicated death on imperfect people.

'But the faces don't trouble yer sleep any more?' Gavon eyed her shrewdly. 'And ye think they ought to?'

She nodded. Apart from Ven, whose face haunted her nightmares, each death became easier to forget. Now, she barely noticed the smells and sounds of battle. Before, they'd caused her stomach to roil and mouth to swim.

'I was raised in Xintou house,' she said, struggling to put her discomfort into words. 'The motto of the house is: *clarity, stability, responsibility, and compassion.* I feel like...' She looked in the direction the slaver ship had vanished. 'I didn't even think about their families. Or whether killing the chuanzhu might have wider repercussions. All I cared about was protecting everyone on this chuan when I shot him. I *should* care, shouldn't I?' Was she becoming as much of a monster as Ven; someone who had little regard for human life?

CHAPTER THREE

ALERE

Gavon snorted a scornful laugh and scratched at his full beard. 'Do the slavers care? Did the Jun First, Ven Zah-Hill, when he tried to invade Shanzhai and take the iron buried there? Or when he had his hands around yer throat, strangling the life out of ye?' His mouth twisted, cynicism glinting in his dark eyes. 'Ye can't afford to care about yer enemies, boyo, or ye won't sleep at night.' Bitterness seeped into his expression. 'And caring for yer allies makes ye vulnerable.'

'But—'

'Ah, ye can't help caring,' he said, waving her objection aside, 'being who ye are and all. But yer enemies'll use us against ye, if they can.' His lips pressed thin. 'And ye've got more than most riding on yer decisions.'

Alere eyed him uncertainly. She'd been raised – as both xintou and weishi – to believe protecting others was her most important function. Before she'd done so out of duty. Now she had people she worried about. Was that wrong? Would it make her vulnerable?

'So why are you here, with me, if you don't care?'

He cocked his head. 'The truth, boyo?'

She nodded.

'Ye remind me of someone. My younger kin-sister.' He twisted one of the leather wrist guards. 'We were taken together by slavers as children. She died in Chengdu in the end-of-year Wushi Games. I couldn't protect her. Ye...' He laid a heavy hand on her shoulder. 'Maybe I can. I owe her. And ye.'

'Gavon, you don't have to—'

He held up a hand. 'Nay, boyo. Save it. If ye'd rather something less guilt-making, then take this: ye've saved my life twice now. I owe ye.'

'No.' She clasped his arm. 'I'm the one who owes you. Your training has saved both of us.'

He bared his teeth in a fierce grin. His eyes vanished in a mass of creases. 'Well, I doubt we're done yet, boyo. We'll tally it up at the end. For now, don't lose sleep over the dead. They can't hurt ye. It's the living and their secrets ye've to watch out for. That's what'll kill ye, boyo.' With that, he marched away and vanished into the cabins beneath the deck.

Alere leaned her elbows on the cool timber rail and followed the swirling green depths of water, willing her mind elsewhere. She ignored the sharp winter wind that curled around from the south and tossed hair into her eyes. A sinuous ribbon of silver-green, longer than the chuan hull, slipped past below. A shaytan-salamander. Dalor had warned they lived in this part of the river. Hiding amongst the rocks, ambushing the unsuspecting.

Like secrets.

Gavon was right. There had to be more to this than she could see and understand. But what? There were too many secrets and pieces missing to the puzzle. Rafi withheld something vital, something even Corin knew, about the state of the Jundom. Mina was tied to it all in some way, too. As Rafi's Jun-Heir, Alere had a right to know.

It was time to confront her father and ask what was going on.

Alere straightened. The awareness of another presence tingled up her spine. Someone approached from behind, with feet silent on the timber. An enemy boarder, unaccounted for? No.

How did he *do* that? For someone as tall and broad-shouldered as Kett, he was remarkably light-footed. She'd never been able to match his stealth. She doubted even Corin could. Sneaking up on her was an old training game Kett used on her back in Xintou House.

Glad of the distraction, she spun and drew her sword in one move. Her blade struck up at an angle. The dagger followed, slicing at stomach height.

Steel met steel in a clarion call to battle. Kett stepped easily away from her sword. He allowed it to float past and brushed her dagger aside with the tip of his sword. Alere let her momentum carry her out of his reach and returned to attack again. She grinned fiercely, striking hard. Kett's grey eyes widened, then narrowed and he blocked. He smiled, wrists twisting and feet shifting as he deflected every blow. He had the advantage of height and reach, and didn't scruple to use it in holding her at bay.

At last he gave her an opening.

Just a slight shift in his weight and lift of an elbow left his ribs exposed.

A flick deflected his sword. She stepped inside his guard and thrust with her dagger. Iron fingers snapped around her wrist. He straightened her arm across his chest, flexing the elbow almost to breaking. His arm snaked around the front of her neck, controlling her head, tipping it backward. All she could see was the back of his shoulder and the pale-green sky. She had to stand on tiptoes to avoid being choked.

'Enough!' She gasped, coughing. Kett released her and she staggered upright.

'Rather jumpy this morning, aren't you?' His deep voice, tinged with amusement, melted her frustration. 'I only came to see if you wanted breakfast. Not very polite to draw steel.'

She laughed and resheathed her weapons. 'I miss our training. Nice move, by the way. Don't think I've seen you use that one before.'

'I've been learning from your interesting yongbing friend, Gavon. I can see why you like him.'

'Yes, he keeps me on my toes.'

Composing herself into a calm she didn't feel, she turned to him. Her weishi leant his back against the railing, arms folded across his broad chest, a faint question in his grey eyes.

She gave an uneasy laugh. 'I keep expecting you to scold me, but I guess you're not my weishi or my shifu any longer, are you?' He'd been her personal guard, shifu and steady friend for so many years it was hard to think of him as anything else.

Kett stilled and dropped his eyes from hers. 'I suppose not. I'll have a difficult time breaking the habits of a decade, too. But now you're Jun-Heir to Rafi perhaps I should be more respectful.' His mouth twitched into a gently-mocking smile. 'Shunu Lianna Koh-Lin.'

Alere hunched a shoulder. 'Don't, Kett. I'm pretending to be someone I'm not. And, as for respect…You outrank me. You should be on your way to the Jun First throne, not Jarran. He's younger.'

He made a hasty, defensive gesture. 'Don't wish that on me, Alli.' Bitterness sharpened his tone. 'I've no desire to be First. I'm not worthy. My birth caused every gouri problem that faces Mamlakah now. Don't add the throne to my burdens.'

'No.' She grasped his wrist. 'That's not true, Kett. I know Hanna Zah-Hill imposed the kin-child laws because she feared your position over her son, Ven. But you were seven. You must let that go.'

'Alli, you can't ignore the fact that you and Mina wouldn't be in such danger if it weren't for those laws. Mina, especially, for she hasn't your fighting skills…' He eyes hardened, bleak as the snowy ground flanking the river. 'I have to make sure she's safe, Alli. I can't undo the bloodshed Hanna unleashed because of me. And I regret letting Hanna live.'

'No, that was the right thing to do. The weishi code is about protecting, not killing for revenge.'

'You forget that I trained for eight years as xiongshou before becoming weishi, and their code isn't quite so noble.'

When she opened her mouth, he cut her off. 'But at least I can protect one innocent, loving woman who doesn't deserve to die.' His mouth twisted. 'And I feel I owe Jarran. He's kin-child and my half-brother and I took away his right to refuse the Jun First throne when I abdicated in his favour. If Rohne poses any threat to him – or Mina – I need to do what I can to right that. I shouldn't have—' He shook his head and closed his mouth.

'Shouldn't have what?'

'It doesn't matter.'

Not knowing what to say, she said nothing and stared at the valley walls. They dropped lower as the river snaked north. Through the bare bones of trees, a broad expanse of ploughed land came into view. Lifeless beneath a thin shroud of snow, it offered little of interest. A few grey-stone farmhouses and barns, sharp-edged and stark as deathstones piled in memory of loved ones. The black footprints of some lone, large animal led down to the water's edge, but not away again. Perhaps taken by a shaytan.

After a short silence, Kett moved closer to her and placed both hands on the railing. He stared across the empty land, his usual imperturbable manner restored. Alere was acutely conscious of him: the warmth of his arm against hers, the solidity of him; the undemanding, enduring nature of his friendship.

Normally, his presence helped settle her nerves, reminding her to slow down, and think. Now, she fidgeted. She couldn't bear to see him take any more blame on himself.

'I'm sorry,' she blurted. 'It's my fault Rohne took Mina. I promised you she'd be kept safe. I was afraid to let her close to me. I didn't listen when she told me how much she hated the killing. So, she left. Or Rohne took her. I don't know.' She shrugged. 'But I feel like I failed you – and Mina.'

The harder subject of Radan Zah-Hill's death lingered on her tongue, unspoken. One day she would have to tell Kett she'd killed his father. But not now. Not when she'd already hurt him by putting the woman he loved in danger.

Kett's gaze softened to rueful understanding. 'You've done nothing but try to help. How are you at fault? No, don't answer. I know how you think.' He rested his hands on her shoulders. 'You owe me no apologies, Alli. Rohne and Mina chose their own destinies.' His gaze flickered away from hers and his fingers tightened. 'You can't control their choices. Nor can you protect everyone.'

She made a dismissive gesture. 'What, you can take blame for the whole of Mamlakah's plight, but I can't own Mina's? Hardly fair.'

He laughed, the pain in his eyes vanishing for a moment. His hands lifted in the traditional sign for surrender. 'Very well. Blame yourself all you like. But in all seriousness.' His fingertips brushed her cheek. 'What really troubles you?'

Alere moved away from the security offered by his touch. 'So many things I can't even count them. Pretending to be Rafi's legitimate daughter, Lianna Koh-Lin, when nothing about me pleases him.' She waved a hand south, in the direction of her father's city-seat of Shanzhai. 'The iron deposit hidden beneath Shanzhai.

What that means to the balance of power in the Jundom. These slavers. Mina and Rohne. Jun First, Ven Zah-Hill's death. His Xintou, Celia Edwards's death. And her warning.'

She inspected her palm, half-expecting to see blood on it, still. 'By killing Ven and Celia, have I created a worse problem than what we already had?' She pressed a hand to her temple. 'I have dreams…'

Ven Zah-Hill's face haunted every night. The glitter of sadistic pleasure in his eyes as his fingers squeezed her throat. The silver-gilt flare of cold decision blazing from somewhere deep within her; from deep within the yanstones; tasting of smoke and iron. Her hand driving the dagger-pin deep into his heart.

Ven always laughed – until his face morphed. Then Rohne Marin-Kin sneered at her, instead. And it was Mina's throat he gripped. And Rohne's skin blackened, crinkling like an old leaf, until he disappeared, screaming, in flickering silver-gilt fire. She and Mina both burned with him, devoured by flames that engulfed the world.

'Ah.' Kett folded his arms. 'Now we're there. You're afraid Rohne will be this "worse than Ven" person Celia Edwards predicted.'

Alere said nothing. Had she made a mistake in accepting Rohne's friendship? Technically, as Xintou House's representative, she was duty-bound to kill any male xintou she found. But how could she murder her sister's oldest friend?

The wind whirled into eddies and flung icy drips from the bare trees. She shivered. Overhead, a massive roc-eagle spiralled, its pale green underbelly rendering it almost invisible against the sky. A qarn-goat leapt from the thorny bushes lining the bank. Its single, silvery horn gleamed; the mottled grey coat, long with winter wool, swept the ground. The roc-eagle wailed a shiver-inducing hunting call. The qarn skipped nimbly back to shelter, one eye fixed on the sky.

That's how she felt: like prey waiting for some unseen predator to swoop down and tear her to pieces. But she had nowhere to hide and nowhere to run. She was heir to the Jun Second now.

'I should have listened to Mina,' she admitted, 'and not killed Ven or Celia. Then she might have stayed. What if Rohne is the worse threat? We don't know what he's capable of, Kett. There has to be a reason why male xintou are forbidden. Yet I studied for ten years in Xintou House and there was no mention of why.'

'Even in the Teachings of Lei?' Kett asked.

She shook her head. 'The Teachings supposedly quote some old journal, but all that's left are a few vague warnings about how bad male xintou are. All Rohne's shown us is some minor telekinesis, precognition, and the ability to Read Outer thoughts at a greater distance than normal. None of the powers associated with great strength, like Broadcasting emotions to control large numbers of people. Or Pyrokinesis. If the Teachings of Lei are right, there must be more, but what? And Rohne stole the Koh-Lin yanstone bracelets from my room in Shanzhai. If the stones in my weapons can give me xintou telepathic powers, what will he be able to do with two bracelets-worth? And what does he want with Mina? Why would he take her like that? Or did she go of her own accord?'

Kett said nothing, his eyes downcast.

She swept her thumbs over the smooth domes of the yanstones set into the hilt of her weapons. The now-familiar shimmer of connection slid under her skin.

Made restless by her own imaginings, she paced the small deck. 'But mostly I know I *have* to get Mina back, Kett. She's in trouble.'

'Alli.' Kett hitched himself off the rail and intercepted her, gripping her wrists. 'You're getting ahead of yourself. We've no proof Rohne has *anything* planned. Mina didn't leave because of you.' His jaw muscles worked and his gaze slid off hers. 'I'm sure he's just escorting Mina home to Gaton, as he promised.'

Alere snorted. 'Please. Without a farewell to any of us?' She touched the yanstones again. 'I've tried to connect with her and all I get is a sense of...I don't know...like there's a wall between us. There's *something* wrong, I just don't know what.' Kett released her and she scrubbed at her bare arms. At gooseflesh brought on by more than the chill winter wind.

She studied her hands, pale and purplish with cold. 'How do I make the right choices? Mistress Li always said "important over what you want". But I can't seem to get that right. I wanted Mina to leave me alone, so she did. Look where that got us. I keep choosing what I want.'

He frowned. 'What about pretending to be Lianna Koh-Lin for Rafi? You can't say you wanted that.'

'No, but I wanted to be recognised and valued. I wanted a family.' She spread her hands wide. 'And to protect them I murdered the Jun First, and his Xintou, and changed the Jundom. How do I tell when I'm doing the right thing?'

Kett sighed and swiped a hand over his head. 'I don't know there's an easy answer to that. But if you keep second-guessing every decision, you'll paralyse yourself. For the moment, just concentrate on getting Mina back. That's all we can do.'

Alere clenched her jaw against a stab of jealousy. She had no right to feel it. Was she really the sort of person who would deny her best friend happiness for the sake of her own comfort? She was no longer a child to be protected from the kin-child laws. He had a chance at happiness. But if Mina returned, would Kett leave with her?

Corin's laughter drifted across the deck and she turned to look. He threw his head back and clapped Gavon on the shoulder, chuckling again. She smiled.

Kett cleared his throat, his eyes on the stark riverbank. 'Alli, if you're keeping Corin at arms-length because of some misplaced loyalty to me, then don't. It's quite clear you admire him. And he, you.' His smile twisted. 'I don't entirely trust him. He's too reckless for my liking and his loyalty will always first be to Rafi. But I can't deny the man has…admirable qualities. You could do worse.'

'But…' Alere hesitated, not sure how to ask the question and half-afraid of the answer, anyway.

Kett kissed her forehead, wistful as he cupped her jaw in one lean, callused hand. 'You and I will always be friends, no matter what, or who, comes into our lives. If he gives you some joy, then take it.' His hand dropped away. 'The lives we lead now are fraught with danger and likely to be more so before they're less. If he's what you want, Alli, don't make the mistake I did. Don't waste what little time you have with him. You only regret what you don't do, so they say.'

He paused, searching her face, then pressed his lips together and turned back to the water.

'Kett—'

'Get away! Get back!' A shout erupted from the lower deck. Alere and Kett spun, swords drawn.

Three people held Rafi by the arms, their bronze daggers laid against his throat, spine, and heart.

'Lower the life-chuan,' the smallest shouted, 'or we'll kill the Jun Second.'

CHAPTER FOUR

ALERE

Alere sheathed her sword and slipped the bow off her back. She nocked an arrow but kept it low and out of sight. The slaver trio edged sideways towards the gunwale, forcing Rafi with them. The smallest, a hook-nosed man, growled something inaudible to the Jun, who curled a lip and shook his head. Rafi's chin was high, his fists clenched by his sides. A bead of blood stained the collar of his shirt.

'They must have hidden when we drove off the others,' Kett said, his eyes scanning the deck. 'Let's hope there are only three.'

'I can take at least one,' Alere muttered.

He laid a hand on her wrist. 'Not yet. They want him alive, but I wouldn't bet his life on it. The question is, why do they want him alive? Who wants him? Hallon Nasim, or his kin-brother, the Shah, Jahil?'

All around the chuan, Dalor's crew stood frozen, ropes half-coiled, buckets of water half-emptied. Dalor, Corin and Gavon were grouped together amidships. Too far from Rafi's captors.

Corin's hand moved behind his back. Was that something in his fingers? Alere smiled.

'Kett,' she murmured, 'can you arrange some sort of distraction? Corin has a throwing knife. He's got a clean throw at the one on the right. I'll take the one on the left.'

'That one's behind Rafi,' Kett said. 'You won't get a clear body shot. Right eye is your best option.'

'I know.'

'You won't need a distraction,' Kett said. 'Just wait. If Dalor's quick, they'll have to climb down into the lifechuan. There's no way to do that and keep using Rafi as a shield.'

Rafi's captors were almost at the gunwale, now. Dalor signalled his men, who lowered the lifechuan. Bronze pulleys rattled and the little magnal metal vessel splashed into the water. Kett made a noise of satisfaction and Alere smiled. They should have climbed aboard, first.

'Right,' hook-nose yelled. 'One of us is getting in. Then your Jun goes into the water. Let us go and we'll fish him out before the shaytans get him. Kill us and he'll die.'

'Gouri...' Alere muttered. 'Kett?'

'Take the shot,' he said. 'No-one could get Rafi out fast enough. Dalor says this stretch of water is a death sentence. Wait. Give me one of your throwing knives.'

'In my cabin.'

He swore and snatched up an empty bamboo bucket with a long rope attached. He dropped into a crouch and ran across the deck, bent double behind the railing, until he was close to the scene.

The largest of the three slavers climbed awkwardly over the gunwale, keeping his knifepoint pressed against Rafi's ribs the whole time. The third, a stick-thin woman with a shock of white hair, then emerged from behind Rafi.

Kett held the length of rope looped loosely in one hand. The bucket dangled by a short length from the other. He glanced across and nodded.

Alere drew back on the string, relaxed her shoulders and sighted. Her hands trembled. She held her breath and slowed her heart. Even a fraction out and she would kill her father. She couldn't reach Gavon or Corin by telepathy without touching the yanstones. Shouting was the only option. Hopefully Corin would understand.

'Corin!' She released the string.

His knife flicked through the cold air. Kett's bucket arced towards the slavers.

Rafi grabbed the knife-hand at his throat and wrenched it away.

The arrow struck first, impaling the short Melcori through the eye. He screamed and dropped the knife, clutching at the shaft. Rafi spun aside and Corin's blade stabbed hilt-deep into the thin woman's stomach. Her blade drew blood across Rafi's midriff. Alere gasped.

The largest man stuck his head back up. Kett's bucket glanced off his shoulder. He screamed an oath and wrapped a thick arm around Rafi's waist from behind. He hurled himself backward, pulling Rafi overboard. A crack, then a splash, followed. And a series of splashes. A scream.

'Rafi!' Alere leapt to the lower deck and sprinted to the railing.

Kett reeled the bucket back in and joined her. 'There!' He pointed.

Rafi's head broke the ice-green water's churning surface. He snatched at the life-chuan's gunwale. Behind him, the slaver thrashed in the water, arms flailing, mouth agape. A thick, silvery-green coil snaked through the water near Rafi. He grunted and hauled himself half-into the chuan. The little vessel tilted, almost capsizing. Water sloshed over the gunwale. A long, silvery tail flipped and slapped at the water. A gaping mouth full of dagger-fangs snapped at air and disappeared.

Alere whimpered, her heart pounding.

The slaver screamed. A flurry of white-green water and smooth, greenish body splashed around him. The water turned pink and his cries fell silent. Something tugged his body below the surface.

Rafi collapsed into the rocking chuan, coughing.

'Get him up, Dalor!' Corin yelled.

Dalor's crew hauled the chuan back up and secured it, helping Rafi onto the *Kuailong's* deck, where he stood, shivering and soaked. One of the crew produced an insect-eaten blanket and wrapped it around Rafi's shoulders. He clutched it close, his face pale.

Alere swallowed. 'Get the healer.'

The crewman nodded and vanished belowdecks.

'Are you alright?' She hesitated a step away from Rafi, unsure.

He grimaced and touched a fingertip to the bloody cut across his ribs. 'Humiliated, more than anything. And freezing.' He managed a wry smile.

He toed the woman lying groaning on the deck with Corin's knife in her gut. 'Corin, see what you can get from this one.'

Corin crouched. 'My knife, for one.' He cocked his head and grinned at the injured slaver. 'Shall I remove it so you bleed out, or leave it in and let you die slowly of infection? Or would you like to tell us why you're here?'

The woman pressed her lips tight and narrowed startling blue eyes into slits.

'I'll take that as a "no", then,' Corin said. He addressed Rafi. 'You go get dry and stitched up. I suspect Gav will quite enjoy dealing with this chouhuo. C'mon, you. Up you get.' He hauled the injured slaver to her feet. 'No, don't take the blade out. Our healer is quite good unless you bleed to death first. We have a lot of questions for you.'

'You gouri wisix hundan!' The slaver wrenched her arm free of Corin's grip. She stared desperately around but every exit was blocked. She swore again and threw herself over the gunwale.

Another splash.

Alere rushed to the side – in time to see the woman swimming strongly towards the rocky riverbank. Kett threw the bucket to her but she ignored it. The current caught and swept her downstream. She submerged and rose again, sputtering. A flash of silver-green swirled the jade water nearby. She kicked furiously, leaving a smoky-red trail of blood in the water. The bank was only five bodylengths away.

She screamed and clawed at the water. Then vanished and didn't reappear. A thick cloud of red billowed to the surface.

Alere slumped and closed her eyes. Who would do something so mad? What sort of person was this Hallon Nasim that he inspired such fanaticism in his people?

'Gaisi,' Corin muttered. 'That was my best throwing knife.'

Rafi scowled. 'And our only chance at finding out why Hallon Nasim is trying so hard to kidnap me.'

There was a long pause as they all stared at the dark waters. Kett pulled the bucket back in and handed it to a crewman.

'Shenshi? Kett said quietly. 'Didn't you say you'd received a flitter from Shanzhai this morning? Did Shunu Yasmin send any news that might shed light on this?'

Rafi sent him a cool look. His jaw muscles worked. 'Possibly. You know Jun Fourth Hassan Wen-Gates – the kin-brother to our previous Jun First, Radan Zah-Hill?'

'We met him when we passed through his estates on our trip to Shanzhai,' Alere said. 'I wouldn't trust him. He doesn't seem…stable.'

'It runs in the family,' Rafi said, drily. 'Hassan has called for a Jun Council. He wants all twenty-one ruling Juns in Madina. And all the Trades House leaders as well. And Mistress Li of Xintou House.'

'Why?' Alere frowned. 'There hasn't been a full Jun Council as long as I can remember. I didn't think he'd leave his fortress.'

'I suspect he's going to make a bid for the throne,' Rafi said. 'With the anti kin-child laws removed, he's got as good a claim as

Jarran does.' His blue-tinged lips stretched into a mirthless smile. 'I know Hassan of old. He won't get the throne. None of the Juns trust him. I'm more concerned about Jun Fourth Bren Gray-Saud. His mother was Radan Zah-Hill's younger fullblood sister. And he's fullblood, himself. He's smart, ambitious and with a strong support network in Madina. The younger generation of Juns and Jun-Heirs have all been raised with Hanna's anti-kin-child laws drummed into them. It will be difficult to garner support for Jarran if Bren Gray-Saud contests.'

Alere cocked her head. 'But how is that related to Melcori slavers trying to kidnap you?'

'Hassan Wen-Gates knows he's not well-liked.' Rafi's eyes narrowed. 'If he has allied with Shah Jahil of Melcor then this attack would make sense. If he kidnapped me, he could force me to support his claim. Which also means that Jarran – and Mina because she's on the same chuan – could be in more danger than I thought.' He shivered and pulled the blanket closer. 'Jarran's the next logical target. And – even with her hair dyed blonde – Mina could be recognised and held hostage for my co-operation.'

'All well and good, shenshi.' Gavon jerked his chin southward. 'But yer thinking too small. Something tells me we won the battle at Shanzhai, but not the war. I've got a bad feeling. This is bigger than the Jun First throne. Bigger than Shunu Hanna and Shenshi Ven Zah-Hill wanting the iron deposit under yer castle to make weapons with. They lit fires under other pots, too, and I think they're coming to the boil, now.'

Alere swallowed. Could he mean Celia's warning?

Corin scratched at the three-day growth on his chin. 'Gavon's right: there's more to this than we see now. I doubt squabbling Juns is your worst problem, shenshi. I've had the feeling something is brewing, but I haven't been able to pin it down.' His glance at the northern skyline was thoughtful. 'Perhaps Melcor's involved. These attacks… and I've heard rumours of unrest amongst the slaves. Then again, that could be unrelated.'

'Guesswork is of no use to me,' Rafi said shortly. 'I can't solve problems I don't even know exist, yet. Find me facts. For now, I have to focus on getting Jarran established.' He laid a hand on Alere's shoulder. 'And there's one more thing you should know. Yasmin says news of the kin-child laws has leaked. There are protests in Madina and other cities. People angry with the change. People who would lose a great deal if any kin-children came out of hiding to claim an inheritance. Mina could be in grave danger. I'm sorry.'

CORIN

Rafi left in search of the healer and Corin sauntered up to Alere and Kett. Both of them seemed far too serious. He bowed extravagantly – mainly because it annoyed them. Kett ignored him. Alere merely gave him a troubled look and returned to watching the river.

'Nothing like a brisk spilling of blood to start the day, eh?' He didn't miss Alere's shiver and frowning glance downriver.

Kett's lips thinned. 'I'll check on the horses. Make sure they weren't too disturbed by the battle.' He strode away, heading towards the makeshift shelter on the lower deck, where his and Alere's animals were stabled.

Not loath to see him leave, Corin leaned on the rail by Alere's side and watched the riverbanks slip past. It was a relief to be back on the road…well, the water. Shanzhai was home, but if he stayed too long Rafi always started making noises about administering his own spy network. Which sounded like very dull work.

He turned forward, drinking in the snow-chilled taste of the wind off the water, and the winter-sun's gentle warmth on his skin. The sounds and smells of battle were long gone, leaving only the splash of water, the twitter of startled birds in bare trees lining the riverbanks, and the creak of chuan timbers. The only human noises were the occasional shout from Dalor as he directed his small crew to fend his pride and joy off massive black rocks jutting from the riverbed. Orange sunlight turned the snow into a glittering field of topazes.

Corin studied Alere as she stared pensively at the snow-covered, rocky bank. Since she was rarely motionless, he took a moment to admire her, unawares. Her midnight hair, cut short when she impersonated a boy on the trip from Newmec, now curled to her shoulders. Stray locks escaped the leather thong tying it into a man's mawei. A crease marred her smooth forehead. She tucked her fingers under her arms and, catching his eye, flushed and sent him a half-hearted smile.

'Alright?' If only he had the right to kiss the troubles from her brow.

Alere pressed her lips together. Her hand strayed, as it frequently did now, to the sword hilt at her hip. To the yanstones. Did she realise it?

'Just...' She scowled. 'Just worried about Mina. And Jarran.' She scraped her wind-blown hair back.

'We all are.' Corin hooked his arm through hers, not unhappy for an excuse to do so. 'Nothing we can do until we catch up with them, though. Fretting won't help, and you know it. This isn't like you. What's really wrong?'

She laughed ruefully. 'I must be transparent. Kett asked me the same thing. It's...' She slipped her arm free and grimaced. 'This thing with the slavers keeps cropping up. Have you noticed? First in

Shanzhai with that weishi from Ven's army. Now here. Do you think Mina's in danger from them?'

'Doubtful.' He didn't want to alarm her even more. 'They're not likely to attack a chuan carrying ten elite weishi now they've lost so many men. Ignore Rafi. He's a pessimist.'

Her hands lay on her weapons and she stilled. 'You don't believe that, Cor. I can tell. Even with your wards up, I can tell.'

'Alere—'

'Don't treat me like a child.' Her night-black eyes hardened and her chin lifted until she looked every inch the Jun-Heir.

'I'm not.' Corin slid his hand along her jaw, his thumb caressing her cheek. 'There's nothing wrong with wanting to shelter people you love, Alli. Believe me, if I could have saved my betrothed – Shasa – and my parents a decade ago, I would have. But it's not your responsibility to protect everyone. And Mina leaving wasn't your fault.'

She batted his hand aside. 'Everyone keeps telling me that, but you're wrong.' She pressed a hand to her stomach, frowning. 'I don't know how to explain it. There's a bond between Mina and I. Something that pushes me to get to her; to take care of her.'

'That's only natural—'

'No!' Alere made a hasty motion with one hand. 'No. You don't understand. It's…no, never mind.' She sighed and tugged at a stray lock of hair as she did when she was troubled. 'Have you been to Chengdu?'

'Of course.' Corin shrugged, accepting the change of topic. 'Chengdu, in Melcor. Also Adeghal, the capital of Shemal to the northwest. But I try to avoid them in summer. Both are hotter than I like, even in our regrettably-short winter. Sweating is so unpleasant, don't you think?'

She merely smiled so he continued, hoping to distract her.

'I normally spend the two months of winter in Shanzhai, Madina or Jiali. But I've spent a couple in the other cities.' He grinned. 'There's not a lot of spying and travelling to be done hereabouts once the blizzards sweep up from Jadid.' He leaned on the railing again. 'I liked Adeghal's people – very easy-going and fun. Chengdu, not so much.'

'Oh?' She tilted her head. 'Not enough skulduggery for your taste?'

He gave a short laugh. 'Actually, Chengdu has one of the best spy networks in the world. We don't know who runs it, although the name Liu Gray gets bandied around. But no-one can – or will – describe him and that's frustrating as jahim. Rafi buys information from him. No, Chengdu sets my teeth on edge for other reasons.' He checked to make sure Gavon wasn't around. 'It's the slave industry. I've had an exciting twenty-six years of life. Seen a lot I'd rather forget. But slavery gives me nightmares. Rafi's forbidden me to go there except under the direst of need.'

'Why?'

He chuckled mirthlessly and fingered the steel dagger at his hip. 'He doesn't trust me not to take out my disgust on the four Slavemasters who run the system. He thinks assassinating them is a waste of time, since they'd be replaced by new ones two minutes after they were dead. He's wrong, because *I'd* feel better. They are the lowest wisix guisunzi I've ever encountered.'

She swallowed, paled and gazed downriver again.

CHAPTER FIVE

CORIN

Realising his mistake, Corin laid a gentle hand on her shoulder. 'Hey, it'll be alright.'

'Of course.' Alere pasted on an obviously-fake smile and slapped her palms on the railing. 'So...Kett mentioned breakfast?' Lifting one bare foot she grimaced. 'And I could use some shoes. My feet are freezing. Last time I go rushing into battle without boots.'

Ignoring the ache in his chest at the tacit dismissal, Corin jerked his head towards the lower deck. 'The cook's got something unrecognisable, but possibly edible, bubbling on the stove if you're brave enough.' He yawned hugely, leading the way belowdecks. 'I might go back to sleep while the others are awake. At least you get your own cabin.' He chuckled. 'Kett, Gavon, Rafi, and I are sharing. So, I get to listen to Gavon snore, and watch Rafi and Kett be incredibly polite to each other.'

'I don't understand why Rafi doesn't like Kett.' Alere ducked to follow him through the low door, into the gloom. 'And you don't like him either, do you?'

Corin laughed. 'I like Kett well enough. It's just fun irritating him.'

'Don't tease him, Cor. He's overprotective of me – and Mina – but for good reason. You know that.'

Corin smiled, lit a mel-oil lamp and held it high in the dark hallway. 'As for Rafi...I know you've only known him a few days, but haven't you noticed your father tends to dislike what he can't control? Kett epitomises that. Technically he should be Jun First, yet he refuses. Rafi sees that as shirking his duty. But he's also afraid Kett may change his mind and take the throne back.'

They collected bowls of steaming yenna-nut porridge from the harassed cook and took them to Alere's cabin. Corin followed her in and resumed his explanation where he'd left off.

'Kett would be someone on the throne who owed Rafi nothing and cared nothing for his good opinion. Someone over whom he had no control or influence.' Corin blew on his porridge. 'To do him justice, though, Rafi's people have thrived. But he's had to watch helplessly for twenty years while Hanna Zah-Hill and Ven wrecked Mamlakah's economy. He wants to help. To make sure the Jundom's run well. He is very good at that.'

Alere unbuckled her swordbelt and placed it and her bow on the narrow upper bunk. After a moment's hesitation, she pulled the dagger from its sheath and laid it on the lower bunk. She rummaged in her things until she found socks.

'I see.' She tugged her boots on. 'And do you think that's why he's along on this trip? To keep me and Kett and Jarran under control?'

Corin sat at the opposite end of the bed. 'I think Rafi's already learned he has little hope of controlling you, shunu. He is worried about Mina and Jarran, though. Typically, he believes he's best qualified to handle the situation.' He finished eating, licked the spoon and dropped his bowl onto the floor. Interlacing his hands behind his head and crossing his ankles, he relaxed against the curved wall as the chuan shifted direction in the rushing stream.

She frowned, spoon dipping in and out of the gloopy mess in her bowl.

'It tastes better than it looks,' he said gently. 'The cook has a deft hand with spices.' She was too pale and tired. She ate a few spoonsful in silence, her gaze abstracted. The yanstone dagger lay in her lap, now, the stones catching and amplifying the mel-oil's golden glow.

Corin pointed at the dagger. 'Have you had a chance to test your limits with the stones?'

Her fingers closed possessively around the hilt and she put the bowl aside. Lifting the dagger, she stared into the stones' silver-gilt fire and frowned.

'Not really.' She cocked her head. 'I guess I'm not sure how. I trained my whole life to be a telepath without actually being one. Now...' She shrugged. 'The only real reason I need it is to track Mina and she's blocking me. And they only work when I'm touching them. So, I don't know what to try. Xintou House is big on what *not* to do.' Her mouth twisted. 'And I don't seem to have any of the useful powers like telekinesis, pyrokinesis, or broadcasting. Just telepathy.'

'What about influencing people's thoughts and emotions? Like you did with Ven when you implanted false memories.'

Alere sent him a sharp look and said stiffly, 'I haven't tried again. And I'm not proud of what I did. That's something Xintou House does *not* condone.'

Corin leaned forward and gave her a sympathetic smile to soften his next words. 'You're not a true xintou, Alere. Do remember that.'

'As if I'd ever forget,' she snapped.

He sighed. 'I didn't mean it like that. I just meant you need to use every advantage you have. There may come a time when you *need* to influence people – for the right reasons. Don't throw out the option because Mistress Li has brainwashed the xintou women.' When she glared he held up a hand. 'Don't get me wrong. I understand *why* the xintou shouldn't use that power. If they did, the Jun First would be xintou, not a normal person. I'm just saying you shouldn't discount influencing people's emotions as a weapon.'

She shuddered. 'I don't even know if I can. Leaving false memories is just a type of telepathy. Not the same as Empathy – influencing emotions. Not all xintou can do that.'

Judging the seed well-planted, Corin changed the subject and proffered his own dagger with its yanstone in the pommel. 'Do more stones strengthen the connection? I must admit, being telepathic would be handy.'

She sent him a shrewd glance. 'You're not fooling me, you know. When we were in the conference room in Shanzhai, after the battle with Hanna and Celia, you touched the yanstones on your weapons. I *felt* your mind connect to them. You do have the xintou gene they unlock. Why did you lie to Rafi?'

Corin stilled then raised a hand, conceding defeat. He quirked a grin. 'I confess my motives are impure. I'm a spy. Minor though my abilities appear to be, Reading others' thoughts is a lot easier than sifting through the lies they tell.'

'Yes, and that's the problem, isn't it?' She rose and paced the small room. 'I've had xintou morality literally beaten into me. I know where to draw the line: when to Read and when to respect others' privacy. You, though…'

He laughed, hoping she wouldn't Read the tiny flash of hurt her words engendered. 'Are you implying I'm less moral than you? I do believe I'm offended. Here I thought you even liked me.'

She raised a scornful brow. 'Given your occupation, I'm not sure you have the right to be offended.' She turned around and back again, waving her hands. 'And of course I like you but…you're… feckless and irresponsible. You have dozens of women chasing you. You treat everything like a joke and act as though nothing is important. You… you're impossible and I…' She jabbed a finger into her own chest and glared. 'I have to be better. Do the right thing by the Jundom. I can't…. even if I want to…I have responsibilities. You and I…we…' She made a helpless little gesture and petered out.

Corin watched her for a long moment until she shifted uncomfortably. She wasn't normally given to outride rudeness. Clearly something bothered her and, from her almost-incomprehensible speech, he had a rough idea what it was. He needed to tread with care.

He rose slowly. His heart skipped a beat and he hesitated. For ten years he'd guarded himself against falling in love again. Guilt over Shasa's death. Long years searching for her. Fear of being hurt. Was Alere worth the risk?

Her cheeks were flushed, her eyes glittering, a frown pulling her straight dark brows together. She swallowed and her hands trembled.

She was afraid, too. And, somehow, that helped. If she didn't care for him, deepening their friendship to intimacy wouldn't bother her. He closed the gap between them. She raised her chin defiantly, arms tightly crossed.

'Don't, Alli.' He kept his voice low and calm. 'You know my reputation with women is a cover. And you know I do whatever is needed to fulfil my responsibilities to you and to Rafi. In my line of work, you either find a way to cope, or you get out. I have to laugh at the world, otherwise I couldn't live with the things I've had to do to keep the Jundom safe. So…' He took a step closer.

She backed away until she bumped against the bamboo wall, and stared up at him, wide-eyed.

'Whatever you're afraid of, let it go and stop pushing me away. I know you're not sure about us…about me.' He rested his hands on her shoulders and slid them up to her jaw, stroking her cheeks with his thumbs. 'I'm hoping I can change that, if you'll give me a chance.' He smiled gently. 'I'm quite likeable you know.'

Her eyes darkened and she searched his face for something, hesitant still.

Slowly, so she could stop him if she really wanted, he leaned down. Her lips parted, her breath brushed his cheek, warm and sweet.

She looped her arms around his hips. Her frown softened to a rueful smile.

'Ah, diyu. I can't stay mad at you, Cor. Stop being so melodramatic, you shazi. Leave that up to me. It doesn't suit you at all.' She lifted her face and fitted her body against his.

A knock fell on the door.

'A...Lia?' Kett's deep voice sounded outside, changing his query from her name to her half-sister's in mid-word.

Alere flinched and pulled away, her cheeks pink.

Corin grimaced. Neither of Kett nor Alli were comfortable with the masquerade of Alere pretending to be Lianna Koh-Lin. While it pained Corin to see Alere's troubled reaction to being called by her sister's name, he quite enjoyed watching Kett's strict weishi sense of ethics struggle with the deception.

'Now who has the bad timing?' he muttered.

Alere flashed a tight smile. 'Yes?' she called to Kett.

'Gavon asked if you wanted to continue your unarmed combat training now you're well enough. He's on deck.'

Alere lit up with the first genuinely-happy smile Corin had seen since their trip from Newmec. He chuckled, half in delight at seeing it, half in amusement that the prospect of being slammed to the timber held the power to dispel her worries, but he did not.

She slipped out of his embrace, yanked open the storage cupboard beneath the bed and laid the yanstones and her weapons inside. Opening the cabin door, she edged into the narrow hall, tucking her shirt into her trous and tightening her belt. She smiled at Kett and ran out onto the deck.

Corin emerged more slowly and turned the bronze key in the lock before pocketing it. Catching Kett's cool speculation, Corin straightened his own clothing unnecessarily. With a knowing grin and wink, he waved the weishi ahead. Kett's expression hardened to stone and he strode away.

After retrieving his oud from his cabin, Corin emerged into the morning glare and settled himself on a pile of ropes on deck. He tuned the instrument and idly strummed, wincing in sympathy as Gavon put Alere through her paces. Kett, seated on the other side of the chuan, watched the lesson with professional interest.

The sun was as warm as it got at this time of year, the pale green sky clear of clouds, the breeze off the river cool and crisp. Corin laid one ankle across his knee to support the instrument and plucked out a carefree little dance tune that had been rattling around in his head the last few days. It was good to be alive.

'She is...' Rafi's voice above his shoulder made Corin squint upward '...extraordinary.'

Corin strummed a joyful, major chord sequence and studied the Jun thoughtfully. Rafi could use a dose of his daughter's humility.

'She is indeed.' He switched to a complex run of minor chords and caught Rafi's eye. 'Y'know it wouldn't hurt to tell her. She's risked everything trying to help you. And all I've heard you do is berate her for being reckless or forbid her from doing something.'

Rafi directed a cold, unyielding glare on him.

Corin twanged a dissonance. 'Don't look daggers at *me,* shenshi. After all, one of the most enjoyable parts of my rather thankless and underpaid job is being able to point out when you're being a zift.' He watched Alere rise, panting and laughing, to leap at Gavon yet again.

'She blames herself for Rohne and Mina's disappearance, and Jarran's endangerment. You could help with that.'

Rafi's eyes softened to consideration as he regarded his daughter. His mouth thinned. 'She *is* reckless, though. And you're just as bad. You encourage her.'

Gavon called Corin's name, gesturing him over.

'Yes, shenshi,' Corin responded. 'But, unlike me, *she* is never reckless impulsively.' He rose, laid the oud aside and dusted his trous off. 'Nor does she flout your authority because she finds it irksome, as I do. She takes responsibility seriously. When she does something reckless, it's because she believes it's the right thing.

'Frankly, shenshi,' he continued, 'it would do her good to relax a little. She was a lot happier and more fun on the road. Before Shanzhai.'

'Before agreeing to pretend to be Lianna, you mean,' Rafi said bitterly. Pain and loss pulled at his mouth.

'Honestly? Yes,' Corin said gently. 'You see headstrong disobedience. I see a girl desperate to prove herself and be accepted. She's already saved your life, your Jundom from war, and given up her freedom. But she can't *be* Lianna.'

Rafi stilled, his hands clenching and unclenching by his sides.

'You need her, Rafi,' Corin added. 'But she doesn't need you. And if you're not careful, she'll realise that one day soon. And it might just outweigh her sense of duty.'

Figuring he'd given Rafi enough to think about, he sauntered over to Gavon and Alere.

Kett approached from the other side, his booted feet silent even on the pitching deck.

Ignoring him, Corin bowed to Gavon. 'What can I do for you?'

'I need both of yer,' Gavon said. 'Time we did some multiple attacker training on m'boyo here.'

'Oh dear.' Corin reached for the buckle of his sword-belt. 'I knew I should have stayed belowdecks. This is going to hurt, isn't it?'

An hour later Corin deeply regretted his impulsive moment of mischief in teasing Kett. Not content with training Alere, Gavon insisted all four of them take turns in handling multiple attackers. Somehow Corin felt he'd received more than his fair share of Kett's strikes and throws. He lost count of the number of times he'd been knocked to the ground. A new cut behind his ear dribbled blood down his neck. Several bruises would show themselves tomorrow.

Afterward, Alere vanished belowdecks, taking her key. She left Corin with the chuan's healer, Lars, who treated his injury with deft experience and kept his lecturing to a bearable minimum.

Retrieving his oud, Corin watched as Kett grilled Gavon. The weishi went over and over the sometimes-unorthodox unarmed techniques the yongbing had picked up during his long years in the slavepens of Melcor. Corin's respect for Kett increased. Not only was the man a skilled fighter already, but he was openminded enough to learn from someone Weishi House would sneer at: a self-taught streetfighter.

Corin made the oud laugh with a chromatic run of chords. Yes, the weishi was difficult to dislike, even when he tried. If only Kett openly returned Mina's affection, the whole situation would be less…awkward. As it was, Corin wasn't sure which sister Kett loved, if either. The man was impossible to read.

Now that was a thought. Corin laid casual hands on the yanstones set into his weapons. Although he lacked the rigorous Xintou House training, he had no difficulty recognising in Kett's mind the same rock-hard Outer wards that characterised Alere's.

Hardly surprising, given she and Kett had both been trained by Xintou House. He put the weapons aside. Worth a try.

He observed the two men awhile longer, finished composing the dance-tune and decided he would catch up on lost sleep. As he passed Alere's cabin he paused. Should he intrude? Continue what they'd started, before training? Silence from within convinced him not to. She was visibly heavy-eyed these days. Given her part in Ven's death, he was fairly sure she suffered from nightmares. If she slept now, she needed it. He left.

When the *Kuailong* tied up for the night, Dalor grudgingly invited his passengers to dinner. The chuanzhu, who rarely spoke, glowered equally at all of them. His cabin was small and the presence of so many large men and strong personalities shrank it further. Corin, who knew the taciturn chuanzhu from previous trips, laughed inwardly at his discomfort.

By the dark circles beneath her eyes, Alere had not slept at all. She seemed reasonably cheerful, though she picked at her food and yawned frequently. If nothing else, the attack by the Melcori served to bring the small group closer and loosened tongues. The talk ran easily enough, even without jiu, for Dalor kept a dry ship. Dalor's company meant the conversation mostly dwelt on the effectiveness of this fighting technique over that, the chuans's attributes, or amusing travel anecdotes. Even Rafi relaxed enough to contribute a few stories from his youthful trips to Jidad and Melcor. Gavon's dry observations about the habits of his native Jidadans made even Dalor laugh.

The table broke up early and Dalor retreated abovedecks to check on the chuan and his crew. Gavon and Kett went to feed the horses. Rafi held Alere back, outside Dalor's cabin. Corin lingered in a darkened corner, shamelessly eavesdropping.

'Li....' Rafi cleared his throat and tried again. 'Alere.'

Her eyes widened. 'Shenshi?'

Rafi cleared his throat again and frowned. 'Please. Shenshi is too formal. You're my daughter.'

'Of course,' she murmured. 'What did Lianna call you? I should do the same.'

Rafi sighed. 'No, that's not what I meant. Call me Rafi if you wish. It's up to you. Choose something you're comfortable with.'

She paused, her fingers straying to tug a lock of hair. 'Very well...Rafi. Is that all?'

He nodded then shook his head. 'No. I...I also wanted to let you know how much I appreciate everything you've done for Shanzhai...for me.' He raised his chin. 'You've sacrificed a great deal and taken enormous risks. I haven't told you enough how much I value you.' His expression softened.

'But I—'

He cut her off with an upraised hand. 'No, let me finish. This isn't easy for me.' He frowned. 'And I realise now how little I did it with Lianna, too. Praised her, I mean.'

'I don't deserve it, shenshi,' she said. 'I let you down. I should have kept a closer eye on Mina and I shouldn't have encouraged you to trust Rohne. Without him on the battlefield at Shanzhai, I almost lost everything for you – your Jundom, your life. Everything.'

'But you didn't,' Rafi said, gently. 'We succeeded because of you. But even more important to me than what you've done is who you are. You're a caring, extraordinary, gifted young woman, Alere. I'm proud to be your father. Proud to have you as my Jun-Heir. That's what I'm trying to say. I'm sorry I'm not very good at letting you know it.'

'Oh.' Tears glistened in her dark eyes and she pressed white fingers into red-flushed cheeks. She choked out an almost-incomprehensible 'thank you' and fled to her cabin. Rafi stared after her, his brow knitted.

Corin eased out of the shadows, shoving his hands into his pockets. 'See?' He elbowed Rafi lightly in the ribs. 'Not so hard, was it?'

Rafi spread his hands wide. 'But she's crying. How can that be good?'

'Never fear. They weren't tears of unhappiness, trust me. She knows you care about *her* now. Not just what she can do for you.' Corin linked their arms and led the Jun to the cabin they shared with Kett and Gavon. 'Hopefully she'll sleep better knowing that. And, as the old saying goes, morning will bring light into darkness. I'm sure everything will be fine.'

He parted ways with Rafi and returned to knock on Alere's door. She opened it but didn't invite him in.

'Alright?'

She nodded and gave him a weary smile, shadowed with regret. 'But we still have bad timing, Cor.' Her half-laugh was self-deprecating. 'My father just unsubtly reminded me I'm Jun-Heir.'

Corin stiffened. 'I don't think that was his intention.'

Her eyes caught his. 'You heard?' When he nodded, she continued, 'No, I'm sure it wasn't. And I appreciated the words. But…' She shrugged one shoulder. 'Maybe we should wait until we find Mina and get Jarran settled into Madina. That way Rafi will have something other than my behaviour to focus on.'

Corin hesitated. If he backed off now, she might keep finding excuses. Did that mean she didn't care for him, after all? But he'd never pressured a woman in his life and he wasn't about to start with Alere. She was too important. He shoved a hand through his untidy hair and took two paces away.

'Alere, I—' He turned back to find her standing close, her eyes dark and wide, her cheeks flushed.

'Ignore that, Cor,' she murmured. 'I'm a shazi. As Kett said, we deserve some happiness with all the madness that's going on.' She slid her hands behind his neck and moulded herself against him.

He frowned and held her away. 'Kett? What does he have to do with this?'

'Nothing.' She held his gaze openly. 'He just said our lives were…that I shouldn't waste time. That if I wanted to be with you, I should.'

Corin stilled. 'Huh. Kett said that, did he?' He pulled her close, searching her face. 'You sure you want this?'

She nodded and flicked a mischievous look beneath her lashes. 'But you'd better not stay all night. Not with Rafi as your roommate.'

Corin chuckled. 'Don't remind me.' He kissed her, tasting the salt of recent tears. When he raised his head, her heart was racing, her body soft and pliant in his arms, her smile sensual. He pushed a stray hair from her eyes. 'Are you going to invite me in?'

She took him by the hand and towed him into her cabin. But, even as she kissed him and melted into his embrace, a small twist of fear knotted in his chest.

And when, hours later, she bid him good night and he slipped from her side, part of his heart stayed with her. He was an utter zift. But loving Alere was the best thing that had happened in a decade.

Now he just needed to make sure nothing broke their fragile new accord.

Several hours later a hoarse, feminine scream of pure terror woke Corin from a profound sleep. Leaping from his bunk, he shouldered Gavon aside only to find Kett already before him in the hallway.

Rafi crowded close behind. The four men reached Alere's door and found it unlocked.

The cabin was too small to admit more than Kett, so Corin stood in the doorway while Gavon and Rafi craned to see past him. Inside, Alere shrank against one wall, knees drawn up, eyes wide. Her breath came in short, gasping sobs. She held her dagger in one hand, thumb on the yanstone set into the pommel's end. Silver-gilt lights in the stone flared as the mel-oil lamp Kett held fed the stone's fire. The glow turned Alere's thumb blood-translucent.

After removing the blade from her shaking fingers, Kett gathered her into his arms, murmuring soothing reassurances. Gradually, the blank-eyed terror faded and her body relaxed. She dropped her head onto his shoulder with a shuddering sigh only to raise it again, tears tracking down her cheeks.

'Something's happened to Mina. She's in so much pain!'

CHAPTER SIX

ROHNE

Rohne sighed and stretched his neck, bumping his head yet again on the upper bunk. He swore and rubbed at his scalp. The cabin was far too small but he didn't dare go up on deck carrying the Koh-Lin yanstone bracelets. Not with ten Shanzhai weishi loitering uselessly about up there. And it was nearly dark, so the moronic senior weishi who shared this cabin would show up soon.

He turned the iron and yanstone bracelets over, admiring the play of light as they caught and refracted the mel-oil lantern's warm glow. They felt cool, even though he'd held them for several minutes. So far he'd only been able to snatch a few minutes in private to test their powers. Not enough to gauge their usefulness. But they did seem to augment his own abilities significantly, which was exciting. When he held them, his mind felt...larger, stronger somehow. And his headache eased. But how did they work?

They had enormous potential. Of that he was certain. But how to unlock it?

He stretched, ligaments crackling, and grinned. Even without the yanstones he was already more powerful than any female xintou. With the possible exceptions of Nasra Connor – his mother – and Mistress Li. Over the last few weeks, his skills had grown considerably. More than he'd shown to his companions. A heavy blanket had lifted from his mind with every step he took away from Gaton. Clearly the stifling, small-mindedness of his birthplace had held him back.

As his mother, Nasra, had always said: he had the power to change the course of history. To be humanity's guide. Now he could see the truth of that. Both his telekinesis and telepathy were stronger. As was his empathic ability to insert emotions and thoughts into others' minds.

Precognitive Seeings also came with more frequency, although they were always about Alere and Mina, not his own future. Annoying, but also useful at times. It wasn't always possible to put the images into any meaningful context until their time was upon him. He would get better at interpreting them, with practice and with the yanstones.

Perhaps it was time to ask Mina how they worked. She obviously knew something about the jewels. Her words back in Shanzhai – when Alere was injured by Ven – seemed to indicate she and Alere were telepathically linked when they wore the bracelets. Yes, if he was going to harness them, he'd have to speak with her. She would understand why he'd taken them. She would know how important this was to him.

Rohne dropped them into a pocket and left his cabin, seeking out hers. But it was empty. He frowned. Probably pandering to Jarran and his whining children again. He stalked along the hall to Jarran's cabin and paused outside the door. Mina's laugh sounded clearly, followed by the amused rumble of Jarran's deep voice. Rohne rapped on the door.

A yawn overtook him and he rubbed at gritty eyes. He shouldn't be this tired. He'd done nothing but sit around on deck, chatting with Jarran and watching the scenery slide past for days.

The warped yar-pine panel opened and Mina edged into the narrow corridor, one finger across her lips. Her face was shadowed and tired, her skin pale. But her eyes sparkled with a glow of laughter that had been missing since they'd left Gaton four weeks before.

'Shh,' she said. 'Rhea and Ashi are asleep. They've both been seasick again, the poor little things. I don't have the right herbs to help, either.'

Rohne scowled. 'I know, but you've spent almost every waking hour minding them. They have a father. He's been looking after them on his own since his wife died. I think he can cope.'

The chuan rolled and sloshed as the crew tied it up for the night. Rohne braced himself against the dark walls. His head spun and he blinked to clear it. The sound of orders rang out abovestairs and timber creaked as the vessel found her place in calmer waters and settled.

Mina kissed his cheek, her velvet-dark eyes melancholy once more. 'Don't be jealous, Rohne. Jarran's not used to being his daughters' sole carer. His sister-in-law lived with them in Shanzhai, but she stayed behind to run his bakeries. He's lost, especially with the girls being so ill. I'm a healer. I have to help.'

Yawning hugely, Rohne tried to keep up the irritation, but exhaustion dragged at his eyelids. 'Well, the chuanzhu said there's some whitewater ahead tomorrow, so you might want to get some sleep tonight. Have you eaten yet?'

'The chuanzhu sent food down. I've had a few bites. I'll eat the rest now the girls are asleep.' Mina smiled gently. 'Don't worry about me. I'm quite enjoying the trip. I don't know why I was so worried when we started. I thought I'd be sick, but I'm not.' She glanced over her shoulder at the closed door. 'And I like being needed.'

'I need you, too.' Rohne snapped his teeth shut, annoyed that he sounded like a child. 'I mean: I miss you. I feel like, since you got back to Gaton, we've hardly had ten minutes together to talk.'

Her eyes softened. She flung her arms around him and squeezed. 'I'm sorry, Rohne. I know. It's all been such a whirlwind – meeting

Alere and Kett. Then Kett being wounded. And all the fuss at Shanzhai.' Her brow clouded. 'Ven Zah-Hill's death.' She shuddered.

'That wasn't your fault,' he said, reluctantly releasing her as she pulled away.

'It was. At least a little,' she said, sighing. 'I should have known Corin was lying when he said they wouldn't kill Ven. They were all so keen to make Alere into a killing machine. Thank you for taking me away before the battle. I just couldn't…' Her lips thinned and she scrubbed her palms down her thighs. 'Never mind. I'm out of it and so glad to be going home.'

Rohne put an arm awkwardly around her shoulders. 'I didn't mean to remind you.' He yawned again. 'I know you feel bad about leaving Alere. And what about Kett? Do you regret leaving him behind?' Now she'd realised Kett wasn't the man for her, they could make a fresh start. Once they got to Madina they would have time together, as adults. Mina would help him achieve his true potential.

'I…I'd rather not talk about him. I thought…It doesn't matter. I just want to get home. Once we're back in Gaton, everything will be alright again.' Mina raised pleading eyes. 'Can we just get to Madina and find a way home?'

'Of course,' Rohne said, fighting to keep his eyes open. 'But I wouldn't mind spending a few days in Madina. You've been there. I haven't. Besides, we have to see Jarran safely installed in the Alcazar.' He grinned. Meeting Jarran on the chuan had revealed possibilities Rohne hadn't even dreamed of before. As Jun First, Jarran had the potential to easily open doors otherwise breached only by force. Rohne had spent the last few days cultivating a connection and a friendship. He intended to make the most of this trip to Madina.

Alarm passed across Mina's face. 'But Madina's not safe. The kin-child laws, remember? I'm Rafi Koh-Lin's kin-daughter. If I'm caught, they'll execute me.' Her voice dropped to a whisper and she checked the corridor. 'And you're a male xintou. You can't—'

'They'd have to catch me, first. I've yet to meet anyone who's mind is stronger. I can control anyone.' He curled a lip.

Mina stared at him.

With a derisive laugh, Rohne shrugged, talking around another yawn. 'And as for you being kin-child...didn't Jarran tell you?'

She raised her brows.

'Whoops. I forgot.' He smiled ruefully. 'He's not supposed to tell anyone. I Read him. That letter he carries from Rafi rescinds the laws. And I think you're safe enough while we're travelling with the new Jun First.'

'Oh,' she said in a small, relieved voice. 'You shouldn't Read people without their permission. But I am glad to know that. And I keep forgetting his new title.' A smile flickered the corners of her mouth. 'He's so ordinary and easy to talk to. I've only known him a few days, but it feels like years. I feel so comfortable it's impossible to think of him as the ruler of Mamlakah.'

'He's not...yet,' Rohne said, sniffing. 'I don't think it's going to be easy, walking into the Alcazar with Ven's blood barely dry on Alere's hands. Do you think the Juns are going to be happy about her killing him, even if he was crazy?'

Mina cast him a doubtful look. 'Do you think they'll do anything to Jarran, or Rhea and Ashi?' She rubbed her palms down the front of her grey and white healer robe. 'Maybe they shouldn't go—'

'They'll be fine,' Rohne snapped, his patience wearing out. His eyes drooped and his head pounded. Every muscle in his body felt heavy. What was wrong with him? He hadn't had that much wine to drink at the chuanzhu's dinner table.

Mina flinched, her eyes huge.

'We'll talk about it in the morning,' he said shortly, 'I can't stay awake, anyway.'

There was a loud thump on the deck overhead. Rohne blinked, frowning. Lethargy seeped through his limbs and clouded his thinking.

Someone screamed, hoarse and masculine.

Mina gasped, hand over mouth. Rohne staggered a step toward the narrow ladder leading abovedecks, his head thick and feet clumsy. She grabbed his arm and dragged him back.

'Don't,' she whispered. 'You can barely stand. What's wrong?'

His tongue cleaved to the roof of his mouth and he squinted at her, trying to focus. 'Wine. Dinner,' he managed. 'Only had one glass.'

Stealthy footsteps creaked across the deck. Another scream, this time cut short. The chuan rocked and sloshed in the water. Rohne's knees sagged. He reached out with a thought, trying to determine what was happening overhead. But his mind was fog and sinking sand, his powers mired.

Mina pushed open the door to Jarran's cabin and dragged Rohne inside. She shut and locked it with trembling hands.

'Stay awake, Rohne. Jarran!'

Rohne propped himself against the wall and leaned his head against the timber, fighting the urge to drift into sleep.

Jarran Zah-Hill lifted his head from his folded arms and blinked blearily at Mina. He rose from a desk in one corner of the spacious cabin, angling his head to stand beneath the low ceiling. He frowned at Rohne.

'What's wrong with him? What was that noise? Did someone hurt themselves?'

Mina shushed him. 'We don't know what's going on, but I think Rohne's been drugged. He says he only had one glass of wine. Where's your wine from the dinner the chuanzhu sent down?'

Jarran waved a hand at the desk where a food tray and glass of dark purple wine waited. She dipped a finger in and tasted it, screwing up her nose.

'Sabat.' She wiped her lips. 'Sleeping drug. Acts more slowly than istilqa but it lasts longer. Enough to knock you out for a day by the taste of it. You drank some?' She peered at Jarran.

'Only a sip.'

'Who would do this?' She set the wine down.

Rohne squinted muzzily at her and forced his mouth to move. 'Slavers,' he managed, though the word was blurred. 'Chuanzhu told me slavers sometimes raid boats. Need to get you out.'

Mina exchanged a horrified look with Jarran. Both of them turned towards the two, small, sleeping girl-children curled up together on the lower bunk of Jarran's cabin.

'We can't let them be taken,' Mina said.

Jarran produced a small, curved dagger and held it in his fist, his face grim. 'I won't. I know where to hide them. You get Rohne out through the aft hatch. Slip over the side. The cold water'll wake him up.'

'What about you?' She wrapped her arms around his waist and pressed herself against him. 'I can't leave you and the girls here.'

Jarran's eyes widened and an incredulous smile curved his lips. 'Mina, I—'

Something thumped against the door. A voice called out a command to open it.

Mina and Jarran rushed to the children, woke them and stifled their sleepy voices.

Rohne's knees buckled. He put his back against the door, slid down and fell sideways onto the polished timber floor. His body refused to obey. His thoughts oozed sluggishly as he struggled to comprehend what was happening. He had to stay awake; had to protect Mina.

The door burst open, jamming into his back. Splinters of wood sprayed across the room. Rohne lay, helpless, as four men kicked him aside and crowded in.

One of them bore a bucket of smoking coals and a bronze poker. The metal glowed red-hot.

Mina screamed.

ALERE

'No.' Alere interrupted the argument amongst the men. 'It was *not* a nightmare. My sister and I are twin-bonded. I *know* she's hurt. Stop wasting time.' She slammed her hands onto Dalor's thin, magnal desk.

Dalor glared back, his short black beard jutting forward with his outthrust jaw. 'We can't run the *Kuailong* at night on this stretch of river, shunu. We have to be able to *see* the rocks in order to avoid them. No amount of shouting at me will change that.'

With a wordless exclamation, Alere threw up her hands and paced around his cabin, caged and powerless. Somewhere downriver, Mina was terrified and in pain, her fear a flame in the depths of Alere's mind. There had to be a solution.

'Jiche! Fine,' she snapped. 'Give me one of your lifechuans. I'll go, myself.'

Dalor gave a short laugh. 'Have you ever manned one before in your life, shunu? Do you even know how to row? Or how to handle it in the whitewater ahead? Can you swim in near-frozen water when you capsize it? Or fight off a shaytan?'

Alere groaned and sank into a chair, trying to think clearly and slowly – through the desire to *do* something. Overhead, a mel-oil lantern swung as the river rocked the vessel like the mother of a sleepy babe. Her shadow leapt and moved on the wall, as she wished she could. She willed Dalor to accede. Her hands rested on the yanstones in her weapons, and she was tempted by the stones' golden warmth. It wouldn't take much to slide into Dalor's mind and change it for him.

'Alli,' Kett's low warning made her jump guiltily. He knew her too well.

'I'm begging you, Dalor,' she said, trying to master the tremor in her voice. 'My sister is in danger and we have to get to her as fast as possible. What are our options?'

'Lass.' Dalor pinched the bridge of his nose. 'I do understand and I'll do everything to get you there but...' He walked around to stand beside her. His heavy hand came to rest on her shoulder. 'I won't run at night because that'll kill all of us. We're only three days behind their chuan. Grounding on these rocks would be the worst thing I could do for you, and her. Trust me.'

'Then how?' Alere spread her hands, wanting a solution.

'We'll run at first light and put men on the oars.' He eyed Rafi, Gavon, Corin and Kett askance. 'That is, if you're willing to help, shenshi. I don't have enough crew. You'll have no-one to spell you, but with even four oars we can catch them up in a day and a half.'

The men all gave their willing assent.

She gripped Dalor's proffered hand. 'Thank you. I'll help as well.'

'The best thing you can do is to get what sleep you can. You'll need it.' His grim expression did not soothe her anxieties.

Before the first hint of light, Dalor roused the grumbling crew, fed them and set them to work. Alere's four companions he took into the belly of the *Kuailong*. There he set them to the oars and bid them pay close attention to the instructions yelled, through a speaking tube, by the first mate. Normally they'd have a drummer, but they hadn't a man to spare and Alere hadn't the experience. Her, he put to work as a runner, supplying the four rowers with water and food, spelling them so they could rest.

When faced with the rowing benches, Gavon muttered something astoundingly rude. He took a deep breath and grimaced. He removed his leather armguards and tossed them aside, rubbing restlessly at old, pale scars on his wrists.

Drawing him apart, Alere touched his wrist. 'I'm sorry, I should have thought. You don't have to do this, Gavon.'

The older man's eyes slid to the hard benches lining the hull then back to her. His mouth split into a thin, fierce grin and he shook her hand off.

'I know, boyo,' he muttered, 'and believe me, I wouldn't do it for anyone but yerself. Now get out of the way before I change my mind.'

By late afternoon Alere was glad of the nagging presence of Mina's pain in her mind. It kept her going even when her hands blistered and her shoulder muscles spasmed and shot pure agony through her back. Corin's witty banter had long since vanished into grim silence. His demeanour now matched the others for blank, mindless determination.

All four men had stripped off their shirts. Alere wore only her breast-binder and loose bamboo-cloth trous that clung to her legs, damp with sweat. For all it was snow and ice abovedecks, below was clammy and steamy. Refreshed only in the brief intervals when a gust of air slipped in off the icy water, through the oarlocks. Alere had regularly doused the men with buckets of river-water throughout the day.

Darkness washed across the valley and Dalor called a halt. Alere sighed and leaned against the curved magnal wall, too exhausted to even walk to the nearest bench. Corin shipped his oar. With a groan, he collapsed to lie on his back on the bench, bare chest rising and falling, skin glistening in the half-light.

Kett peeled his hands off the oar and inspected them. He shipped the oar and rested his elbows on his knees, head bowed. His smooth, broad shoulders curled around his exhaustion and his fingers dangled loosely between his legs.

Gavon's xiao-bear-pelt back was crisscrossed with pale whip-scars. He rotated his shoulders, groaning, and held up a hand.

'Long lost all me calluses. It's blisters for me as well, boyo. If ye've the energy, see if the healer has any luhui aboard. He ought to. If we get it on now, yer hands'll be right in the morning.'

Alere shoved herself upright. Barely able to stand, and drenched with sweat, she staggered onto the deck. Icy wind sliced through her wet clothing, sucking the last strength from her body. Her knees buckled as she descended into the cabin area and found the healer. A thin, cynical young man, Lars was in the middle of stitching a deep cut one of the crew had sustained when a stretch of whitewater had tossed the chuan around like a cork a short while before sunset.

He demanded to see her hands. She held them out wordlessly and he slathered cooling luhui-gel onto the blisters. Giving her the jar and instructions, he pointed her out the door and returned to his previous task as though she hadn't interrupted.

Clambering back into the hold, she painstakingly applied the gel to four pairs of blistered, twisted hands, murmuring words of thanks and encouragement as she moved among the men.

When she forced herself to rise from the bench next to Kett, he laid the back of his hand on her arm. His palm glistened with purplish gel.

'Have you learned anything more about Mina? Can you reach her?' His voice was as weary as his slumped shoulders, but his eyes were calm, as ever.

Were her hands less painful, Alere would offer to massage his shoulders, as she had in years past when he'd come back from Weishi House training, exhausted and beaten. Instead, she shook her head, pressing three fingertips to her temple.

'When I use the stones, I can feel the distance between us is less. And that she's alive. Somewhere dark. But I can't reach her. She's too afraid and in pain. It's making a natural ward I can't get through. I'll keep trying, I promise.' She kissed his cheek. 'I'm sorry.' After such a day she ought to have better news for him.

A sponge bath in her cabin, and a meal of cold meats and bread were all she could manage before collapsing into her bunk. The exhaustion was essential, otherwise Mina's low-key fear and pain would keep her awake through the night. As it was, she dreamed of darkness, fire, and laughing faces that twisted and morphed into her own as the flames danced. Whether it was a product of her mind or Mina's was impossible to know.

The next morning was worse. Aching muscles seized overnight and all five companions felt the stretch and tear as they took to the oars again. True to Gavon's prediction, their hands were blister-free, but only for a short time. It wasn't long before each oarstroke tortured anew.

Sooner than expected, Dalor's hail of 'hard-a-port, chuan ahead' had them drawing in their oars and struggling onto the deck. The feeble sun played hide-and-seek behind heavy, snow-laden clouds and Alere could barely make out the hulk half-hidden in a tributary. It listed to one side, tied to a tree to stop it from floating away, cabin and deck partly burnt.

As they approached, several bodies became visible on the remains of the deck. Alere counted eight, all wearing Koh-Lin weishi black and green uniforms. Metallic-red bot-flies swarmed around the bodies, their buzzing audible even over the river's gurgling. Something moved on the deck and Alere tensed. Then three huge nasiri squawked shrilly and launched from the deck to circle above, their curved beaks and claws red with blood. Their leathery black-and-grey furred wings were mired with gore.

Rafi's knuckles whitened on the railing and Corin groaned low in his throat.

The river-bottom rose and the *Kuailong* could approach no closer. One of his men threw a lasso around a tree stump and tied the aft line securely. Dalor, after inspecting the waters downstream, lifted the keel and let the vessel float with the current. A poleman kept the prow away from the rocks.

Dalor lowered the lifechuan and Alere collected her weapons and joined Kett, Corin, Gavon and one of Dalor's crew in it. Rafi protested. Alere ignored him. The crewman rowed, sympathetically declining their assistance.

They landed downstream. The crewman leapt to shore, tying the little vessel firmly to a silverbark tree.

'Stay out of the water,' he warned as Alere prepared to slide over the gunwale. 'Get to shore over the prow. There're straight-eels in this stretch of the river. They'll rip a chunk out of your calf if you're in the water more'n a few seconds.'

Alere shivered and clambered over the prow. A flash of mottled blue-green fin and multiple rows of jagged scarlet teeth splashed in the dark water by her foot. She jumped high onto the shore and the crewman steadied her.

The others followed. The crewman stayed with the lifechuan. Alere followed Corin, struggling through the bare-leafed, thorny thickets growing along the water's edge. Snow slid off the branches, wetting her clothing and hair, soaking her boots, and turning the soil underfoot to mud. A pair of jin-birds, brilliant gold in the weak sun, flew from their hiding place. Their furred wings and pointed beaks beat in Alere's face and she ducked, her heart racing. They fluttered away, squealing. No other sound disturbed the heavy, cold silence.

By the time the group reached the hulk, cold, exhaustion and foreboding soaked Alere to the bone. As she neared the vessel, certainty grew.

CHAPTER SEVEN

ALERE

Alere touched the damp, blackened timber as Corin hunted for a way to climb onto the deck. Her other hand rested on the yanstones in her dagger and she sought for life aboard the chuan's gutted carcass. Nothing. Her stomach knotted. She pushed further, searching. No... wait...there was someone. A mind she didn't recognise. No, two minds. Young and half-dead with thirst and hunger. Hiding. And a third. A man, barely alive.

As she followed Corin and Gavon over the gunwale, Alere called out softly. 'There are three alive, just. One's a man. The other two are Jarran's daughters. They're hiding on board somewhere. Did anyone—' Corin passed a mel-oil lamp over. 'Oh, thanks.'

She drew her dagger out, just in case.

The stench of day-old death and burnt wood wafted up and she had to swallow against nausea. As they searched belowdecks, the body count rose to fifteen – nine of the ten weishi, plus six of what must be the crew. All killed efficiently and quickly, with little sign of resistance. Most of them still wrapped in cloaks and blankets where they'd slept.

Gavon inspected one of the bodies. When he rose, he held an oddly-shaped knife in his palms. A double-edged bronze blade, sinuous and etched with an intricate design of stylised waves. His expression was one of bleak distaste. Wiping the blood off, he handed it to Alere.

'A Melcori kris.' He pointed at the carnage. 'This was done by raiders from Melcor. Probably the same boat that attacked us, the *Nasir*. But we killed most of their men. That's why they've slaughtered the Koh-Lin weishi as they slept on deck, rather than risking a fight.' Gavon waved a hand at the fast-flowing river. 'The man posted to watch would have been taken overboard, first. Straight-eels and shaytans would have got him.'

Alere stifled a horrified gasp. To a trained weishi, being murdered in his sleep was the most ignominious of deaths. It was hard to believe none of them woke and fought back. She took in the bodies' relaxed poses. Something wasn't right.

'Gouri,' Corin muttered. He closed the eyes of one dead weishi and swallowed hard. 'I knew these weishi. Some of Rafi's best. Good men and women, all. They didn't deserve this.' He stood abruptly and stalked to the side, staring blankly out at the stark landscape and icy waters.

'And what of Mina, Jarran and Rohne?' Kett put in quietly, inspecting the non-uniformed bodies.

'If they were in cabins, they were fair game,' Gavon said. 'They've either been taken hostage for ransom or taken as slaves. If the slavers missed the wee girls then we need to find the poor things.'

'Wait.' Kett waved Gavon over to where he crouched by a crumpled form. 'This man's still alive and he's not dressed like the rest of the crew.'

Gavon inspected him, turning over the man's arm to reveal an embossed leather bracer. 'Melcori. Paid mercenary, not a mhareb-slave. Slaves and mhareb-slaves get a tattoo instead of the bracer. Ye can tell who they work for by the letter.' He tapped the embossed letter N. 'Master Hallon Nasim's man, like the others. Hallon Nasim's not the worst of the Slavemasters, just the most powerful. Hallon sits in Shah Jahil's pocket: his kin-brother. Some say he's the power behind the throne.' He ripped the man's shirt to expose a sluggishly-bleeding, stinking wound under his ribs. 'One of the weishi must've fought back. He'll not live more than an hour or so longer.'

Corin inspected the wound and shook his head. 'More like Jarran's work. He favours the karambit blade – close-fighting. Nasty weapon.' He checked the other bodies again. 'He's not here, which means he's probably with Rohne and Mina on the slaver chuan. Hopefully.'

'Right.' Kett jerked his head at the cabins. 'Alere, you and Corin find the children. Gavon and I will get what we can here. There has to be a reason they're so far upriver at this time of year. Why they tried to kidnap Rafi. We need to get to the bottom of this. Something's not right.'

Relieved to hear her own thoughts echoed, Alere followed Corin into the cabins. Her boots slipped on the smooth, tilted floor. The boards creaked. A chunk of burnt wood dropped from the ceiling, landing in front of her, spraying charcoal dust into the air. She coughed and waved Corin on, rubbing her eyes as she followed.

The chuan was smaller than Dalor's and the number of places to search, fewer. As Gavon predicted, Mina, Jarran and Rohne were all missing. The cabin that must have been Mina's was torn apart and held nothing but her shredded clothing and, tucked into the corner of a storage cupboard, her healer's bag. Alere clutched it against her stomach.

As they approached the largest cabin, Alere touched the yanstones and gripped Corin's arm.

'Do you know Jarran's daughters' names? Have you met them?'

'Only once. I don't know if they'd remember me, though. Rhea and Ashi.'

Alere pointed to the cabin on the left. The door stood open, torn off its hinges, the lock splintered. 'They're in there. Hiding in a small, dark place. Maybe a smuggler's hold under the floor?'

It took several minutes to find the hidden panel under the bed, and another few to extract the limp little bodies from the airless cavity. Corin brought the first child out and handed her over. Her eyes were closed, limbs and lank hair dangling. Were they too late? The girl's thin chest rose and the dry, cracked lips parted on moan. Relief set Alere's legs trembling. Corin retrieved the other child. He carried her onto the deck and handed her to Gavon, who waited on the riverbank. Alere followed with the younger child and Mina's bag.

The small lifechuan wallowed low and the crewman struggled to row it upstream as they made the return trip to the *Kuailong*. Freezing water splashed and lipped over the sides, soaking Alere's boots and trous. Her shivering translated to the thinly-clad, unconscious girl in her arms. Someone on deck threw a rope, which Corin caught and twined around his arm as they bumped against the hull. They passed the unconscious children aboard and climbed up.

Lars took charge, directing the crew to carry the girls below. Before disappearing with his new patients, he hastily reminded Alere to slather luhui onto her hands again or suffer blisters. And to get dry and warm.

Corin frowned after him. 'I should probably go with him. They'll be frightened and might remember me.'

Rafi stayed him, his clear blue eyes troubled. 'Let me. I know them well. They'll trust me.' He regarded Alere. 'I gather you didn't find Mina, Rohne or Jarran, though?'

Alere shook her head regretfully and handed him the kris, letting Gavon take over to restate his opinion. She found it difficult to maintain her composure. She'd been too late to save Mina. If only she'd pushed harder. Or stopped Mina from leaving Shanzhai in the first place. The insecurity and fear that had kept her from opening up to her sister had driven Mina away.

'Aye, shenshi.' Gavon grimaced. 'They're gone and all the weishi and crew dead. I'm sorry. Slavers again. I misjudged them.'

In the heavy stillness after his words, Rafi paled and turned away to blankly watch the shore slip past as Dalor got underway again.

'Where?' he finally asked, his voice low and strained.

ROHNE

Rohne awoke to a headache that drove spikes into his eyes and twisted nausea into his stomach. He kept his eyes closed, hoping the sensation would fade. Yes, the headaches had been getting worse since he'd left Gatton, but this was like nothing he'd ever experienced. Mina. Maybe her healer bag would have some willowbark. He disliked taking medication, but…

Beside him, someone groaned. He froze, trying to think through the haze of pain. He drove a thought outward. Agony obliterated coherence. Why couldn't he *think?* Why couldn't he sense anyone else's thoughts? It felt like someone had ripped out his xintou powers and stuffed thornbushes into his head. Momentary panic seized him. Without his powers he was helpless. Ordinary.

No. He took a grip on his spiralling emotions. Whatever caused this, it would pass. It had to pass.

He opened his eyes. Light stabbed in and he fought the urge to vomit. Closing them again he tried to get a sense of where he was. Instead of his thin chuan-bunk mattress, he lay on hard, damp wood. His fingers touched slime. The smell of mould and wet cloth filtered into his awareness; along with the unpleasant stench of human excrement, urine and vomit. That was too much. He sat up and retched bile onto the bare boards between his ankles.

'Rohne?' Mina's thready voice barely reached him.

He squinted in the dim light. 'You alright? Where the jahim are we?'

She lay beside him, huddled in the foetal position, shivering in her grey and white healer-robe. Her eyes were dark-shadowed, her cheeks mottled with tearstains and dirt. Beyond her, Jarran Zah-Hill snored heavily, his big body lax in sleep. Rohne peered into the dimness beyond. At least thirty people, dead-eyed and miserable, lay on the curved floor. Water sloshed somewhere nearby, outside the room. The ceiling, low overhead, was also timber, set with gratings at regular intervals. Voices called out instructions up there, somewhere.

'Are we on a chuan?' He pressed a thumb into his temple as the headache flared again. Bronze chains clanked around his wrist. He grabbed one and yanked at it, swearing.

'Oh, don't, please?' Mina whispered. 'The guards come if you do that. They hit Jarran so hard they knocked him unconscious.'

Rohne studied the Jun. A dark, spreading bruise shadowed one eye and cheek. Zift.

'Khara!' Rohne touched Mina's face. 'They didn't hit you, did they?'

'No, but they branded all our feet. You were lucky,' she added bitterly, 'you slept through it. I think they gave you a stronger dose of the sabat.'

Rohne frowned, trying to remember. He checked his feet, only now noticing the dull throbbing pain. Livid red burnmarks marred the soles. 'The chuanzhu. That filthy kalet. The wine.' Relief surged. Drugs wore off. He would be fine, soon.

Mina grimaced. 'I think he must have been in league with the slavers. Or maybe one of his crew was. But they killed him and the crew, anyway.' She trembled and swallowed. 'The food must have been tampered with as well. Jarran had eaten, but I hadn't. You came downstairs. Do you remember that?'

Rohne shook his head. 'But why give me more, unless...' He stared at her in horror.

Her eyes widened. 'One of the side-effects of sabat is mild suppression of xintou gifts. But how could they know who you are?' She glanced at Jarran. 'They do know who Jarran is, because they called him by name. They don't know me. But you?'

'Maybe it was a mistake. I did drink the wine. He didn't.' Rohne dismissed her fears impatiently. 'No-one could possibly know who I am. As soon as it wears off, I'll take control of this gouri ship and get us out of here.'

Doubt flickered in her eyes, but she didn't argue.

Rohne contented himself with playing scenarios in his head. Handling these slaver scum would be simple. If this didn't show Mina the truth, nothing would. She would see him clearly – as a man of power and ability – not through the distorted lens of childish memory. He would look after her.

'What about Jarran?' she asked quietly, touching the Jun's shoulder.

Rohne nodded. 'We'll get him to Madina, too. Then the Jun First will owe us a favour, and that's useful.'

Things had been going well... until the slavers showed up. But now he understood: this was just another opportunity.

Mina smiled gratefully. She squeezed Rohne's hand. 'Thank you, Rohne. I'm so glad you're here.'

Rohne kissed her cheek and lay back on the boards, smiling to himself.

ALERE

'Where, Gavon?' Rafi repeated, his fists clenched around his sword and dagger hilts. 'Where would they take Jarran. And Mina and Rohne?'

There was a long silence. Gavon regarded first Alere, then Rafi.

'Dalor says the *Nasir* is small and fast.' He inspected his blistered hands. 'But they're short-crewed now. And with that burnt sail canvas they'll be hard-pressed to use the sail well. So, we might catch them when they reach Madina. They'll have to stop there to take on more crew, replace the sail, and supplies to feed the slaves.'

Alere covered her mouth and closed her eyes briefly.

Gavon's lips thinned. 'But if we miss them there, their next stop will be Dalcin, then Chengdu. The big end-of-winter slave markets are on in a week.' He folded his arms over his barrel chest. 'If we don't get to Chengdu in time, it'll be tough to find them once they're sold. They could end up on the bamboo and rattleberry plantations to the west. Or out on the seaweed floating-farms, offshore.'

Rafi ran a hand over his short hair. He prowled across the deck and back again, his brow furrowed. He stood at the rail, staring downriver as though trying to see the future.

At last he turned back to Alere and the men, his face firming. He'd made some sort of decision. Alere quashed her irritated reaction to his arrogance. She should hear what he had to say before objecting. As Jun Second, he did have the right – and many years of experience.

'Let's assume the worst. What do we do if we can't catch them at Madina? Recommendations?' His gaze swept all four of them interrogatively.

'We go after them, of course.' Corin answered first.

Alere agreed wholeheartedly. 'But we have to get to Madina. We have to stop them, there.'

Gavon scowled at his own weatherbeaten hands, not meeting her eyes. His mouth pulled down and his fingers wrapped around one of his leather wrist guards. At last, he nodded once. 'Aye, we must.'

'What of Jarran's daughters, shenshi?' Kett indicated the cabin. 'If we miss the chuan in Madina, we can't take the girls with us into Melcor. They're now Jun-Heirs to the First.' He laid a hand on Alere's shoulder. 'Lia shouldn't go, either. She should take the girls to Madina. You should come to Melcor, shenshi. You may be the only person who can negotiate for Jarran's return, if the Shah of Melcor is involved.'

Alere glared at him. His grip tightened on her shoulder. He shook his head a fraction, forestalling her angry protest. She closed her lips, reluctantly and only out of trust in him.

Rafi surveyed him in silence for a long moment. 'You make a good point, Tekettan.' He addressed Kett rarely. When he did, he used Kett's childhood full name, though it sounded formal and awkward.

The Jun raised his chin with all the cool assuredness natural to him. 'However, you'll need Alere's connection to her sister to find Mina. With Jarran absent, I must deal with the unrest resulting from Ven's death and Jarran's abduction. And I'll have to chair the Jun Council when that convenes.' He looked down his nose at Kett. 'Which is why *I* will take the children ashore at Madina and stay there. Jun Second Petar Ma-Safra is in the city, so he and his wife, Leah, can take charge of the girls and assist me.'

Kett's grip relaxed. He inclined his head, reluctant agreement writ on his handsome face. 'Very well, shenshi.'

Rafi swept a hand over his head. 'But, with any luck, we won't need to send anyone to Melcor.' His frown deepened. 'And if we do catch the *Nasir* in Madina, I want Lia and Mina out of the city and heading back to Shanzhai the next day.'

'Why?' Alere asked. 'We can help.'

'I received another message from Yasmin this morning. Hassan Wen-Gates has sent a flitter to the Law Mistress at Xintou House in Madina. It confirms he is claiming a right to the throne.'

Kett spoke. 'He won't be the only one at the Jun Council with a claim, though. You're walking into a zanbur's nest, shenshi.'

The look Kett received bordered on the contemptuous. 'Which is why I want Lia out of the city, back home where she'll be safe.'

Dalor sprang onto the deck with a shouted instruction, interrupting whatever Kett might have replied. The crew lifted what appeared to be a long, central beam running the length of the deck. Within moments it stood vertical and slotted into a hole with a dull thud. Seconds later, its purpose became clear as a small, green sail unfurled and billowed out.

Corin groaned, holding up his blistered hands. 'Really Dalor? *Now?*'

The chuanzhu smiled sourly and thumped him on the back. 'Wind's fickle on the river. Rarely comes steady from the right direction this time of year.' He squinted upriver at the sky. 'But we've got a storm coming up from the south and we can run before it awhile. River's wide and clear from about four gongli further north, and both moons'll be up. Long as we can stay ahead of the storm and have light to see, we can run through the night. Should get to Madina early tomorrow.' His expression darkened. 'Best chance of catching those hundan. Be a rough ride, though.'

'Do you need us to row, as well?' Kett asked.

Dalor shook his head. 'Wouldn't make enough difference to be worth the blisters. This storm's going to be pretty nasty. The trick will be keeping the sail from tearing. You get some sleep. I'll wake you if the winds die off.'

'Well done.' Rafi gave solemn praise then waited until the chuanzhu left. 'I'll speak with the healer about the girls. The rest of you best talk with Gavon about your plans – just in case. That is…' He directed a piercing stare at the yongbing. 'If you're prepared to help, Gavon. You're not in my employ so I can't order you. It's your choice. I would have more faith in Jarran's return, though, if you did go.'

Beside Alere, Kett stiffened, but said nothing.

Gavon sighed heavily. 'Aye. I'll go to Chengdu, if we must.' He sent the Jun a shrewd look. 'But ye'll need to send for more of yer own men if yer to stay in Madina. As ye said, it's an unrestful place. Kin-child law protests. And who knows what rumours are flying around about Ven's death. Being in yer house at yer daughter's hand, as it was. If ye'll take any advice, mine would be to send for yer second-in-command weishi, Maha. And some good men. Maybe even a few of those junren ye've already trained up.'

Corin nodded. 'You'll need trustworthy men to keep the peace in Madina and Jun Third Han-Asad's city weishi are a pitiful lot at best. The Alcazar weishi won't be loyal to you. Nor to a couple of girl-children of Jarran's get, given he's the old Jun's kin-child. And who knows how bad the protests are over those new laws.'

Rafi nodded. 'Sound thinking. There are six weishi stationed in our Madina residence, but I'll send a flitter to Shanzhai. Though, if the roads are snowed, I may need to hire ronin weishi. And I'll keep the girls' presence secret. Perhaps even send them to Jiali if Leah Ma-Safra is agreeable.'

'A good thought, shenshi,' Corin said. 'Can we also send a message to the Madina Portmaster? He can delay the *Nasir* vessel long enough for us to arrive.'

Hope fluttered in Alere's stomach.

'Excellent idea.' Rafi gestured to one of the crew, instructing him to bring a flitter bird trained for Shanzhai and another for Madina. Messages sent, he vanished belowdecks.

Alere rubbed at her arms and gazed at the relentless river that pulled her north. Towards Mina; towards uncertainty; towards…something.

CHAPTER EIGHT

ALERE

When Rafi was gone, Alere sagged against the gunwale. 'Nice bit of reverse psychology, Kett – getting Rafi to stay in Madina.'

Kett's mouth twisted wryly. 'He knew what I was doing. He wanted to stay. I just gave him the opportunity to save face and disagree with me at the same time.'

'I suspected as much.' Corin gave a rueful laugh and slapped Kett on the arm. The weishi remained unmoved. 'You're good at this Kett, that I will admit. It's that inscrutability thing you do. I must try it sometime.'

Kett said nothing.

'Rafi is right about one thing, though.' Corin glanced back over his shoulder at where the Jun Second had disappeared. 'Madina needs him now.' He tilted his head at Alere. 'You too, if we're being blunt. Rafi could use you by his side. You know the Alcazar staff better than he does. And the xintou. He'll need a new Xintou for Jarran. I know Celia's daughter should take precedence, but...' He shrugged. 'What's her name? What's she like?'

'Tali. I don't know her very well,' Alere admitted. 'The senior xintou all say she's intelligent. She hardly ever spoke to me.' She twisted a loose strand of hair around her finger. 'But she was one of the few who left me alone. She used to come and watch me train, sometimes. She's beautiful. Oh.'

'What?' Corin asked.

'I just remembered. When I was leaving Xintou House to go to the Alcazar, Tali tried to tell me something about Celia. I think she was warning me, but Mistress Li stopped her.' She screwed up her nose. 'I don't know. She might be worth talking to as an ally. Did she ever speak to you, Kett?'

'Not beyond polite greetings.' Kett shook his head. 'About a week after you left for the Alcazar, she did ask if I'd heard from you. When I had no news she seemed upset.' He addressed Corin. 'But she's too beautiful to put in the Alcazar. Jarran is young, widowed and in a vulnerable state with all the upheaval in his life. It would take an extraordinary man to ignore her.'

Corin scraped loose hair back into his mawei. 'Makes sense. And her loyalties would be questionable. Though you have given me a strong desire to meet her.' He chuckled as Alere sent him a dry look. 'Lia, you could help with choosing the right person. You know your House sisters. You should go with Rafi.'

'Oh no.' Alere backed away. 'There is nothing you can say that will convince me to go back to that thueban-pit in the Alcazar.' She shook her head vehemently. 'I spent two weeks of diyu in the Alcazar, pretending to be jiaoji to the Jun first. His other jiaoji are saafil kalbs and the staff factions are at each others' throats. I'd be a complete shazi to voluntarily go back there.'

She wrapped both hands protectively around the yanstones on her weapons. And she was not yet ready to confront Mistress Li and her sisters at Xintou House. Not until she'd mastered the yanstones. And not until she'd found out the truth of Celia's claim that Mistress Li had some hidden agenda.

Corin chuckled, guileless and untrustworthy. 'Such language, shunu. But you wouldn't be going back wearing the red-robe and veil of a mistress to Jarran. You'd be Jun-Heir to Rafi. It'd do you good to learn how to handle the politics.' He folded his arms and propped himself against the railing, legs crossed at the ankles.

'He's right, boyo,' Gavon said, scowling. 'Ye should stay. Melcor is no place for ye.'

'But we might not need to.' She frowned at him. 'And why don't you want me to rescue my own sister. What's going on?'

Gavon drew himself up to his full height. 'I just want ye to be safe.' He flicked a glance at Kett, who said nothing. 'If we miss them in Madina, getting Mina and the others back won't be easy. Keeping ye safe is just as important as rescuing them. The Jundom needs ye.'

'I ran away from Xintou House – which is pretty much the safest place on the planet – five times. I've got years of safe ahead of me as Jun-Heir. Many, dull years.' She turned away, appalled by the surge of bitterness that accompanied the realisation. It was true. She would marry some Jun's son and produce the next Heir. All the while running the Second Jundom and answering to its people. This, right now, was her last chance at any sort of freedom, any sort of adventure.

Her throat tightened. She cleared it and lifted her chin. 'Mina needs me more than Rafi does. Besides,' she said, smiling to lighten the mood, 'I'd far rather go to the slavepens of Melcor than back to the Alcazar, any day.'

'Ye say that now, boyo,' Gavon said, his brow dark and teeth clenched. 'But I guarantee that'll change if ye find yerself in the pens. Stay behind. Ye've no gouri idea what ye've agreed to.' He stalked away, back stiff, hands clenching and unclenching by his sides.

Corin watched him go. 'I'd best go after him. We'll need his expertise and I want to know as much as possible in case we do have to go to Chengdu. I've stayed away from Melcor and that choice is now going to be a liability for us. I hate going into a mission blind.' He made a circular motion with a finger as he sauntered away. 'Do feel free to talk amongst yourselves until I get back.'

'Kett?' Mindful of the way voices carried on wind, Alere waited until Corin was gone then turned her back on the deck. 'Is it my imagination or is there something else going on here? *All* the weishi on Mina's chuan dead without a fight? What did the slaver on the ship say? Why didn't you tell Rafi?'

Cold wind from the south played with her hair and sliced through her damp trous. Kett wrapped his cloak around her and tucked her under his arm with absent-minded familiarity. He hunched his shoulders, creating a shelter from the wind. His face was composed, his eyes on Dalor, not far away.

'The dying slaver didn't say much. Only admitted that the men who took Jarran and Mina were Hallon Nasim's. And were under orders to take Jarran, specifically. Which means the Shah of Melcor could well be behind the attack on both chuans. And the attempt on Rafi. But whether he's allied with Hassan Wen-Gates or not is anyone's guess.' He tightened his grip around her shoulders when she started. 'Remember the conversation you overheard in the Alcazar? When Hanna talked about waging war against Jahil? And when she mentioned the Selb? And I think you said Celia told you about the slaver raids?'

Alere nodded. At the time she'd been focussed on finding out what Hanna and Ven were hiding. The prospect of war had shocked her and she'd almost forgotten Celia's mention of raids. Now she clutched at Kett's arm as the rest of Celia's comments returned to mind.

'Celia said Jahil was training an army. I thought she was lying.' She frowned at her weishi. 'So why is Jahil sending slave-raiders this far south? How does it tie in? What does he want and what's this Selb thing got to do with anything?'

Kett contemplated the shoreline. The snow-dusted banks slid past. Blackened leaves, silver-black tree branches and white snow contrasted starkly against the soft blue-green of sky and water. A small grey bird darted out and snatched an insect hovering a handsbreadth above the water. The winged reptile took the insect back to a bush and impaled the twitching body on a thorn then tore it to pieces.

Kett's gaze followed the bird's path. '*Selb* is an old Rabic word meaning 'steel', or perhaps 'crucifixion'. I honestly don't know how it connects. But that the slaver today said the word as he died.' He paused. 'No, he said Selb and then he said, '*I am gangzhi*' – which is old Mandrin for steel.'

'Well, that doesn't help,' Alere said.

'Actually,' Kett added, 'it's more like: *made of steel.* You're right. It doesn't help. I don't understand the significance. But this is the fourth mention we've come across, if you include those men who attacked Mina when we first met her. They said a similar thing. I'd like to find out why.

'As for Jahil, it's not what he wants, but who.' He lowered his voice further as a crewman ran past. 'The only way nine trained weishi are taken in their sleep is if they're drugged. Someone on that ship worked for Jahil and Hallon.'

'You think a Shanzhai-based chuanzhu took bribes from Melcor?' Alere pressed her palms against her temples, hardly able to get her mind around the ramifications. 'But that makes it even more important for Rafi to know.' She half-turned, intending to tell him.

Kett's hand clamped her hard against his side. 'Wait. Think about it, Alli. At the moment, Rafi doesn't know for certain that Jarran was targeted. It's all been guesswork and supposition. If the Shah of Melcor has *deliberately* kidnapped the Jun First of Mamlakah, what would Rafi be obliged to do when he finds out?'

'Oh.' Alere cursed her slow-wittedness. She thought too much in the immediate and not enough in the wider picture. Kett was much better at that. 'If negotiations with Jahil for his return failed, then Rafi would have to go after Jarran with an army. You think that's what Jahil *wants?* War? Or has he allied with Jun Fourth Hassan Wen-Gates to back his bid for the throne?'

'Impossible to know,' Kett replied. 'Could be both of those. He may be backing Hassan to get a war started. If he withdrew his support at the right time, the other Juns would massacre Hassan and leave a power vacuum that would throw Mamlakah into chaos.'

Icy wind gusted under his cloak and slid up her spine. Her feet were numb in wet boots. She shivered again, but not just from the cold.

'But if Jahil knew where Jarran was, that smacks of an incredibly efficient spy system in Shanzhai and Madina,' she added. 'Jahil must have known what was happening – and who was nominated Jun-Heir – as soon as the battle with Hanna's men was over. It's the only way he could get a chuan here fast enough and even then...Unless...'

'Unless?' Kett prompted.

'He had men stationed in Shanzhai, ready to send word.' She gripped the hilts of her blades. 'Which means he'll know I'm here, along with Rafi. No.' It wasn't possible. Sick despair twisted her stomach. 'It's insane, Kett. Jahil couldn't possibly be that good, could he?'

Kett angled his shoulders, blocking her from view of the crew, his face impassive. 'Think it through, Alli. You've studied the politics and economics of Melcor as well as Mamlakah. Who's gained the most by Hanna's destructive policies? Who has the most to lose if a decent Jun First sits on the throne?'

'Jiche.' Alere swept her palms blindly back and forth along the railing as the implications sank in. 'Jahil encouraged Hanna's extravagance. She put the Jundom more and more into debt to him.

That explains the ridiculous trade deals in his favour. Jarran would stop all that. Jahil must have known Radan Zah-Hill was dying. Known Hanna was building an army. Maybe he even knew about the iron deposit. The armies were just in case Hanna succeeded in taking Shanzhai and making steel weapons.' She scowled at Kett. 'He's aiming to take the throne, isn't he?'

'Perhaps.' He stared into middle distance. 'Or to control who's on it.'

'But,' she said, 'I've met Jahil's Xintou, Valera. She came to visit Mistress Li five years ago. She spoke of him as a reasonable man. Intelligent and cultured. Why didn't Mistress Li counsel Valera to stop him?'

Kett lifted a brow. 'I think we've aready established no one understands what goes on in Mistress Li's mind. Or what she's trying to do. After all, she counseled the Bonded Xintou to allow those gouri kin-child laws to go unchallenged twenty years ago. See where that's brought us.' His fingers whitened on the railing. 'I should have done as I vowed years ago and killed every gouri person involved in implementing those laws. Why did I let you talk me in to letting Hanna live?'

'Because it was the right thing to do.'

He said nothing.

Alere leaned into him, but there was nothing she could say that hadn't been said before. It would take time for him to stop blaming himself for the kin-child deaths.

He tucked the cloak tighter about her. 'You could be right, though. If Jahil's not behind this then perhaps it's his kin-brother, Hallon. It doesn't really matter. If they already have Jarran, then the only people to stand in the way are Rafi, and Petar Ma-Safra.'

'And that,' she said, 'is why you wanted Rafi in Madina rather than chasing after Jarran.'

'He's safer in Madina. It's where he can do the most good.'

'And me?' she asked. 'Do you want me to stay with him in Madina?'

With a quiet, rueful laugh he raised his face to the sun. 'Don't ask me what I want for you, Alli. I long ago gave up hoping for that.'

She rested her head on his shoulder, feeling closer to him than she had in many weeks. 'I'm sorry I'm such a difficult charge. You've spent the last ten years babysitting me, teaching me, getting me out of trouble. And all I do is drag you into more. I'm not surprised you've given up on me.'

A low chuckle rumbled through his body as he pulled her closer to his warmth.

'Never. As I've said before: we're bonded, you and I. We're in this together. We'll go together and get Mina back, along with Jarran. She'll be alright.'

Alere stilled, her heart sinking in a way she didn't like or want. 'Mina. Yes.' She disengaged from his arm. 'I should check and see if I can reach her yet.'

Several hours had passed since she'd last tried. She tugged the suede covers off the yanstones. They caught the weak orange light of the midday winter-sun and flared to silver-gilt life, their internal fire hypnotically beautiful. A knot of tension in her stomach dissolved as she caressed the stones' smooth curves and liquid warmth oozed through her veins.

She relaxed her mental wards and let her mind slide into union with the stones. Their gilded heat wrapped her in a full-body embrace from the inside: intimate and, oddly, loving. The taste of smoke and iron teased her tongue and her connection to the stones glissaded across her skin like a warm summer breeze. The world around her: Kett, the chuan, the snow-scented air, the rush of water;

all disappeared into darkness. Unburdened by worry and fear, she floated in ease and security for an immeasurable time.

A thin silver-gilt thread appeared in her hands. She tugged on it and felt movement. Hand-over-hand she followed it. In the distance, a different of sort darkness approached. It enveloped her and she slipped inside a familiar, yet not-familiar mind: Mina's. Yet Mina's thoughts were absent, the space in her mind where her Outers should be was empty. Alere occupied it.

The darkness was now the red-black of closed eyelids. With the body came pain and a strange, pervasive lassitude. Alere extended her new senses and flinched. Mina must have retreated into the back of her own mind to hide from the hurt. She was a healer, not a warrior. Used to other people's pain, but not her own. Untrained in coping with the agony flaring from burns to the soles of her feet. Her jaw ached, too. Alere fought the impulse to groan, to move. Instead, she drew on her weishi training to block out the pain.

Able to bear it at last, she focussed on her surrounds. Rough, damp timber beneath Mina's body, along with a rocking motion and sloshing of water. A chuan. Warm air stinking of human waste suggested the hold. Pressure and rawness around her wrists and ankles spoke of metal restraints. Soft, organic sounds from close by implied she wasn't alone. Were Jarran and Rohne there?

'Mina?' Rohne's whisper by her ear made her jerk involuntarily. 'I know you're awake.'

Alere lifted her eyelids a fraction. Dim light filtered from a grate in the low, wooden ceiling, less than a man's height above her. She turned, the movement jerky. Controlling Mina's body was more difficult than she expected. Pain flared again. If only she could heal Mina's body as she had her own, in Shanzhai. But she had no idea how to do it.

Rohne's amber eyes were vague as he squinted at her. His face was shadowed and bruised. Dark auburn hair hung matted and limp. His clothing was torn and filthy and he, too, wore bronze chains around wrists and ankles.

His expression shifted from concerned relief to shock as his gaze and mind met hers.

'*Alere?*' His bloodied lips fell open. 'How?'

She fought for control of the vocal cords and mouth, finally managing to whisper. 'Later. Are you alright? Jarran?'

He grimaced. 'Feet burnt, same as Mina. It's how they mark slaves and stop them trying to escape. Someone drugged us on the chuan from Shanzhai. I woke up here.' He gestured around the airless hold, chain clanking loudly in the muffling, miserable silence. 'They keep us partly sedated with sabat. I can fight it enough to stay awake more than the others. But it affects my abilities. I can't influence anyone, so I can't get us out of here.'

'What's wrong with Mina?'

Anger flashed through his eyes, followed by a flicker of guilt. 'I was making too much noise, rattling the chains. The guards came and hit both of us.' He touched his swollen lip. 'Knocked her unconscious and she hasn't woken since.'

She flexed Mina's limbs. 'She's alright, physically. Where's Jarran?'

'On the other side of you but I haven't seen his daughters.'

'They're safe with us,' Alere murmured. 'We found your chuan. We're following. Have you still got the yanstone bracelets?'

Rohne flushed. 'They took them.' His brows snapped together. 'How can you be in Mina's mind and controlling her body if she's not wearing her bracelet? And aren't you at risk of Fusion with her?'

Her mouth felt gummed and dry. 'She's retreated, hiding from the pain. There's no danger of Fusion. Listen: whatever you do, don't let the Melcori know who you are, who Mina is, or that you're a xintou.'

He raised a scornful brow. 'I'm not stupid. I thought they might already know because they gave me extra drugs. But I'm not sure.'

She shook her head painfully. 'You don't understand. The Shah of Melcor could be behind this. He's after Jarran, control of the throne and possibly the iron deposit. It's political and Jarran's a pawn. You and Mina would add to the Shah's leverage against Rafi. Keep your heads down and we'll come for you.' The tenuous silver-gilt connection to her own body tugged on her mind and she rushed to finish. 'Help Mina manage the pain. She'll need to be ready. I can't do *this* easily but, if she's alert, we might be able to communicate and arrange an escape.'

Footsteps sounded nearby. A harsh voice commanded her to silence. A heavy hand struck her across the cheek and she tasted blood. The shock brought Mina's mind surging from its hiding place, forcing Alere out.

The silver-gilt thread stretched tight and snapped her into the void. She returned to her own body, standing on the deck of Dalor's chuan. All of Mina's anguish stabbed through Alere. She cried out. Pain exploded in every corner and shadow of her body and mind. Kett gathered her into his arms. The world deepened to darkness and vanished.

CHAPTER NINE

ALERE

'I already told you.' Alere winced as the motion of talking tugged at her bruised cheek. 'I *don't* know how I took over Mina, and I *don't* know how I took on her injuries.' She plucked at the coarse blanket. Her legs twitched uncontrollably as Kett, sitting on the end of the bunk, smeared luhui on her feet. 'Any more than I know how I healed myself when I was injured in Shanzhai. If I did know, I'd do it again, believe me.'

Crowded into her tiny cabin, Rafi, Corin and Gavon all stared at her with expressions ranging from disbelief to surprise and, in Gavon, a hint of fear. Kett remained unmoved, his hands gentle on her feet.

She had apparently dropped unconscious on the deck and slept the rest of the day and night while he and Corin took turns watching over her. Now it was morning and, with Madina a few gongli downriver, Rafi was demanding answers.

Kett clamped down on her legs as she twitched again. He had medicated the burns, bruise and chafe-marks on her wrists and ankles several times through the night, though she had no memory of it.

'The healer says they're almost better,' he said. 'There will be scars, though. The twitching is the nerves regenerating.' He studied her. 'Tell us what you saw on the chuan.'

'They were there and alive. I didn't see Jarran, although Rohne said he was there. All I had time to do was warn Rohne not to reveal himself. The stones did this, I think.' She gestured at her feet. 'I only remember wishing I could take away Mina's pain.'

Rafi vanished into the narrow hall. His footsteps echoed as he paced. Finally, he reappeared, grim.

'We must make ready. We'll be docking at Madina shortly and I don't want to waste time. Corin, you, Tekettan and Gavon go straight to the Portmaster and find out if the *Nasir* is still in port. I've sent a flitter for my six weishi to meet us. If the *Nasir* is still in port, I'll board her as a Madina official, with the weishi and you three. We'll get Jarran and the others off that gouri chuan.'

'I'll go, too,' Alere said.

'No,' Rafi replied shortly. 'You're injured and you girls are my heirs. It's madness for all three of us to be on enemy territory at once.'

'But—'

'No!' Rafi's blue eyes were ice and Alere subsided, fuming.

He turned to Gavon. 'Gavon, make a list of what you think you'll need for Melcor, just in case. You too, Corin. If the *Nasir* has already left, I want you to cast off again within two hours. Lia, keep trying to get back in touch with Mina. We must know for certain what's become of Jarran. Corin, use your contacts to find out who can be trusted in Melcor, in case you need help. I'll try to get word to Liu Gray.' He made a noise of frustration and rubbed a hand over his short hair. 'We have little time. With the Jundom so close to chaos we need Jarran back here for a coronation and a show of stability as fast as possible.'

He turned sharply away and vanished.

Alere set her jaw. Her father hadn't even mentioned his own daughter, in pain and enslaved, other than as a tool for gathering intelligence, or as a potential Jun-Heir. His thoughts were all for Jarran, the Jun-Heir. She thrust down resentment. He was right, of course. The Jun-Heir was vital for the stability of the whole Jundom. Mina would be alright. Uncertainty quivered deep in her stomach.

Corin jerked his head at Gavon. 'We'd best make that list.' Patting Alere's leg, he smiled. 'Let me know if there's anything you need from Madina.'

'The horses,' Kett put in. 'They should be offloaded and sent to the Ma-Safra townhouse. It would be cruel to subject them to an extended trip in that makeshift shelter.'

'Stop!' Alere said. 'All of you. Stop talking like the chuan won't be there. It will.' She scrubbed a hand over her face, trying to force down the sick worry knotting her stomach.

'Alli,' Kett said, gently, 'we have to. Weishi code is to plan for the worst and try for the best.'

She sighed. 'I know. I just...oh, fine.' She leaned over the side of the bed and hauled out her travel pack. She had only two changes of clothes, both in material too thick for Melcor's warmer weather. 'Some lighter clothing for me. Trous and shirts. Not weishi black. Too obvious. And some spare clothing for Mina and the others. Oh, and maybe some disguises that could be useful in Melcor,' she added. 'I'm sure you'll know what's suitable.'

Corin's eyes lit with laughter and he swept her a low bow. 'Indeed, I do.' He kissed her forehead and caressed her cheek with the backs of his fingers. 'And, some makeup, I think.'

She frowned. 'Why? I don't need makeup. Jiaoji pride themselves on never wearing the stuff.'

Corin laughed. 'That's because Jiaoji House chooses only the most fascinating women and men to be jiaoji. In Melcor, ordinary folk don't have the House's training, so they resort to...other techniques.'

Alere mock-narrowed her eyes. 'Are you trying to say I'm ordinary and need makeup.'

Kett coughed a laugh. 'Perhaps you should stop talking, Cor.'

Corin waved dismissively. 'She's stuck in bed. I'm safe. Besides, she knows she's not ordinary.' He leaned down and kissed her, one hand caressing her neck and sliding into her hair. She shivered. Corin pulled back and smiled. 'But everyone wears makeup in Melcor. Everyone over the age of ten. They use it to show marital status as well. Three white dots on the forehead means you're unattached – not bound in the hunli ceremony. Two blue dots means you are. One red dot means you're an unveiled jiaoji, available for hire.' He raised a brow. 'Preferences?'

'White for me,' Alere said quickly, before either of them could make a smart remark. 'But I think you two and Gavon should wear the red.'

Corin laughed again and kissed her once more, lingeringly. Then, with a sly wink, he vanished into the hall, leaving Alere flushed and uncomfortable under Kett's even scrutiny. Kett finished bandaging her feet and knelt on the floor beside her. He touched her arm briefly.

'I'm glad you took my advice about Corin.' His expression was an inexplicable cross between amusement and something she couldn't work out. Sadness?

'I don't know,' she said, twisting the blanket. 'It might have been a mistake. It's just all so…' She let her hands fall to the bed. Corin cared for her and – she couldn't deny it – she for him. And their one evening had been everything she'd hoped. But, while her life was in turmoil, was she mad to take the relationship further? She hadn't had time to talk to him, though.

Kett rose. 'Like I said, Alli. If you love him, don't let anything stop you from being together.' He straightened and stroked her cheek – exactly where Corin's fingers had. 'There's never a right time. There will always be important things that get in your way. In spite of what Mistress Li says, sometimes you deserve to get what you want.' He turned on his heel and left.

Alere fell back onto her pillow and stared sightlessly at the low ceiling, her throat tight.

Half an hour later, she heard and felt the commotion associated with docking at the Madina wharves. Unable to stand the inactivity, or the solitary company of her thoughts, she changed into the formal, dark-green-and-silver Koh-Lin robes given to her by Yasmin Koh-Lin in Shanzhai. Reluctantly, she brushed her hair, pinned it into neat coils, and added the silver-green silk veil over her eyes. No matter what happened, Lianna Koh-Lin needed to leave the ship, so Alek Marin-kin could continue the journey unwatched.

Should that be necessary.

She eased still-tender feet into silver silk slippers, grabbed what she needed to change herself into a boy again, and shoved her sword and dagger into the bag as well. She hobbled onto the deck and paused at the sight of Madina's familiar skyline. She'd never thought to come back. At least, not so soon. And not under such desperate circumstances.

Kett and the others had already left to talk to the Portmaster. How long would they be?

Where was the *Nasir?* She scanned the docks. They extended down the Kabir River and were crowded with chuans nudging and pushing each other like tracker-doquan puppies eager for food. The *Nasir* wasn't in sight.

Great bamboo and bronze gantries hauled nets loaded with bales of seaweed and silk off flat-bottomed chuans that bore the Melcor golden salamander flag. Chuans marked with the Madina roc-eagle symbol were being loaded with live runiu herdbeasts. Twice the height of their handlers, the animals jostled up the loading ramp, their massive, spiralled horns newly-hacked off and some still bleeding. Their plaintive lowing and nervous stamping echoed off the port buildings.

Dozens of men, women and children carried burdens of all sizes on and off the vessels. Dozens more stood in line at the port gates, wrapped in ragged clothing, hoping to be offered work. Their desperate eyes and hollowed cheeks made Alere shiver and turn away. If she failed to retrieve Mina and Jarran, things would only get worse for the people of Madina.

War profited only the wealthy.

The Alcazar's twin silvery towers, hazed in smoke and gleaming in the burnt light, held up the sky. They were the last remnants of the great colony ships that had carried thousands of refugees away from the wars and overpopulation of old Earth. Now they housed the fractured Jun First's court and dominated the skyline of Madina. A city in chaos. Was Kalima destined to follow in Earth's footsteps?

She dragged her gaze away, unwilling to think about it.

Closer to the wharves stood a jumble of bamboo-and-brick slums and warehouses. Buildings built atop each other, overhanging narrow, filthy streets. The Zalams. They obscured the larger, sandstone and sulcrete buildings of wealthier merchants and tradespeople, further away.

From almost every chimney in the city, the lavender smoke of burning seaweed firebricks tainted the last clouds and glimpses of pale green sky to an unpleasant brown. Here at the docks, the acrid smoke combined with the stench of sewage and rotting fish. The storm gusted its last breaths and blew the clean smell of snow across the city. A light flurry of snowflakes dusted the ground and melted immediately.

A port worker emerged from a Melcor chuan, carrying a small dirty-white bag, and approached the locked gate. A clamour arose amongst those waiting. Hands shoved through the bamboo fence, offering him copper tongbi and silver yinbi. He snatched the coins and replaced them with lumps of something dark. The buyers tore off fragments and shoved them into their mouths. Fights broke out. Women and children scrambled, clawing amongst the men for their share.

Blackweed. The illegal narcotic grown in Shemal and northwestern Melcor. Being openly sold at the wharves of Madina. Alere huddled in her cloak, suddenly reluctant to go ashore. The disturbance settled, with many of the blackweed buyers drifting away towards the Zalam slums, their steps uneven, eyes glazed.

Corin, Kett and Gavon appeared at the foot of the gangplank. Corin caught her gaze and shook his head as he ran onto the deck. She sagged against the gunwale, hope dissolving to leave only a bloom of fear that threatened to derail logic. She reached into her bag and gripped the yanstones. The comforting warmth of their silver-gilt reassurance oozed under her skin, calming, soothing, distancing her fear.

Corin arrived at her side and wrapped an arm around her waist, taking her weight.

'What the jahim are you doing on your feet, woman?'

'I wanted to check for the *Nasir.*'

Kett gazed north, downriver. 'The Portmaster wasn't inclined to talk much. He was dealing with some major problem.'

'A chuan was stolen last night,' Corin put in. 'A private one belonging to Master Yar, head of the Merchant House. Pompous hmar. But I've seen the chuan. Nice vessel. I don't blame him for being upset.'

Kett continued as though Corin hadn't spoken, his grey eyes on Alere. 'Portmaster says the *Nasir* stayed only a few hours in the middle of the night.'

'He was lying,' Corin said shortly. Kett raised his brows. Corin grimaced. 'I Read him as he was talking. I'm not great at it, yet, though. Couldn't tell exactly what he was lying about. His mind was full of Master Yar's threats to go to the Xintou House Law Mistress over the theft.'

'Let me try,' Alere said. 'Let me talk to him. I have to go ashore anyway – as Lianna Koh-Lin – in case the *Kuailong* is being watched. I'll change once I'm out of sight of the port and come back as Alex Marin-kin.'

'Wise thought.' Corin scratched at his jaw. 'Things are a little uneasy around here, though. Probably not safe for you to be seen in the Zalams. And you shouldn't be walking. The Portmaster's office is two blocks downriver. I'll find a closed chair for you. You can change and get out around the corner. The chair can go on to Koh-Lin House without you.'

Corin helped Alere across the gangplank onto the dock. Gavon and Kett joined them as Corin handed her into a dilapidated, leather-curtained chair. Corin bowed and made a show of loudly calling her Shunu Lianna, then let the curtain fall. The bearers lifted the palanquin. Corin, Kett, and Gavon strolled alongside while she changed. When she called out she was ready, the chair settled to the ground and Gavon shepherded the bearers out of earshot.

She climbed out, dressed once more as Alek. Corin waited in a noisome alley overshadowed by derelict warehouses. At his back stood a disused, white-brick warehouse that smelled strongly of runiu dung. Nearby, a zibal scavenger-lizard scurried along the wall, its red tongue flickering and mottled black fur torn by fresh claw-marks. It vanished into a pile of rotting lumber and cloth. Kett stood at the opposite end of the valley, keeping lookout.

'Nice neighbourhood,' she said.

'Mmmm,' Corin said absently, holding her at arms length as he inspected her costume. 'Ports are some of my favourite places. So unsavoury. So full of excitement.'

'I'm a little over excitement,' Alere said drily. She tugged the brown linen shirt into place across her shoulders and settled her dagger and sword on her hips. The ankle-high leather boots were tight, but once her feet healed they would be fine again.

'Now *that* I don't believe. Young Alek, tired of excitement? Never.' Corin pressed his fingers to her upper lip. 'Your little moustache is a little skewy.'

Alere touched the gum and hair-clippings she'd hastily smeared onto her lip.

Corin chuckled. 'I'd forgotten how much I like Alek. I was almost sorry when we got to Shanzhai.'

'Me too. I—' She stilled, uneasiness stealing over her. A quick glance over her shoulder showed Gavon staring warily down the street, hands on his weapons.

'Yes,' Corin said. Steel slithered and he drew his sword. 'Gav?'

'Aye,' the yongbing said. He muttered something to the chairboys, who hurried away, leaving the covered chair sitting in the alley.

Alere unsheathed her sword and dagger and put her back against Corin's. Gavon and Kett joined them.

'Kett and I met Mina, not far from here,' Alere murmured. 'Some Zalam slums people had killed her escort and were going to sell her to a slaver waiting at the docks.'

Corin sent her a startled glance. 'Here, in Madina? Bold.'

A shadowy figure scuttled past the mouth of the alley. More appeared. Ten, altogether. Metal and ceramic glinted in their hands. Not the ragged mob Alere expected, though. These were dressed in plain leathers and street clothes, but well-made and clean. Seven men and three women, all carrying shortswords and daggers. Every one had a leather bracer on their left arm. One of the men hung back, ordering the others. His red hair glinted in the weak sunlight.

Alere gasped.

'Gouri slavers,' Gavon muttered. He spat.

'They're persistent, I'll give them that,' Corin said.

Alere gripped his arm. 'Corin—'

He shook her off. 'Leave this to me. Gentlemen. Ladies.' He bowed without taking his eyes off them. 'Can we assist?'

'We want the woman,' the tallest man said. He pointed at the covered chair. 'Give her to us and you can live.'

Alere stiffened and resisted the urge to touch her moustache. They wanted Lia Koh-Lin, not Alek.

'Kett,' she whispered, watching the slavers.

He leaned in.

'We have to take one of them alive this time,' she said.

'Why?'

She nodded towards the man at the back. 'The redheaded man. He was on the *Nasir*. I'm sure of it.'

'Jiangui!' Kett muttered.

'Ah,' Corin said in reply to the slaver's demand. 'Unfortunately, you're out of luck.' He lunged and thrust his swordblade deep into the slaver's chest. The man gave an incoherent gargle, clutched at Corin's steel blade, and slid to the ground with blood spattering his lips.

'Cor,' Kett snapped. 'We need one alive. It's important.'

Alere shifted her weight. Her feet were too painful to move much. But she didn't have to. With a cry of anger, a blond man leapt at her, sword swinging. She waited then stepped aside. His blade missed. Hers didn't. He stumbled past and scrabbled at the warehouse wall. Blood gushed from a precise puncture wound in his chest, smearing scarlet on the dirty-white wall.

Beside her, metal rang on metal and echoed off the close brick walls. A cry of pain. One of anger. An oath and scuffing footsteps. Another man thrust, jabbing his sword like a fencer. Alere danced aside then hissed in pain. He saw her weakness and closed the gap. His bronze blade grazed her arm and she cried out. Anger flared, obliterating pain. Her dagger found his throat and his triumphant laugh cut off in a choking burble. He fell against her. Alere staggered back under his weight and let him slide to the ground.

A blade pressed against her throat. An arm looped around her waist from behind. 'Where's the woman? The chair's empty. Tell me!' The sweet-sick smell of blackweed oozed from her attacker's clothes and skin. If he'd chewed recently his reactions would be slow. Did she bet her life on that hope?

His arm tightened around her waist. 'Hey, wait. You're a—'

She reversed the dagger and jammed it into his forearm. He stiffened and gasped. The blade at her throat fell away and he dropped at her feet. Alere turned, surprised. Corin withdrew his sword from the body and wiped it fastidiously on the fallen man's clothing.

'Thanks,' she said. 'I had it, though.'

Corin grinned. 'I know. But I was done already, and Gav was bored. You know how he hates to be left out of a fight.'

She rolled her eyes, cleaned her blades matter-of-factly and sheathed them. How different this fight was from the first she'd had, here in the Zalam slums. How different she was. Gone was adrenalin-fuelled trembling and nausea. Gone was the need to prove herself in battle. She was just grateful it was over.

'Did we get one alive?'

'Yes,' Kett replied. His dagger lay against the redhead's throat. The man stood frozen, his dark eyes wild.

Gavon checked each body, ensuring the rest were dead. He tapped an embossed-leather bracer and nodded grimly. 'Nasim's people again. And this time they wanted Lia.'

'Gouri…' Corin's jaw worked and he stared blankly at the two dead men at Alere's feet. 'Someone in Chengdu is certainly laying out the welcome mat for the Koh-Lins. First Rafi, now Lia? Why?'

'Leverage? Control?' Alere suggested, repeating the gist of her conversation with Kett. 'If Jahil wants war and Jarran's out of the way, Rafi's the only one left to mount a defence if Melcor attacks. Or, if Jahil is backing Jun Fourth Hassan Wen-Gates for the throne, then taking Lia – me – would control Rafi's vote in the Jun Council.' She cocked her head. 'Either way, it means Jahil and Hallon might have Mina, but they don't know yet who she is.'

'Makes sense.' Corin frowned at her. 'Let's find out where these fellows were going to take you.'

Alere, Corin, and Gavon surrounded the redheaded slaver. Corin tapped his nose with the tip of his dagger. Alere slipped the suede covers off her sword hilts and gripped the yanstones. She reached towards the slaver's mind. It was chaotic with fear – not only of Kett's blade, but also of what Hallon Nasim would do if he talked. Getting coherent information would be difficult. His mind leapt and skittered like a sky-monkey.

'Where's the *Nasir?*' Corin asked, politely.

The redhead spat in his face. 'Long gone.'

Corin wiped it off and sighed. He raised his brows at Alere. She frowned, concentrating, sifting through the scattered half-thoughts.

There. She smiled fiercely. 'His job was to take either me or Rafi to Chengdu, as well as Jarran.' She pointed down the next alley. 'There's a private berth at the end of this alley.' She grabbed Corin's arm, her heartrate tripling. 'The *Nasir!* It's still there!'

CHAPTER TEN

ALERE

With a look of satisfaction, Gavon drove his dagger deep into the redheaded slaver's chest. Kett frowned and Alere turned away, swallowing down nausea. But it was hard to blame Gav at the moment.

Corin pursed his lips and eyed the bloodied bodies littering the alley. 'Not much we can do about the mess.'

Alere agreed. The murders would go unnoticed except by Zalam-dwellers. Madina junren rarely patrolled this area, anyway. The bodies would be looted and tossed into the Kabir before long. The *Song of Passing* was rarely sung in the Zalams. So many died each day there would never be silence.

Corin nodded towards the alley. 'Let's go. We'll come back for the chair.' He frowned at Alere. 'Can you walk?'

'Try and stop me,' she growled.

The four companions hurried towards the river. The narrow alley continued between two warehouses for a few dozen paces, then widened into a covered slipway surrounded by derelict chuan-building paraphernalia. A forgotten, forlorn space that stank of wet, rotting wood and algae. Corin slipped behind a workbench piled high with lumber and the others followed. Their footsteps echoed off the high walls. Alere gasped. She clutched at his arm and pointed.

At the end of the slipway, tied to a bollard, lay the *Nasir*. The vessel rocked in the wash of chuans passing on the Kabir behind. The charred sail sagged half-unfurled from the mast; the lay deck empty and quiet. A child's broken, abandoned toy.

Alere stopped, and grabbed the yanstones on her weapons, seeking Mina's mind. Then she closed her eyes. Disappointment fisted in her stomach.

'It's empty,' she said, flatly. 'There's no-one aboard. That must have been the whole remaining crew that attacked us.'

'Gouri…' Corin muttered. 'Stay here. Gav and I will check…for bodies.'

Alere swallowed. 'She can't be dead, Cor. I'm sure I would have felt it.'

'Jarran might be,' he said.

Kett wrapped an arm around her waist. 'I'll wait with her.' He glanced at the sky. 'But hurry. We need to get this news to Rafi.'

Corin mounted the gangplank cautiously, sword drawn. He and Gavon vanished below decks. Alere gripped Kett's arm until her fingertips turned white. He held her close.

Corin and Gavon reappeared, running down the gangplank, faces grim.

'Nothing,' Corin said. 'Crew cabins were empty. Abandoned clothing in some of the bunks like some of the crew left quickly.' He exchanged a hollow look with Gavon. 'Belowdecks is full of piss and shit. Where the slaves were kept. Bronze shackles. No bodies, though.'

Kett swore and Alere breathed a sigh of relief.

Gavon nodded. 'Aye,' he said. 'And I'm betting we know who took the Merchant Master's chuan, now. They probably couldn't get the burnt sail replaced. The Melcor ships use an odd-shaped sail. I doubt the Madina sailmakers had any handy in the middle of the night.'

'You're right,' Corin said. 'And Master Yar's chuan is fast. They've got a good headstart. We need to get moving.'

Alere cast her mind north, seeking Mina again, but felt only the faintest echo of her sleeping mind, haloed in pain and fearful misery. She sucked a deep breath and straightened and lifted her chin.

'Go, then, Cor. Get what you need. Get us underway again. We're going to Chengdu.'

Corin caught her into a swift hug and released her, holding her troubled gaze. 'I'll be back as soon as I can.' He squinted at the sun's glow, weak through thin, icy clouds. 'I'm running out of time. It's only a few steps back to the dock. Gavon and Kett will go with you.'

Kett nodded to Gavon. 'We'll go get the chair. Wait here.' They jogged away.

Corin stroked Alere's hair. 'Don't worry. We'll catch her. I'll escort the chair to Koh-Lin house, have them make a fuss, and run my errands from there.'

'What if you're attacked again? You'll be on your own.' Alere's heart skipped a beat and she gripped his arm.

He smiled quizzically down at her. 'You're worried about me? I'm touched.'

'Stop it, Cor. Just be careful.'

'Always.' He bowed flourishingly. 'Did you have any messages to send?'

'I thought about sending a message to my mo…adoptive mother, Elmira,' Alere said. 'But as Bonded Xintou to Jun Second Petar Ma-Safra she'll be in the middle of all this.'

'And the Ma-Safra place is over the other side of the city.' Corin said. 'Not sure I could get there and back fast enough. I could send a runner?'

Alere considered. 'No. There's no guarantee she'd be home. And what could I write that would make sense? At best it would ease her mind.' She wrapped her arms around herself as the cold southern winds whistled around the corner and rattled the doors and windows of the surrounding warehouses. 'At worst it would alert the wrong people of our plans. Better not.'

'And Xintou House?' He lowered his voice, eyeing her curiously. 'Mistress Li must be worried about you.'

'No. Not until I know what's really going on. Celia Edwards accused Mistress Li of having some hidden agenda.'

He chuckled. 'Now there's a person to listen to.'

'That's the point,' she said, exasperated. 'I can't really trust anyone, even Mistress Li.'

'You wound me.' Corin put on a hang-dog expression.

Kett and Gavon reappeared with the chair-bearers.

'Oh, shut up.' She shoved Corin in the direction of the chair, grateful for his ability to lighten her mood. 'And hurry back or we'll leave without you.'

He blew an airy kiss and vanished into the chair to complete whatever tasks were necessary to prepare for the trip to Melcor.

Gavon and Kett helped her walk back, hands discreetly under her elbows. Both kept their blades unsheathed until they got to the busy-ness of the dock.

'I'll go inform Rafi,' Kett said. 'Gavon, get Alli back on the *Kuailong.*'

After one last scowling check of the surrounds, Gavon swept her off her feet and carried her onto the ship, glaring her down when she protested. Once on board, he plonked her unceremoniously on a crate on the high deck.

'Ye'll stay here boyo. I'll send Lars up to stitch that cut on yer arm.' He pointed a thick finger at her. 'Stay, or I'll tell Rafi to take ye ashore here and we'll leave ye behind. If the Hallon's men are after ye, I still think ye should stay here.'

Alere uttered a wordless protest, but raised her hands in submission when he glared. He, of any of her friends, was most likely to carry out such a threat. So, she stayed put and watched the bustle as Dalor shifted cargo on and off the chuan. Lars came, rolled his eyes, cleaned and stitched the injury, and left again, muttering.

Alere fidgeted. The sun dipped towards the western horizon. Every second wasted here took Mina further away. Closer to slavery or worse. She groaned aloud when Dalor vanished ashore in search of more crew to row the vessel downstream in order to make up time.

Would Corin never get back? Where was Kett?

Rafi climbed onto the deck. Under one arm he carried a bulky parcel wrapped in the Koh-Lin family green-and-silver colours. In the other hand he hefted his travel-bag.

'Your cabin was empty. I was worried.' He sank onto a nearby storage locker and cocked his head. 'Almost didn't recognise you.'

'Not recognising me is the idea. Lia Koh-Lin has officially left the ship. She's going to have a mild relapse of her illness and be confined to the Koh-Lin house in Madina. We have to assume people knew I was onboard.' Probably best not to tell him of the attack.

'Yes, I suppose we must.' Her father grimaced, sitting on the crate beside hers. 'I've come to bid you farewell and wish you luck.'

'Do you mind that I'm going, rather than staying to help you?' Alere wasn't sure what answer she hoped for. He wasn't a demonstrative or open person.

Rafi gave a sardonic snort. 'Believe me, I'd rather come with you than face the diplomatic nightmare that awaits me. It will be difficult to build support for Jarran, especially when he's not here.'

Alere hesitated then gripped his hand. He raised a brow in question.

'Shenshi,' she said, 'I'll bring Jarran back for you, I promise. And Mina. You have enough to worry about.'

Rafi groaned. 'I'm sorry if I've seemed more concerned about Jarran than about you and your sister.' She was startled to see tears gather on his lower lids. He cleared his throat and squeezed her fingers. 'I've already lost Lianna. I can't bring myself to even think about losing another daughter, let alone two. Focussing on Jarran and the Jundom stops me from...' He stopped, his smile twisting into self-derision.

Her heart warming, Alere kissed his knuckles. 'Don't fear for me. I'm tougher than I look.'

He caught her into a ruthless hug. 'I know, my dear girl. It's one of the many things I've come to admire about you.' He cleared his throat again and thrust the parcel into her hands. 'Here. Yasmin gave this to me, for you. I wasn't sure if I should pass it on, but I trust my wife's instincts in these matters.'

'Thank you,' she said. She squeezed his hand. 'We'll get underway as fast as possible. With more crew, Dalor should get us to Dalcin in less than a week.'

Rafi grimaced. 'Faster, if you can. If you have to continue to Chengdu, then keep your ear to the ground and see if you can find who's behind these attacks. What Jahil and Hallon are planning. The last thing I need is trouble from that quarter as well.'

He stood abruptly, his eyes dark beneath lowered brows, then raised a hand and strode away.

Alere watched him leave, foreboding in her heart. She picked up the package and turned it over. Uneasiness itched under her skin and she hesitated with her fingers on its green silk ribbon.

As Alere sat, stroking the silk wrapping, a soft footfall signalled Kett's approach. He took the seat Rafi had vacated.

'Going to open that?' He pointed to the parcel.

'Later.' She put it aside, unwilling to be reduced to tears in front of him if it contained something personal.

'Dalor's hiring enough extra crew that we can row night and day.' Kett glanced at her. 'He thinks we might be able to catch the stolen chuan. It's named the *Jin Bird.* Dalor thinks perhaps we can beat them to Dalcin if we pass them during the night. Wait for them there and get the Dalcin portmaster and Sharif to hold the chuan.'

'Good. Can we send a flitter to Dalcin?'

Kett shook his head. 'Dalor checked with Messenger House. No Dalcin-trained flitters in at the moment. It's a small town. He left a message but there's no way of knowing when it will go.'

An icy shiver slipped down Alere's neck and she pulled her cloak tighter, hunching her shoulders.

'Alright?' Kett asked.

She hesitated, then forced words through an uncomfortable constriction in her throat. 'I have a horrible feeling…'

Kett hitched one knee up on the bench, took her hand and faced her. Concern marred his brow. 'Are you regretting your decision to come along? You can still stay. If Dalor's plan works, we won't even need to go as far as Chengdu. We'll bring Mina back.'

Alere snatched her fingers free. The laugh that escaped her was more bitter than amused. 'Mina. Of course not. I wasn't going to run. I just…' She stared at the towering silvery edifices of the Alcazar as the southern storm blew itself out, hurling last, wild windgusts against the squalid dockside buildings, like a child throwing a tantrum. 'I'm just…I feel like something awful is coming and I don't know what.'

She was committed now. To a life in service as Rafi's Jun-Heir. To recovering Jarran. Committed to following Mina. And somehow each choice she made seemed equally wrong and right. Each choice bound her more tightly to Mina and to a future cast in iron, when all she'd ever wanted was to be free of restrictions. But her connection to Mina went deeper than she could describe. Even if she'd wanted to, she couldn't sit this out and let Kett bring her sister back.

Kett's frown deepened. 'I don't understand, Alli. Are you saying the yanstones have given you precognition? That you've Seen a future we should be wary of?'

She shook her head, her tongue once more intractable. What was wrong with her? Every time she tried to speak to Kett or Corin about her fears for the future and her close tie to Mina, a pressure in her mind tied her tongue in knots. The words to express how she felt evaporated, leaving only growing unease. She absently stroked the yanstones on her sword and dagger. Warm reassurance crackled beneath her fingertips and burned under her skin. Iron and smoke.

She straightened and smiled brightly at him. 'Nevermind. I'm being foolish. Go. Dalor, Corin and Gavon are back. Corin's trying to get your attention.'

He hesitated. She flipped her hands at him. With a backward look, he strode over and consulted with Corin.

'I'm fine,' she whispered.

As Dalor got the chuan underway, she stayed on deck watching the familiar skyline of Madina fall behind and the land slowly turn back to farmland. Pregnant Runiu herdbeasts lowed and bleated in their winter-brown paddocks. Crop fields lay ploughed and dusted in white, ready for planting. The fecund world waited for rebirth in the coming spring.

Dalor called out to his drummer and the steady thud-thud began, dictating the rowers' pace. Alere inspected her hands, still raw from the day before, and grinned in relief.

At last the sun vanished behind the western ranges. The temperature plummeted as the sky darkened to purple and the first stars glittered in the east. Luna-Er rose, cold and white, quickly followed by the smaller, reddish Luna-Yi. Together they bathed the landscape in a clean light bright enough to allow Dalor to navigate well into the evening and make up lost time.

But was Dalor just being optimistic? Was it possible to catch or pass Mina's chuan?

CHAPTER ELEVEN

ALERE

Cold and hunger drove Alere belowdecks. Her feet were only stiff now, though they did throb. She dropped the parcel from Rafi onto her bed, sat down, kicked her boots off and lifted her feet up with a groan. The healer had told her to keep them raised and she now regretted ignoring that advice.

A knock fell on the open door. Corin stuck his head around the frame, cheerfully triumphant, juggling food platters and parcels. She waved him in. He shut the door and sank onto the other end of the bed, shedding wrapped packages and carefully placing the bowls.

She listened in amusement to the highly-coloured tale of his trip into Madina, and the lengths to which he'd had to go to procure some of the items he'd bought. And, as she ate, Alere considered Kett's advice from days before. He was right. Life was, quite possibly, short and brutal. She'd spent too long already being the dutiful daughter, xintou student, weishi student, spy for Mistress Li, and now Jun-Heir to replace Rafi's lost daughter. Maybe it was time she thought, just a little, of herself and what she wanted. Even if only for a short while. One night with Corin wasn't enough. She cared too much about him for that. Being with him couldn't do any harm. Wouldn't affect any big, important issues. Or was she just being selfish because she was afraid to face those big issues?

CORIN

Corin glanced up from his meal to find Alere watching him, a fierce, haunted expression on her lovely face. He stopped in mid-sentence, fascinated by her once again. Even the yellowing bruise still disfiguring her cheek took nothing away from her allure. It simply reminded him how extraordinary she was. Jahim! He smiled ruefully. He couldn't help wanting to be with her, even though she was clearly in two minds. Undoubtedly, he was a zift.

He picked up the one parcel he had not brought into the room, feeling its softness.

'From Rafi?' He tossed it into her lap. 'What is it?'

She shrugged, swallowing a mouthful of runiu stew. 'No idea. Yasmin evidently thought it might be useful.'

She laid her bowl aside and tugged at the green ribbon. The silver silk wrapping parted and her mouth dropped open.

'Oh!' With reverent hands, she lifted the thick, gold silk robe and shook it lightly so the hem fell to the floor. A gold veil floated down and something heavy and metallic tinkled to the bamboo floor.

Corin leaned down, but Alere was there before him. She snatched up the steel links and cradled them to her chest, crumpling the gold silk xintou robe without care. Corin raised his brows. He picked up the veil instead and laid it on the bed. Alere's fingers curled tightly around the yanstone chain that had fallen from the robe. Her expression changed to one of relieved delight.

She tossed the robe aside and tugged her shirt up to expose the smooth, golden skin of her stomach.

'This is Rafi's bracelet and Yasmin's necklace linked together,' she said, breathless. 'There are enough stones in this to give me xintou powers, without needing the ones in my blades. With these...with these we may have a chance, Corin.' With shaking hands, she clasped the chain around her hips, where it fitted flat against her skin.

The yanstones caught mel-oil lamp's glow and flared white-gold, their hypnotic flickers lighting even the darkest corners of the small room. An abstracted smile played on Alere's mouth. She stroked the stones then dropped her shirt, hiding them.

She glanced down and picked up another chain from the floor – two bracelets, linked. A frown creased her brow as she rubbed a thumb over the stones. She held the length up to the light.

'These are exactly like the Koh-Lin bracelets Rohne took.' She held them out to Corin. 'But they don't feel right. I don't understand.'

Corin held them up to the light. The milky-translucent stones remained stubbornly dark, refusing to catch, hold, and refract light the way yanstones did. He hefted them in his hand.

'Ah. I remember now. These belonged to Lia.'

'But what are they? No.' Alere refused when he tried to hand them back. 'They're fakes. Why did Lia have them?'

'Rafi had them made for her,' Corin said. 'They're silver and quartz chosen to resemble yanstones. She loved Yasmin's bracelet. She was going to wear one and give one to her friend, Farima Han-Asad, for Farima's nameday. But Lia got sick and didn't get a chance to send it. Yasmin must have found them when she started cleaning out Lia's room before we left.'

'But why would she give them to me? I have the real yanstones, now.' She touched her waist.

'She does have the same xintou gene you do,' Corin said. 'Perhaps she thought they would be useful – along with the robe. It's possible she had some sort of Seeing, or even just a hunch. These might be fake, but they do look exactly like the real ones.'

'Well,' Alere said, brushing them aside, 'you keep them.'

Corin tucked the bracelets into his inner coat pocket.

She gathered up the gold silk robe and held it against her shoulders. Her smile broadened into a soft laugh.

Curious, Corin laid his palms on the pommels of his weapons and stretched his mind towards hers, but Alere's Outer wards held hard and smooth against intrusion. He retreated and shored up his own. He had neither the skill, nor the inclination, to try and break hers. Alere would see it as a severe breach of etiquette if he did.

What worried him was how possessive she had become of the stones. Was there something addictive about their use? He ran his thumbs over his own, feeling their warmth and the sense of connection they aroused. He hadn't fallen into the habit of touching them, as she did. And it didn't bother him to be separated from them. Perhaps he read too much into her actions. After all, she'd been brought up thinking she should be xintou and was somehow flawed. It was only natural this new ability meant a great deal to her.

'You have no idea how much I desperately wished I was entitled to wear the Gold, Corin.' She echoed his thoughts, stroking the shimmering cloth reverently. Her expression segued into resignation and she held the robe away. She folded it with sharp, angry movements and stuffed it into her pack. 'But I don't know why Yasmin thought it would be useful. I can't wear it. It's too conspicuous and there are so few xintou. They all know each other by sight or mental signature. I'd be caught and then I'd have to explain the yanstones.'

Her hand strayed first to the sword-hilt, then to the belt hidden beneath her shirt.

'In Melcor,' Corin said, mildly, 'the Shah is the only person with a Bonded Xintou. Valera, I think her name is. And she almost never leaves the palace, except to accompany him on diplomatic missions. No-one would dream of questioning you. The Melcori hold xintou in even higher reverence than Madina people do. The slaves almost worship Valera. I hear they even believe a xintou will free them.' He laughed. 'Which is probably why she never leaves the palace. And makes the robe a poor disguise, now I think of it. You'd be mobbed.'

Alere cast a bitter look towards the closed bag. 'Good. I'd rather not be reminded of my shortcomings, anyway. I had enough of that in the House.'

He watched her closely. 'I guess it's a pity we've left Madina. You could have consulted with Elmira about the stones. Surely she's trustworthy? You know it's not too late? Dalor can put you to shore and you can still go back to Madina. I'd be glad to know you're safe there.'

'No. I need to bring Mina home. And Jarran.' She smiled bleakly. 'For once, what I want and what's important are the same thing, so it's not a difficult choice to make.'

Corin cocked his head, not seeing the connection. Did she feel she'd made poor choices, before? Hard to see how. Hoping to ease her mind, he pointed at the yanstones. 'Will having these make it easier to reach Mina?

Her gaze became abstracted and a frown knitted her brows. Her eyes cleared.

'Nothing. She's either asleep or unconscious. But it is easier because I have my hands free.' She tilted her head as though listening to voices only she could hear. A small, puzzled smile flickered then she shook her head and blinked.

Corin rose and threw the wrapping and the xintou robe onto the top bunk. He held out a hand and she stood. Her uneasy expression vanished. She swayed into him, a sultry smile playing about her lips.

'Well,' he said, grinning, 'I've heard interesting things about xintou skills in other areas. The bedroom, for instance.' He traced a finger across her forehead and down her cheek. 'It would save a lot of confusion if we knew…exactly…what felt good.'

Alere's eyes flew to his, wide. 'And unwarded connection?' Her cheeks flushed crimson and she pulled away. 'A xintou doesn't do that. It's letting someone that far into your head. It's so…intimate. And there's a Fusion risk for the untrained.'

He laughed to cover a stab of hurt that almost stole his breath. 'I was joking. I had no idea the xintou even had a concept for such things, let alone any taboos.' He tugged her closer again and she didn't resist. 'But, given how restrictive all their other rules seem to be, it's not surprising, I guess.' He couldn't expect Alere to open up to him so soon. He would need to be patient.

She said nothing, but leaned her head on his shoulder and slid her hands beneath his shirt. They splayed across his back, warm, sensual.

He tilted her face up and kissed her gently, putting as much understanding and tenderness into the touch as he could. 'When you're ready, Alli. You can teach me.' He tilted his head and quirked a wry smile. 'But, in the mean time, since your hands are free…'

ALERE

The trip to Dalcin, which normally took two weeks, lasted four days. For Alere they carried a strange mixture of pleasure, guilt and worry. The pleasure came from Corin's companionship. Although they were discreet, the knowledge of their liaison had to be obvious. Having trained as a jiaoji, Alere was aware Corin betrayed his feelings in ways he probably didn't even realise: a softening of his expression when he saw her, a closer personal space, fewer sarcastic quips and self-protective jokes.

Kett remained impassive. The only alteration was that he spoke less and kept his distance more. That was painful, but understandable as Corin clearly found their close friendship challenging.

Gavon, however, made no secret of his disapproval and scowled frequently at Corin. Alere once caught the tail end of a sotto voce conversation between the two men that sounded like Gavon threatening Corin. When she questioned Corin, he laughed.

'Gavon was merely pointing out, in graphic detail, the numerous painful things he would do to me should I hurt you in any way. So, do try to seem happy, for my sake.' He laid a hand on his heart.

Alere rolled her eyes. 'Honestly, you men. What's he going to do to me if I hurt you? After all, he's known you a lot longer. It ought to be you he's protecting.'

Corin bowed with a theatrical flourish. 'I think he considers me a hardened rogue, and you a guileless innocent of whom I'm taking horrible advantage. It's rather like a bad play. Especially with you dressed as a boy.' He made a moue of mock thoughtfulness. 'I believe he's cast me as the villain, which I'm not sure I appreciate. I always rather fancied myself the hero.'

'Nevermind.' Alere linked arms with him and they took a slow turn around the deck. 'I'm hardly innocent, rarely guileless, and I always preferred the villains in those plays anyway. The heroes were so dull and so painfully *good*.'

He laughed and, after a quick check to see they were unobserved, kissed her soundly.

So, while her nights were pleasantly occupied, her days were spent in a different form of enjoyment: combat training and knife-throwing practice with the three men. There wasn't much else they could do. Dalor had hired enough crew to work unceasing shifts on the oars. Now the river was wide enough, they rowed through the night as well. He kept lookouts on watch through the day, hoping to spot Mina's chuan.

The four companions did as much planning as could be done, with the limited information they had. Dalor insisted he would catch the slavers up by Dalcin.

Alere wanted to believe him.

She was only once able to contact Mina – the day after they departed Madina. Alere woke up well before dawn and tried the stones again. Finding Mina awake and open to contact was a huge relief.

Are you alright? She tested Mina's Outers, Reading only exhaustion and a low-key, background level of fear. There was also a muffled vagueness to Mina's thoughts. Most likely due to the drugs. *Are they still drugging you?*

Yes. Mina's mental voice was heavy, with layers of reluctance and distress that seemed to have nothing to do with her physical situation. *They transferred us to a different chuan a few days ago.*

We know. Have they said how far away from Chengdu you are?

No. Her response was curt.

You're not well. Alere slid her mind through the stones, along the silver-gilt thread. *Let me try to heal—*

No! Mina slammed up all but the shallowest of her Outer wards. *No, Alere. I'm fine.* There was a long pause, then her voice returned, thin and strained. *Just come for us. Please?*

We are, I promise. Are Rohne and Jarran alright?

Yes. But Rohne is— There was another pause. Mina spoke again, her mental voice formal and stilted. *We're fine. Rohne is taking care of me. I have to go. There's a guard coming.*

I'll contact you tomorrow.

There was no reply and no way of pushing past Mina's wards. Her Outers closed with surprising solidity. Alere had not thought her sister so well-trained. Rohne, also, held his wards against her.

The following two days, neither were open to communication. In fact, both warded with a strength that seemed suspicious. Why would they ignore communication? The only other warded mind on the chuan must be Jarran's but she couldn't get through to him, either.

Her unease grew with each passing hour.

CHAPTER TWELVE

ALERE

They were due to make landfall in Dalcin early on the fourth day. Anticipation poured jiu on the fire of Alere's impatience and she found herself unable to sleep when dawn neared. She slipped from Corin's side and made her way to the narrow prow.

It was possible they had passed Mina's chuan in the night. There was no way of knowing, but she clung to hope. Corin had the Dalcin portmaster's name and would find out when they arrived. Assuming the slaver had registered their landing in order to take on more crew, as Dalor suggested they must.

Their quest might be finished. If they could overtake the slaver ship here, in Dalcin, Jarran would be back in Madina in good time for the Jun Council.

And Mina would be safe.

Alere hugged that thought to herself and paced, willing the chuan to go faster. She braced herself against the chuan's jerk-and-glide motion, watching the distant cluster of buildings on the eastern shore draw nearer. The chuan cleaved through the calm, mud-coloured water. Fog clung to the surface, swirling and drifting as the steady oarstrokes moved air and water. The sun rose and its vermillion fire swept across the plains. It transformed the bleak fog into sparkling jewels and the turgid river to liquid gold.

On the eastern side, the land was flat, the loamy floodplain heavily cultivated, with farms and small villages scattered along the riverbank. It was warmer too, with a hint of salt in the air as they neared the ocean. The western riverbank was too distant to even see.

She felt Kett's silent approach and spoke without turning. 'Do you think we've passed them, Kett? Do you think we can intercept them here?'

He moved alongside, hands resting by habit on the hilts of his weapons, cloak fluttering in the cool breeze. 'There's no way of knowing. If they've already been, Dalor says he can get underway in an hour. Maybe two. If they haven't, he'll head downriver, out of sight, and we'll wait for the slavers to come into port.'

'Jiche!' Alere tried again to reach Mina's thoughts. Nothing. 'I still can't reach Mina. If I could we might know for sure. I can't even tell where she is, just that she's closer than last time.' She flung out her hands. 'I can't stand this! We're so close. Why won't she open her wards to me?'

'Alli.' Kett grabbed her shoulders and stilled her restless movements. 'We have to assume someone on that chuan is preventing you from reaching her.' He'd never been one to lie and give false hope.

She groaned. 'I know. It has to be Rohne. But *why?*' She pressed cold fingertips to her forehead. 'I don't understand. He must know we can't rescue them if he...'

Kett raised his brows.

'He doesn't want us to rescue them?' She shook her head. 'That's ridiculous. What does he gain by being a slave? He loves Mina. Surely he wouldn't endanger her?'

'Now you're asking the right questions, almost. Perhaps a better one is: what does he gain by going to Melcor?' The morning blood-sun illuminated half his face, throwing the other into deep shadow.

'Or by taking Mina or Jarran with him?' she replied shrewdly. 'Maybe I made a mistake telling him the Shah was behind this.' She reached out to her sister, only to be stonewalled again. 'But what does Rohne *want?*'

Kett nodded. Sunlight shone through his eye, turning it eerily translucent and colourless. 'Another excellent question. Even after three weeks on the road with him, I can't be sure I understand him. He's highly intelligent and extremely well-educated by Nasra. But he's also intense, guarded and very angry at the world. He hides it well, though.' He tilted his head. 'He's also surprisingly poor at social interaction. He's used to Reading people who have no wards. And he has little time or patience for people he considers stupid – which is most of them – or the niceties of mere conversation. He kept asking me to lower my Outers so we could communicate more easily. Got quite irritated when I refused.'

Alere screwed up her nose. 'I remember, in Hassan's house, when he used telepathy to tell me the guard outside our door was gone. It made me...uncomfortable for some reason. And again – when he Read me in Shanzhai, when I was with Ven.' She shuddered at the memory. 'I think you were right to refuse him. I don't think Nasra has trained him in the Xintou methods of etiquette. He has no inhibitions about Reading without permission or digging deeper than he should.'

'Yes,' Kett said. 'I wondered about that. Be careful if you do connect with him. You're right, though: if Rohne loves Mina, he won't endanger her. The only problem is, he may not love her as much as he used to.'

'What does that mean?'

He grimaced. 'During our trip from Newmec he didn't hide his annoyance with her attentions to me. If I were him, and having to watch the woman I cared for love someone else...' He turned downriver and folded his arms. 'I'd probably be torn between wanting her to be happy, and wanting to separate them. Perhaps Rohne thinks bringing Mina here will keep her away from me. It won't, of course. But he's angry and I'm not sure he's thinking straight.'

Alere said nothing and tried to ignore the tiny twist of hurt in her stomach.

Kett cleared his throat. 'When you were in telepathic contact with him, were his Outers any more revealing? What do you think he wants?'

'I…I never really thought about it.' She'd been so caught up in her own priorities: warning her father; preventing a war. It had never occurred to her to question Rohne's motives. Her own and Kett's she knew. They were both trained to the protection of others; duty and honour in the weishi code.

'I'm not sure. I was uneasy with him because of what he was, but I assumed he was basically honourable.' She frowned up at Kett. 'He helped us at Hassan Wen-Gates' estate. And when you were injured. He ran the risk of being exposed in Shanzhai, but he still helped bring down Ven.'

'True,' Kett conceded. 'But what if his actions were steps to further his own cause? If they were, what is it? What did he really want from us?'

'Recognition, I think,' she said. 'He's been forced to live his whole life in secret. Hiding his abilities as a xintou for fear of being put to death. He wants to be seen for who he is and what he can do. He wants to be accepted.'

After a long, thoughtful silence, Kett's eyes narrowed. 'Agreed, except I believe he's past wanting acceptance. He had that with us in Shanzhai and abandoned it. He wants more now. What's his ultimate aim?'

'I don't know. I have a strong feeling Mina is important in all this. And that we *have* to get her back, quickly.' She placed a hand on her diaphragm. 'Something here tells me she's heading into serious danger and soon. We have to catch them. Here. In Dalcin.'

'I believe you, Alli. Dalor says we'll arrive at Dalcin in less than an hour. Keep trying to get hold of Mina. Difficult as it is,' Kett said, smiling faintly, 'have patience.'

'I hate it when you say that,' she muttered, scraping wind-blown stray hairs out of her eyes and retying them into her mawei.

He chuckled. 'Then have more and I'll be obliged to say it less often.'

He left her then and she went back to fruitlessly willing the vessel to go faster. And replaying his words about Rohne and Mina.

When they docked in Dalcin, Corin physically held Alere back from accompanying him to see the portmaster.

'We're not in Mamlakah any more, Alere,' he said brusquely, one hand firmly gripping her shoulder. 'Melcor operates by different rules. Bribery will work. Force won't. They're all used to the threat of slavery. Lives mean little. But money goes a long way. If two of us go in, swords swinging, we'll just end up with no information and time in front of the local Sharif. Leave this to me.'

'I could Read him,' she insisted. 'That would be faster.'

'Maybe,' he said, 'but maybe not. People often aren't as straightforward as you think. You have to know what questions to ask. And I can Read him as well, remember? Please?' he said, catching her gaze. 'This is my forte. Stay here. Hallon has already tried once to take you. The trick with sending "Lianna" to the Madina Koh-Lin house may not have worked if his spy system is as good as we think.'

Reluctantly, she agreed and watched him swing down the gangplank, her heart skittering. By the time he'd been gone an hour, even Kett had stopped asking her to be patient. He stood with her by the gangplank, a frown clouding his brow, a hand on his sword.

'Should we go after him?' Alere asked for the fifth time. She reached for his mind, hoping for news, but found only his wards. Closer, though, than they were before.

Kett pointed. 'No. Here he comes.'

She shaded her face from the sun's glare. Corin's expression gave nothing away. He paused at the foot of the gangplank and exchanged words with Dalor. The chuanzhu had already replaced the rowers with fresh men, just in case.

Corin strode up the plank and Dalor followed, his face grim.

Alere's heart dropped.

Corin leapt onto the chuan and jerked his thumb towards the aft deck. 'Let's go up there. Out of earshot. We're casting off.'

Alere hurried after him. Kett and Gavon joined them.

'We missed them,' Corin said bluntly. 'Only by a few hours. But the *Jin Bird*'s already heading across-river to the western bank.'

Covering her mouth with one hand, Alere turned away, half-blinded by tears of anger. She kicked at the solid gunwale and let out a growl. Nausea twisted her stomach and she had to lower her head to stop it spinning. How could they have missed? She'd been so sure.

And now Mina was heading into Chengdu. If she was sold into slavery she would be abused in ways Alere couldn't even bear to think of.

'It gets worse.' Corin produced two tightly-rolled, thin sheets of paper and handed one to Alere. She took it with a shaking hand. Its Koh-Lin seal was broken. He tapped the paper.

'Rafi and I use a code. I had to translate it for you.' He screwed up his nose. 'You're not going to like his news.'

Before opening it, she pointed at the unsealed note he still held. He tucked the list into his coat pocket.

'Merely an updated list of useful contacts in, and outside of, Chengdu. Rafi's still trying to make contact with the infamous Liu Gray, leader of the spy network there. See if he can meet us. I'm not going to hold my breath, since he's notoriously good at hiding.' He shrugged. 'A lot of the others are because I do like to set up an exit route before things go all suilie.'

'A wise precaution,' Kett said, 'but you're assuming things *will* go...suilie.'

'How do you think I've survived as long as I have? I always make that assumption. It could be self-fulfilling, of course.' Corin smiled wryly. 'And usually my own fault. But I'm alive because I'm good at having an exit strategy.'

Alere listened with half an ear as she skimmed the terse message from her father. She sagged against the aft railing, reading the contents again to try and make sense of them.

'The Jundom is in anarchy,' she said, softly. 'Hassan Wen-Gates is marching on Madina with a small army of junren. Rafi thinks Hassan's request for a Jun Council was just a ploy to trap all the Juns in one place and hold them hostage. And Yasmin says Yaku's mountain-raiders – the ones Hanna Zah-Hill paid to let her army through Eagle Pass – are attacking the southern outskirts of Shanzhai. So, Yasmin can't send our Koh-Lin junren to Madina without leaving the city borders unprotected.'

'And the Zah-Hill troops that went with Hanna to Shanzhai?' Kett asked, his brows knitted.

'They haven't arrived back in Madina. Even when they do, they'll be in no fit condition to fight. Storms snowed them under on the march back. The junren are suffering from cold and lack of food.'

Gavon let out a snort and jerked his chin at her. 'What's yer father doing? I can't see him sitting on his hands waiting for them.'

'No.' She reread the cramped script closely. 'Rafi's trying to rally what weishi are in the city, but two of the senior Juns who would support him are still travelling with the Zah-Hill army. Rivalries between the rest are so long-standing and bitter he hasn't been able to unify them. They won't recognise his authority, even with Jun Second Petar Ma-Safra's support. They're afraid Rafi will take the throne.'

Corin grimaced. 'It doesn't help that Hanna encouraged in-fighting amongst her Juns to stop any one gaining enough power to challenge her.' He indicated the note. 'But what sort of madness has possessed Hassan Wen-Gates to think marching on Madina in winter is a good idea?'

Kett looked south. 'He is somewhat… paranoid, I admit, but it has a sort of logic. When we passed through his land, we saw his preparations. He had enough supplies to feed his junren. If he knows the Zah-Hill troops are away, he'll be able to walk into Madina without meeting much resistance.'

Alere waved the paper at him. 'We have to *do* something! We have to help Rafi.'

He regarded her steadily, one brow lifted in a way she recognised. Slow down and *think*. Immediate action wasn't always the smart thing to do. Rushing back to Madina would achieve little but to add four swords to Rafi's defense. Mina was more important.

'I know, shifu. Getting Jarran back *is* the best help, right?' She folded the note and tucked it into her pocket. Turning away, she thumped her hands onto the railing and stared at her own restless feet. 'I feel so gouri useless. Can't we go any faster?'

The sail snapped out, billowing in the wind. Oars sliced through the muddy water with regular, rhythmic motions that carried them closer to Chengdu with each stroke.

'No.' Kett's flat reply was softened only by the faint smile on his lips. 'Patience and trust.' He held up a hand when she opened her mouth to protest and the many years of their shifu-student relationship held her silent. 'We need to focus on getting Jarran and Mina back as fast as we can.' Irony flickered in his grey eyes. 'And we need to trust Rafi can manage without us – at least for a little while. You can't fix everything, yourself.'

He was right, of course. She'd rejected the chance to stay behind. Rafi had far more experience in his field of political expertise. But Madina held much that was dear to her: Elmira, and now Rafi, plus her House sisters and weishi brethren. The thought of the city plunged into war and chaos made her stomach churn. But she couldn't allow fear and emotion to guide her decisions. She was better than this. She needed to get control.

She drew on xintou techniques and dampened her emotions; compartmentalising them for later. Now was the time for clear, logical thinking. She couldn't let fear for Mina cloud her judgement.

'Corin,' she said.

He slowly switched his speculative gaze from Kett to her and raised his brows. She resisted the urge to find out his thoughts through the yanstones encircling her hips. Constant wear in the last three days had improved her abilities to Read, but his wards were strong.

'Assuming we can find and retrieve the others,' she said, 'what *is* your exit strategy? How do we get back to Madina? The *Kuailong* will be too slow, even if Dalor was willing.'

'Which he isn't,' Corin finished. 'By the time we got halfway back to Madina the upriver ice would be breaking up with the spring melt. The river will be too high and fast. Dalor won't risk it. He'd normally row to Madina then go overland back to Shanzhai. This time he'll either wait out the floods in Dalcin, or pull the boat apart in Dalcin and portage from there, instead. Tow it with teams of four xiang. Rafi won't like the bill.' His mouth twisted.

'Now that I'd like to see,' Kett murmured. Xiang were reptiles the size of houses, bred in Shemal for pulling heavy loads. Their leathery white skin tough enough to bear harnesses for days. Their thick-padded feet able to traverse any terrain.

'We'll take horses from Dalcin. Much faster than xiang, no matter how fascinating,' Corin said drily. He continued outlining their trip. He'd foreseen the need for a quick return and had sent flitters and runners to bespeak fresh horses in every major township between Chengdu and Madina. It would be a brutal ride. Several hundred gongli in a matter of a week, through the tail-end of winter. That sort of riding would most likely kill some of their mounts. Alere wasn't even sure she was capable of a journey so difficult. Mina definitely wasn't.

When she voiced that concern, Kett gave it consideration. 'You could be right. If so, then we split up. You and Corin can get Jarran to Madina. Gavon and I will travel with Mina and Rohne at a slower pace. We must get an heir on the throne before Hassan arrives in the city. That gives us two weeks at best.'

Alere opened her mouth to suggest the logical alternative, that Kett himself was the heir. He flicked her a look so cold that she held her tongue. Shaken, misliking the idea of dividing their group in such an unstable time, but unable to come up with an alternative, she could only nod in agreement.

Gavon growled. 'Yer both gettin' ahead of yerselves. We still have to get them out of the slavepens and that'll be no easy task. There are only two ways out of slavery.' He thrust the hilt of his sword forward belligerently. 'Either ye buy them or they die. No one escapes.'

'If I may ask,' Kett said, 'how did you gain your freedom?'

Gavon's expression closed into hardness. He lifted his chin. 'I was mhareb-slave: a fighter. Bodyguard to the Sinclair family. One of the four big Slavemasters. After five years I used the small freedoms given a trusted mhareb-slave and tried to escape.' He grimaced and shifted his shoulders. 'They caught me and put me into the Wushi Games as punishment. Only the Shah's Guanjun – his champion – goes free. If he survives. The rest are Chosen or killed.'

'Chosen?' Alere asked.

He nodded, dark eyes flat. 'Twenty survivors are Chosen for the Seyd-Hunt. The Hunt is held over the two days of the Mianshou celebrations – on Yirun and Er'run. I was one of the Games' survivors, but not the Shah's guanjun. I went into the Hunt.'

'Seyd?' Alere asked. 'What does that mean? What does it have to do with the Mianshou end of year celebrations?' The term "mianshou" literally meant "immunity from prosecution" or "freedom from punishment". Each year the two extra days needed to round out the end of the calendar year, Yirun and Er'run, were given over to a free-for-all celebration. Any destructive behaviour was supposed to be forgiven.

'I didn't factor in the Mianshou,' Corin said, thoughtfully. 'Well...easier to be inconspicuous, anyway. Chengdu will be overflowing with merrymakers. But it does bring out the baser side of mankind. We'll need to keep weapons to hand and purses tucked away. The pickpockets in Chengdu are quite skilled. Children, especially.' He chuckled. 'In fact, there's a network of child-thieves in Chengdu. Almost a tourist-attraction, you could say. They do love the Mianshou.' He rubbed his hands together. 'So many fat purses.'

Alere frowned him into silence. She disliked the event. Xintou House forbade participation and she had witnessed true ugliness the one year she'd snuck out attend. Kett's appearance to retrieve her had been a relief.

She turned back to Gavon. 'What were you going to tell us about the Seyd?'

Now, seeing Gavon's closed, haunted expression, her distaste for the Mianshou season seemed as nothing to what he had gone through. The others waited expectantly, although Corin's sympathetic grimace said he knew at least part of Gavon's story. The silence stretched.

'A Seyd is prey,' Gavon said at last. 'The twenty Games survivors are released at dawn on Yirun. Hunted down for sport over Yirun and Er'run. In my year, the other nineteen were slaughtered on the first day. I killed ten hunters in the Seyd-Hunt, including my Slave-Master.' He ran his fingers over a long, pale scar on his upper arm. 'Stole a horse. Lost the rest of the Hunters in the bamboo forests of Ketheyf on the Shemali border. Spent three days delirious of wound-fever before a villager from Hala'a found me.' He grimaced. 'There's not many Seyd as ever escape. I earned my freedom with blood. Jarran, Rohne and Mina haven't that choice.'

CHAPTER THIRTEEN

ALERE

After a short, uncomfortable pause, Corin spoke up with easy confidence. 'We'll just have to buy them. Rafi gave me enough coin to buy an entire village if needs be, so I do think that's the least of our problems.'

Gavon squinted up at the pale orange sun. 'Yer wrong, lad. Am I right in thinking today is Ahad the twenty-fifth of Shisiyue?'

They all conceded and Alere's stomach sank at his grim expression.

'Then the slave-markets start at dawn on the twenty-sixth. Tomorrow.' He waved a hand at Alere. 'A lass as pretty as Mina'll get snapped up straight away for a jiaoji-slave. The others are strong and young, so they'll be bought for the spring plantings most likely. Or, if they resist, the Games on the thirtieth. They could be on their way to anywhere by the time we arrive in the afternoon. It's a big Jundom. Could take days or weeks to get them all back.'

Alere grabbed at the rail to steady herself, staring blindly at the swirling muddy water. No, that was simply unacceptable. There *had* to be a way. She'd promised Rafi she would bring them back. The Jundom needed Jarran. She needed Mina. And she had to stop Rohne from doing whatever he planned. It was her responsibility and there had to be a solution.

She breathed slowly to settle the fluttering in her stomach. Silence pressed on her ears and mind. She felt the men's eyes on her. Corin touched her arm and she barely resisted the urge to snarl at him.

'Alli,' he said gently, 'we don't know any of that for certain. Even if we arrive late, I know the slave auctionmaster. I can find out who bought them and we can move quickly once we have that.'

'Very well.' She made the decision. 'But if it comes to it, we'll have to split up. Kett and Gavon can find Mina. Corin and I will track down Jarran. That way, when we find him, we can head straight for Madina.' She grimaced. 'Rohne will have to wait. We can come back for him once Mina and Jarran are safe.'

'But you'll want to be there for Mina,' Corin protested. 'And we can't leave Rohne behind.'

'What I want isn't the same as what's important,' Alere said. 'I made the mistake of doing what I wanted in Shanzhai, because I was afraid to do what was important to Mina. And she left. Now we're here.'

'Alli—'

She waved Kett brusquely to silence. 'Getting Jarran back to Madina is important. Getting Mina back is next-most. If we can find Rohne then we will. But he's our third choice, not our first. And not if it will delay getting the others to Madina.' She raised her chin. 'Understood?'

Kett inclined his head, expressionless. Corin opened his mouth then shut it again with a snap. He spun on one heel and marched away.

Gavon glowered. 'I hope ye know what yer doing, boyo. Leaving someone ye care about in slavery is about the worst thing I can think of. When we first met, I asked ye to think on what was worth fighting for. Ye said freedom.'

'I know, Gavon. Believe me, if we can free Rohne, I promise we will.' She touched his arm. The images seeping from his unwarded mind battered on her thoughts before she could block them out. Horrifying scenes of death, blood, agony and humiliation that made her want to retch and back away. 'But I have to put the safety of everyone in Mamlakah before my personal feelings.'

'Aye,' he murmured, 'and that makes ye a good Jun-Heir, boyo, but a poor friend. Think on it.' He walked away, shoulders drooping.

Alere sought absolution from Kett. He returned her hopeful look calmly, letting the silence lengthen until she felt obliged to fill it herself.

'Do you think I'm doing the wrong thing?' she asked, fighting self-doubt. 'I mean, we're pretty sure Jahil will want Jarran, so we should be able to find out where he is. Rhone has the power to manipulate thoughts, so I doubt he'll let himself be separated from Mina. It's a calculated risk, but I think it's right. Don't you?'

Kett stared west across the slow, broad waters stretching towards Chengdu. He lifted his face to the pale sky and straightened. He placed both hands on her shoulders, sliding them down to grip her upper arms.

'I think,' he said, his tone even, 'that you need to worry less about my approval and have more faith in yourself. Yes, seek ideas from others, but you have all it takes to be a good Jun *and* a good friend. Although I agree, the choice leading to both can sometimes be difficult to see.'

He glanced around and kissed her forehead, his lips soft against her skin, warm breath fluttering her hair. She leaned into him, grateful for his support even though his advice took them one step further apart.

Then he held her away and contemplated the direction in which Corin had vanished. 'You'd best speak with Corin.' He pressed his lips together. 'He's not someone who trusts easily, but he trusts you. Return that by sharing your reasoning, not ordering him like a servant. You're more than his Jun-Heir now. That's a rocky path to tread. Heavy steps won't suffice.'

He stroked hair away from her face then turned his back.

'Cor?' She knocked tentatively on the open door of his cabin and peered around the corner. She'd already spoken with Gavon and found him quick to understand. She approached Corin with trepidation. He lay on his bunk, hands behind his head, staring blankly at the underside of the bed above. She took his silence as consent and sat, hunched uncomfortably under the upper bunk, by his feet.

'I'm sorry,' she said, finding it harder to apologise than she thought. 'I should have asked you for input and let you know what I was thinking.'

He said nothing.

'As I said to Kett and Gavon,' she continued, stiffly, 'I doubt Rohne will allow himself to be separated from Mina, so finding him should be easy.'

Corin's gaze remained fixed on the bunk above, but the small muscles in his jaw worked.

'I shouldn't have told you what to do. Missing Mina in Dalcin really shook me. And I'm just...' She sought for the right words. 'I'm not great at...this. Us, I mean. I am great at killing people, though,' she joked feebly. 'If things go really wrong with us, I can always fall back on that.'

His lips twitched.

She gave a low laugh and fidgeted with a loose thread on her shirt. 'I trained for three years with Jiaoji House. I know pretty much every way there is to seduce a man, or woman. Psychologically and physically. I know how to drug, poison, and manipulate people. But I've just realised what they never teach a Jiaoji. Or a xintou.' When he didn't reply, she continued, 'Non-contractual relationships. Real relationships.'

She rose and paced the cabin. Four strides in each direction covered the whole claustrophobic space.

'What I'm trying to say is that I don't know what I'm doing with us. And I also have no idea what I'm doing as Jun-Heir. And I'm terrified I'll mess this up and lose my sister.' She waved her hands vaguely. 'I'm making things up as I go along, so I'm sorry if I do anything wrong,' she finished, stomach roiling.

She still wasn't sure how deeply she felt about Corin, but she did know hurting him wasn't what she intended. 'I tend to make quick decisions because I think I'm right and—' She stopped, coming up against Corin's broad chest.

His green eyes gleamed with rueful humour and he gently cupped her face. 'And it's one of the things I admire about you, Alere. That and an uncountable number of other things.' His grin became wicked. 'Not the least of which is your jiaoji training. And the fact you've saved my life several times so far. However, decisiveness and independence are some of the ways we're similar. I'm used to working alone and I do dislike being ordered around. I guess we'll have to work on that, won't we…shunu?'

He inclined his head ironically, finishing the bow with a kiss that left her breathless.

When he raised his head, his eyes narrowed. 'Did you mean what you said?'

'Which bit?'

'About what you want and what's important not being the same thing?'

Alere paused. She was used to questioning her own beliefs, for Kett had ruthlessly forced her to do the same for many years. A false belief would lead to a poor decision under stress. The truth of a situation was not always obvious until one stripped away the beliefs through which one filtered the world.

'Yes.' She gazed up at him openly. 'I do. I've made too many mistakes in the past, chasing what I wanted.'

He stiffened. 'Does that include me?'

She kissed him and his mouth softened. He groaned and pulled her close. Her body flamed to life beneath his skilled touch.

When she came up for breath, she murmured, 'No. You're not a mistake. And I don't particularly like putting what's important first, believe me. I used to resent hearing it from Mistress Li. But lately, I've come to see it is the truth.'

'I used to think it was as well.' Corin's reply carried a hint of bitterness. 'But sometimes what we think is important…actually isn't.' His eyes held shadows of old grief. 'But people you care about always are. Because often they're gone before you've had a chance to let them know. I left my home village to pursue a job in the Artist House, because music was important, at the time. Shasa and everyone I loved died. I've regretted that ever since.' He held out a hand and she took it, troubled.

He lightened, and the moment was over, his defences back in place. 'Don't worry.' He kissed her quickly and led the way out into the hall. 'You'll get over it. I did. Life's short.'

With good relations restored, more due to Corin's essential optimisim than anything else, they returned to the *Kuailong's* upper deck. Gavon had requested another training session.

Alere faced Gavon hesitantly, for he seemed grimmer than usual.

'Right, boyo,' he growled. 'I've been putting this off. Hoping we'd catch the *Jin Bird* before we reached Chengdu. But if yer going to Melcor then ye need to learn how to defend against these.'

From his carrysack, he produced one of the most evil-looking weapons Alere had ever seen. In his left hand he held an armslength timber shaft, topped by a curved, bronze scythe-blade. Attached to the handle's base was a long bronze chain and weight.

'Kusarigama,' Alere said, recognising the weapon from her weishi studies.

She'd never seen one in action. The weapon had been banned in Mamlakah since the anti-slavery rebellion two hundred years before. At least the weight wasn't spiked as the illustrations in the weishi texts had shown. But she was glad Gavon had told her to wear her alzin armour.

'Right again, boyo.' He circled slowly around the deck. 'This is one of the most common weapons in Chengdu. All the Melcori free mharebi and mhareb-slaves use it. And, if there's one thing the Melcori love, it's to challenge each other to combat.'

Alere groaned, remembering hours pouring over weishi texts of Melcor combat rituals. The Challenge of the Wronged. The Challenge of Equals. The Challenge of the Righteous. There were an unending number of ways to be called to a duel. He was right. She needed to know how to deal with their national weapon.

Gavon whirled the weighted chain in his right hand. 'Focus, boyo. Ye've only got one day to learn what normally takes a body a year or so to master. Move.'

Alere slid her sword and dagger free of their scabbards. She watched his movements, judging the distance, focussing on his chest. Her heart thudded and she drew a slow breath, ignoring the blood-rush of adrenalin. She relaxed her peripheral vision to keep an eye on both the swinging chain and the scythe. Diyu!

It must be a matter of timing. He spun the chain faster. At what felt like the right moment, she sprang forward. He loosed the chain. It wrapped around the hilt of her sword. The weight smacked painfully into her knuckles. She jerked back but was wrongfooted. He yanked her offbalance and she stumbled close to him. His arm blocked her dagger-strike and he laid the scythe blade across her throat.

She swore and straightened, untangling her blade. 'So?'

Gavon gathered the chain and skimmed it through his hand until he had the length he preferred. 'It's all in the timing. Watch the feet as well as the chest. Most will telegraph their next move through their feet as they shift balance for the throw.'

Alere made a noise of frustration and moved back again. Five times more she lunged, trying different angles, different speeds, and different attacks. Each time he defeated her easily, leaving more bruises. Once, he entangled her ankles, bringing her crashing to the deck. Once, he wrapped the chain around her chest and arms, pinning her. Twice, he disarmed her by twining the weight around her weapon and yanking it from her hands. Lastly, he changed the swing angle and looped it around, outside her guard entirely. The weighted chain encircled her throat and smacked painfully into the back of her head.

Dispirited, she took a break, rubbing her head and watching while Kett tried. He'd learned from her mistakes, but only enough to make different ones. Twice he got within Gavon's guard, coming close enough to lay his dagger against Gavon's ribs. Only to find the scythe blade already in place at the back of his neck.

Finally, Gavon called Corin up and Alere watched carefully. The two men had travelled together and knew each other well. She suspected Corin already knew how to deal with the kusarigama. She was right. Faster than she could comprehend, Corin closed the gap. He wrapped the chain and Gavon's right arm up. His sword lay across the yongbing's throat. Four more times against four different attacks, Corin achieved the same result.

'Good,' Gavon muttered. 'Nice to see ye haven't forgotten. Alek.' He jerked his chin at her. 'Yer turn again.'

Alere rose. If Corin could do it, so could she.

An hour later, battered and frustrated, she had only once succeeded in getting through his guard. More by dumb luck than skill. It was like being back on the road from Newmec, but worse because this time Kett watched her humiliation. She glared at Gavon. He chortled. At least he was sweating, too. Probably more from the warmer sun this far north than any effort she had caused.

'That's enough for today, boyo.' He wrapped the chain around the scythe handle and stowed it away. 'Ye'll get it, ye always do. Don't be too hard on yerself.'

'But I need to get it now,' Alere protested. What hope did she have of rescuing Jarran and Mina if she couldn't best a Chengdu-trained fighter? 'We don't have time to waste. We'll be in Chengdu tomorrow.'

'Aye.' Gavon hefted the carrysack over his shoulder. 'I know, believe me. I can think on little else.' He trod heavily to the railing and stared at the river ahead.

CHAPTER FOURTEEN

ALERE

Alere hesitated. How did she handle this?

Gavon gazed blankly across the expanse of water towards Chengdu. The river had widened and slowed further, the water sluggish and swirling, heavy with the mud and debris carried by the merging of Mamlakah's three main rivers. The east and west banks were ragged purplish lines of salt-tolerant mangrove plants, low in the distance. The cool breeze lifting Alere's hair came from the northeast and had a salty tang, both invigorating and unfamiliar.

Other chuans skirted theirs, ferrying goods back and forth across the river. Small canoes and two-man rafts were most common, often stacked high with dark purple bales from the seaweed farms, or baskets of fish and fruits. Sometimes they came alongside, their gold-skinned, lean-bodied crews offering wares and glowering in angry incomprehension when Dalor brusquely sent them away. Mostly, they stayed away from the larger chuan; watching, with hands on weapons and mistrust in their startling blue eyes.

Gavon looked through them.

Alere waited for him to say more but he didn't. She sheathed her weapons and joined him.

'You don't have to come, Gav,' she said, treading with care on what she guessed to be sensitive ground. 'We won't think less of you for not wanting to confront old terrors.'

Gavon laughed, an ugly snarl of a sound. 'It's not the old terrors that worry me, boyo.' He ran a hand over his faintly-stubbled chin. He usually wore a short, thick beard and had shaved it only this morning. 'If my time's up, then it is.'

'What, then?' She fell silent, respecting his habit of thinking before he spoke.

Wavelets rippled and glittered, breaking against the chuan's magnal skin. A small school of black fish leapt from the water and disappeared again into its opaque depths. A brilliant green sea-bird swooped down, missing both fish and chuan by a hairsbreadth, turning aside on a wingtip to wheel back into the sky and circle again.

Gavon scraped both hands through his hair, head bowed. 'My worry is that I'm endangering ye three. To be a Seyd is to be sentenced to death. Escaping challenges the Slavemasters' authority. Especially since I killed my Master during the Hunt. His son, Bahad Sinclar, will want revenge. If I'm caught, I'll be put back into the Wushi Games to be executed. There's a chance they'll do the same to anyone with me.' He grimaced self-deprecatingly. 'I'm a decade older and a mite slower than I was. I don't think I'd make it through another round of the Games.'

'Ah.' She inspected his face. 'That's why you shaved?'

He had also, from the day they'd found Mina's wrecked chuan, let his wiry dark hair grow. Instead of being so short as to be almost shaven, it was already over a fingerswidth long and beginning to curl. His appearance was dramatically altered.

'Aye.' He stroked his chin again. 'I always had a Jadidan's beard and short hair, as a slave.' He rolled one sleeve up his arm as far as it would go, revealing a faded, grey-blue tattooed letter S, with a smaller M beneath it. 'But if they find this and the scars on my feet they'll know I was mhareb-slave to the Sinclar family.'

Alere touched the tattoo. 'Couldn't you have had this changed to something else?'

'Aye.' Gavon pulled the sleeve down and smoothed it absently. 'But it's part of who I am. The Melcori made me what I am today. I didn't want to forget. In hindsight changing it would have been smarter, eh?'

'Well…' She steeled herself against a quiver of uncertainty. 'As much as I appreciate your skills and knowledge, I can't let you risk yourself. It would be best if you stay on the chuan and let us find the others.'

Her task would be more difficult, for his skills were formidable and his knowledge of the city and culture invaluable. But giving him the option to withdraw was the honourable thing to do.

'Very weishi of ye, boyo,' Gavon said with weary, scornful amusement. 'How many times have I told ye to let that go if ye want to survive? Besides, ye need me and yer not my Jun-Heir for I claim no land as mine and answer to no master.' His smile twisted. 'I make my own choices.'

'I know. If I can't change your mind, then I'm glad to have you with me.' Alere laid a hand on his shoulder. 'We'll just have to make sure you don't get caught.'

She turned to leave and a thought occurred to her. 'Gavon, have you heard of something called a Selb?' When his head snapped around, she added quickly, 'It's only…I know that dying slaver mentioned it. I've been wondering if it was a Melcori thing and maybe you knew what it was.'

'Aye.' He straightened, glowering. 'And I've been hearing more of them lately than I'd like to. They're a filthy cult.' The hardened warrior, survivor of slavery and of countless skirmishes in his role of yongbing to a trade caravan for the last five years, shuddered at the word. 'They have some mad belief that the slaves will be freed one day by some mysterious champion. That they'll rise up to form an army of justice.'

'Cult?' Alere rolled the unfamiliar term on her tongue, trying to find a definition for it. 'Isn't that something like a religion? Our ancestors deliberately left religions behind on Earth. Where has this come from? Oh.' Hours of tedious study of the history of Kalima now sprang from her memory and her heart sank. 'I remember now: the Selb worship steel, don't they? Something about using it to purify people of evil. But I thought they were wiped out a couple of hundred years ago in the failed uprising of five-oh-six? When Madina outlawed slavery.'

Gavon sneered. 'That's what the history books say, boyo. And that's what the Juns'd have us believe. Religions were one of the main causes of wars on old Earth. Kalima was meant to be free of them.' He spat over the side. 'Truth is, we're too gouri stupid as a species to know when we're being stupid. Banning religion was never going to work. And not just because we lost the good of it along with the bad – for there *was* some good.'

She opened her mouth to ask what, but he cut her off.

'We're bred to be followers of one thing or another. When times get tough, we seek something outside ourselves to fix things. That's why yer hearing about the Selb, now. In good times it festers amongst the slaves. In bad it spreads out into the free folk when they lose hope in their leaders.'

'Well,' Alere said, 'it sounds like the best thing we can do is get Jarran back and give them a strong leader who can improve things. Then it won't spread further into Mamlakah.' She glanced at the crimson sun. 'It's getting late. Morning will bring light into darkness, so they say.'

He uttered a short, cynical laugh. 'Around here morning brings nothing more than the Slavemaster and another day under the whip. Darkness is better. It brings respite.'

He stalked away.

She went to bed early and alone, grateful for Corin's lingering goodnight, but needing some time by herself to think. Once abed she lay awake for a long time, unable to sleep. Another attempt to reach Mina or Rohne – this time closer to an all-out attack – ended in failure. The strength of both their wards nailed solidly to rest her last doubts about Rohne. He warded her from Mina. He'd shielded one other mind on the chuan, too. Jarran's, probably. Was Rohne afraid Alere would incite Jarran against him? What was he doing to fear that?

She sought out the *Jin Bird*'s chuanzhu but found his mind numbed by the effects of some narcotic. Maybe jiu or blackweed. Overcoming her xintou scruples, she tried to influence his thinking or his emotions. Tried to convince him to stop the chuan and wait. But, whether it was the drugs or her lack of skill, he didn't respond.

As the midnight change of watch rang out abovedecks, Alere closed her eyes and meditated to settle her thoughts. The burden of responsibility was too heavy to bear, yet not heavy enough to weigh down her eyelids. Concern for Mina, Rohne, Jarran and now Gavon filled her mind with possibilities too horrific and varied to allow sleep to hold her for long. When she did doze off, her dreams were haunted first by Ven Zah-Hill's death, then by scenes of Mina, hurt and in tears; then by images of the deaths of people she'd never met; and the firey destruction of buildings she'd never seen.

In the small hours of the morning, she woke with tears on her cheeks, the blankets twisted and tangled about her legs, and the smell of hot metal curling through the cabin. She rolled over on the thin mattress. The clasp of the yanstone necklace dug into her skin. Half-awake, she unclipped it and shoved it to the bottom of the bed. After that, she dropped into a deep, dreamless sleep.

She woke late. A knock on the door was followed by Corin's concerned voice softly calling her name. She answered and sent him away with an assurance she would be on deck for training soon.

After he left, she tossed the blankets aside and found the yanstone necklace. She ran its smooth warmth through her fingers and stared into its flickering silver-gilt fires for a long time. Was it linked to her recurring dreams? The dreams of fire and destruction began when she'd taken to sleeping with the yanstone dagger in her hand. Worsened when she wore the necklace to bed. Was there a connection or was it just her own fears for what lay ahead?

She dropped it into a pocket of her carrybag and made ready. As she gathered her weapons, a smudge of charcoal-black on the curved magnal wall near her head caught her eye. Had that been there yesterday? Of course. It must have been.

Hurrying through ablutions and breakfast, she arrived on the upper deck and blinked against the morning glare. Gilded sunlight split into a million tiny orange suns and danced on the river's surface. Alere sank onto a storage crate next to Corin.

He stroked her cheek. 'You look tired.' Blond hairs escaped his mawei, fluttering and catching in his lips as he spoke.

'Didn't sleep well.' She raised her face to the sun as the warm breeze off the water caressed her skin. Shading her eyes and squinting northward she pointed at a smudge of brownish-grey on the horizon. 'Chengdu?'

Corin aligned one eye lazily with her arm. 'Chengdu, indeed.' He leaned back on the heels of his hands and stretched his legs out, crossing them at the ankles. 'Should have let me stay last night.' His smile was wicked with shared secrets. 'I could've helped with the sleeping problem.'

Still dream-troubled, Alere gave him a half-hearted smile. They approached the rivermouth and slowed as Dalor navigated mud and sandbanks in the broad delta. The city-smudge seemed to come no closer and the distant riverbanks drifted past with painful sluggishness. But half-rotted wrecks, poking out of the sands, attested to the need for care.

Giant golden salamanders, longer than the *Kuailong*, slipped off the mud islands and splashed into the river. And once, a massive coastal roc-eagle – its fur white above and pale green beneath – swooped down and snatched a half-grown salamander in its claws. It struggled skyward, heading for a rocky islet covered in thick, purple-leafed trees.

'Hey.' Corin interposed his head between her and the view, one brow raised. 'Have I failed to hold your interest for even a week?' He pressed a hand to his heart. 'My reputation.'

Alere turned away. 'Don't be flippant, Cor. I'm worried and you know it. What if we can't find them fast enough?'

'All the more reason to be flippant, if you ask me. Worrying never helps. Nor do what-ifs.' He directed her attention towards Gavon and Kett, who circled each other nearby. 'Be here and now, Alli. There's nothing else to be done and learning this may help when you do get there.'

His words held more sense than her dreams. She focussed on the others in time to see Gavon entangle Kett's leg and yank it from beneath him. Kett hit the deck hard. He rolled away from the slicing blade, hooked his other ankle around the chain and jerked it out of Gavon's hand. The blade sailed through the air, landing point-down in the timber, vibrating, next to Kett's ear. The weishi untangled his leg, freeing himself only to find Gavon's dagger at his throat. He raised his hands in submission.

'I concede…again,' he admitted. 'I don't know that we can learn to best someone of your skill, Gavon.' Nevertheless, he took up a fighting stance once more.

Alere blinked. It was the first time she'd ever heard Kett admit defeat. His ability to learn any weapon was legendary in Weishi House. His singleminded determination, humility and skill earned him the respect of even House Master Anh. Concerned, she paid closer attention as Gavon continued to instruct.

After a few minutes, she sighed in relief. Kett feigned some of his difficulty in dealing with the weapon. He skilfully and subtly allowed Gavon to triumph. To what end, though? Surely Gavon would see it? How did letting him win benefit anyone? Then she observed the older yongbing. Over the course of half an hour, his demeanour changed.

To begin with, he was quiet: intently concentrating on Kett's reactions, frowning, almost hesitant. In anyone else she would label it as self-doubt. But in Gavon...? By the time Kett held up a hand in final, panting submission, Gavon's gruff self-confidence had returned. He patted the weishi's shoulder and sent him to rest, his expression one of wry understanding.

As Kett limped over to join her, Corin stretched his neck. He rose and slapped Kett on the back.

'Not sure I can do better than that, my friend.' Corin winked at Alere as she passed Kett a full waterskin.

Kett grimaced and rotated a shoulder, feeling the elbow joint with his other hand as he watched Corin spar with Gavon. He drank deeply and poured water over his head, wiping it from his face and smoothing his dark hair into neatness again. He passed the skin back to her and she drank sparingly.

'Do you think Gavon knows you threw that?' Alere noted Corin's deft footwork as he closed on Gavon and attempted to disarm him. The two men were evenly matched. As far as she could tell, Corin tried wholeheartedly, losing and winning in equal measure. Gavon's fierce grin broadened with each bout.

'Oh, yes. As does Corin, clearly.' Kett gave a rueful grimace and prodded at his ribs. 'Besides, I didn't. Not all of them, anyway. Gavon is extremely good.'

She frowned. 'So, if Gavon knows, what was the point?'

Kett smiled with resigned amusement. 'I'm sure I've said it before: the mind is just as powerful a tool as that sword on your hip. Any fight – win or lose – goes beyond the weapon you wield. It's your mind and your opponents' that you battle. Not just his blade.'

Alere said nothing. It *was* something Kett had said often, but she'd never understood. She'd always believed the winner of any encounter did so through superior skill or tactics. Now she finally understood the psychology behind it.

The winner was the one likely to have that implacable, unhesitating warrior mindset she'd already come to recognise was needed. And the winner was also the one who could best undermine that same mindset in his opponent.

By allowing Gavon to win narrowly, Kett gave the man back his self-belief. The one thing most critical to any warrior. By allowing Gavon to *see* him throw the matches, Kett also gave back the yongbing's confidence in his ability to read his opponent.

When Gavon called her up, she went thoughtfully. In truth she did little better against the kusarigama than she had the day before, but it didn't matter. For now, besting Gavon was not the objective, setting him free, was.

They broke for lunch, battered and tired. Gavon spoke briefly with Dalor before joining them at the table. He sank into a chair and poured himself a drink of the thick, yellow dawfruit juice Dalor had picked up in Dalcin as part of their supplies.

'Dalor says we'll be at port in less than two hours.' He nodded to Alere. 'Ye'd best make ready, boyo. Ye'll need to be young Alek before we arrive. Yer hair's come loose and ye'd best re-do yer little…' He waggled a finger under his nose, indicating the gum-and-hairclippings moustache. 'It's come unstuck.'

Gavon threw back his drink and screwed up his nose. 'And Chengdu's no place for a woman unless she's veiled. And ye did say ye didn't want to don the red robes again.'

Alere misliked the implication. 'So, all women are either slaves or must wear the veil here?' The veil, in that context, smacked of another form of slavery or servitude. Did it mean women were viewed as inferior to men in Melcor?

'Aye.' Gavon inspected a piece of dried meat before gnawing on it. 'They're a bit behind the fashion here. They stick to the old ways of cosseting and protecting their free women. They think they're best suited to child-bearing, like in the colony's early days. The only exceptions are female mharebi. But they're rare. That path is only open to young women who can't bear children. It's not an easy one. Few survive the training.'

'Oh, joy.' Alere stuffed a last piece of bread into her mouth and washed it down with juice. 'I definitely want to be Alek.'

'Aye.' He gripped her wrist as she rose from the table. 'But don't make the mistake of thinking that makes the women weak, boyo.' He jerked his chin at the shore. 'All Melcori people train from childhood – men, women, and a few select mhareb-slaves. So ye need to be clear about who ye'll kill and who ye won't.' He swept his gaze to include the other two. 'For if someone comes at ye with a weapon, ye can bet they know how to use it. Ye can't afford to hesitate.'

Alere massaged her wrist when he released it. 'Of course not.'

He curled a lip. 'Easy to say, boyo. But have ye ever thought about how ye'd react if a veiled woman attacked ye?' When she shrugged to indicate it wouldn't matter, he curled a lip. 'And what if she were pregnant? Or what if it were a girl-child of seven or ten holding the knife at yer throat?'

Alere shuddered. He was right. The protection of women and children was ingrained into her weishi thinking and training. Woven into the fabric of the colony. Survival dictated it must be that way. Even the thought of raising a weapon to a pregnant woman or a child made her cringe.

Corin's countenance was set in stone, blank and shuttered. A thoughtful furrow creased Kett's brow. His most burning focus had always been the protection of those weaker than himself. She could only hope they never had to test the idea. Hesitation could be fatal.

Alere sought the safety of her tiny cabin.

PART II

CHAPTER FIFTEEN

ROHNE

'Rohne. Oh, please wake up.' Mina's harsh whisper woke him from a half-doze.

He yawned and automatically stretched his mind towards hers, only to find it still like wading through mud. Gouri drugs. Their jailers watched him drink water, so it was impossible to get his system clear. He'd managed to spill some of his water rations surreptitiously. He was thirsty, but his mind was now clear enough that he could maintain the wards around Mina and Jarran's minds. He just wasn't strong enough to influence the guards, as well.

'Rohne?' Mina's call snapped him into full alertness.

'What?' He stretched his neck and wrinkled his nose as the reek of sweat and filth wafting from his clothes. Even with access to a slops bucket, the hold stank.

'The chuan's docked,' she said.

She was right. Water sloshed but the boat's rocking had settled to the merest hint of movement. Overhead, sounds of bronze rattling on timber and footsteps running on and off the deck attested to the movement of men and cargo.

'And?' Rohne glowered at her in the dim light. Pain throbbed through his head as he checked her wards. Still firm.

'I just—'

'We stick to the plan,' he said, coolly. 'I know what I'm doing. Trust me.'

'But I don't understand why you won't let me talk to Alere. She can help,' Mina said.

'Shut up about Alere, will you?' he snapped.

Her eyes widened. She shrank away.

'Don't talk to her like that, Rohne,' Jarran said, his deep voice rumbling. 'She's scared. We all are.'

Rohne rubbed at his head. 'Sorry, Mina. The drugs are giving me a killer headache. You don't need to be scared. I can handle this.' The ship must be in Chengdu, which was perfect. His power to influence the slaver crew had been limited. But, even if he had been able to convince them to let their prisoners go in Madina, it would have done little good. Alere and the others would have been right on their heels. She needed to be delayed. Coming to Chengdu would serve that purpose nicely.

And another, as well.

This was the moment he'd been waiting for his whole life. Now the next phase was about to begin. When they'd swapped to a new chuan in Madina, one of the slavers had whispered a message to him. Nothing that would have meant anything to anyone overhearing. Just the single word, *Erheyi*. But it had dramatically altered Rohne's plans. He grinned, fiercely.

'You three.' A guard stood over them. 'On your feet.'

Rohne complied with alacrity, helping Mina to stand as well. Jarran struggled to his feet, bent almost double beneath the low ceiling. Mina clung to the hands of both men, her eyes darkshadowed and apprehensive. She was too thin after days eating the watery slop fed to the slaves. The first thing Rohne intended to do was make this Slavemaster treat her as a guest and give her decent food and a bath. She'd appreciate that. He squeezed her hand. She returned a tiny, flickering smile.

'Move.' The guard prodded him with a dagger. He held out three black bags. 'Put these on your heads. Master Hallon wants to see you three.'

'So.' A harsh disembodied voice echoed in what sounded like a large room.

Rohne tested his powers again and ground his teeth. He was still barely able to keep the wards up around Mina and Jarran's minds. How was he supposed to control this Hallon person?

'This is the new Jun First, is it?' the voice continued, clipped and impatient. 'Let's see him, then?'

The black bag covering Rohne's head vanished, leaving him blinking in the glare of actual electric lights. With his hands bound, he couldn't push back the hair falling in his face. He shook his head, clenching his jaw against the pain. How dare this slaver scum treat him this way?

Rohne lifted his chin as a broad-shouldered, grey-haired man scrutinised him up close. The man was thickening in the middle. His face scarred. Two faded blue dots were tattooed on his forehead. A warrior gone to seed. But he carried himself arrogantly, like a Jun, looking down his crooked nose at Rohne and sniffing in distaste.

'You don't much look like Radan Zah-Hill, boy.' Hallon tilted his head. 'Maybe a bit around the eyes.'

Rohne didn't react and didn't bother to correct him. The man was clearly a shazi, past his prime and lacking in both intelligence and education. Escaping would prove simple once Rohne had the lay of the land.

'Master,' a guard interrupted hesitantly, gesturing at Jarran. 'This is Jarran Zah-Hill.'

'Ah.' Hallon shifted his attention to Jarran. 'Yes, I can see *your* resemblance. Welcome to my house.'

Jarran stared down at the proffered hand and lifted cold, light-brown eyes to Hallon's. 'You've kidnapped us, branded us like slaves, and you expect me to shake your hand?'

Hallon's genial expression didn't waver but his nostrils flared. 'I branded you so that you'll never forget to whom you owe loyalty. Once you're released, that is. Assuming all goes well in our...negotiations.' He kept his hand out. 'And whether you shake hands depends...do you want to see your daughters alive again?'

Jarran's jaw clenched. 'You don't have my daughters, so that's an empty threat.'

'Really?' Hallon's hand stayed outstretched. 'I know where they are. Do you honestly think I couldn't get them out of the Ma-Safra household in Madina if I wanted to? Come, come.' His smile widened. 'We have much to talk about, so let's start on the right foot. I'm offering you the hand of friendship. Take it.' The last two words carried an unmistakeable threat.

There was a long, strained silence, then Jarran grasped Hallon's hand. His fingertips whitened and his forearm corded. Their joined hands trembled and Hallon's grin showed teeth. He relaxed his grip and laughed aloud.

'I like you, boy.' He slapped Jarran on the shoulder. 'I can see we'll get along fine, once you understand your place. Now.' He turned to Rohne. 'Who are you, then? Oh, yes. You're the one my spy said was dangerous. He said we had to drug you. Why is that? What's so special about you? Are you a xiongshou sent to assassinate me?'

Rohne threw back his shoulders and lifted his chin, meeting Hallon's eye as an equal. 'Here's what I am.'

He took a risk and dropped the wards around Mina and Jarran to give himself enough power to work. A swift probe into Hallon's mind brought him up frustratingly short. The Slavemaster was xintou-trained to ward. Khara! Fine. Rohne switched his attention to the armed guard standing behind Jarran.

The man stepped jerkily forward, his mouth agape and eyes wide. He drew his bronze dagger and thrust it toward Hallon in a spasmodic, clumsy jab. Hallon leapt back with a cry of anger. He snatched out his own weapon – some sort of sickle thing with a chain – and deflected the blow.

Rohne gritted his teeth against the raging pain in his head as he worked around the drug. The guard raised his arm again, even as his mouth formed a denial. Hallon sidestepped the slow strike and sliced his blade across the guard's throat with cool efficiency. Released from Rohne's influence, the guard dropped his weapon and grabbed his throat. Gurgling, he sank to the flagstone floor in a pool of his own blood.

Hallon stared at the body as two of his men dragged it away.

He pointed the reddened tip of his curved blade at Rohne.

'What the jahim was that?' He pointed at the trail of blood. 'He was one of my most loyal men. Are you telling me you did that? How?'

Rohne met Hallon's disbelieving gaze coolly. 'I'm xintou, that's how.'

Hallon froze. Behind him, two of his guards paled and clutched at their weapons. The third, a woman with short, blonde hair, frowned.

'Now *that's* interesting,' Hallon said, stroking his jaw and inspecting Rohne more closely. 'I believe you'll make a most useful slave, boy.'

'I'm no-one's slave,' Rohne said. 'And neither are my friends. You'll let us go or I'll rip out your mind and turn you into a dribbling mess, begging for the release of death.'

A crack of genuine mirth escaped Hallon. He clapped Rohne on the shoulder as he had Jarran.

'You've got guts, boy, but you're not very bright, are you? If you could do that, you would have already.' He grinned sympathetically. 'But thank you for the warning. I'll have to make sure you stay drugged until I break you. You'll come around. I've never met anyone I couldn't break.' He whispered in Rohne's ear. 'And I've had thirty years of practice, so don't doubt I can do it.'

Repressing a shiver, Rohne kept his scornful expression and ignored the man. Only the weakminded gave in to brainwashing techniques.

Hallon chuckled shrewdly. 'And now you're thinking only fools break?'

Rohne started but said nothing.

The Slavemaster shrugged. 'I've found most people – intelligent or not – actually prefer guidance in their lives. People need a strong leader. Someone who knows what's best for them. Takes away the worry of having to think for themselves. Or having to take responsibility for their pathetic lives and predictable mistakes.'

'Feel free to delude yourself,' Rohne sneered.

Hallon simply laughed again and turned towards Mina. He tugged the black silk bag from her head and grinned appreciatively. 'Now that's more like it.' He waved the female guard forward. 'Have her washed and dressed and taken to my room. I'll have her for dessert after this infernal dinner we're hosting for Mianshou.'

'No!' Jarran and Rohne spoke together. Mina whimpered and shrank from Hallon's bulk, her eyes huge.

At Hallon's imperious gesture, guards grabbed Jarran and Rohne and hauled them away from Mina. The female guard wrenched Mina's arm and fisted her hair, forcing Mina towards a nearby flight of stairs leading up to the next floor.

'Don't!' Rohne yelled. He focussed on his guard and the man released Rohne, looking at his hands like they'd betrayed him.

'What are you doing, man?' Hallon snapped at his mhareb. 'Restrain him.'

'You can't take her,' Rohne said, struggling to hold the mhareb off. 'She's—'

'Shut up, Rohne,' Jarran growled.

Mina sobbed, twisting in the grip of the female mhareb. 'Don't, Rohne. I'll be alright. Don't tell him.'

'Hold.' Hallon's deep voice cracked through the tumult. 'She's what, boy? Are you going to tell me she's something special?' He studied Mina contemptuously. 'Because she's just another woman. I don't care if you love her. She's mine, now.'

Rohne bit his lip.

'Rohne,' Jarran yelled. Hallon nodded and Jarran's guards dragged him away, still yelling and thrashing. There was a thump and the cries stopped.

Rohne swallowed, weighing up the options. He couldn't let Hallon hurt Mina. There was only one choice.

'She's Rafi Koh-Lin's daughter,' he said. 'His kin-child, not his heir. But he cares about her. You harm her and you'll have a war on your hands.'

'You say that like it's a bad thing.' Amused interest flickered across Hallon's coarse features. He strode over to Mina and grasped her jaw, turning her face this way and that in the light. He laughed.

'I can see the resemblance, now. Oh, this is excellent. You may be my best prize of all, girl.' He nodded to the warrior-woman holding Mina. 'Put her and Jarran in the room next to mine. Get them clothes suitable for formal wear.'

As the woman dragged Mina up the stairs, Hallon turned on Rohne, rubbing his hands together. 'You three, my boy, are coming to dinner. There are some people who need to see your friends. And you're going to make sure those two behave. Because if you don't, your lady-love will spend time in my bed.' His smile widened. 'And I suspect that would cut at you most, wouldn't it?'

CORIN

Even half-blinded after stepping from the street's brilliant chaos into *The Monkey's Wing* tavern's smoky gloom, Corin easily spotted his three companions. Laughing softly, he drifted over to the bar and leaned on it, ordering drinks and taking the opportunity to run a professional eye over the other patrons.

The taproom was full of end-of-day diners and drinkers: boisterous, loud and already half-drunk. At one end, two androgenous slaves danced on a small, raised dais, accompanied by a talentless oud-player and a drummer. In one corner, a woman with short, blonde hair watched Corin, her light eyes sultry above a brilliant orange veil that obscured her nose and mouth in the Melcori style. She wore a bright orange and silver silk robe wrapped in the complicated fashion favoured by upper class Chengdu women. She winked and tilted her head. Corin turned away. The two blue dots on her forehead meant she was married and dallying with married women in Chengdu was tantamount to a death sentence if the husband issued a Challenge of the Cuckolded.

Not that he was interested, anyway. He looked around for Alere.

She, Kett and Gavon sat in wary silence in the opposite corner, watching the entrances. With cowls raised, drinks untouched on the table, and hands resting on weapons. They might as well be wearing a sign saying 'trouble'.

Corin ordered drinks. The tavern's tame sky-monkey swooped down from its perch near the ceiling. The blue-green skin webbed between its limbs gleamed almost iridescent in the afternoon light. It landed next to Corin and barked at him. He scratched its indigo-furred head, keeping clear of the poisoned spikes on its neck. The animal purred and attempted to steal his purse. Well-trained. Corin flicked its black nose with a fingertip and gave the barkeep a wry look. The man had the grace to blush as he pushed over four glasses of the green wine favoured in this part of the world.

Corin exchanged lighthearted Mianshou greetings with several cheerful drinkers, and scooped up the glasses. He raised them high and made his way over to the table. Sliding in beside Gavon, he passed out the wine and pushed ale tankards to one side. Then he raised his glass, smiling as he crooked an elbow over the seat back.

'My friends,' he said quietly, in between laughing at nothing, 'do stop looking like foreigners. You stand out. And get rid of the hoods and the scowls. Relax. This is the end of the year. The entire jundom is here in Chengdu, getting ready to celebrate Mianshou. There will be trading, laughter, dancing, sex, and far too much drinking of this horrendous green wine. Anyone who is not doing the same will be suspicious.'

To her credit, Alere caught on first. She flipped back her cowl and raised her glass, doing a reasonable job of appearing relaxed. Kett followed suit. Gavon, after a moment's hesitation and a quick, darkling look around the room, did the same. Corin laughed again and the others joined in, albeit forced, raising their glasses in an imaginary toast.

'Oh, and keep an eye on that gouri sky-monkey. Thing's trained to pick pockets,' he muttered.

'Any news?' Alere said, sipping at her drink. She screwed up her nose. 'Bleh.'

'Yes, it's awful. Pretend.' Under cover of drinking, he filled them in. 'You were right, Gavon.' He scanned the room and their nearest neighbours to make sure no one listened in. 'The slavemarkets finished about three hours before we got here. Their chuan made better time than us and arrived just before dawn. My contacts say all the slaves on board were brought to sale this morning.'

Alere's fingers whitened on her glass. 'Jarran and Mina?'

'Ah.' Corin lifted his drink to hide his mouth. One never knew who could read lips in a room like this. The Shah usually kept a close eye on foreigners. And Liu Gray's spy network, did as well. Best to assume they were watched.

'Therein lies the mystery,' he continued. 'My good friend and mildly untrustworthy contact, the auctioneer, assures me that no one matching their descriptions – or Rohne's for that matter – came across his board today. His Outers Read truthfully, too. If they were sold, it was a private transaction.' It was also safe to assume anything he asked about would be reported back. With its layers of intrigue and doubledealing, Melcor required an extremely agile mind to stay ahead of the game. Corin savoured the familiar flutter of excitement, low in his belly.

'Jiche!' Alere's forceful interjection turned an amused glance or two their direction. She waited until they lost interest. 'So, we don't know who has them?'

Corin put his feet up on a seat opposite. 'Now I didn't say that, did I?'

She glared, so he relented.

'Another little friend of mine says three slaves were taken directly to Hallon Nasim's house in the city, as soon as the chuan arrived. They were hooded, but he was fairly sure it was two men and a woman.' He raised a finger to forestall questions. 'Here's the interesting bit: only one of the men was chained.'

'Master Hallon,' Gavon growled. 'Should have known.'

Alere paled. Her wineglass shook and green liquid splashed onto the scarred tabletop. Kett gently took the drink from her. She twisted at a stray lock of hair by her ear.

'Gavon said,' she murmured, 'that Hallon's the most powerful Slavemaster in Melcor. That he's never had a slave escape.' She raised wide, frightened eyes to Corin. 'If he's working with Jahil – with all their resources behind this – how can we four possibly get them out?'

'We need more information,' Kett said. 'Gav? Any suggestions?'

Gavon said nothing. His skin was waxen and the small muscles in his jaw jumped. Alere gripped his clenched fist and he sent her a swift, empty smile. He downed his wine in one long swallow. Then he rolled his shoulders back and placed both hands carefully flat on the table.

'Aye. We need more information. I've never been inside Hallon's…establishment. We need to know what his security's like.'

'Which means,' Corin said, grinning, 'now comes the fun part. We pay a house call on Master Hallon.'

CHAPTER SIXTEEN

CORIN

'And this was *really* the best idea you could come up with? Not exactly original,' Alere muttered.

'What can I say? Short notice.' Corin glanced at her slight figure striding beside him and laughed. 'The purple suits you, though.'

She shot him a narrow glare and twitched her cloak closer to hide the skimpy Artist-House purple dancer's costume. Her kohled eyes were huge and dark above the sheer purple veil over her nose. The three white dots on her forehead proclaimed her unwed status. He bore the same marks, and tried not to let it bother him.

Corin moved aside to let a harried merchant, leading a herd of silver-grey qarn-goats along the street, pass by. Catching up with her again, he checked to see Kett and Gavon still followed. Even by the light of Luna-Er, and the torches lining the streets, it would be easy to get separated. Kett and Gavon – under protest dressed in the purple – fell into step again.

Chengdu teemed with people. Market stalls crowded into every possible space as distant farmers and craftsmen sought buyers for their wares. According to rumour, every conceivable thing was available for purchase this week, somewhere in Chengdu. Corin believed it. Tantalising opportunities to spend, make, or steal money lay everywhere. It hurt to bypass them.

He led the way through a cluster of stalls devoted to exotic spices; the heady smells of cinnamon, sweet-xun and clove intoxicating. Nearby, food vendors waved roasted rong, skewered night-wings, and stir-fried red-root under their noses and Corin's stomach growled. Wine and jiu sellers tried to press sample cups into his hands. Beyond them, brilliantly coloured birds fluttered in cages alongside those holding barking sky-monkeys in all shades of blue and purple. Wild xiao-cat kittens mewed plaintively in solid timber boxes, ready to be taken home and trained as guard-cats. Musicians danced and wove their way through the crowds, their melodies sometimes clashing, sometimes blending.

And, practically invisible to the locals, countless slaves wended through the marketplace, burdened with wares. They were easily identifiable by their cream bamboo-cloth shifts which bared the left arm so their tattoo remained visible at all times. Their faces were devoid of makeup or marital marks, and they were careful to step aside, eyes lowered, whenever a free citizen passed. Corin clenched his teeth and turned away. There was nothing he could do to help any of them, right now.

Maybe one day.

A boy of about ten bumped into Corin, fingers fumbling at his pockets. In no mood to teach an aspiring thief a lesson, Corin simply elbowed him aside, sending the youngster sprawling onto the cobbled road. The pickpocket scrambled to his feet and flicked Corin a rude hand signal. His white-blond hair and grey-green eyes stood out amongst other Chengdu children, who tended towards dark hair and gold skin with white-blue eyes. Standing out was a liability for thieves. Someone ought to tell him.

Corin shrugged, adjusted the oud across his back and tugged his purple cap lower. He patted his pockets, just to make sure. Something crinkled. Interesting. He pulled a grubby piece of bamboo paper from one pocket. Not such a bad thief, after all. He glanced back. The boy was gone.

Alere, Kett and Gavon had paused at a weapons stall, so Corin took the opportunity to skim the note. A strong hand with good spelling and grammar. So, someone educated. Probably not the boy.

Rafi Koh-Lin has requested I assist you and I'm always pleased to oblige a regular customer. A message left at The Monkey's Wing inn will also reach me with alacrity.

If you require a safe house during your visit, please follow the directions below.

LG

Ahhhh. Corin read the directions and carefully tore up the paper, letting it scatter. So, Rafi had reached the elusive Liu Gray. Hopefully a safe house wouldn't be necessary, but it was useful to have as backup. And Rafi paid Gray enough, so he ought to be trustworthy – for a given value of trust.

Corin tapped Alere on the shoulder and jerked his head.

'We need to keep moving,' he muttered. 'Still a few blocks to go and my source says Hallon likes to start his feasts on time.'

She raised a brow. 'Of course. Can't keep the nobility waiting for their fried runiu-balls and rong brains.'

Corin grinned. 'Do be careful around here. Slightly unsavoury neighbourhood for the next couple of blocks.'

Blackweed sellers lurked in shadowed alleys, offering less legal wares. Children scurried past, laughing and thieving. Girls and young men, most marked with the single red dot and wearing the closest possible shade to the true jiaoji red, caught at Corin's and Alere's clothing, trying to drag them into unveiled jiaoji flophouses. Alere sent them a scornful, pitying look. She cocked her head and Corin followed her gaze. One unveiled jiaoji wore little more than a Shemali quetzal snake. The animal was draped strategically about the girl's body, its metallic-blue and black fur shimmering in the lamplight. The wide crest lifted and fanned out and the animal bared sharp, finger-length teeth. Alere flinched back, wide-eyed.

'Not poisonous,' Corin said, 'but it will take a chunk out of you. C'mon. We need to keep moving.'

Alere nodded.

With a quick glance at Luna-Er, shimmering over the river, Corin hurried past the last market stall and picked the pace up to a jog. Six blocks later, he dragged Alere into a shadowed doorway.

'Right, we're here.' He waited for the other two and pointed their destination out. 'According to my source, all the houses in this block belong to either the four Slavemasters or their sycophants. This one is Hallon's.'

'Aye,' Gavin grunted. 'And the wall's a good bodylength higher than when I saw it last.'

They were in a more affluent area of town. Far cry from the crowded, mudbrick-and-bamboo constructions jammed tightly together around the port area. The houses were large and set on wide plots of land. Several had small wind-capture arms buzzing and spinning on the roof; the sea breezes providing electricity to the richer houses.

Across from where Corin stood, a high sandstone fence surrounded a two-storey house of the same pale rock. Spikes of bronze protruded from the fence top, giving it a barbaric, fortress-like appearance. They were linked by thin wires. Several guards, armed with crossbows, paced a raised walkway inside.

'The real entertainment for Hallon's dinner guests is due any time now, so watch for them,' Corin murmured. 'We need to either take their place or join with them.' He inspected the street. 'First, I want to see if there's a way out.'

Kett's soft laugh rumbled behind him. 'For, I assume, when things go suilie?'

'Exactly.' He flashed the weishi a grin. 'Gavon? What do you know about Hallon's methods of dealing with new slaves?'

The yongbing inspected the high walls and grimaced. 'If he still does things the same as he used to, he'll keep them here for about a month, training them before he either onsells or sends them to his country estates. He owns a good third of the rattleberry farms and produces most of Melcor's silk.'

'And his security?' Kett asked.

Gavon jerked his thumb at the building. 'There are more men on patrol than I remember. That wind-arm is new. He's electrified the top of the wall. It's a house in front, but there'll be a training facility in behind. Security around the slave quarters will be tight.' He scratched his chin. 'Seeing it now, I don't know that there's going to be a way out, if ye want to know the truth. Master Hallon has been a Slavemaster for twenty years or more, and his mother before him. He's made improvements. If he wasn't good at keeping them, he wouldn't be one any longer.'

Corin swore. 'In that case, I recommend we use this as a reconnaissance only, so we can work out how to get them out safely, later.'

'What?' Alere scowled at him, fists clenched at her sides. 'No. We have to get them out. That's the whole gouri reason we're here.'

'Alli.' Kett's warning hand on her shoulder stopped her short, but she continued to glare at Corin. 'Corin has a point. We don't have an exit plan. We don't know whether they're even in a fit condition to move. Or if they're still there. Or if Rohne has some other agenda. If we go in without knowing more, we're likely to get ourselves captured. Patience.'

'I could use the stones to subdue him,' she retorted.

'And how confident are you of that?' His fingertips whitened on her shoulder.

She made an abortive, angry gesture, but held her tongue. Corin smiled wryly. He understood the feeling. Only years of experience prevented him from acting as impulsively as she wanted to.

Alere touched the yanstone chain she'd tucked beneath the hip-belt of her costume. 'Give me a minute. I can Read them.'

'Thought you were worried about Rohne sensing you?' Corin reminded her.

'No time anyway, boyo,' Gavon warned. 'The entertainers are almost at the gate and there's too many to overpower in this busy a street. Time to move.'

Corin followed his pointing finger. Six folk in the purple strolled casually up the street, only half a block from Hallon's door. Too many and too close to take them out unobserved. The four companions sauntered across the road, timing it so they arrived as the artists reached Hallon's gate. In the confusion of being allowed entry, they weren't questioned by the others.

Once inside, however, the entertainers' leader looked askance at them. 'Who are you? Did the House send you?'

With a flourishing bow, Corin pasted on a broad, sincere smile. 'Indeed, they did. They felt such an important event should be dignified by a full display of the House's talent. But, with so many of the purple required at other functions, they've called us in from out of town.'

The man was small and thin, with arms and legs that seemed out of proportion because of his skin-tight, purple-and-red motley costume. His dark eyes were sharp and deepset over a blade of a nose, his dark hair short and styled to spike out in all directions. He could have been any age from thirty to fifty, but his forehead bore the white marks of the unwed.

He flung out his hands dramatically. 'The House Master listened to me after all, did he? Wasai! I'm Porro the acrobat. You are?' He sucked a quick breath. 'Wait. The fee? Are we being paid more?'

'Of course.' Corin threw an arm around the man's shoulders. 'Double in fact. Now, tell me what you plan to do, so we can fit our skills in with yours. We have a wonderful dancer with us.'

He guided Porro up a short flight of stairs to the entrance to Hallon's house. The vast blackwood door swung open and warm golden light poured into the night. A stick-thin female servant, sombrely clad in dark red, scrutinised them – and Porro's papers – then bowed them in. She pointed out the dining room where the guests awaited their entertainment.

Another servant appeared, led them around to a back entrance, and ushered them into the vast room. Corin and Alere followed Porro. Kett grabbed Gavon's arm and the two men slipped away, vanishing into the house.

Massive and oppressively warm, the dining hall ran the house's full length. The room rose two stories high, with a timber-beamed ceiling and jewel-bright tapestries covering the stone-and-zitanwood walls. Long tables, arranged in a U shape, dominated the space. Most seats were occupied, the diners laughing and talking loudly. Their voices echoed, merging into an unintelligible babble of noise.

Porro capered into the middle of the open space and turned a few backflips.

'Shenshis, Shunus, and gentlefolk all!' A somewhat manic giggle burst from his wide mouth. He bounced into an impressive series of flips and rolls, landing in a full leg-split on the wooden floor. Corin winced and Alere stifled a laugh.

The crowd applauded politely.

'For your entertainment,' Porro yelled, 'we have the beautiful and mysterious Callia, all the way from steamy Shemal in the northwest. Her dancing will delight and mesmerise. But be ware...' He lowered his voice and drew all eyes '...for you may lose your heart—'

'And your coin!' someone shouted.

'—to her beauty!' Porro ignored the interruption, laughed wildly, and flipped his way off the floor.

After a quick exchange with the acrobat about song choices, Corin unslung his oud and tuned it. He returned to Alere's side.

She sent a darkling glare towards the door. 'We're the distraction, are we?' She flung off her cloak and dropped it onto a chair, lifting her chin and smoothing the long, blonde wig Corin had purchased in Madina.

Corin tightened a slipping string, swept a finger over his ridiculous fake moustache and grinned. 'You are, anyway. I'm the background noise.'

She adjusted her veil. The Melcori favoured a veil covering the lower half of the face and leaving the eyes exposed; opposite to that used in Mamlakah. Above it her kohl-lined eyes were watchful. She checked the set of her gauzy, black and purple skirts. Her gold-skinned midriff lay bared and the purple halter-top covered little more than the essentials. Corin was glad he'd secreted his dagger and hers under his tunic. She also carried four slim blades as part of her jewelry. The bronze zills on her fingers were honed to a razor's edge. In that outfit she was likely to start a riot, so at least she could finish it as well.

The tambor player took up a dance rhythm.

'Next time,' Alere murmured as she passed Corin and headed for the open space in the middle of the room, 'they get to be the distraction while we sneak around. I *hate* this.'

'I'm not sure I'd ever get the image of Gavon in that costume out of my head.' He was glad to see a smile flit across her lips as she stepped into the dance.

ALERE

Alere raised her chin, softened her lips into a sultry smile, and lowered her eyelids. A swift scan of the room showed around fifty men and about a third that number of women. In the centre of the head table sat a man who must be Hallon. He was flanked by two women on his left, and three younger men on his right. By the resemblance, one of the younger men had to be his son. He wore dramatic grey eye makeup and the white marks of the unwed. The other two men were obscured by a large candelabra set on the table.

The women were, perhaps, a wife and daughter, although their age was hard to determine because they both wore the veil, heavy make-up, and gauze hair-coverings. The older woman sipped from her wineglass, eyes half-closed in either boredom or watchfulness. The younger barely blinked, apparently disinterested in the entire proceedings, not even touching the food on her plate or the wine in her glass.

Hallon appeared to be around fifty, broad-shouldered and fit for his age. His blue marriage-marks were tattooed onto his scarred forehead, his eye-makeup minimal. He was clean-shaven and kept his salt-dusted dark hair tied neatly back with a band of some silvery metal. Possibly iron. His wife's jewelry was also iron – and set with three small yanstones that flickered in the light of a few warm electric bulbs dangling overhead.

Electricity, iron and yanstones. A display of status and wealth.

Behind Hallon and his family, stood four armed weishi. They must be mharebi, who took the role of weishi in Melcor but did not have the House tattoo and training. The three men wore leather armour and carried the kusarigama, plus a long kris dagger.

The fourth was a woman. Slender and leanly muscled, she too wore leather and what appeared to be an alzin vest. At her hip she also carried the kusarigama and kris. Her blonde hair was cut close to her head and her light-coloured eyes scanned the room restlessly. They came to rest on the small group of entertainers. She stilled and glanced at Hallon, seated before her. She took a half-step forward, her lips parting. Then she paused and moved back into the shadows. A frisson of fear prickled down Alere's spine. What could the mhareb see to alarm her?

Apart from the mharebi, it appeared only Hallon and his red-faced son bore weapons. Both carried ornately-decorated bronze swords slung across their backs. All the other guests seemed to be unarmed, but Alere doubted they were. In their place, she'd bring any number of concealed weapons into a function like this. A certain brittle tension in the air carried the taste of mistrust with it.

Close behind her, the drum took up a beat, thrumming through her body. The first notes spilled from Corin's talented fingers. A pipe picked out the tune, its clear, lilting tone cutting through the hubbub of chatter, drawing all eyes to the entertainment.

Corin nudged her with a shoulder, his fingers flying across the strings while his eyes swept the room.

'Make sure Gavon stays out of here,' he murmured. 'The man five seats to Hallon's right, wearing black and a frown, is Bahad Sinclar. Son of the Slavemaster Gavon killed in his escape. Opposite him, wearing puke yellow and clashing red eye makeup, is Alcona Ebrahim, the third of the big four Masters of Chengdu. Four seats to *her* left, scowling like an underfed xiao-cat, is Chan Ling, the last of that lovely group of sweet and adorable folk who trade in others' lives. This is *not* a room Gavon wants to be in.'

'Understood.' Her stomach churned. The Slavemasters were all more focussed on watching each other, but it wasn't worth the risk of drawing their attention. 'Stay close,' she murmured.

Corin nodded and moved with her as she spun across to the nearby table. With the drummer and piper trailing behind, they worked their way along the board.

Whispers swept around the room, followed by coarse laughter. Corin twanged a sour chord on the oud. Alere checked her audience. The lull in conversation and the lascivious looks were enough to show she had crossed a line. She had learned to dance from Jiaoji House, where every movement was just one more seduction technique. Here, seduction was the last thing she wanted to achieve.

She shifted her movements from languidly sexual to sharper and more energetic. Corin picked out a quicker, lighter tune. The tambor player and piper, after a moment of confusion, caught up the change and went with it. Tension in the room palpably eased as men lost interest. The babble of voices rose again over the music.

With attention no longer solely on her, Alere felt able to split her concentration. Dropping into contact with the stones nestled under the glittery skirt-band, she reached for Kett and Gavon. Kett, as usual, had solid Outer wards she had no hope of breaching. Gavon, however, had no such training. His mind was open. In fact, his thoughts were so open as to be a liability. She kept forgetting to teach Gavon the basics of warding. Should Rohne be Reading, he would know where they all were and what they did.

She slipped into Gavon's Outers. A quick review of his surface thoughts showed he'd not yet found Mina, Jarran or Rohne. She made him aware of her presence.

How much longer?

She lived his uneasiness with him. He pulled himself together and gave her an estimate of five minutes before they completed their scouting. She warned him to stay clear of the ballroom, and to think lost-artist type thoughts. He couldn't hide his dismay at her mention of Bahad. But he mastered it and his fear segued into cold anger. He acknowledged, and she withdrew.

Swaying close to Corin, she let him know the timeframe. He gave a quick nod, following as she moved further up the table. She danced closer to the head table and used the opportunity to inspect Hallon.

Everything about him screamed of someone used to power, control, and obedience. Those closest checked his face frequently for his reactions. Strong-jawed and warrior-fit, he gave away little that wasn't deliberate and superficial. His mouth seemed set in a permanent, knowing half-smile. Alere had the distinct impression he was aware of every person in the room, what they plotted, and how he could manipulate them. This was not a man she wanted to cross, and yet they had to. His mind was warded, too. But if he was the Shah's kin-brother, that wasn't surprising.

Since he was so close to Shah Jahil, the odds were he'd either already handed his prisoners over or would in the immediate future. If they were still here, what reward was the Shah promising? Alere would either need to offer Hallon something better or break her friends out. She seriously doubted she could outbid Shah of Melcor. Yet, if what Gavon said about security was true, breaking Mina and the others out would be impossible.

She danced closer and directed her attention to Hallon's table mates. One quick viewing sent her spinning away with her back to the head table. As fast as possible, she danced to the end of the other side, and returned to the servants' door. A bemused Porro hurriedly ushered his other entertainers onto the floorspace.

'What was that about?' Corin demanded, slinging his oud across his back and following her behind a decorative screen.

Alere glanced apprehensively at the top table, but the diners paid her no attention.

'The three people sitting near Hallon at the top table.' She paused while Corin peered around the screen. 'It's Rohne, Jarran and Mina.'

Corin checked, swore and hurried her into the darkened outer hall. Kett and Gavon emerged from the shadows and joined them.

'We need to go,' Corin murmured. 'Hallon's displaying Rohne, Mina and Jarran like prize runiu at the head table.'

Kett's brows lifted and he took a half-step towards the dining hall. Corin grabbed his arm and shook his head. 'Trust me. Not a chance. Not even you.'

'But we can get them now,' Alere protested. 'It's too good an opportunity.'

'We can't,' Corin said, glancing back over his shoulder at the dining hall. 'The house is full of mhareb, guests and servants.'

The servants' entrance swung open, releasing a blast of laughter and the clatter of dishes. A woman hurried past, carrying plates. She glanced at them curiously and continued towards the back of the house.

Porro stuck his head out and squinted at them. 'You alright?'

Corin heaved a sigh. 'Callia is feeling quite unwell. I do apologise.' He swept a bow and sent Alere a warning look. She clutched at her stomach and groaned. 'We'll escort her home. Apologies for leaving you short-handed.'

The acrobat shrugged. 'You'll forfeit your part of the fee, you know.'

A quick frown tightened Corin's face, but he shook his head resolutely. 'It can't be helped. Spend it well, my friend.'

'Oh, I will. Watch yourself on the streets tonight.' Porro cocked his head and winked. 'Lot of nasty types out there during Mianshou, just waiting to steal an Artist's hard-earned coins.' He grinned and retreated.

'We can wait here,' Alere hissed, indicating the shadowy hall. 'Until it's over. There'll have to be a chance. We can't leave.'

Corin's fingers dug into her arm. 'We can and we will. Now. We'll split up to throw off any spies. You and Gavon make your way back to the inn.'

'He's right,' Kett said. 'This isn't the time. We need a plan.'

Alere clenched her jaw and spun towards the door. She brushed past the serving-woman at the entrance and stalked out of the house, into the street.

CHAPTER SEVENTEEN

ALERE

'Are you saying Jarran, Rohne and Mina are *guests* in Master Hallon's house?' Kett threw the question over his shoulder from where he stood watch by the window.

Their room, above the *Golden Salamander* – one of the less seedy taverns around the port – was small and clearly designed for short term stays by chuan crew, rather than luxury. It smelled of old sweat and jiu. Two sets of bunkbeds, without blankets or pillows, were jammed into a corner, leaving enough space in the centre of the room for a small table and four mismatched chairs. A narrow storage cupboard stood next to the door.

'Yes,' Alere said, slumping into a chair and resting her head on her fist. 'No. I don't know. All I know is that they were sitting at the head table with Hallon, his wife and son.'

She and Gavon had only just returned to the inn, having spent the better part of an hour navigating the city's back streets. Alere had even stopped in the street markets to dance while Gavon checked for followers.

The return trip had, at least, given her time to regain control of her temper. It hurt, physically, to be so close to Mina and Jarran and yet unable to help. Kett and Corin were right, though. A rescue would never have worked.

'And they were well? Mina?' Kett turned back to watch the street through the dirty-white curtains. His brow was troubled, his arms folded. The room's two windows overlooked a street in a constant state of riotous celebration. So much so Alere doubted she would sleep at all.

She scrubbed at her face, blinking as kohl smeared into her eyes. 'She seemed physically fine. But she wasn't…there.'

'Meaning?' Corin dropped into a chair beside her.

Gavon stayed by his position at the second window, peering into the street below. Outside, screams of laughter and the tinkling of smashed glass marked the progress of another group of merrymakers.

Alere yanked the blonde wig off and flung it aside. 'Before we left, I tried to connect with her.'

'And?' Corin lay his oud on the table, where it twanged dissonantly, as though in protest.

'And whatever Rohne is doing, it's beyond anything I've heard of in xintou abilities,' she admitted. 'He's somehow keeping both Mina and Jarran under mental control. It's like…' How to describe it? 'It's like he's suppressed their consciousness and is operating them as a puppeteer. His mind controlled their bodies. It means he's well into their Inners. I didn't think you could do that to one person without risking Fusion, let alone two. It must take tremendous concentration.'

There followed a long silence as the three men digested this unpleasant news. Alere moved restlessly over to a small washstand in one corner of the room. Reflected in the scratched, spotted mirror above it, her makeup-streaked face stared back, showing lingering fear.

'Jiche.' She closed her eyes briefly. 'I've just realised: he learned it from me.' She met Corin's puzzled gaze in the reflection. 'When I contacted Mina, on the *Nasir*, she had retreated. I was able to control her body. I thought it was because of our twin-bond, but he must have worked out how to do it on anyone. This is my fault.'

Hastily, she wet a cloth and wiped at the makeup, rubbing until her skin was red.

'I tried to break through his wards around their minds.' She wrung the cloth out and wiped her eyes again, trying to rid herself of the memory. 'I couldn't even get close.' She threw the cloth into the sink. 'What's the point of having xintou powers or weishi training if I can't *do* anything to save my own sister? And if everything I can do makes things worse?'

She grimaced, swiping back sweaty hair. 'At least he was so busy concentrating that I don't think he felt my attempt. What he's doing isn't easy. I doubt he can keep it up all day and all night. Maybe we can free them when he's sleeping?'

Corin rose from the table and laid a hand on her shoulder. 'Stop punishing yourself. What Rohne does is not your fault. There's nothing any of us could've done to get them out of there tonight.' He kissed her softly and gathered her into his arms. She rested her head on his shoulder.

'With what you learned, and what Kett and Gavon saw of the compound, we'll come up with a way to get them. I promise.' He kissed her again. 'This is what I'm good at, remember? Being sneaky.'

The slick noise of a drawn sword made Alere turn in surprise. Across the room, Kett stared at the sword in his hand, his grey eyes icily distant. When he saw Alere watching he sheathed the blade and wordlessly stalked to the door.

'Kett?' Alere ran to him, shocked by this uncharacteristic display of anger. 'Where are you going? You can't possibly rescue her tonight, on your own. You said it yourself: we have to come up with a plan.'

He ignored her and reached for the door handle.

She hesitated, not sure what to say to calm him. He was always so cool, so restrained. Focussed, determined, even obsessive in his role as weishi-protector, yes, but furious? Mina's plight must be affecting him more deeply than she'd realised.

There was a knock on the panel. Kett froze, anger shifting to surprise and thence to wariness. Stepping back, he drew his sword again, his expression one of anticipation.

'Who is it?' he ground out.

An unfamiliar female voice replied. 'I've come to see Corin. Corin Johnston.'

Corin sucked a sharp breath and murmured, 'I never go by that name.' He drew his weapon. 'Ever. No one, apart from Rafi and Alere, even knows it *is* my name. I left it behind ten years ago.'

'There's no-one here by that name,' Kett finally replied.

The female voice came again. 'Yes, there is.' She laughed throatily. 'Tell him Shasa Meron-kin is here to see him. If that doesn't bring him back into existence, then I'll leave.'

The colour drained from Corin's face.

He staggered back, impossible hope blooming in his green eyes. Alere picked up her blades from the table and stood behind the cupboard. Kett flattened himself into the dark space at the end of the bunkbeds. Gavon ducked into the opposite shadowed corner and vanished from sight.

Corin, after a long hesitation in which any number of emotions flickered across his face, opened the door.

The woman slipped through the gap, closed the door, and swiftly reviewed the room in the manner of a seasoned warrior scanning for threats and exits. She wore leather and alzin with a cloak of dark red silk flung back over one shoulder. Through a cut-out in her leather armguards, a tattooed letter N showed blue against her golden skin. Close-cropped, dark blonde hair, and two small gold studs glittering in each ear and another in her nose, lent her an air of barbaric intensity. Alere tightened her grip on her sword.

The female mhareb from Hallon's house.

The woman held her empty hands out, palms up, and smiled coquettishly at Corin. She tilted her head to one side.

'Corin.' Her voice was low and husky. 'Good to see you. Glad you're not dead.' She surveyed the room again. 'Tell your friends to come out. I'm alone.' She pulled a dagger from her leg-sheath and laid it on the table. 'And only lightly armed. A girl would be mad to walk around this place unarmed, after all. What a miserable little inn. Are you so badly off?'

Alere sent a swift thought to Gavon. He stayed in hiding while she and Kett emerged into the dim light of the single mel-oil lamp burning on the table.

Corin reached out hesitantly. Shasa took his hand and laughed, the sharp wariness of her softening into beauty.

'You zift, it *is* me. I'm not a ghost.' She lifted his palm to her cheek. When he still didn't speak, she flung her arms around his neck and buried her face in his chest, her muffled laughter shaky.

After a moment's hesitation, Corin wrapped his arms around her and held her as one might hold a precious, fragile work of art. Tears slid down his cheeks. Alere quashed the sick flutter in her stomach. This was Shasa, his lost first-love; his betrothed, believed murdered a decade before. Another victim of Hanna's kin-child laws. Of course he cared for her.

Alere mett Kett's questioning gaze and managed a smile. Yes, it was difficult to see Corin with another, but she couldn't even imagine what he must be feeling. To see him at a loss for words, his protective facetiousness stripped away, was both heart-breaking and joyous. He deserved the chance to be free of grief and loss.

At last, Corin broke the embrace, holding Shasa at arms length and inspecting her. He ran his fingers wonderingly down her cheek.

'How?' His question emerged broken and thick.

'Perhaps,' Alere put in quietly, 'we should go and leave you two in private awhile.'

Corin took an uncertain half-step in her direction, his brow creasing.

'No.' Shasa shifted away from him, but kept his fingers entwined in her own. Her ice-blue eyes lingered on his face. 'Our reunion will have to wait. I have little time. As mhareb I've earned trust. But I'm watched, so I can't be caught out after my ten curfew.'

'I don't understand.' Corin shook his head, his eyes stricken. 'How did you find me? Have you been here, in Melcor, for all these years? Why didn't you come home?'

A sad smile played at Shasa's mouth and she touched his lips. 'I've missed you so much, my love, but there's no time for the full story. Later, I promise. I followed you here from Hallon's house. You didn't make it easy. Yes, I've been here, in Melcor. I was taken prisoner, not killed.' She raised her chin coolly at Corin, clearly expecting him to react. 'Hanna Zah-Hill's men sold me. It's taken me eight years to work my way into the position of head mhareb-slave for Master Hallon.'

'Slave!' Corin's grip on her hand tightened and she winced.

His expression froze then closed into detachment. Shasa's golden skin flushed pink and she withdrew her hand from his.

'If you're blaming yourself,' she said matter-of-factly, 'then don't. You were away. We were both children. You would have died or been enslaved. There were too many of them, Cor. The only thing good about that day was knowing you were still alive. I hope you haven't wasted the years pining and feeling guilty over me.' Her eyes slid away from him and she fussed with straightening her armguard.

Corin said nothing but his lips pressed thin and he turned aside. Alere ached for both of them, her eyes stinging.

After a long moment, in which the sounds of wild laughter out on the streets were the only intrusion, Shasa smiled tightly.

'So, enough with the embarrassed silence. Done is done and we have other things to speak of. We can exchange our pathetic life-stories later.' She jerked her chin at Alere and Kett. 'Who're your friends?'

'Alek Marin-kin.' Alere introduced herself then gestured at Kett, not taking her eyes off the woman. 'And Tan Peter-kin.' She gave the names the names currently listed on Dalor's register and on the foreign visitor papers they each carried in their pockets. They had been checked on arrival at port and would be again on departure.

Shasa surveyed them both shrewdly. Alere still wore her dancing outfit, but Shasa didn't comment. There were, after all, far stranger people wandering the streets of Chengdu at the moment. Kett earned a longer look, a sultry little smile and the merest flicker of a wink.

'Well, Corin,' she murmured, 'you are keeping... interesting company, aren't you?' She opened her stance toward Kett, rolling a shoulder back and tilting her head to peek at him from beneath her lashes.

Alere found her hands curling into claws and forced herself to relax. Corin had once described Shasa as sweet and shy. She may have been so – at sixteen. But Shasa was twenty-six now and must have used everything at her disposal, including her sexuality, to survive an ordeal that would have broken a lesser woman. She deserved Alere's respect, not her enmity.

Regardless, she reached for Shasa's Outers. The mhareb's mind was closed and strongly warded, which was unfortunate, but not unexpected. Her Jun Fourth kin-father, Meron Gray-Saud, must have tried to hide her from Hanna. His Xintou would have taught Shasa to ward as part of that attempt.

Now that was an interesting thought. Could Shasa be the oldest, or was the heir really Bren, her kin-brother? Alere pictured the new Jun Fourth as she'd seen him last on the battlefield outside Shanzhai. No, although close in age, Bren was probably the elder.

Shasa turned to Corin. 'I must go back to Hallon.' Her eyes sparkled. 'But you've given me hope of escape for the first time in ten years. That is, if you're willing to help?'

She took Corin's face in her hands and kissed him with lingering expertise. His eyes glazed. Pulling back, she gave him a loving smile and patted his cheek.

'Yes, I have missed you.' She collected her dagger from the table and slid it into the sheath strapped to her thigh. 'I'll be back in the morning, after breakfast. Hallon will be in a meeting for a couple of hours, so he won't notice I'm gone.' She nodded to Alere and Kett. 'We have much to discuss – including how we can help your friends escape Hallon's…care. Oh.' She paused with the door partly open, a hint of mischief in her eyes. 'And tell your friend lurking in the shadows he'll need to bathe more often if he wants to hide successfully.'

The door clicked softly shut behind her, leaving them gaping in silence.

Gavon emerged from the darkness and stalked to the window, pulling the curtain aside. 'She's leaving. Alone. Heading back in the direction of Hallon's. We need to get out and find a different place to stay.'

'What?' 'Why?' Corin and Alere spoke at the same time. Kett remained silent and thoughtful.

With an easy laugh, Corin strolled over and slapped Gavon's broad back. 'You're being more paranoid than usual, Gav. Shasa's no threat to us, my friend. She was my betrothed. She obviously recognised me tonight at the feast. But she said nothing to Hallon.'

'And yer blinded by yer emotions, Corin,' Gavon growled. 'Of course she said nothing to Hallon. There was no advantage to it. She didn't know why ye were there, or who ye work for. For all she knew, ye could *be* a musician.'

Corin spread his hands. 'And how has that changed? She can't be certain we're here to rescue Mina, Jarran and Rohne.'

Gavon slashed the air with a hand. 'It doesn't matter. She followed ye. She could've caught up any time and spoken to ye in the street. But she came all the way here to see who ye were with. She can't be trusted. The mhareb training includes twisting a slave's mind to ensure loyalty, otherwise they couldn't bear weapons around the master. If she's survived the training, then she's not the girl ye knew. Took me years to think straight again.'

Kett added his opinion, low-voiced and calm. 'Regardless, you're also forgetting Alere. Mina wears her face. Plus, all our weapons are in plain view in this room. We're clearly not of the Artist House. It wouldn't take much to realise our task is to rescue Alli's twin and, by extension, the others with Mina. Shasa's offer to help us free them may have been a guess, but it was a good one. We don't know what her true agenda is. Gavon's right. We shouldn't stay here.'

Corin glanced at Alere.

She hesitated, folded her arms across her bare midriff, then sighed. 'She has strong wards so I couldn't Read her intent. Her body language was truthful. But Jiaoji training teaches control of that so it's not impossible she could have learned. If you want my honest opinion, Cor...' She grimaced. He wouldn't like it. 'We shouldn't stay. We don't know what she wants. We can't be sure where her loyalties lie, and we can't jeopardise our task. If she followed you, and Hallon has her under observation, then we aren't safe. I'm sorry.'

He closed up into coldness, turned his back on all three and stood at the window, hands jammed into his pockets.

'Are you truly so jealous that you'd condemn Shasa to this life and leave her behind?'

Alere ran to him. She gripped his arm and he raised haunted eyes to hers.

'No, Cor,' she said gently, hating the torture there. 'I'm not jealous, I promise. I have to consider the safety of all of us. As well as Mina, Jarran and the people of Mamlakah. If she truly is still your Shasa, we can come back for her, I promise. I'll help.'

He froze, searching her face. Then he gave a short, incredulous laugh. 'No, you're not, are you? Having my betrothed reappear in my life didn't bother you at all.'

'Corin, that's not what I—'

He backed away and threw a hand up. 'No, no. You're all quite correct. I do apologise for my momentary lapse into sentimentality.' He swept them deep, satirical bow. 'Please don't let my little life-trauma interfere with the good of the Jundom. By all means, do let's find somewhere else to stay.' His tone became lightheartedly cheerful. 'I know exactly the right place. A safehouse address given to me by a trusted informant. Let's not delay. Be warned, the streets of Chengdu are far from safe at this time of year, so do keep your weapons handy.'

Without further discussion, he stuffed the few things he'd unpacked into his carrybag. Alere changed into her boy's clothing and threw on her cloak, flicking the hood up to hide her face. Painfully aware of underlying tension, she could only follow as Corin strode out the door. She had hurt him badly by being unaffected by Shasa's appearance and nothing she could say would fix it. The truth was: she didn't love him as deeply as he did her.

But what would he do, now?

CHAPTER EIGHTEEN

ALERE

Corin led them out a back entrance, avoiding the inn's staff. Once in the narrow street behind the building, he took off silently through a confusing, twisted array of back alleys. His dark-clad form ghosted from shadow to shadow. Alere did her best to follow, astonished at his skill. He didn't glance back to ensure his companions kept pace. Not even once.

Thunder drummed and lightning flickered, high in the clouds. A light drizzle drifted down, making the stones slippery underfoot. Alere pulled her cloak tighter, squinting to keep Corin in sight.

He paused, checked a battered wooden street sign and turned towards a narrow, northbound alley. A dark body hurtled from the alley mouth. Moonlight sheened off a bronze dagger. Corin sidestepped, caught the arm and jammed his own dagger to the hilt in the man's chest. Catching the body, Corin lowered him to the ground. He yanked the knife out and wiped it before Alere and the others even arrived. It was all done so quickly, and in such deadly silence, that Alere was left stunned. This was a side of Corin she didn't recognise. A frightening, deadly intensity.

He peered down the alley, shook his head and continued west, instead.

Alere exchanged a worried look with Kett and hurried after him.

Corin turned into a broader lane heading north. When Alere caught up, she almost bumped into him. Ahead in the street, five armed men and women were knocking on doors, questioning the inhabitants.

'Back,' he said softly. 'A contingent of mharebi. Probably hunting for an escaped slave.'

He didn't wait for an answer, simply reversed course and headed west again.

Less than a minute later, another attempt to turn north found their way blocked again. This time a huge stack of crates containing some sort of purple-leaved vegetable, bright orange fingerfruits, and bags of rice, had fallen off a cart and lay strewn across the road. Three people stood amongst the chaos and screamed abuse at each other while the carter's che-ma shook it's red-striped mane and whickered uneasily.

Corin frowned, hesitated, then returned to the westward road.

The next alley he tried was clear and he picked up the pace.

A few seconds later, he strode into the centre of a crossroads and slowed, allowing the others to catch up. He held up a hand when Alere questioned him. She shut her mouth, uneasiness stirring. Faint moonlight struggled through the clouds and between the buildings, casting odd shadows in places where they shouldn't be.

'Khara!' Corin's muttered curse was accompanied by the slither of metal as he freed his sword from its sheath. 'I thought it was suspicious. We were being herded. We have company. At least ten. More. All sides. No way out and no way to get up against a wall. Get rid of your gear. Back to back.'

Alere dropped her carrybag and cloak and drew her dagger. There wasn't a lot of space. A sword was more likely to injure her friends. There was no high ground from which to shoot, so she tossed aside her bow and quiver. Kett did the same. They would only hamper movement. She slipped a throwing knife free of her belt. Alere took up a position with her back to Kett and the others, in the middle of the crossroads, facing outward.

Shadows slid off the walls.

At least thirty figures appeared, hooded and clad in darkened leather armour. They emerged into the flickering, uncertain glow of lightning that chased rain and led thunder. Metal gleamed.

Corin groaned. 'Clearly my ability to count is questionable.'

'But who are they,' Kett asked.

'Slavers,' Gavon growled. 'Too dark to tell whose, though. Gangs target foreign visitors who wander away from the festival during Mianshou.'

Alere let that slide. She was too busy assessing her options and potential opponents. There were no escape routes. She glanced swiftly around at the weapons. Only clubs, sticks, daggers and a net or two. No swords and no kusarigama.

Alere smiled. That meant they would fight to incapacitate, not kill. The soft chuckle from Corin and the way Kett shifted his balance said they'd realised as well.

For a long, tight-wound moment no one moved.

With a growl of irritation, Alere flicked her throwing knife. It embedded deep into the nearest man's neck. He choked and collapsed to the cobbles. Blood, black in the half-light, spilled from his lips.

She threw her second knife into the shocked silence and all diyu broke loose.

The remaining men in front of her faltered, allowing Alere time to throw her last knife. Her target moved and it took him in the left shoulder instead of the chest. He yelped, wrenched the blade free, and flung it inexpertly back at her. She caught, flipped, and threw it again. This time he toppled over in mid-stride and hit the cobbles face-first. Part of the blade protruded between his shoulderblades.

Her heart raced, pouring adrenalin into her blood. She sucked a deep breath and calmed the trembling in her hands. She swapped her yanstone dagger to her right hand and dropped into a fighting stance.

Behind her, Kett, Corin and Gavon fought their own battles. Only the scuff of bootleather on stone, the *chink* of metal on metal or ceramic, and mewling gasps of the dying broke the silence. The stink of blood and wet leather rose from the ground. Alere couldn't afford to check on the others. With any luck they were still close enough to protect each others' backs.

There was still only space for two enemy to reach her at once. A third hung back, watching for an opening. More waited behind him. Both the closest wielded heavy clubs. They struck in concert, one at her shoulder and one at her legs. She stepped back, out of range.

The higher club skimmed her shoulder, fluttering her sleeve. Her dagger blade sliced at the club-bearer's arm as it passed, severing tendons and muscles. She sidestepped and jammed the blade into the second man's exposed ribs. A kick smashed his knee and he screamed, club clattering to the cobbles.

Something heavy and soft fell against Alere's legs and she trod on what felt unpleasantly like a hand. She checked to be sure it wasn't one of her own people. Her third attacker launched himself forward, taking advantage of her distraction. His hood fell away revealing a face twisted into savage ferocity. He swung a pair of short hardwood sticks at her head.

Something clamped onto her ankle. The man on the ground was alive enough to grab her foot. She stamped with the other at roughly where his head had been. Her heel drove into something that gave and crunched. The hand relaxed. Too late. All she could do was duck and raise her blade and an arm to catch the brunt of the stick strikes. It wasn't enough. One of the sticks flexed around and caught her behind the ear. Flashes of scarlet and yellow spiked behind her eyes. Agony blazed in her elbow as a stick found the pressure point there. Fingers numb, she barely managed to hold onto the dagger, unable to wield it effectively.

But her forearm pressed against his. She caught his elbow and twisted it skyward. Tendons snapped in his shoulder. He screamed and flailed at her with the stick in his free hand, connecting with her skull again. Stars and pain flashed. Left-handed, she snatched out her sword and drove the pommel into his chin.

The instant it connected, a kind of peace stole over her and the confusion dropped away. She was able to observe the situation with calm detachment. She became aware of the various injuries in herself and in her friends. Alive to their pain. And their vulnerability. More men swarmed in from every direction. Far too many for four to overcome, no matter how good they were. But she saw it all as though through a window.

The moment of clarity slipped away. Her silver-gilt connection with the yanstones flared, overwhelming her mind, consuming all that was her, moving through, seeking out enemies, defending. Iron and smoke filled her mouth. Thunder broke close overhead, rattling windows and bones. Heat flared through her. Eye-aching light flashed from the stones in her sword and dagger. Lightning crackled through her attacker and arced into the three men behind. Limp, blackened bodies smacked into a building and fell into smoking heaps. Their clothing caught fire and yellow flames licked up the timber walls.

A confused pause ensued as everyone blinked away the purple after-burn and reorientated. In that moment of distraction, a high-pitched voice called out. The buildings rained a thick fall of arrows and crossbow bolts into the alley.

Kett's arm swept around Alere's shoulders and dragged her to the ground. His body and Corin's sheltered her as metal and wood embedded into flesh all around them.

Then there was only stillness and the distant clatter of running feet as their last attackers disappeared into the dark alleys.

When only silence and their own hoarse breathing remained, the weight lifted off her back and Alere raised her head. Kett stood over her, gasping, blood dripping from sword and dagger. He gazed around the crossroads, brows raised. Alere struggled to her feet. Dizziness darkened her sight. Corin gripped her elbow, holding her steady. He ran his hands over her face and shoulders. She managed a faint smile. He caught her into a hug and murmured a broken apology into her ear. She held him, grateful to be forgiven, not sure she deserved it.

Her lightheadedness cleared, leaving only faint nausea, and she was able to see clearly the carnage. Everywhere, bodies lay sprawled in the slack, impossible poses of death. Black smoke spiralled in the air. The sickening smells of offal, blood and burning flesh caught in her throat, driving nausea to the forefront. She turned away.

The drizzle eased and clouds drifted apart, giving glimpses of Luna-Er's pale face high in the darkness. Gavon limped over. A deep gash on his thigh glistened in the moonlight. His hands and arms were covered in gore. He inspected the smouldering, blackened bodies, his thick brows lifting.

'Waa faqri! What happened? How did the fire start?' He peered at Alere, who couldn't find enough mental acuity to do more than shake her head dumbly. 'Are ye alright? All of ye?'

Corin and Kett both affirmed. A bruise already darkened Corin's cheek and a shallow slice across Kett's forearm dripped blood. Alere's head throbbed. The lump behind her ear was tender but, apart from that, she seemed uninjured. Her memory of the last few seconds was hazy, though.

'I...I don't really know what happened,' she admitted. She shook her head, struggling to recall. 'I think lightning struck them. But who shot the arrows?' Was it her imagination or did the shadows move again?

'We did.' A treble voice floated from a darkened doorway. 'Sorry we were a bit late getting here.'

A second later, a boy of about ten or twelve emerged. Barefoot and dressed in ragged leathers, he swaggered into view, casually shouldering a crossbow far too large for him. White-blond hair framed a dirt-smeared, angular face set with piercing eyes of a pale colour indeterminable in the moonlight.

'Glad we could help.' He flashed a quick grin. 'Any enemy of Hallon is a friend of ours.'

'Hallon?' Corin ripped the sleeve off the nearest body's arm, revealing an N emblazoned on the skin. Yet another bore the embossed armguard. He raised his face to the sky, devastation writ clearly in his eyes. Alere pressed a hand to her mouth. Shasa must have sent them. She had betrayed Corin. It was the only explanation.

The boy cocked his head. 'Sure. A couple of them were following you. I followed them. When they cut you off, I figured you could use a hand. Took awhile for us to get into place, though.' He lifted his chin. 'Now, we need to get out of here before the fire-crews arrive. Even with the rain, that'll catch.' He pointed at the fires.

'I'm Saric Wuming.' He gave them a jerky little bow and swept a hand vaguely around. 'This is my team. Please, follow me. There's someone who wants to meet you.'

Clambering down from every roof and nearby window, twenty more children appeared. Boys and girls, ranging in age from around six to early teens, all dressed much as Saric. All, with a nonchalance at odds with their age, carrying bows, crossbows, kusarigami, and krises.

Corin brushed past Gavon and gave the boy a perfunctory nod. His tone brusque to the point of rudeness, he said, 'Thank you for your assistance and your invitation, but we have more pressing matters to attend to.' He gestured at the bodies. 'We have... unfinished business with Master Hallon.'

He paused, looked more closely at the boy and pointed a finger. 'I know you. You're that kid in the market.' He frowned. 'You're the one who put the note into my pocket. The directions were meant to take us to a safe-house. You led us into a trap. You—' He lunged for Saric, but the boy danced back and levelled the loaded crossbow.

Saric gave a short laugh. 'Sorry, I think you misunderstood. Please, follow me. There's someone who wants to meet you.' He aimed the bow at Corin's chest. 'Polite, yes, but an order not an invitation.'

Corin swore. 'You little—'

Kett grabbed his arm.

'Corin,' Alere murmured. 'It's fine. We'll go.'

His jaw clenched but he nodded shortly and sheathed his weapons.

'What note?' she whispered.

He ignored her.

They left the alley behind. The burning building was now well-alight and served as a beacon as they moved deeper into the maze of tenements and warehouses behind Chengdu's port area. The *clang-clang* of a fire-crew's huoche echoed through the alleys, drawing closer.

In a show of good faith, Saric allowed them to keep their weapons, and even had their bags carried.

The children shadowed and guided them through the backstreets of Chengdu; some always visible, most not. Ridiculous as it seemed to be taken captive by children, escape was impossible.

Alere studied Saric as he led the way. 'Wuming' literally meant 'nameless' and was the family name given to foundling or orphan children of unknown parentage. If a stigma existed around being a mother-kin-named child, it was nothing compared to being a Wuming. Alere shuddered. Such children were sometimes abandoned and left to die. Or neutered so they couldn't pass on their unknown genes to offspring. A barbaric practice rarely seen these days except in smaller, more backward villages. Yet this boy-child flaunted his name, indifferent to their reactions.

There was an air of the ruthless warrior about Saric that sat strangely on his slim shoulders and innocent face. The ragtag group of twenty or so children obeyed his orders implicitly. Almost unwillingly, Alere admired his poise. How had someone so young come to be in such a position?

Saric shoved open a small door, inset into a much larger one, in the front of a dilapidated warehouse. After a swift check of the moonlit street, he ushered them inside and led them to a small, windowless room made of solid sandstone. It held four chairs, a small table and a lit mel-oil lamp.

'Wait here,' he said. 'Your host will be along soon. Leave your bags and weapons outside. They won't go anywhere.' His mouth quirked in an ironic smile. 'Thief's honour.'

Twenty loaded bows pointed in their direction. There wasn't a lot of choice. Alere dropped her gear and led the way in. The door locked and a clunk spoke of a heavy bar across the outside.

Corin swore and sank onto one of the straight-backed wooden chairs. He dropped his head into his hands. Kett helped Gavon sit and checked the gash on his leg.

'We'll need to clean and bind that, Gav,' Kett said.

'Mina's medical bag is in my gear outside,' Alere said. 'Do you think they'd let us have it?'

Corin's head snapped up. 'No!' He rose and stalked around the small room. 'Don't you get it? They aren't our allies. This...' he waved his hands at the room '…this was all a setup. And I walked right into it. I'm an utter hmar.'

Kett stood and grabbed Corin's shoulders. 'Talk sense, Cor. What did you walk into? Who set us up?'

Corin smacked the weishi's hands off and continued pacing. Alere stayed where she was. He was too angry to be reasoned with.

Thunder crashed outside again, muted by the thick sandstone walls.

'That kid,' Corin growled. 'He slipped a note into my pocked in the market. When we were heading to Hallon's. It was signed by Liu Gray. Gave directions to a safe house if we needed it. Talked about Rafi as his customer. Which he is.' His steps slowed but his frown deepened. 'Rafi buys information about Melcor from Liu Gray's spy network.' He scrubbed both hands over his face. 'I cannot believe I fell for it.'

'Fell for what, Cor?' Kett asked, calm as ever.

Corin spread his arms wide and gave a bitter laugh. 'It had to be Shasa. All of it. Well, Hallon, really. She paid that Saric kid to give me a fake note from someone I'd trust. She must have suspected we'd leave the inn once she followed us there. Then she set up an ambush. Three different roads blocked? I should have listened to my gut.'

'But that makes no sense, Cor,' Alere said. He'd calmed down, now, so she took his hand and caught his troubled gaze. 'Why would she send us into an ambush, then also send Saric and his friends to rescue us? What's the point?'

Corin snatched his hand away and began pacing again. 'I don't know. Gaisi! I can't believe she did this to me.' He dropped back into the chair and shoved his fingers deep into his hair.

Alere drew a chair close and laid an arm across his shoulders. 'It's not your fault, Cor. We played right into her hands by leaving the inn. You didn't want to, remember?'

He pushed her away and shook his head, his face a mask of hurt. 'Just don't, Alere. Don't patronise me. I've been in this game too long to make such a stupid mistake. You three were right. Seeing Shasa compromised my thinking. She manipulated my emotions and I wanted to believe her.' He sighed and looked around the room. 'If this is Hallon's doing…Shasa's doing, then we're in big trouble and I have no-one else to blame.'

Kett frowned and tilted his head. 'I suspect—'

The door opened. Saric poked his head around. 'We've taken your bags to your rooms. Your weapons are just out here. Dinner's ready. Coming?'

CHAPTER NINETEEN

ALERE

'Ah. Our guests. Thank you, Saric,' a cheerful, adult male voice called out from the far corner of a vast, dark room in the centre of the warehouse. His words were almost drowned by the roar of rain on the high, clay-tiled roof. Here and there, rain dripped through and splashed, invisible in the gloom.

In the isolated pool of light cast by a bronze candle-chandelier, a man rose from a threadbare wingback chair. He gestured them over. Nearby, a seaweed-brick fire crackled in a small, bricklined clay stove, but did nothing to abate the cold of the enormous space. Around him, stood various other mismatched pieces of furniture: a scarred dining table and eight chairs; two more upholstered pieces, their cushions tattered and gilding tarnished; a rug made of hand-knotted, multi-coloured rags, hiding the bare sulcrete floor. The overall impression was one of impoverished culture. Like the great hall of a Jun whose fortunes had waned, but who clung to his noble upbringing.

'Porro?' Corin raised his brows. 'What on Kalima are you doing here?'

Alere squinted against the light and the haze of lavender seaweed-smoke that hung about the chandelier. It was the entertainer they'd met at Hallon's house earlier that evening. No longer wearing the purple, he now dressed in a many-pocketed leather vest and unremarkable grey streetclothes. He wore a short sword at his hip and a blowpipe strapped to his back. A dozen darts – with coloured feathers of green, red, grey, and black – slotted into a belt around his hips.

'Well done,' he said, smiling. He tucked his thumbs into his belt, dark eyes narrowed shrewdly. 'You do have a good memory for faces, don't you?' The man no longer came across as the foppish, laughable character he had at Hallon's function. Quite the opposite. In his late fifties, he was unremarkable, with sharp facial bones and a hint of grey in his smooth dark hair. His face was clean of all makeup, even the marital-status mark. The only sign of ostentation about him was a small, silver-metal double-bladed axe pendant hanging around his neck. His smile was particularly open and charming as he inclined his head in greeting.

'Porro's my stage name. I go by several. But Liu Gray is the one you might know best. I'm the humble guardian to the unmanagable band of young rapscallions who escorted you. Please, join me. Sit.' He waved graceful hands at the dining table. A modest array of fruit, bread, wine and cheese awaited them.

Corin gaped. '*You're* Liu Gray? You're an acrobat. You're telling me *you're* the mythical leader of the Melcori spy network.'

'Not so mythical, huh?' Saric sauntered over, picked up a hunk of cheese and flopped into a chair. He put his feet up on the table and rested the crossbow on his knees. The bolt pointed directly at Corin.

Corin ignored him. 'Why should we believe you. I've never been able to get a description of Liu Gray. How do I know you're him?'

'Frustrating, isn't it?' Liu said, waving them over. 'But I have no way of proving my identity and I don't actually care if you believe me.' He gave Corin a rueful smile. 'So, it's your choice. I hide for a good reason, which has nothing to do with impressing you. I'm allied with several Houses and go by many different names. It makes my work much easier. Come, come. Sit. You must be tired.'

'Your work?' Kett unwrapped Gavon's arm from across his shoulders and eased the yongbing into a chair, lifting his wounded leg onto another and inspecting it. He picked up an open bottle of wine and tipped a cupful over the wound, ignoring Gavon's hiss of pain. Tearing strips from his shirt, Kett dressed the wound, but it was deep and still bleeding. Gavon paled and his fingers shook as he accepted a glass of water. Alere frowned. He needed a healer, not a social gathering and a chat.

Kett sent her a grave look. She drew a long breath, deliberately relaxed her shoulders and released her weapons. They were at Gray's mercy and no amount of impatience would change that. Kett nodded and sat. He calmly put together a bread and cheese sandwich, handing it to Gavon before making a second. Then he used his dagger to slice a calla fruit, apparently at his ease. Blood dripped from his arm, onto the table, but he appeared not to notice.

Corin stayed standing, inspecting Liu narrowly. Alere pulled out a chair for herself and took a piece of bread.

'Cor?' She held out the food.

He grimaced and took a seat opposite Saric, eyeing the boy with mistrust.

Liu folded himself into the head chair and rested his chin on one fist, watching them all in apparent fascination. He didn't ask their names. Alere considered trying to reach his mind to find out what was going on, but the pain in her head flared. Let him talk, instead.

'You know.' He picked up a calla fruit. 'I was quite annoyed with you this evening.' He pointed at each of them. 'You disrupted a long-planned, well-paid mission with your appearance at Hallon's party. If I hadn't realised who you must be, I might have turned you over to Hallon's mharebi by accident. *That* would have been disastrous.'

'What?' Alere put the bread aside as her stomach rebelled. 'What *are* you talking about?'

Corin tilted his chair back, watching the man from beneath half-lowered eyelids. 'I told you Rafi trades for information from Gray's spy network. And, I assume, other rich benefactors do the same?'

'Trading it for what. Money?' Kett asked. Inspecting the cut on his arm, he tore another strip off his shirt and bound the injury. His eyes swept the darkness beyond the warm pool of light.

'Weapons, medical supplies, food.' Liu took a bite of his fruit and wiped a trickle of yellow juice from his chin. 'And assistance in smuggling the children out of Melcor.'

Alere pulled her wandering attention back, focussing with difficulty on him. 'Children? I don't understand? Why are you smuggling children?'

'They're slave-get, aren't they?' Gavon's rough voice intruded. He grunted, tightened the makeshift bandage on his leg, and winced as he shifted in his seat. 'I'd heard someone was getting them out.'

Seeing Alere's confusion, he elaborated. 'Sometimes midwives take pity on the children of slaves and take them away. They give them to sympathetic free citizens to raise and tell the master they've died. That way the child is never branded. But they also have no free citizen papers, so they can't live a normal life here. The child has to get out before they turn ten and need papers.'

Liu's delightful smile widened. 'Very good. Entirely correct. We have more and more midwives willing to help. Our resources are stretched thin. It's difficult to get them out safely. May I say, Gavon Abdul-kin, as Wushi winner and escaped Seyd, you're either insane or extraordinarily brave to come back.'

Gavon tried to stand, startled fear flickering over his face. The whisper of many bowstrings spoke of instant death from the shadows. He froze. Kett spoke his name in a low, warning tone. Gavon raised empty hands and sank back into the chair, his skin sweating and waxen. Blood stained the floor beneath his seat.

Leaning back on his chair, Liu nibbled on the core of his fruit. 'I'm honoured to be in the presence of so many noble families.' He pointed. 'Corin, last of the Johnstons, one of the most notorious colonial First-Families. Tekettan Zah-Hill, abdicated heir to the Jun First seat. And last, but certainly not least, Alere Koh-Lin, the redoubtable favourite protégé of the extraordinary Mistress Li.'

Alere gasped and even Kett paused in his casual consumption of food to stare levelly at the man. Corin stilled, letting his chair legs thump back to the sulcrete floor. The sound cracked through the silence like a whip.

Liu sipped at his wine. 'Now there is a woman whose powers of control and manipulation have earned my deepest admiration.' He waved Mistress Li aside. 'But I was speaking of you, Alere Koh-Lin currently masquerading as Jun-Heir Lianna Koh-Lin. Or is that Alek Marin-kin, yongbing for hire?' He studied her with frank interest. 'Don't you find that confusing?'

'How do you know us?' Kett's voice was steel and silk. He laid aside the last piece of bread and dusted off his fingertips.

Liu laughed softly. 'My dear boy, I've been doing this for over forty years. I was slave-get myself, you see. Just think of how many of my very grateful youngsters now live in Mamlakah, and the other Jundoms. Many hundreds, I assure you.' He pointed at Gavon. 'Jacksa, the merchant running the caravan from Newmec. He hired you six years ago on my recommendation.' His finger swung to Alere. 'Ruth, the serving girl who waited on Elmira Connor when you were brought to the Ma-Safra household as an infant.' He switched to Corin. 'Timon, the healer in your village who attended the unfortunate death of your loved ones at Hanna Zah-Hill's hands.'

Corin clutched at the table's edge. His jaw worked and his green eyes narrowed, but he remained silent.

Liu indicated Kett. 'And Radan Zah-Hill's Shangwei, Boran, who saw your potential over young Ven Zah-Hill, even when you were just a seven-year-old. He hid you away in Weishi House twenty years ago.' He smiled and steepled his fingers. 'I hear everything, eventually.'

Alere checked on Kett. His utter stillness and the tension about his mouth betrayed him. He'd believed his father had instructed the Shangwei to save his son from Hanna's death-order. To find it untrue – to discover his rescue was the result of a moment of calculated foresight from a near-stranger...

She grasped his hand. He let it lie under hers for a moment, then withdrew it and sliced his fruit again, as if nothing untowards had been spoken. He, like a book, holding himself emotionally distant.

'Surely, though,' Liu continued blithely, apparently unaware of the effect his words had on them, 'it's rash of Rafi to send you all here, into such danger?'

'Is that a threat?' Corin's voice was low but held an unmistakable undercurrent of rage. He laid his hands on the pommels of his weapons and his eyes glazed slightly. If he Read Liu, his face gave away nothing and Alere's head still pounded too hard to even think about trying it herself.

Liu waved a languid, dismissive hand. 'Of course not. I could have killed you many times over, if I wanted. Just a demonstration of the extent of my information network – so you'll understand I have the power to do what I say I can.'

'And what's that?' Alere jumped in. Corin rode the edge of losing control and probably shouldn't speak. Anger and betrayal emanated in waves from him and she wasn't even trying to Read. His emotions battered on her wards. She pressed her thumbs to her temples as the ache grew into a flame that ate at the edges of coherent thought.

The older man's dark yes gleamed and his mouth twitched into a sly smile. 'Help you free your sister and the nominated Jun-Heir, of course.'

'What? But why?' Corin broke in. 'What's in it for you? What the jahim do you want from us? Enough games!'

'Ah.' Liu raised a finger, sounding like a Housemaster instructing a stubborn child. 'Now we get to it. Revolution, my friend, that's what's in it for me. We help you save Mina, Rohne and Jarran.' He spread his hands. 'You help us overturn the social order and free the slaves.'

Corin barked an incredulous laugh.

Gavon snorted. 'Simple as that? Yer mad.'

'Just a quick little revolution. To put who on the throne? You?' Corin leaned forward. 'We're on bit of a deadline, Gray. We don't have time for this. Let us go, now.'

'Or what?' Liu sipped blithely at his wine. 'You're hardly in a position to bargain, are you?' He put the cup carefully aside and leaned forward, matching Corin's intensity. 'I don't want the throne and it's not even Jahil we're interested in. Strange as it may seem, he's quite open to the idea of abolishing slavery. But his kin-brother, Hallon, has been in control of this Jundom for the last thirty years. He runs the slavemarket, holds the purse-strings, and orchestrated Jarran's kidnapping. Hallon is setting things up to bring both Jundoms to war and to lay the blame on Jahil. When things go suilie, Hallon is waiting in the wings and has a son to inherit. Jahil has no recognised son to take the throne. And believe me...' Liu relaxed, once more urbane and cool. 'We do *not* want Hallon on the throne.'

Gavon gaped at him and Alere blinked in shock. Even Kett seemed startled by this revelation. Although they'd had some doubts, they had all come here expecting the enemy to be the Shah. Now Liu wanted them to believe the Shah's kin-brother was the greater danger?

Alere had to admit the possibility. She had yet to meet the Shah, but his Xintou, Valera had spoken warmly of Jahil, praising his openmindedness and forward-thinking. Since hearing of Jahil's involvement in Jarran's abduction, Alere had assumed Valera's vision of the Shah to be skewed by their Bonding. Perhaps that assumption had been wrong.

'Look,' Liu said quietly, all posturing falling away into seriousness. 'We have a common enemy in Hallon. Let's start by getting your friends out. Then you'll know you can trust us. How does that sound?'

Corin raised his brows. 'You'd do that?'

'Of course.' Liu nodded. 'There's a reasonable chance you'll have to kill Hallon anyway, to achieve your ends. And it's in our best interest to have someone like Jarran Zah-Hill as Jun First.'

'But how?' Corin scraped his chair back and stood abruptly. 'We don't have a plan, or resources enough to get into Hallon's compound to get them out.'

Liu rose and walked around the table. Corin topped him by half a head but somehow Liu dominated the space. The older man laid a hand on Corin's shoulder, compassion deepening the lines in his face.

'I'm sorry,' he murmured, 'forgive me for putting you through this. I needed to see for myself what sort of people you were, before I put mine at risk. My people and the Selb will help us, of course. But there's someone else I'd like you to meet who will be the key player.' He patted Corin's shoulder. 'Wait here, all of you. I'll be back momentarily.' He turned away, then clicked his fingers and came back. 'Please stay at the table. Saric's team are…edgy.'

'Are we prisoners?' Corin snapped.

Liu cocked his head and smiled sympathetically. 'If you enjoy righteous anger, by all means consider yourself prisoners. But I'd prefer us to be allies. Saric's team are merely here to protect you from yourselves. Hallon does have men searching for you, remember?'

He vanished into the gloom and Saric skipped after him, with a backward grin for Corin.

Corin glared after them.

Alere nibbled at a slice of dark, sweet bread stuffed with dried fruits, more for something to occupy her hands than from hunger. Her stomach roiled and her skull ached. The darkness around the dining table danced with purple and red shapes when she moved her head. The drum and roll of rain and thunder pounded against her ears.

'So,' Corin said, spreading his arms wide, 'now what?'

'We wait,' Kett replied, imperturbable.

Corin gave a dry laugh and exchanged a glance with Alere, who shrugged.

'I see why you hate it when he says that,' he muttered. He sighed and sat down. 'At least now I know the note about the safe house was genuine.' A frown knitted his brow. 'But I still don't get how Hallon's people knew where to ambush us.'

'Saric did say they were following us,' Alere said, mindful of the small ears listening from beyond the light.

'Following, perhaps,' Kett said. 'Although I didn't see anyone, and I'm reasonably good at spotting tails. Corin's right. There's something not quite right about the story. I can't put my finger on it, though.'

Alere swallowed and stared into the darkness again. 'Could Liu have a spy in his midst?'

Gavon snorted. 'Why would slave-get children ever spy for a Slavemaster like Hallon?'

She shrugged. 'True. I'm not thinking straight.' She pressed a thumb to her temple.

Kett's warm hand gripped her shoulder. 'You alright?'

'Just tired. Cold.' She gave a quick smile.

His grey eyes warmed. 'Liar.'

'Do you think it's possible?' she whispered. 'This revolution he wants? I mean, we're only here a couple of days. How do we achieve something like that?'

Kett's eyes narrowed. 'I get the feeling Liu doesn't leave much to chance. If I had to guess, I'd say he's been planning this a long time, waiting for the right figurehead to lead the Selb and the slaves in revolt.'

'Figurehead? Who?'

With a sympathetic look, Kett continued. 'Slaves are indoctrinated to fear. Creating the right crowd mentality to break that takes a lot to get started, but it's an unstoppable force once it's rolling. He needs someone both the Selb and the slaves will follow without question.' His calm gaze turned on her. 'If his information is as good as I think, then he probably knows about your xintou powers. And Gavon did say the slaves believe a xintou will lead them to freedom.'

Alere froze, her heart thudding. 'No. I can't! I don't have time to lead a revolution. I have to save Mina and get Jarran back to Madina.'

Kett shrugged. 'If that's the price of our freedom and his help, I don't see we have much choice. From what we saw of Hallon's security, we won't release Jarran, Mina and Rohne without an army.'

'I—'

His head snapped around. 'Someone's coming.'

Alere gripped her sword-hilt and set her feet for balance.

Saric emerged from the darkness, ignored them all, and slouched back into his vacated seat. Next came Liu Gray, his feet silent on the sulcrete floor.

He paused and surveyed the four companions. 'Thank you so much for waiting.'

'Like we had a choice,' Corin muttered.

Liu didn't dignify that with an answer. He gestured at the impenetrable darkness.

'Here's the person I wanted you to meet.'

Shasa emerged into the light, her chin raised defiantly, a mocking smile on her lips.

Corin snatched at his sword. 'You!'

Saric shot up from his seat, his small body and large crossbow interposed between Corin and Shasa. Corin skidded to a halt with the bronze-tipped bolt poking into his stomach. Sword half-drawn, he looked coldly at the boy. Saric stared straight back without flinching, green-grey eyes hard, finger curled around the trigger. Corin's eyes dropped to the bow. His fingers whitened on the sword hilt.

Bow limbs creaked subtly in the surrounding darkness.

CHAPTER TWENTY

ALERE

Alere broke the silence, groaning and dropping her head into hands. 'I'm sorry to interrupt the moment, Corin, but I think I'm going to be sick.' She was unwell, but her words were more a ploy to distract Corin.

'You're injured. I apologise.' Liu's tone was contrite. 'Saric, send for the healer. Gavon and Kett will need their wounds tended as well.' He gently pushed Saric's bow to one side and guided Corin back to his seat.

Corin sat, his eyes glittering and mouth thin. Alere watched him through her lashes. Years of guilt and hurt meant he wasn't thinking straight. He needed to calm down. Corin did not take his eyes off Saric and Shasa, watching them both with a cold distance unlike his normal good humour.

Liu thrust a glass of sky-green wine into Corin's hand. 'There are explanations to be made.'

Saric gave a derisive snort and vanished into the darkness, only to reappear a few moments later and drop back into his seat. He produced a six-pointed shuriken and picked his nails with it, eyes fixed on Corin. The bow rested across his knees, cocked and ready.

Shasa eased into the seat opposite Corin, between Saric and Liu. She gave the others around the table a swift, assessing scrutiny. Her eyes widened when they fell on Gavon. When she encountered Corin's mistrustful gaze, she raised one brow and leaned back, lids drooping and mocking smile back in place.

Alere saw the struggle taking place in Corin and ached for him. He'd found his betrothed, only to be betrayed by her within an hour.

He'd turned to Alere for support and she had let him down, too; forced to reveal her heart was not deeply bound to him. Perhaps the emotional distance of her xintou upbringing had isolated her more than she realised.

She shivered. The cold-dark of the enormous warehouse space pressed in, while the fire in her brain grew. Burning pain threatened to consume her from the inside, making it hard to follow the conversation. A prickle down her spine and under her skin foreshadowed something important, she just didn't know what. The taste of iron and smoke made her want to vomit. Swallowing hard and trying to ignore the pain and tension, Alere focussed on the words being spoken.

'Fine. Explain, but make it fast.' Corin sent Shasa a cool sneer. 'I'm sure I heard mention of a curfew. It's late, we're all tired and we have a long day tomorrow – with or without you.' He took a long draught of the wine and grimaced, setting the cup aside. 'That's revolting.'

'Apologies,' Liu said, chuckling. He returned to his seat. 'We can't afford much. And children will want to eat.' He lapsed back into seriousness and indicated Shasa. 'As I was saying: we have someone on the inside to help us to free your friends and to kill Hallon.'

'You're a xiongshou.' The flat statement came from Kett. 'Why don't you kill Hallon, yourself?'

Chin on folded fingers, Liu rested his elbows on the table and tilted his head, inspecting Kett as a Tradesman might study a machine he didn't understand. 'Interesting. I didn't believe the stories I'd heard of you, but I'm beginning to. Yes. Being born non-existent has its advantages. Weishi House has always been good at finding invisible people to train for their invisible section: the xiongshou-assassins.' He pulled up his sleeve, revealing the faded shuriken tattoo of Weishi House on his wrist.

'And yes,' he said, grimaced, 'I did try, when I was younger. But I was less experienced and Hallon was well-guarded as a young man in the Shah's household. Now, we're both older.' He indicated the darkness. 'He's more arrogant, but I have little responsibilities that rely on me. I can't risk capture.'

'So.' Corin sipped the wine and made a face. 'Why not send one of your little responsibilities, then?' He raised a cool, sardonic brow at Saric.

The boy paused in his nail-scraping and returned an equally-contemptuous stare. He flicked the shuriken. It *thunked* into the tabletop a handsbreadth from Corins chest.

Corin didn't flinch.

He plucked the weapon free. 'Y'know what, kid?' he mused, his normal good humour reasserting itself. 'I like you. I do. You've got guts. But you're also really starting to annoy me and that...' He flicked the shuriken. It stuck in the chairback less than a fingerswidth from the boy's ear.

Saric jumped.

'...could be a bad thing,' Corin finished.

Shasa brought her hands together in a slow clap. 'Oh, very good. Such a big man.' She pursed her lips into a moue of mock innocence. 'But you're angry at me, not him. Why not see what *I* can do instead. I'll even let you search me for weapons.' She leaned forward, drawing focus to her ample cleavage.

Even through pain, Alere had to admire the woman's technique. She was good. A little unsubtle, but good.

Corin's eyes flicked down and jumped straight back to Shasa's face.

'How about,' he replied, matching her sarcasm, though anger showed in the tightness around his eyes and thin-stretched smile, 'you start telling me the truth about what the jahim is going on.'

The mounting tension in the room found its echo in Alere's head. Their razor-edged voices sliced through her wards, leaving her mind flayed and exposed. The internal flames were fuelled by their emotions until she could do nothing but grip her head and fight to hold onto herself.

Shasa shrugged, dropping her overt jiaoji act. 'I walk a fine line working for Hallon and helping Liu when and where I can. I saw you first at the inn, this afternoon.'

Corin groaned and slapped his forehead. 'The noblewoman in orange. That was you.'

She nodded. 'I couldn't speak to you. I was there as a spy for Hallon, but he has me watched. I didn't know *why* he had me spying on you. Or who your companions were. When I saw you again at the entertainment, I realised what you must be here for. I had to act. As I said, Hallon has me watched. If I did nothing he'd suspect me. I had to send his mharebi after you.' She held up a hand at Corin's inarticulate growl. 'But I also got a message to Liu, so he could send the youngsters to help you. That way I preserve my place as mhareb.' She laid both hands, open, on the table and spoke with disarming candor. 'I can't help you free the others if I'm not on the inside.'

There was a long silence and Corin eyed Shasa narrowly. His shoulders relaxed slightly and he leaned back in his chair.

'No.' Kett said quietly, his eyes on Shasa. 'How did Hallon's men know where we were going? That's what's been bothering me.'

Shasa flicked a quick look at Liu but said nothing. Her expression stayed calmly innocent.

'What are you saying, Kett?' Corin asked.

Kett's gaze stayed fixed on Shasa. 'You planned this. Even before you followed Corin to where we were staying tonight. You arranged the whole thing. They didn't follow us.'

'What?' Corin stilled. 'Is that true?'

Gavon scowled, growling a curse low in his throat.

'But that's not all,' Kett added, thoughtfully. 'The ambush. It wasn't for us, was it?'

Shasa's eyes widened and Liu leaned back, a satisfied smile playing on his lips.

Alere gasped. Of course. He was right. How had she missed it?

Corin swore long and inventively.

'My compliments. You're correct,' Liu said. 'Shasa has been trying for years to slowly infiltrate trusted Selb into Hallon's mharebi. But he's suspicious and rewards those of his men who betray their fellows as Selb members.' He spread his long-fingered hands. 'Tonight was too good an opportunity. I sent you the note with directions for the safe-house. Shasa let Hallon know where you were going. Then she filled the ambush with Hallon's most loyal mharebi. And I sent Saric to help you kill them. Now we can make sure his new mharebi are Selb loyal to us.'

'Why?' The word cracked through the pause. Corin leaned forward. 'Why do you want to help us?' He flung out an arm. 'Why should we trust you after tonight? You set us up as bait. Those hundan mharebi you sent almost killed us before the kids stepped in.'

Liu grimaced. 'I apologise. It did take Saric's team a little longer than expected to get into place on the roofs without Hallon's mharebi seeing. You were not meant to be injured in the fighting.'

Corin ignored him, his attention on Shasa. 'I'm asking *you*, Shasa. Why the gouri did you set us up like that? Why didn't you just ask us for help. I'm all for killing off slavers. You could have trusted me.'

'Like you trusted me by leaving the inn?' Shasa's mouth twisted. 'I'm a *slave, Corin. I can't trust anyone and I *belong to Hallon.' She indicated her whole self with a disdainful wave. 'With everything that entails. I've done the best I could to make this life bearable. But I was born into freedom.' Her scorn softened and she tilted her head, regarding her betrothed. 'And, in spite of everything Hallon has done to me, I still want to be free again. Up until now, I couldn't see a way to achieve it – for myself or anyone else.' She glanced briefly at each of them. 'Now, I can. But I couldn't exactly tell you everything, could I? It's been ten years, Cor. We hardly know each other.'

Corin dug his fingers into his hair and sucked a deep breath, gazing up into the darkness above for a moment before letting the breath go on a heavy sigh.

'You could kill Hallon, yourself.' Kett's low, reasonable words fell softly into the tense silence. 'You don't need us.'

She flicked dismissive fingers, not taking her eyes off Corin. He stared back at her, but the sharpest edge of his anger had been dulled.

'There's no point in me killing Hallon,' Shasa said. 'It needs to be public and have meaning. If it's done by a slave, in private, his family will simply cover it up and say he died of a heart attack or something. I'd be executed. His son, Feddor, would take over and things will stay the same. Possibly worse. Feddor is stupid, but ambitious.'

'And how does us killing Hallon make any difference?' Corin's tone was less hostile. 'They could cover it up no matter who does it.'

Alere pressed the heels of her hands into her temples, trying not to let the whimper in her throat escape her lips. Tongues of fire stabbed out of darkness behind her eyes. The lump on her head ached and throbbed. But now was not the time to distract Corin. If only the pain would stop so she could *think*. There was something more here. Something floated around the edges. Flickering in and out of someone's thoughts. Something important. She couldn't concentrate enough to find it.

Now would be a useful time to learn how to heal herself. She focussed on the yanstones around her hips. The golden whispers flared again into a seductive temptation to let them take over, but the pain in her head didn't abate.

'There's a rumour among the slaves,' Shasa said, 'and the Selb. A hope that a champion will come to free them. And I think there's one person here who could be that champion. Someone who could both kill Hallon and unite the slaves and the Selb members to revolution.'

Alere raised heavy lids, her heart sinking.

Shasa inclined her head respectfully to Gavon. 'Gavon Abdulkin, it is an absolute honour to meet you. Your escape has been a symbol of hope for every slave in Melcor for the last decade. We need you.'

Gavon leaned back in his chair, shaking his head vigorously. 'Oh no, girl. I'll not be anyone's figurehead, thank ye. I escaped for myself, so I could live again. And I want nothing to do with the Selb.' He scowled and gestured to his leg. 'Besides, yer little stunt tonight means I'm in no position to do much, anyway.'

'The Selb are the only ones who can pull together a fighting force quickly, should you need them,' Shasa said. 'So, you'd best lay aside your prejudices. Many of them owe their lives to Liu, and will come at his call. And I'm sorry you were injured. Liu didn't tell me you were part of Corin's party or I wouldn't have risked your life.' She sent Liu a sharp look.

'I don't care,' Gavon snapped. 'Ye were willing to risk yer betrothed's life for some gouri Selb and that makes ye untrustworthy in my book.'

'You do care.' A hint of pity coloured her words. 'Or your arm wouldn't still bear the Sinclair mark. It says you're still a slave. In here.' She thumped her own breast.

Gavon started, grabbing at the sleeve he'd rolled up to inspect a cut on his arm. The tattoo was partly visible. 'I belong to *no-one.*'

'That says you belong here, with us. Why did you come, if not to help us? You must have known you risk being thrown back into the Wushi Games. Why take that chance if you aren't here to do more?'

He slammed a fist on the table. 'I came to help m'boyo here free her sister, and to get Jarran back. Mamlakah needs a Jun First. That's all. I'm *not* here to free any guisunzi slaves too weak to free themselves.'

A flicker of thought from someone speared through Alere's broken wards. The yanstones around her hips flared their silver-gilt connection, slipping into the flesh of her with honeyed warmth. She let out an involuntary whimper as the flames in her mind grew to a conflagration that threatened to consume her. The world burned. Not only with pain of injury but with the screams of the dying, and the uncontrollable fire of justice. She resisted, struggling to think.

Something important needed to be said.

'Alli?' Kett knelt beside her, concerned. 'What is it? Your head? Where's that healer?'

'Yes,' she mumbled, her tongue thick. 'No. It's something else as well.' She squinted at Liu. The truth was written in his mind.

'You're wrong, Gavon.' She forced the words out, though her tongue felt awkward. Words were the wrong form of communication. 'We're all here because Liu wished it.' She switched her gaze to Liu. '*You* arranged everything, didn't you? It was *your* spy network that told Hallon where to find Jarran. It was *your* idea to kidnap him. Why?'

Kett's hand dropped to the hilt of his sword. Corin's chair scraped and Saric tightened his finger on the crossbow, still pointed at Corin's chest.

Liu contemplated her shrewdly, tapping on his chin. 'Because I needed Rafi to have a stake in this game. Planting the idea in Hallon's head to take Jarran was my decision, yes. I was hoping you four would come after him. Gavon to act as figurehead for the revolution. You three to free Shasa and Jarran and return the Jun First to Mamlakah safely. I knew Gavon wouldn't come voluntarily.' He sighed heavily. 'Mina and Rohne, I'm afraid, were unexpected inclusions. I apologise for endangering them.'

This time she couldn't block the outburst of noise and anger as all three of her friends leapt to their feet and laid hands on weapons. Gavon collapsed to the floor, his agony a sword into her wards. The flames in her head exploded, driving Alere to her feet with a cry of pain.

Under her clothing, the yanstone necklace burned with a cold-fire that sleeted across her skin. Responding to an internal order she had no hope of disobeying, she pulled the suede covers off the stones on her weapons and laid her hands over the smooth domes.

The world vanished in silver-gilt flames; engulfed, wiped clean of all hatred and anger; all pain and all humanity. With emotion cleansed, it seemed so much simpler. As it had in Shanzhai when she battled with Celia.

She reviewed the others in the room. Only Kett watched her, a frown knitting his brows. Yes, it was easier this way. But there was much to do and understand.

The time had come to take control of this situation. Freeing Mina was of paramount importance. The rest subsidiary. To do that,

Liu and Shasa would be required. Determining their motivation was key. She could not fail again.

Angry voices drifted into stillness as she stepped away from her chair and the others turned to watch her. Walking around the table she touched Shasa's arm, holding on even when the woman flinched away. Through the connection she was better able to pierce Shasa's wards; to read her Outers. Truth coloured her thoughts; passion drove her purpose.

Shasa was honest about being willing to help them free Mina. And she did want to be free. There was something more, though. Something important to her. But she'd buried the knowledge deep, as though to hide it even from herself. Extracting it would risk Fusion and take time Alere didn't have. For now, what mattered was that Shasa could do what she said.

Shasa half-drew her knife and wrenched free. Alere moved on to Liu even before Kett's warning to the mhareb left his lips.

Liu rose from his chair. His hand strayed to his dagger, but he paused and his expression segued into one of almost-academic interest. Alere touched his arm, sliced straight into his unwarded Outers, and examined him. He'd clearly had no training. Since there was only one Xintou in the city, he had no need. However, the sheer complexity of his mind was its own defence. Much lay hidden within his Inners. So many interwoven plans and games it would take hours to sift through them. She did not have hours, for this body weakened and needed rest. So, she did no more than establish the veracity of his promise before releasing him.

The flesh could not sustain this level of power for long. It needed healing, which would take most of the remaining. Before she completed the task and let go, she faced the small group. Suspicion, fear and confusion lay written in every face and mind.

'Alli?' Kett spoke the name uncertainly.

Smiling she opened her hands to them. 'Liu and Shasa speak truthfully about this, if not everything. We need them. Let them help. Freeing Mina is the only thing that matters.'

She allowed the silver-gilt warmth to envelope her whole being.

Briefly, she stretched out and touched Mina's sleeping mind. Her twin was alright. The silver-gilt thread connecting them was still intact. She strengthened the tie.

Then the energy withdrew, taking her strength with it. A word appeared in her mind as the body drifted into unconsciousness.

'Erheyi,' she breathed.

Blackness claimed her soul and fire released it.

CHAPTER TWENTY-ONE

ROHNE

Sitting up in the luxurious bedchamber of Hallon's guest-quarters, Rohne sought for whatever had woken him. Was someone else in the room? Flicking a lightswitch, he checked, just in case, but part of him knew already there was no-one. He pressed a thumb into his temple, trying to squeeze the ubiquitous headache out of his brain. He checked on Mina.

Ah. There. Someone connected with Mina. Their intrusion disturbed the wards he'd established around her sleeping mind. Even from that fleeting touch, he recognised Alere's mental signature. Rather, almost hers. It felt like Alere worked in tandem with another, stronger mind. Unfamiliar and without emotion; distant, detached. Who, though?

Had she somehow convinced the Shah's Xintou to help?

He'd need to find a way to keep Alere out of Mina's head until he was ready. Which shouldn't be difficult. Even with Valera's help, Alere wasn't skilled enough to compete with him.

He lay back down but sleep proved elusive. So, he gave up and stared blankly at his surroundings. Ornately woven silk rugs littered the floor. Much-gilded, tasteless furniture squatted about the room, and heavy red velvet drapes obscured any light from the barred windows. The single door was locked and guarded. A guest he might be labelled, but Hallon took no chances he might lose his new asset.

The Mianshou dinner had gone so well that the Slavemaster undoubtedly wove new plans around Rohne's xintou skills and would continue to use Mina as hostage.

Rohne ground his teeth.

With his mind still sluggish from the drugs, controlling Jarran and Mina had taken all his concentration and strength. Jarran had a strong mind. His fear for his daughters made him even stronger; determined to live and to escape. He'd fought Rohne's control every moment.

Mina's wards were less solid, and he'd known her so long that he understood her weaknesses. It had been simple to merge right through and bury her consciousness. Her resistance and shocked fear gave him a twinge of regret, but his actions were for the best. She just needed to trust him. She would understand, soon. When they were in Madina together. When she understood what he was trying to achieve.

Rohne folded his hands behind his head and smiled fiercely. One more day of not eating, and of drinking only water from the bathroom tap. Then the drugs would be cleared out of his blood. After that, he would be free to return to Madina.

Pity he had to leave Mina behind for now. If he escaped and brought Mina along, Alere would follow, like a xiao-cat on the scent. Mina would be alright. He would arrange to bring her to Madina, eventually. Then she would see his true worth. Then she would respect him.

Jarran's fate was neither here nor there. Mamlakah needed a good Jun First, but there were spares if he didn't make it back. The man was too strong-willed anyway. Rohne's purpose would be better served by someone more malleable. Someone who would be grateful to have a powerful Bonded Xintou by his side.

He threw aside the blankets and got out of bed. All of this would be easier with the yanstones, though. They were close, somewhere within this building. He would get them back. It was annoying to have lost them so soon. With them, every corner of his mind lit up like fireworks and everything he'd ever dreamed of being as a xintou came within reach.

Right now, though, he had to decide what to reveal to Hallon about Alere. How did he manipulate the man once his full powers returned? Where did the advantage lie? How could he use the knowledge that Alere was in Chengdu – undoubtedly with Kett and Corin? There had to be a way he could turn this game the right way. She had to be kept busy – at least until he made it to Madina.

But preferably, forever.

An idea sprang into his head, full-blown and perfect. Ahhhh. Yes. That might work nicely. If he managed it well, he could use Alere to release Mina and also hamstring Alere's ability to act against him.

Rohne ghosted a laugh. He flicked off the lightswitch, dropped back onto the bed and stretched out a thought. Time to draw Alere into this.

Let the games begin.

ALERE

Alere woke with a familiar, heavy lassitude dragging at her limbs and groaned. This had to stop. Dropping unconscious every time she received an injury was not a useful habit. It was nice to wake up whole, but surely there was a better way? She squinted at the flickering, honey glow of a nearby mel-oil light. It took a minute to fit her surroundings into some sensible world-view.

She lay on a bottom bunk-bed in a room full of sleeping girl-children. Craning her neck, she counted thirty beds, arranged dormitory-style, along a narrow, high-ceilinged room. No light came from a series of small windows set high in one wall. Either it was dark outside or the windows were blacked. Her internal body-clock said morning must be close.

The predominant colour of the room was grey, even in the warm yellow of the mel-oil lamp. Walls, floor, bedblankets; all grey. Yet, here and there, spots of colour showed the place to be more than a temporary sleeping-space. A small painting of pink flowers hung next to one bed; a red scarf from another; a vibrant blue silk robe from yet another.

Most incongruous, however, was the array of weapons. Bows, arrows, miniature kusarigama, short-swords, daggers, and shuriken lay scattered around the room much like clothing, shoes, or toys would be strewn around the chamber of an ordinary child. A sobering reminder of what sort of life these girls led.

Alere flicked the blankets aside and checked herself and her possessions. The lump behind her ear was gone. The clothes she wore were her second set, which meant someone had removed the bloodied ones she'd worn last night. Her sword and dagger lay by the bed, along with her bow, knives and bag.

The yanstones! She untied the bag and dumped the contents out. Nothing but her clothes and Mina's healer bag. She shoved a hand into one boot and sighed. The yanstones were warm and smooth against her fingers. With the memory of last night still fresh, she tipped them onto the bed and hesitated. But their seductive warmth and hypnotic flame was impossible to resist. She settled them around her hips and the internal oneness/duality wormed its way into her thoughts again. A sliver of unease raised hairs on her arms. She rubbed at gooseflesh and frowned.

Last night was mostly a haze of pain. But she recalled the moment of clarity and decision brought on by close connection with the stones. Though she wasn't sure why, it felt utterly right that Mina was her priority. Freeing Jarran would happen as well. But, no matter what, Mina needed to be released.

The time for dithering and second-guessing herself was done. Important and what she wanted were the same thing, now. She couldn't let Mina down again. Or Kett. Or Rafi.

She gathered up the rest of her equipment and crept from the room. Outside the door, she paused, taken aback by the sight of a sleepy young girl, no more than nine or ten, sitting on a chair. Her huge, dark eyes were fixed solemnly on Alere and a crossbow rested on her knees. A half-grown sky-monkey lay curled up asleep under her chair.

The girl rose, tucked her long, black hair behind one ear, then placed both hands on her chest and bowed, weishi-style. 'I'm Wei Nahas, your friendly weishi for the night. Well, the early-morning watch, anyway. I hate the midnight shift.' Her face lit up as only a child's can. She pointed to the sky-monkey. 'This is Pell.' The animal cracked an eyelid, gave a sleepy bark, and closed it again. Wei grinned. 'Bathroom is two doors up. Liu is in the room at the end of the hall, waiting for you. Your friends are there, too. It's the kitchen. They're having breakfast. Hungry? Rest of the girls will be up soon. Best eat now. I already did. And Pell did, too, but he doesn't much like bread.'

Alere had the feeling there might never be a break in which to respond politely, so she returned the weishi bow and said, 'Thank you. I mustn't keep them waiting.'

She found the bathroom then followed the corridor until she heard Kett's low voice and smelled the enticing aroma of eggs. Steeling herself against the inevitable questions, she opened the door.

Kett, Liu, Corin, Gavon, and Saric were seated around one end of a long, narrow table. Shasa was absent. Presumably she'd had to return to Hallon's house before morning. Where had she slept, if she'd stayed long enough to do so? Alere bit back a groan. How petty. Corin had a right to happiness, and a right to resolve any old issues. It was none of her business.

Corin smiled at her, all his old humour firmly back in place. He winced and touched the black eye developing over his bruised cheek. Rising, he pulled out a battered chair, bowed her into it and dropped a quick kiss on her head.

Kett merely nodded a greeting. His arm was neatly bandaged, but his face was lined by fatigue. Gavon was still pale. Crisp beige bamboo-cloth bandages swathed his leg and he smelled of bitter herbal healing ointments. The healer must have arrived sometime after she'd fallen unconscious.

The kitchen was large and basic in its amenities, with a seaweed-burning clay oven and fireplace the central features. Nearby, a gleaming brass sink echoed the cleanliness of floor and table, as though scrubbing could make up for lack of luxury. At one end, a door stood half-open, revealing a pantry of mostly-bare shelves with just a few bags of rice, golden ren-tubers, and flour visible. Liu had said they couldn't afford much. How did he feed so many children?

Saric slid a plateful of eggs across the table. Alere took it guiltily. What would the small girls in the dormitory eat when they arose? Kett passed her a pair of bamboo chopsticks, then lancha tea in a cracked, heavy pottery cup.

'Eat, child.' Liu smiled. 'Eggs are one thing we do have plenty of. Some of the children aren't suited to this city life, or the xiongshou training. They manage a farm for us, under the aegis of some of the grown youngsters. In the outer regions, where the regulations on papers for free citizens are not so strict. They keep us supplied. Extremely good at raising chickens.' He lifted a mouthful on his chopsticks.

Reassured, she ate.

'I see,' she said between mouthfuls, pointing at Liu and Corin, 'that you made up your differences and are speaking civilly to each other. What happened?'

'You did.' Corin shrugged. 'And we see that you have, once again, terrified everyone with your new and wonderous abilities. Do tell. What happened?'

She screwed up her nose at him. 'Are you *ever* serious?'

He sipped from his cup and made a show of thinking about it. 'Tried it a few times. Very overrated and no fun at all. So, I'd have to say No to that one. Not if I can help it.' He used the cup to gesture at Kett and Gavon. 'There are more than enough serious people to make up for my lack.'

Kett's lips twitched, but he didn't reply, only regarded her steadily. 'So?'

Corin chuckled. 'Succinct as usual, but to the point, which I like. Yes, Alere: so?'

She glanced warily at Liu. How much could she say in front of him?

'Oh.' Corin gave her a sly smile. 'Don't fret about Liu. In the light of last night's events, we were obliged to tell him of your late-blooming xintou abilities.' He grinned. 'Apparently something he actually didn't know. Which annoyed him.'

There was a slight emphasis in his words that said Liu remained unaware of the yanstones. She agreed with Corin's decision to keep them secret. Although Reading had shown her some of Liu's motivations, much remained hidden.

'I don't really know what to tell you.' She rotated the cup, focussing on the milky-blue liquid inside. 'We weren't getting beyond yelling and fighting. You needed to know if Shasa and Liu could be trusted. Reading them was the fastest way. I'm xintou, yes, but there's a limit to what I can do – and what my mind can take. My head still aches.'

That last was a lie but it seemed politic to downplay her abilities.

'Yes,' Corin said, 'we noticed it comes with a rather challenging side-effect.'

Alere gave a weak laugh. 'Only if you call falling unconscious a challenge.'

'Aye,' Gavon growled, smacking a fist on the table and making the plates jump. 'I do, boyo. Ye can't do that again, y'hear me? What's the point to these powers if they leave ye vulnerable? Ye don't need them and I'll not allow ye to put yerself in that sort of danger.'

'Which reminds me: I need to teach you to ward.' She smiled, ruefully. 'I'm sorry if it bothers you, but I have to use them. You're not my shifu any longer, Gavon. And you know I won't stand by and watch my friends endangered. You're too important. Are you well enough this morning? How's your leg?'

'I'm fine and don't change the subject. If we're talking about who's important, I don't think it's a contest.' He pointed at her. 'If it *ever* comes down to a decision between saving my sorry ass or yers, ye'd better make the right choice, boyo.'

Kett laid a hand over her wrist and echoed Gavon's sentiment. 'He's right. Of all of us, you are the key, here. You're Jun-Heir and getting you, Mina and Jarran back has to be the priority.'

'Speak for yourself.' Corin put his feet up on a chair and cradled his mug to his chest. 'I consider myself to be quite important, thank you. Although in this case I do admit it is slightly possible I may be wrong.' He feathered a wink at Alere.

Saric choked on a mouthful of water and sprayed it onto the table.

Corin sent him a sarcastic look.

He brought his feet down with a thud. 'Anyway…beside the point. While you've been sleeping and lazing away the night, my love, we've been planning. Sleep is overrated too.'

Glad to see him back to his buoyant self, Alere forebore to rise to his teasing.

Liu unrolled a sheet of yellowed paper on which the outlines of several buildings were drawn. 'Shasa has given us detailed building plans. These are the guest rooms, on the second storey, where your three friends are being held. She says Rohne is separate from the others. She thinks Hallon is using Mina as leverage against Rohne to make him co-operate. Hallon's good at finding peoples' weaknesses.'

He pointed to one of the rooms. 'The guest quarters are much less secure than the slave cells. Although most of the windows are barred, there is one – in the master bedroom – which is not. That wall of the building itself also forms part of the outer wall of the compound. Which means a descent from that window will place you in the alley outside. Then my youngsters will provide a distraction while you extract your friends.'

Corin took up the explanation, outlining an idea for an incursion.

After a few minutes she interrupted the flow. 'So, am I right in thinking your plan essentially boils down to: sneak in, get Jarran and the others, sneak out, don't get caught?'

Corin cocked his head and pulled his mouth down. 'Pretty much. We don't have time to gather an army, and Hallon would just hold Mina and the others hostage against an army, anyway. The trickiest bit is getting in. We're hoping you can help, in a xintou-kind of way. Encourage the guards to look the other way. That sort of thing.'

'I don't have the ability to influence thoughts on a large scale. Maybe one or two? But Hallon had dozens of guards.' Alere shook her head. 'And you're forgetting something: Rohne. He's warding

Jarran and Mina. I touched her mind last night and he knew I was there. He'll be aware the minute we wake them up, and we don't know what his plan is. Why is he co-operating with Hallon? Why is he controlling the others? We can't be sure he would let them go. He could bring every mharebi in the place down on us in a minute if he wanted to.'

CHAPTER TWENTY-TWO

CORIN

Corin sat on the floor, legs crossed beneath him, back against the rough sulcrete and claybrick warehouse outer wall. He plucked at his oud distractedly, watching Alere spar with Saric. The boy was tall for his ten years, and well-trained by Liu. But it would still be many years before he could match Alere for speed and technique. A dozen children stood around the makeshift dojo, observing the pair intently as they threw each other to the woven-reed mats. Alere clearly enjoyed her unusual role as instructor, and the children could only benefit from her skills, so Liu had not objected.

They were just playing around, though. Passing time until Shasa returned. After Alere's mention of Rohne, they had decided to suspend further planning until Shasa came back and could add to their information.

Now, Corin watched Alere and thought about Shasa. What the jahim was he supposed to do? Obviously Shasa was not the girl he'd loved at sixteen. Yet there was still a tie of remembered love and new chemistry between them. She had grown into a beautiful, strong woman and he'd long had a thing for beautiful, strong women. But his feelings were coloured by guilt. Now he wasn't certain what he felt, and it annoyed him to be unsure.

One of the oud strings loosened, souring his chords. Corin twisted the tuning knob and grimaced.

He owed Shasa. He had given up searching too soon and the awareness of where she'd been gnawed at him like a cancer. He'd even been in Chengdu several times in the last ten years. How had he never seen her? With a twisted smile, he admitted the truth: he hadn't been looking. He'd probably seen her, yet not seen her, in Hallon's entourage when he'd been in the city three years ago, spying on Jahil. If he'd recognised her then, he could have saved Shasa three years of huozui.

Then there was Alere. While he didn't doubt his feelings for her, she hadn't committed her heart to him. Would she ever? Was he kidding himself to think he had a chance at happiness with a woman trained to put duty before her personal desires? Trained to keep people at an emotional distance?

Restless, he put the oud aside and left the room, ignoring Alere's questioning call. After wandering aimlessly through the vast, maze-like warehouse complex that served as Liu's main base of operations, he climbed a rickety set of stairs and found an exit to a small widows' walk running the length of the building's eastern end. Coming out into the cool morning air was a relief after the cold darkness of the warehouse. He'd never liked being stuck inside.

The day was yet early and the pale orange morning-sun laid a glittering path across the opaque river surface. Corin raised his face to the sky and tasted the cool, salt-tinted, human-tainted air. The walkway overlooked the distant port. He closed the door and leaned on the railing. Dalor's chuan was still moored at the dock, bobbing gently in the river's tidal rush. His crew were no-where to be seen, probably hung over and sleeping off the first night ashore at the end of year festivities. Corin smiled. Dalor would be mightily annoyed.

His dilemma forced its way back into his thoughts and he sighed. How did he deal with Alere and Shasa? In a short space of time he'd gone from keeping all women at armslength, to having two in his life at once. Both of whom held a place in his heart. How did he choose? He laughed silently at himself. Choose? What made him think he even had the right? It was hardly up to him. Both women were strong-minded and would do whatever the jahim they wanted.

Alere still didn't know her own heart. She gave herself wholly when they were together, and cared a great deal for him. But she kept a small, secret part hidden. Of course, he'd gone in knowing that; hoping she would grow to love him. Now, he wasn't sure it would ever happen. And that affected his feelings for her. He held back as well, guarding himself against the hurt to come.

Shasa, on the other hand, hid everything. She had been destroyed and rebuilt. She was so used to protecting herself behind that defensive, sultry front that it would take years of patience to gain her trust. Even then she would never *be* the Shasa he'd loved so long ago. Then again, he was not the idealistic, naïve boy she'd loved, either. Even though he found her physically attractive, he had no idea what went on in her head.

He laughed wryly and watched a bird soar past. It floated effortlessly up into the clear teal-green sky and Corin wished himself on its wings, back to the freedom of life before he'd met Alere. It was a useless thought and one he didn't mean. He'd lived in limbo for ten years, unable to wholly let go of Shasa. Meeting and loving Alere was one of the best things that had happened. She had opened him to the potential for living again.

Now it was all going…suilie.

It was entirely possible he would end up with neither woman.

'You seem troubled.'

Corin half-turned, his knife already free of its sheath, before his brain caught up with his ears. Kett. He must have been standing there the whole time, still and silent against the building just five steps away. With a soft chuckle Corin turned the blade over in his hand and relaxed against the wall, resting his head on the silvered wooden slats.

'You could say that.' He shoved the knife back into its scabbard with more force than necessary and stared towards the ocean, north of the city. The bird was now no more than a dark dot against the growing brightness. Dark clouds gathered over the vast blue-green expanse of ocean, promising storms later.

Kett's profile was pensive. What was he doing here, alone? Then again, Kett wasn't the sociable type, so it was probably normal for him to seek time on his own.

'I'm sorry.' Corin hitched himself off the wall. 'You must have come here to be alone and I'm intruding. I'll go.'

'No.' Kett held up a hand. 'It's fine. Stay. Something on your mind? Alere by any chance?'

Corin sagged back and folded his arms, inspecting his own feet. 'Good guess.'

'She has a habit of getting under people's skin.' Kett's expression softened. 'When she was seventeen, she snuck out of Xintou House to attend a Selection party being thrown in Jiaoji House. It was meant for graduate jiaoji, ready to be hired. She'd just started jiaoji training and wanted to know what to expect. When I arrived to fetch her home, she'd received one offer of marriage and three offers of a permanent jiaoji contract to various senior Jun and merchant families.'

'What'd she say to them?'

'Well,' Kett mused, 'one of the men didn't take refusal kindly. He eventually got control of his larynx again. The others got the message and backed off. When I arrived, Alli was bored and happy to come home. Told me she didn't see what all the fuss over jiaoji was, anyway. She's never been one to rate her own charms very highly.'

Corin frowned. 'Is that what makes her hard to reach? Or is it the xintou training? There's some part of her I can't get through to.' He met Kett's shadowed gaze.

The weishi looked away. 'Her life at Xintou House wasn't easy. She had to protect herself – mentally and physically – to survive.'

'Xintou House is hardly a slave-pen,' Corin said, indicating Chengdu. 'She was living in luxury.'

Kett folded his arms. 'Lack of freedom comes in different forms, Cor. Being non-xintou, she was the target practice for xintou techniques by the other girls. Never their equal. Her life was a long series of humiliations and degradations.' He grimaced. 'In the first six months she ran away three times. Every time I brought her back, she begged me not to.' The muscles in his jaw worked. 'Ripped my heart out, but I had to protect her. I asked Mistress Li to let me train her as a weishi. Otherwise she was either going to succeed at running away or commit suicide.'

'Suicide!' Corin gaped. His chest ached. She'd never said. He'd assumed her unhappiness at Xintou House stemmed more from the impossible desire to be xintou.

Kett nodded. 'She's not the type to just give up. But she puts herself in the path of danger. A lot.' His troubled gaze caught Corin's and he shrugged one shoulder. 'Risk-taking. Sneaking out. You name it. I spent the first four years worrying that a runner would show up at the House saying she'd been kidnapped or murdered in the Zalam slums. Mistress Li wouldn't let me give her a sword or dagger until she turned eighteen.'

Corin shoved his hands into his pockets and stared blankly at the glittering river. 'So, she keeps people at a distance—'

'Because she believes she's not worthy of being loved,' Kett finished. 'She feels like her only worth is in her ability to do things for others; to protect them. That's why she chose to be Lia even though it meant giving up her freedom.'

Corin managed a half-smile and slid a sideways look at the weishi. 'Only worth is in protecting people? Sounds familiar.'

Kett's mouth pressed thin and he shifted, angling his body away from Corin. Aware he'd crossed a line and not sure how to recover, Corin let the awkward silence sit between them.

All around, Chengdu awoke; doors opening, windows being thrown back to let the morning light in. Neighbours called out to one another, relating memories of the night before. The first market stalls opened for business and the scent of baking bread drifted up, making Corin's mouth water.

He scuffed one bootheel on the flaking wooden platform. 'How do you do it?'

'What?'

'Have two women in your life?' Corin straightened and paced a few steps in each direction, trailing his fingers along the rough timber railing. 'I mean, Mina's obviously in love with you and Alere thinks you can do no wrong. You love them both. How do you manage it?'

Kett stepped forward and leaned both elbows on the railing. He stared out across the portside rooftops for a long while then contemplated his own hands, clasped together over the void below.

'I do...care...for both, of course.' Kett's smile twisted with irony. 'But what I feel isn't relevant in this case. What Mina thinks is love, is infatuation. I appeared, like a hero from a play, to rescue her. Twice. She cast me in that role and endowed me with all the attributes she wanted of a hero.' He gave a quiet laugh. 'I'm afraid I can only fall from that pedestal. When I do, and she realises how poorly she chose, I hope there's someone decent around she can turn to.

'Alere...' He flicked a quick, narrow glance at Corin and pulled his mouth down. 'Well...we've known each other a long time. She's far from blind to my faults. But I agree she needs to have more faith in her own decisions. She doesn't need me any more. In fact...'

Closing his lips he left the thought unfinished. 'I'm not really the best person to ask about how to handle Alere and Shasa, I don't think.'

It was, perhaps, the most open Kett had ever been and Corin was impressed by the man's level of honesty.

'Strangely enough, it sounds exactly like what I needed to hear,' Corin admitted. 'Except in my case I think it's Alere who's infatuated, and Shasa who's hanging on to me as an illusion of the past. After everyone went to bed last night, she clung to me like she was a girl of sixteen again. But she's not that child any more. She just wants me to rescue her.' He held up his hands to forestall any comment. 'Which I'm more than happy to do, but—'

'You're not sure how to feel about her,' Kett finished for him, 'and you're in love with Alere.'

Corin chuckled. 'We're a sad pair, you and I. Both being led around by the nose by these women of ours. Perhaps I undervalued my freedom when I had it.'

Kett straightened and sent him a sympathetic smile. 'Perhaps you're not as in love as you think, then. A relationship is about walking side by side. You can only be led if you don't have common goals and your own path to follow.'

He disappeared back inside and leaving Corin to regret he'd opened his mouth at all.

ALERE

'You twist like this.' She demonstrated on Saric. 'And pin him like this. He shouldn't be able to move. If he resists, you can use your weight to break the arm. Now you try.'

Glancing up at her class of small people, she smiled at their intent eagerness. She hauled Saric up and bowed formally. He returned it, grinning from ear to ear.

'Bai, shifu,' he barked, waving the others onto the mat.

Alere moved amongst them to begin with, correcting and assisting. Then she stood back and watched, admiring how quickly the youngsters picked up the new technique and how ruthlessly they applied it. There were sixteen on the mat, now. Boys and girls ranging in age from six to ten. But all behaved as though they were years older. They paired off without being told, first into roughly matching sizes. After they had grasped the technique, they swapped into grossly mis-matched pairings so the smallest could practice against a larger opponent.

None of them complained – as she had when she'd first trained with Kett. They practiced with a focussed intensity that sat oddly on their childish features. Of course, they had more at stake. Her training had merely been a device to keep her out of trouble.

'Saric likes you.'

Shasa's voice at her shoulder came as no surprise. She'd felt the woman approach several seconds earlier, but had chosen not to turn, waiting to see what Shasa would do. Almost-palpable tension emanated from the mhareb's slender form.

Alere steeled herself. The moment had come sooner than she'd hoped. Shasa had spent the last ten years fighting for everything good in her life. Of course she expected to have to fight for Corin. And she probably felt threatened by Alere's work with Liu's children, too, for they clearly admired Shasa.

Alere unfolded her arms and turned. She gave Shasa a friendly smile. She didn't entirely trust the mhareb. The woman had secrets. However, the success of this task rested on her co-operation. Alere would just need to be on her guard.

For now, the aim was to fold this prickly, defensive woman smoothly into the team. It would entail a painful sacrifice, though. But what she wanted was not always the same as what was important. Mina, Jarran and the people of Mamlakah were important. Her own lovelife hardly rated a mention.

'Saric's a good kid.' She indicated the group on the mat. 'He's bright and a natural leader. They're all amazing. It took me five tries to find something you hadn't already taught them. You and Liu should be proud of them.'

Shasa studied the children in their training, her cheeks flushing. Alere hid a smile. Shasa recovered her irritation but took her hands off her weapons and folded her arms. The spark of anger in her faded to wariness.

Since keeping her offbalance was the result Alere wanted, she added, 'Shasa, I want you to know I'm not here to tread on your toes – in any way.' She locked gazes with the woman, letting her see honesty. She opened her palms and tilted her head to show vulnerability. 'I know you're smart enough to have guessed Corin and I have been spending time together.' She held up a hand as Shasa gripped her knife-hilt once more. 'But that's a very recent development. You and he have a far deeper history.

'So...' She hooked her arm through Shasa's, ignoring the older woman's reflexive stiffening. Alere led her down the narrow hall towards the kitchen, where they had agreed to assemble on the mhareb's return. 'If it's alright with you,' she continued, 'I'll take a step back and give you two space to sort things out. There's a lot going on right now. The last thing we need is tension between you and I if we're going to work as a team to rescue Jarran and Mina.'

She snuck a quick, assessing peek at Shasa, relieved to see a wry smile.

'I know. Frustrating, aren't I? Kett says so all the time,' Alere said. 'Look, I like Cor and I want him to be happy. He loved you deeply and he has some unresolved issues to fix before he can get on with life. The best thing I can do for him is give you two the chance to work out how you feel about each other. I'll talk to him then I'll stay out of the way.'

Shasa paced silently beside her for several steps, but didn't unlink her arm. Finally, she let out a low chuckle.

'That was a masterstroke,' she said at last. 'I can't possibly hate you and I have no reason to even pick a fight with you, do I?'

Alere laughed aloud, hiding the pain in her chest. 'That was the idea.' She withdrew her arm and held out a hand. 'Let's be friends and terrify Corin.'

After a moment's hesitation, Shasa gave a rueful smile and grasped her hand. 'Very well, but don't expect me to actually like you.'

'Never. Oh.' Alere patted her hips. 'I left my weapons in the dojo. Will you please tell the others I'll be right in? They're waiting for you in the kitchen.'

Turning away, she strode back through the hall. When she made the corner, and Shasa couldn't see her, she stopped and wiped the tears from her cheeks. She rested against the wall, arms wrapped around her waist, staring up at the dusty warehouse ceiling, willing the constriction in her throat away. It had been the right thing to do, hadn't it?

'If you're wondering if you did the right thing...' Kett's low voice emerged from the shadows nearby. '...then the answer is: yes. They do need to resolve whatever is between them.'

Alere straightened, sniffing a watery little chuckle.

'I know. I just...I don't know.' She groaned. 'I guess, when he was chasing me, it was easy to be ambivalent. To keep a distance, just in case. Now I could be about to lose him I don't want to…but I'm still not sure.' She sniffed again and used her sleeve to wipe away the last tears. 'Maybe it's my competitive nature.'

Moving closer she dropped her forehead onto Kett's chest. He stroked her hair soothingly. Eventually, she leaned back, interlacing her fingers with his and inspecting the scars and calluses there.

'Why does doing the right thing always hurt so much?'

A smile flickered on his lips. 'Always? How many times have we discussed the folly of using extreme statements?'

'A million.' Alere laughed at the years-old banter. 'And I did notice you didn't answer my question.'

Kett pulled her hand through his arm, drawing her along the corridor towards the dojo. He smiled slightly, his eyes fixed forward. 'Maybe because I've never been ambivalent in how I feel about someone, so doing the right thing is easier.'

Alere envied his unruffled surety. How would it feel to be so unwavering in love that no room for doubt existed? Mina was lucky.

Tears pricked at her eyes again.

She withdrew her hand and hurried ahead to pick up her weapons. Saric spotted her and bowed himself off, running to join her as she returned to Kett's side. Fussing with the buckle on her belt allowed Alere to avoid Kett's gaze. Together, they joined the others in the kitchen, though she found her throat too tight to speak for quite some time.

CHAPTER TWENTY-THREE

ALERE

'Today's the twenty-seventh of Shisiyue.' Shasa smoothed out a large map of Chengdu on the scarred kitchen table. 'Hallon will have functions every night until the Wushi Games on the thirtieth.'

Saric fetched cups and weighted the corners, earning himself a smile from the mhareb.

'After that, on Yirun and Er'run, he'll take part in the Seyd-Hunt and be gone for two days,' Shasa continued. 'Hallon will bring men in from his estates to cover for those with him on the Hunt. And he's recruited half a dozen new mhareb already, after the slaughter last night. Five are Selb, so they can help, as well. And the new mhareb won't be quite as familiar with the routines, so there may be holes in the security. That's our best chance. While he's away.'

'But,' Gavon rumbled, 'if yer his head mhareb-slave, then ye'll be riding point on the Hunt. So how were ye thinking of joining us and getting yer freedom?'

'Yes, I'll be with him,' she admitted. 'But it's the only time that Hallon, his son, and most of his men will be away. I'm trusting you'll come back for me, later.' Before anyone could object, she continued briskly. 'We're here. His compound is here.' She pointed to a street on one side of the map, close to the river, upstream of the port facilities and across the other side of the town from Liu's warehouse. 'It backs onto the river, but the wall on that side is more than four times a person's height. Unclimbable. The top is patrolled, wired with electricity, and glassed.'

'What about sewage or stormwater outlets?' Alere put in, remembering Shanzhai.

Shasa made a negatory, chopping gesture. 'Hallon has them all guarded, gated and well-maintained. There *is* no way to get a small force in and out again safely, believe me. I've spent ten years living there.'

'But we got in and out again last night at the feast,' Alere put in.

Shasa nodded. 'You also didn't do anything. A lot of visitors sneak looks around the house. But if you'd tried to enter the slave compound, or the guest rooms, you would have been caught.' She eyed Liu doubtfully. 'If you contact the Selb leadership and get them to spread the word amongst all the slaves, we could organise a mass uprising?'

Liu shook his head. 'That would take more than three days to arrange. And too big a risk of indiscriminate killing. Mina, Jarran and Rohne could be caught in the crossfire.'

Shasa went on to explain the security around the compound and they argued over various plans to get in and, more importantly, out again. Alere studied the map. Shasa was right: no plan involving anything less than an army would achieve their goal. Hallon had inherited the compound, already functioning, from his mother's family. He'd only improved on the security in the last thirty years.

'I see why you think we should act on Yirun,' Kett said, 'but that means a wait of three more days.' He glanced at Alere. 'I don't think we have that much time.'

Alere agreed. They had already been absent from Madina for a week. To get Jarran back to Madina before Hassan entered the city, they had to leave Chengdu within the next two days.

'Believe me,' Shasa said bitterly, 'the *only* way to do this properly is to take time and plan, and wait. Rushing will just get all of us thrown into the Games.'

Alere regarded the woman. 'When you became mhareb, and had more freedom to move about the city, why didn't you leave?'

Shasa lifted her chin. 'As I said, I'm usually watched. Even when I can evade surveillance, the roads and ports out are closely guarded. Without papers I can't get out. Liu slips small children out hidden amongst goods. But the guards check everything big enough to fit an adult. Papers can be forged if you have enough coin, which I don't.' She pointed at the tattoo on her arm. 'This, and the burn scars on my feet, give me away anyway.'

'Scars…' Alere let the rest of the conversation wash over her. The seed of an idea slipped sideways into her mind, seeming to spring from nowhere. She stood and paced the length of the long room twice, trying to chase it down.

'We didn't get checked on the way out last night.' She interrupted a heated discussion between Saric and Corin about using the children to storm the compound. 'When we left Hallon's. No-one checked us for brands or tattoos. Why not?'

'Remember Denna?' Shasa said. 'The servant who met you at the door and escorted you out again?' Shasa waited for her nod and continued. 'She has an eidetic memory for people. It's how Hallon has guests into his house without insulting them by inspecting their feet on departure. If Denna saw you, then she knows you. Even with a veil. Yes, even though you wore a blonde wig. I guarantee she'd still recognise you. People have tried everything. She's uncanny.'

Alere couldn't even picture the nondescript little woman who'd greeted them at the door.

'Why didn't she recognise me as Mina, then?' How could anyone be recognised by just their eyes? Hers had been heavily made-up. Surely changing wigs, makeup and veil colour had to have an effect. No one was that good. Or using her boy's disguise. That would be better.

'I doubt she's ever met Mina,' Shasa said. 'Mina and Jarran came in with their heads covered and have been kept apart in the guest rooms, except for last night. Denna doesn't leave the front door.' She put her hands on her hips. 'Why? What did you have in mind?'

'Could we use istilqa to put all the mharebi to sleep for awhile?' Corin put in, inspecting the more detailed drawing of the compound itself. He pointed at a section of the wall. 'If we could, then a rope thrown over this section of wall would give us the quickest exit route.' He tapped on the main building. 'Or…what was it you said this morning about the window out the master bedroom, Liu?'

'There are food tasters,' Shasa replied to Alere, ignoring Corin. 'And the mharebi are not allowed visitors, alcohol or jiaoji. You'd never get the istilqa to where it needed to be.' She smiled in such a way that Alere flushed. Someone must have told her how Ven had been tricked and defeated.

They were running out of options.

Kett, who had been watching Alere closely, rocked back on his chair, frowning. 'Alli? What are you thinking?'

Her heart pounded as she anticipated their reactions. Kett's expression darkened as it did when he suspected her of mischief. This was more than mere mischief, though. This was insanity. But she couldn't think of anything else.

'I know you're not going to like this…but hear me out.' She hung her head, trying to table the words in such a way as to make them palatable. 'I think I can get Mina out. She's the weakest link for she has no weapons skills. If we can get her out – and someone else in – then they can help Jarran escape.'

'How?' Kett's chairlegs thumped on the flagstone floor.

CORIN

'Just for the record,' Corin said, folding his arms, 'I think you taking Mina's place is an *extraordinarily* bad idea.'

They had spent the better part of the day trying to come up with an alternative. To no avail. Having exhausted all other plans, they were forced to come back to Alere's, though no one particularly liked it. Shasa had been obliged to return to Hallon's compound before midday. Now it was late afternoon. Time to leave, and Corin liked the plan even less. However, a message had been sent to Shasa, so there was no turning back now.

In a short while, they would go again to Hallon's feast as entertainers. This time with more of a purpose. There were an appalling number of things that could go wrong. So many, Corin shuddered to even think of them.

Alere clasped the mock-yanstone bracelets on her arms and adjusted her skirts, checking the material's fall.

'You've already said that. As has Kett, Gavon, and even Saric.' She raised one ironic brow at him. 'In fact, Shasa's the only one who thinks it might work.'

They were in the girl's dormitory. Which seemed to irritate the youngster, Wei, who lounged on a nearby bed, reading what appeared to be a Weishi House instruction book. A young sky-monkey, still more blue than adult purple, leapt and swung from bed to bed in a highly distracting way.

Turning back to the mirror propped against one wall, Alere tweaked the veil lower on her nose.

'Look Corin, we've gone over and over it. This is the *only* way any of us can get in and stay inside long enough to get Mina and Jarran out.'

'What about Rohne? Before, you said he'd sense the minute you touched his wards around Mina. What the jahim are you up to, Alli?' Corin grabbed her arm.

'Cor.' She twisted free of his grip. 'Stop fussing. I can do this. That's why I'm going in, and not trying to reach her telepathically. I can get her and Jarran out without alerting Rohne. Trust me.' She patted his cheek, her dark eyes gleaming.

She tugged again at her skirts, tidying the many, gauzy layers. The way she shifted her tight-fitting, midriff top and the bejewelled knife pinning the blonde wig in place made him groan. Wei made an exasperated noise and put her book aside, leaving the room with what sounded suspiciously like a huff. At least the monkey followed her out, barking piteously.

'It's too dangerous.' Corin scraped at his hair and paced back and forth, struggling to find the words without sounding too needy. It had been many years since he'd invested so much of himself into someone. 'I…I can't lose you, Alere. Gaisi! Don't you know I love you?'

She laid her palms flat on his chest. 'Corin, stop.' Her eyes were soft.

He wasn't going to like the next words out of her mouth.

She caressed his jaw and ran a thumb over his lips. 'Love takes time and we've had too little to be certain of our feelings. I'll be fine and you have to think of Shasa now. You two have things to work out. You owe it to each other and she deserves a chance to be happy, too. Just…No, nevermind.'

'What?' He held her close, but she drew back, searching his face.

'Be careful. Shasa is hiding something… well, be careful.'

He pressed his lips together to prevent the automatic denial. She hurried on, flushing and watching from beneath her lashes.

'Until you two have decided what you want from each other, you and I should go back to being friends.' She tugged the veil down, cupped his jaw with cold hands and kissed him swiftly.

He gripped her wrists. 'What about what I want in this? Don't I get a say?'

'What *do* you want, Cor? Do you know?' Her smile quivered and tears shimmered in her eyes.

He thrust her away and swore.

'Can we talk about this later?' She cleared her throat and carefully dabbed at her eyes. 'I need your support. Be there to help me get my sister and the Jun-Heir back. Can you do that?'

'What's important over what you want, huh?' He gave up, accepting the inevitable, little though he liked it. Standing against her on this would be pointless.

'Something like that.'

He ran both hands over his face. 'Gaisi, Alere, this was *not* what I signed up for. It should be me, or Gav or Kett. Not you. I can't help if I'm stuck outside watching. It will drive me insane.'

'I'm beginning to think you really do want to see Gavon in this.' Alere spread the skirts of her dancer's outfit in a curtsy. 'Besides, you and Kett were the ones Shasa followed and told Hallon about. You can't go back in or you'll be recognised and the whole thing will fall through.

'Tell you what.' She touched his hand, where it rested on the hilt of his sword. 'Check with these every few minutes. I'll let you into my Outers so you can keep an eye on me.'

It was the best offer he would get. Corin grasped her face and kissed her, releasing her before she had time to react, and before he had time to get so involved he wouldn't let her go.

'Go, then. But you'd better come back safely.'

She gave a shaky laugh and resettled the veil beneath her eyes. She swirled a cloak around her shoulders, fastening it at her throat and flipping the hood up. 'I will.'

He followed her into the main warehouse and stalked past Kett without speaking. Gavon had to remain behind because of his leg injury. He'd been quite vocal in his disapproval of their scheme, demanding they wait until he was better. He'd retired to his bed and could be heard swearing vociferously at the healer who'd arrived to dress his wound.

Liu joined them, clad once again in the ridiculous acrobat's outfit, with his hair darkened and sticking out in all directions. As they exited through a side door, Saric appeared. He wore a smaller version of Liu's costume. When Corin frowned, he gave back an irrepressible grin.

'You're short a man.' The boy turned a series of backflips on the street outside. 'And I'm useful.'

Corin snorted. 'You're short, but not a man, kid. Go home.'

Saric sauntered alongside. 'Make me.'

Not in the mood to argue with a ten-year-old, Corin shrugged and watched Alere hurry ahead into the evening gloom. 'Your neck, kid. Don't get in my way.'

'Funny,' Saric said, skipping to keep up with the adults' longer strides. 'I was going to say the same thing to you. Meet you there. I'll do some scouting.' He ducked into a narrow side alley, and vanished into the night without a sound.

'Is that kid always such a pain?' Corin growled.

Liu laughed. 'Oh yes, but you do have a way of bringing out the worst in him.'

To the north, a rumble of thunder and a distant flicker of lightning signalled the approach of the thunderstorm that had brooded on the horizon all day. Fitful breezes gusted, bringing the smell of rain on earth. Clouds tumbled over each other like barking doquan puppies, piling high into the dimming sky. Lightning flashed white-purple in their depths. Probably an hour at the most, before it hit. Maybe less. Great. Not only did he get to stand outside, waiting while Alere risked her life, now he had to do it in the rain. Oh joy.

They arrived at Hallon's house without incident after deliberately taking a route to avoid the most popular eating and market areas. In the street opposite Hallon's compound, they paused in the shadows and watched the front gate. Once more the house blazed with light, and the sound of laughter floated from within.

Light rain had fallen that afternoon, a precursor to the front rolling in now. The cobbles were slick, and shiny with golden reflections from lanterns fixed to the wall and house. The scent of roasting meats wafted out into the street, reminding Corin he hadn't eaten for several hours. That meal had been little more than bread, cheese and vile green wine again.

Saric appeared from nowhere and gave them a cheerful greeting. 'Nothing strange. Guests are all here. The other entertainers are waiting around the corner.'

'Good, signal them.' Liu inspected the street. 'Let's go.'

Corin grabbed Liu's arm, dragging him close. 'You make sure she gets out or, I swear, this will become more painful than you bargained for, old man.'

Liu waited in cool, amused silence, until Corin let go. Without deigning to reply, he ran lightly across the street, leaving Kett and Corin in the shadows. Alere followed, her skirts fluttering about her ankles.

Corin spat out a curse.

Kett said simply, 'Yes' and relaxed against the brick wall beside him, intent on the building across the road.

The first drops of rain splashed on Corin's head and dribbled down his neck.

CHAPTER TWENTY-FOUR

ALERE

Heart pounding, Alere followed Liu across the road, where they were joined by four others in the purple. Genuine entertainers, she assumed. Liu rounded his shoulders and dropped into a half-scuttling, sideways walk. He became Porro, the flustered, disorganised, cheerful acrobat. At the gate, he fussed about presenting their entertainers' invitation. Then they were ushered inside by a bored-looking mhareb. At the front door, Denna greeted them with that same piercing scrutiny. After a moment's heart-stopping hesitation, she waved them brusquely towards the great dining room.

In the short distance between the door and the dining hall, Alere eased herself into a shadowed corner. Porro ignored her. He greeted a house-slave loudly, talking at great speed about his plans for the evening and leading the way into the event. The others were obliged to follow him, like the straggling tail to an agitated comet.

Alere glided along the hall to the back stairs. According the Shasa's map they led directly up to the second floor and emerged close to the guest quarters. Shasa had earlier sent a message to say Rohne, Mina and Jarran would not be attending the function. They should be in their rooms. That would make things easier.

Now the main variable was Rhone. Was he paying close attention to Mina's Outers? Was he warding or controlling her, still? Alere couldn't risk checking in case she tipped him off too early. Timing was everything.

At the base of the broad, zitanwood stairs she paused, ears straining. So far, so good. But kitchen staff had to pass this point to serve the dining hall with food, so she'd best hurry. She sprinted up the stairs, sticking to the extreme sides of the risers and leaning on the handrail to prevent betraying creaks.

At the top, she crouched low and peeked around the corner. Leaning back against the wall again, she processed what she'd seen. Four doors on the western side: three along the hallway and one at the extreme end. Three guest rooms and the master bedroom, if Shasa was telling the truth. Jarran and Mina should be in the one next to the master. Rohne right next door. The final room belonged to Hallon's wife. Posted between Mina's and Rohne's rooms, a mhareb drooped on his chair, visibly fighting the sag of heavy eyelids.

Below Alere, someone opened the servants' door to the dining hall. Golden revelry escaped into the bleak, grey back of the house. A serving-boy carried trays, teetering with empty plates, into the kitchen. If he looked up, he would see her. She relaxed. Tension was as much of a betrayer as movement. The kitchen door closed behind him, cutting off a comment both innocent and frightening.

'You lied Brettan, that dancer's not here again tonight, more's the pi—'

If Denna heard such gossip at the front door, a search would be mounted. Time to move.

She drew a short tube, courtesy of Liu, from her hip-belt and telescoped it open. From her hair she produced two green-feathered darts. Fitting one into the tube, she held the other ready. The distance was daunting and the blow-pipe far from her favourite weapon, but there were no other options. Pursing her lips, she lay down on her side. The stairs dug into her ribs and shoulder, but she ignored the discomfort and concentrated. She slid the pipe slowly around the corner, angling it upward and taking careful aim.

Phuut. The dart flew true and embedded into the mhareb's fleshy thigh. A much easier target than the neck. The istilqa would act more slowly, though, which was a problem. The guard gasped, leaned forward and plucked the dart free. Alere loaded and shot again. This time it lodged in his neck. He gargled and scrabbled at his throat. His eyes glazed and he slumped in the seat, the first dart falling to tinkle loudly on the timber floor.

Alere froze, awaiting an outcry. Nothing. She rose and ghosted along the hall, treading on the boards closest to the wall. Shasa had warned of several nightingale centre-boards, rigged to creak loudly if trodden on.

The sleeping mhareb twitched as she collected the darts. She wiped away the bead of blood on his neck and murmured a suggestion to forget. She tried the door handle. Locked. Hardly surprising. Shasa had provided a spare key, which turned with no more than a faint *click.* With a quick glance down the hall, Alere slipped inside, closed and locked the door again.

Behind her, a stifled gasp and flicker of movement. A fist flew at her face. She grabbed the arm, turned, twisted and dropped her assailant to the floor. She wrenched on an armlock and knelt on his back, her dagger to his throat.

No. He couldn't possibly be mhareb. Not unless Hallon's men now wore orange silk robes on duty.

'Don't hurt him!'

The plea made her look up, into the desperate eyes of her sister. Alere leapt free, putting space between herself and her assailant in case she was wrong about who he was. The man on the floor rolled over, massaging his arm. Fury knitted dark brows over deep-set gold-brown eyes. Mina crouched beside him, running her hands over his arm. He scrambled to his feet, eyes widening as he inspected Alere in her ridiculous outfit.

Somewhere in his mid twenties, he stood a good head taller than herself, with the broad shoulders and muscular arms of a warrior. Or a baker. Even wearing the gaudy house-robe, he exuded strength and competence. His dark brown hair was tied back into a short, blunt-cut mawei. A man more concerned with practicality than appearances.

'Mina, it's me.' She yanked down the veil. 'Jarran, I assume? Rafi sent me to get you both back.'

Jarran watched her with intelligent wariness. He was, undoubtedly, Radan Zah-Hill's son. The resemblance was uncanny, though his angular jaw had a strength and firmness that had been lacking in his father.

Her sister peered around Jarran, her expression shifting from fear to joy. Tears shimmered in her eyes. She threw herself into Alere's arms, sobbing. Alere held her tightly for a moment then, pried herself free and held her sister at arm's length. They had little time.

'Are you alright? Is Rohne holding you in thrall?'

Mina's eyes were reddened and cheeks tear-streaked. She held out a hand to Jarran. He softened and allowed her to draw the three of them together.

'We're alright. But I don't understand what's happening.' She clung to Jarran and to Alere. 'One minute we were on the chuan to Madina. Next, we were in the hold of that slave ship. Rohne wouldn't tell me anything. Wouldn't explain what was happening. Wouldn't let me speak with you. Then we were here and he was somehow...' she shuddered '...in my head, controlling my body. All I could do was watch from the inside. Why is he doing this? *How* is he?' Her voice rose into hysteria.

Alere shushed her, glancing at the door apprehensively. The guard was under with only a small dose. Enough to keep him out for ten minutes at the most.

'I don't have time to explain.' She willed her sister to comply. 'Please. We only have a few minutes. If you want to get out of here, you *must* do exactly as I say. Will you trust me?'

Mina drew a slow, shuddering breath and visibly pulled herself together. 'Yes. What do we do?'

Alere threw off her cloak and shed her costume, explaining in quiet, rapidfire words as she did so. She wore little beneath but underwear, breast-binder, yanstones, and a knife strapped to her thigh. Jarran flushed and faced the door.

Mina gaped at her in appalled non-comprehension. Alere growled, yanked the turquoise blue house-robe from her sister's body, and man-handled her into the costume.

'But I can't do that,' Mina protested, her voice muffled as Alere dragged the bodice over her head, tugged it into place over her breasts and tightened the front lacings.

Next, she dropped the skirts to Mina's hips and fastened the belt with adrenalin-shaken fingers. Too slow. Any minute the mhareb would waken outside the door and they would all three be stuck here.

'You *can*,' Alere said. 'All you have to do is walk down the stairs and to the dining hall entrance. You'll find a short man in a red and purple acrobat costume waiting for you. With a young blond boy. Then you stroll out the front door. You have no scars on your feet, I do. So, they have no proof you're the girl they took from the chuan. Kett is out there, waiting to take you to safety.'

'But what about Jarran?' Mina protested.

Ignoring the question, Alere clipped her own cloak around her sister's shoulders, shoved sandals on her feet and fixed the veil over her nose and mouth. She used a few copper hairpins to twist Mina's dyed blonde hair up into a knot, hiding the black regrowth and mimicking the style of Alere's blonde wig. Alere kept the wig in place to improve the chances of the substitution going unnoticed, should anything go wrong.

She shivered at the thought and concentrated on her task. Pulling the stub of a kohl pencil and a small piece of dried white clay from her breast-binder, she marked Mina's eyes and added the marital status dots. Then she wiped her own face clear of makeup when she was done.

Finished at last, Alere checked Mina over and was satisfied. It wasn't perfect, but it would do. Hopefully enough to fool Denna. Next, she threw on Mina's robe and stowed away the blowpipe and two remaining darts as best she could.

'You can turn around,' she informed Jarran. He did so, gaping at the transformation.

'You understand?' she asked him.

'Yes. She'll be safe?' His voice was deep and mellow.

Alere sent Mina an impatient glare. 'If she leaves right now. The guard will be awake any second. Please, Mina.' She grasped her sister's hands. 'This is our only chance. Jarran and I have to leave a different way. The servant at the front door would know Jarran hadn't come in that way. If they stop us, she would find the scars on his feet and mine. Please, go now.'

Mina glanced at Jarran, who nodded. He pulled her into a quick hug and kissed her troubled brow before holding her away again.

'Go. I'll join you soon, I promise.' He had the intensity of a goal-driven man. A good person to have onside and a good person to have as Jun First.

Mina shivered, her eyes huge, the veil fluttering over her lips. Alere unlocked the door and peered out. The mhareb slept but he twitched. A sure sign he was coming around.

They eased into the corridor and Alere relocked the door, tucking the key into her breast-binder. She pointed Mina in the right direction and gave her a shove. With a frightened look at Jarran, Mina wrapped the cloak close about her body and tiptoed along the edge of the hall, as Alere had instructed. She disappeared around the top of the stairs at the same time as the mhareb gave a faint groan.

Alere jerked her head at Jarran. They covered the short distance to the master bedroom door. The second spare key from Shasa opened it. A rapid survey put Alere in possession of the room layout. She ran to the large, street-facing window in the bedroom's western side. Thick, blood-red velvet curtains obscured any hint of light from the street. She shifted one curtain so she could see the street gate below. Jarran arrived beside her. For a big man he could move quietly.

'Has she left?' His voice was soft in her ear, his breath tickling the hairs on her neck.

She shook her head. Opening her mind, she reached for Corin through the stones. His relief was almost palpable and she had to cut through it.

Cor, be ready. She should be coming out any moment.

We are. What about you?

We're in place. Won't be long. Make sure you get her away as fast as possible, as far as possible. I don't want Rohne taking control of her again. I'm hoping distance will attenuate his ability.

We'll wait for you.

You'll jiche-well go, Corin. Don't wait. Leave Saric to guide us if you must, but get her away. And watch your back. This has been too easy.

There was a long, anger-tinged silence. Had she pushed him too far? Now was not the time to worry about his ego.

Lightning flashed and a gleam caught her eye. The bracelets! The fake yanstones were still on her wrists. Would Denna notice and stop Mina to question her? Alere's heartrate tripled and she held her breath.

The wait seemed interminable. Jarran shifted beside her, pushing the curtain further back. Alere yanked it from his hand.

'She should be out by now,' he whispered.

'Shut up. The mhareb might hear you.'

Below, the street-gate opened and Liu, Saric and Mina emerged. They walked briskly across the street towards the alley where Corin and Kett waited. As her sister disappeared into the darkness, Alere released the breath held captive in her chest by anxiety. Mina was safe. The knot of tension that had twisted in her stomach for the last two weeks, finally loosened. She would not lose her sister. She swallowed the unexpected tears clouding her vision. Silver-gilt warmth and approval flickered from the yanstones around her hips; slithered under her skin, into her heart.

Time for celebrations later. Mina might be away, but Jarran was not.

Turning from the window she gave Jarran a bright smile to hide the anxiety that fluttered her belly and slicked her palms.

'Our turn.' She gestured at the window set into the southern wall, next to the bed.

The room was massive and opulently-masculine; decorated in deep reds and rich golds, with heavy carved wooden furniture. The central feature was the blackwood bed on a dais next to the window. The room was clearly meant to intimidate any woman brought here. There were restraint loops bolted to the wall on either side of the bed head. Alere found it confronting, even with her training in jiaoji techniques. No wonder Hallon's wife slept in the third guest room.

Jarran cleared his throat. His cheeks reddened. She took pity on him and led the way to the window. Flipping up the silken quilt covering the bed, she found a coil of thin rope on the floor where Shasa had said it would be. The thick bed-leg would make an ideal anchor. She tied off the rope and tugged on the knot. Checking outside, she dropped the end out.

'It's about two bodylengths short of the ground,' she whispered. 'Be careful about how you land. Bend your knees and roll. It's raining so the rope will be slippery. Go.'

He peered out into the downpour then hesitated. 'You should go first.'

Alere pointed to herself. 'Jun-Second Heir rescuer with no children and with weapons.' She indicated him. 'Jun-First rescuee with children and with no weapons. Stop being chivalrous. You're wasting time and it's not necessary. Your daughters are fine, by the way. They're safe in Madina.'

Jarran laughed softly, his intensity lightening into humour. 'I begin to see what Mina said about you is true. Very well. Under protest, though. And thank you, Mina told me you'd found the girls.'

'I like a man who doesn't argue with me.' It would be interesting to know how her sister had described her.

'When you're down,' she said, as he gathered up the rope and swung his legs over the sill, 'don't wait. Head straight across the street to the alley opposite. Walk like you belong and have a purpose – head up, shoulders back. Ignore the mharebi at the front gate. Saric – that blond boy I mentioned – will be waiting for you. He'll guide you to safety. I'll be right behind you.'

The rope was too thin and would be pulled too tight by his weight for her to go at the same time. She had to wait until he was on the ground.

She checked the room again. Unease prickled at the back of her skull. A black-lacquered box, sitting open on a set of drawers beyond the window, caught her eye. The Koh-Lin bracelets. She hissed at Jarran and he stopped, lifting his face, rain dripping off his chin. Snatching the real bracelets, she replaced them with the two fake ones she'd forgotten to give to Mina. They were almost identical. Leaning out the window, she dropped the real ones into Jarran's outstretched hand and instructed him to give them to Mina. He put them between his teeth and lowered himself down the sheer wall.

Alere kept half an ear out for footsteps in the hall and an eye on the alley below to make sure no random passerby saw Jarran, stranded halfway up the wall. Twice she twanged the rope to signal him to stop as someone wandered past. Luckily, they were drunken partygoers who could probably barely see their own feet as they stumbled through puddles and laughed uproariously at the splashes.

Finally, he was at the rope's end. He dangled for a moment before dropping to the ground and rolling neatly to his feet. He scanned the alley and gave her a wave. She swung a leg over the sill, preparing to follow. She gestured for him to leave. After a moment's hesitation he did so, though he glanced back several times. The rain thickened to a deluge, making it impossible to even see the other side of the street. Lightning arced overhead, sizzling through the air, tasting of ozone. Thunder rolled a second later.

Cor? She sent him a swift thought as vague uneasiness spiked into fullblown awareness of danger close by. *I know you're still there. Jarran's heading your way. Get him to safety. And tell me Mina is gone.*

Gaisi, woman, you're impossible. I see him. Yes, Kett took Mina back to the warehouse. She's safe. Where are *you?*

Coming. But she could tell he didn't believe her. *He has the Koh-Lin bracelets. Take them and watch him. If you think Rohne's controlling either him or Mina, sedate them and get them the diyu away.*

What? Where are you?

She cut the connection as a babble of angry voices broke out in the hall. Footsteps sounded. She eased over the edge and lowered herself. The doorhandle rattled and turned.

Jiche! She'd forgotten to lock it.

CHAPTER TWENTY-FOUR

The bedroom door flew open and crashed against the stone wall. A rough voice ordered a search of the room. Alere clung to the rope, afraid to keep moving lest the rope's motion draw their attention.

Her fingers and forearms ached, muscles burning. With all her weight suspended on her hands, the thin rope cut deep into her fingers. The coarse sandstone wall scraped against her arm and frayed at the rope where it fell over the windowsill. She twitched her legs, wrapping the rope around one foot and anchoring it with the other, taking some of her weight there. Rain pounded on her head and ran down her neck, cold and unpleasant. The silk robe clung to her skin. She rested her cheek against her forearm and focussed on the harsh sound of her own breath. Anything but the cutting pain in her hands.

Alere? It was Corin in her head again. She shut him out.

A voice raised in surprise dashed her hopes. They'd found the rope. Putting more weight on her feet, she unwound one hand, drew out the blowpipe and darts, and dropped them. They were most obvious clue she wasn't Mina. After a moment's hesitation, she also discarded the knife in its thigh-sheath. She couldn't bear to drop the yanstones for fear they might shatter. She should have given them to Jarran or Mina.

The one weapon she had left was a tiny, jewelled knife wound deep into her wig. Well-enough hidden it would escape a cursory inspection. Apart from that, her last recourse was the tiny sac of watu poison stitched into the lining of her breast-binder.

The rope shuddered and slipped through her grip. She clung tightly. The ground was a long way below. Even if she'd started down the moment she'd climbed over the sill, she wouldn't have made it more than halfway.

'Very brave, shunu.' A smooth bass voice dropped from above. 'But not very intelligent.'

Hallon's harshly-lined face peered at her from an unflattering, upside-down perspective. He signalled to someone and the rope jerked, hauling her upward. Stone scraped at her arm, tearing skin. She twisted, bumping off the wall until she could get her toes beneath her body and half-walk up the surface. Hands grasped her arms and dragged her over the windowsill. She fell, gasping, onto the smooth floor, the rope still twisted around her fingers. Someone unwound it and tingling pain followed as blood returned.

'Start searching for Jarran,' Hallon barked at his men. 'He can't have gone far, barefoot and in a house-robe.' He eyed her disdainfully. She huddled on the floor, dripping and shivering. 'We will find him, girl, even if we have to raze the city to do so. If you know where he's gone, you'd best tell me now and save innocent lives. Don't doubt me. I will *kill* every man, woman and child who shelters him. You're a healer, surely that has to mean something to you?'

He wrapped large hands around her arms, hoisting her upright. Her face was level with his, his wine and meat-scented breath hot on her cheek. His nails dug into the soft flesh under her arms.

'Where *is he?*' Hallon shook her until her head rocked.

Alere gasped, acting frightened and cowed, allowing tears to gather and fall. Her best hope lay in convincing Hallon he still had Mina, gentle and compliant, in his grip. Mina, second kin-child to Rafi, was of far less strategic value than was Alere-Lianna, Jun-Heir.

'I…I don't know!' She moaned. 'The door opened and the guard was asleep. We heard the party and thought maybe one of your guests had opened the door. We came into this room and…' She glanced at the bed, letting her words be interrupted with sobs. 'Jarran found the rope. I made him go first. I don't know where he is. I don't. Please.'

'Bah!' Hallon thrust her away and she collapsed to the floor, hiding her face and watching him through her fingers. With any luck, he would suspect one of his guests and blame his own stupidity in leaving the rope under his bed.

His mharebi hoisted her up. She didn't struggle, but merely begged and cried, as they thrust her back into the guest bedroom. The door clicked shut and the lock snicked. Outside Hallon questioned, then berated, the mhareb on duty. There was a frightened protest, a slick, organic sound, followed by the thud of something heavy falling to the floor. A shadow fell across the gap beneath the door. A dribble of blood. Footsteps retreated, dragging something.

She was left alone. Soaked, bruised, and shaking with cold.

A quick search of the bathroom and cupboards produced towels and a dry robe, but no real clothing. She threw the sodden robe aside, dried off and dressed, winding the little knife back into the bedraggled wig when she was done. Able to think clearly again, she considered her situation and found it grim.

Outside, the rain eased. She moved to the barred window and peered into the darkness. Lightning flashed and illuminated a street swarming with mharebi. Had the others made it to safety?

Corin? She reached for him but found nothing. *Cor?* The mental space where he had been, only minutes before, was empty.

He wasn't warding, he was simply gone.

CORIN

Corin swore eloquently when Alere cut their thought-connection. Jarran hurried across the road, garish robe flapping and clinging to his legs. Saric emerged from the shadows and ushered him to Corin. Luckily, the mharebi at the gate were transfixed by a gaggle of half a dozen barely-clad unveiled jiaoji hurrying past the house.

Corin gave Jarran a nod of recognition. The man shivered, drenched and ridiculous in the thin orange robe. Corin shrugged out of his leather jacket and swung it around Jarran's shoulders, ignoring his protest.

'After the trouble Alere's gone to to get you out, I doubt she'd be happy if you died of a lung infection. She's already killed one Jun First,' he said acerbically. 'How far is she behind you?' He hunched his shoulders against the rain, huddling close to the building to get beneath the narrow eaves. It didn't work.

'The rope wouldn't hold both of us,' Jarran said. 'She insisted I go first and she's a hard lady to argue with.'

'You're telling me. Still, she should have been on the ground by now. I can't see through this rain. Saric, will you go see if the rope's still hanging from the window.'

The boy dashed across the road, into the side alley and vanished into the gloom. Moments later he was back, panting and shaking off rain like a small xiao-kitten. He held a blowpipe and the basic thigh-sheathed bronze dagger Alere had taken with her.

'Not there. These were under the window. By the sounds of Hallon's yelling, he's found Jarran's missing. We need to get out of here.' He pointed at the house front gate. 'He's sending search parties out.'

Corin swore again as the gate opened. A squad of thirty mharebi assembled, barely visible in the uneven light of sheltered mel-oil lamps fixed to the wall. Their leader, Shasa, gave instructions at the top of her voice. She pointed to the directions she wanted the mharebi to begin; undoubtedly trying to warn Corin and Jarran if they were still in the area.

'I'm not leaving Alere,' Corin snapped. 'I don't care if you're heir to the whole gaisi world, Jarran. Saric can lead you to safety.'

'Not a chance,' Saric retorted. 'She's my friend, too. I'm not going anywhere.'

'Nor I,' Jarran said. 'I feel guilty enough about going first. Mina would never forgive me if I left her sister in captivity while I went free. Is Mina safe?'

Corin's respect for Jarran went down a notch. What on Kalima did that girl have to attract men? Personally, he found Mina sweet but on the dull side. 'Kett got her away.'

Relief swept across Jarran's craggy face. Corin eyed the man curiously. Had Rafi informed Jarran of his half-brother's existence? Was he aware of Mina's infatuation with Kett?

'Right. Since we're all in this together...' Corin caught Saric's attention. 'Kid, you're up. You know the lay of the land best. Run or hide? We'll also need a weapon for Jarran.' He took in the man's broad shoulders and strong hands. 'Sword?'

'If you can find one. I'm better with a karambit, though.' Jarran swung his hand in an arc at throat height. 'It's a knife. They use them in Adeghal, where my mother was born. But even a rolling pin will do. I've had a lot of practice with them.' His golden-brown eyes sparkled with self-deprecating humour and Corin liked him better for it.

Saric checked the street. 'Even the alleys around here are too open and wide. They'll see anyone running. Hiding's our best bet for now. Follow me.'

He ran to the alley's end and ducked around the corner. He tried the handle to a stout, silvered timber door set two steps below street level. It was locked. Pulling two thin pieces of what seemed to be actual steel from within his clothing, he inserted them into the brass lock.

Corin posted himself at the building's corner and peered back the way they'd come. A lantern bobbed in the rain, surrounded by a halo of glowing water. Two mharebi walked directly towards them, only moments away. He drew his sword and stepped in front of Jarran, shielding him from view.

'Any time now, kid.'

'Got it.' The boy pushed the door open.

They slipped inside and shut the door quietly. Saric re-locked it by touch, the tumblers loud in the darkness.

The room was cold, ink black and without sound. What sort of building was it? Corin pictured the outside: two storey, sandstone, red-tinted sulcrete mortar, with a slate-tiled roof. A private house, most likely. They had probably entered some sort of back storage room or servants' entrance. A musty, soapy smell, and a faint drip-drip of water pervaded. Maybe a storage room for cleaning products, or perhaps a laundry. Should be safe enough for a while.

Footsteps approached on the cobbles and paused outside the door. The three held their breath in the darkness. The handle rattled and a short discussion ensued between the mharebi. One argued that a locked door meant no-one could be in there. The other stated pedantically that the master had ordered a full house-to-house search. The first won and the footsteps retreated moments later.

Saric sighed exaggeratedly. An almighty crash of metal on stone pounded against Corin's eardrums. He jumped, heart lodging in his throat. Saric swore. He must have knocked something over. Outside, the footsteps returned, running this time. The mharebi shouted for help. More footsteps approached.

'Khara,' Corin muttered as the handle rattled again. A thump against the wood tested the frame's strength. 'Find us a way out.'

'I'm s-sorry,' the boy squeaked and Corin didn't have the heart to berate him.

'Never mind, kid. Just get us out. Let's start with light.'

There was a scraping sound and a spark jumped into a tiny flicker of flame as Saric lit a little tinder kit. He held the light high. The door rattled again. More shouting. More feet splashing and running. Lights flickered beneath the ill-fitting door.

A feeble, yellowish light came to life overhead. Saric had found the switch for a lone bulb dangling from the low ceiling.

Corin groaned. 'This is what I get for not planning the exit strategy better.'

The room was a long-disused laundry turned storage room. The stone walls and floor were thick with grey mildew. A pile of haphazardly-stacked furniture lay at the base of the only other exit: a narrow, rotting flight of steps leading up to a trapdoor in the ceiling. A leaking copper tap dripped into two large stone tubs standing against one wall. The whole room was no more than five paces in each direction and barely over head height. Corin ducked instinctively. He and Jarran had been lucky not to crack their heads on the support beams.

Outside, the shouts and thumping redoubled, the noise deafening in the small space. The door frame made ominous splintering noises.

Saric scrambled nimbly over the pile of furniture and pushed against the trapdoor.

'No good. Bolted from the outside. Sorry Corin, I thought it would be open. This room was still in use when I was last here a year ago.' He seemed, for the first time since they'd met, genuinely contrite and frightened.

Resigned to the inevitable, Corin drew his swords and addressed Saric. 'You hide behind the furniture, kid. They're not hunting for you. When they leave, go tell Kett what happened.'

He checked the Jun-Heir, relieved to find him calm. Jarran picked up a chair and coolly snapped off two legs, twirling them experimentally.

'Not the way I envisioned dying,' Jarran said conversationally.

Corin snorted. 'Don't worry, they won't kill *you*, unless it's by accident – or if you wave those gaisi sticks at them. You'll be put back in your nice comfy guest room until Rafi sends someone else to rescue or ransom you.'

'Will he, do you think?' Jarran's tone held a sliver of doubt.

'He sent us, didn't he?' Where had that question come from? Had Rafi done anything to warrant Jarran's mistrust?

The door shuddered again. What annoyed Corin most – apart from dying – was that his family heirloom swords would now end up in the hands of an arrogant saafil hundan like Hallon. He'd meant to, one day, have a family – a son or daughter to give them to. Well, that was clearly doomed to failure as a life-plan. There had to be a dozen or more mharebi out there. He couldn't count on Shasa being one of them, or being able to step in and save him if he came out swinging.

'Wait!' Saric leapt onto the floor and heaved an upside-down table aside. He pointed eagerly. 'What about that?'

Corin followed his finger, hopes rising, only to be dashed again. Set into the floor was a square timber grate, half-rotted and slimy. By the sounds of rushing water, the hole opened into the storm drains running beneath the city. But the entrance was too narrow for either him or Jarran to squeeze through.

The doorframe bulged and twisted. The door creaked under repeated impacts. One or two more and the ancient timber would give way.

Corin made a quick, easy decision. 'You go, kid. And take these.' He sheathed his weapons and handed them, belt and all, to

Saric. 'They might not kill me if I'm unarmed. Drop yours, too, Jarran. Prisoners is better than dead.'

He bent over so he was level with Saric. 'These blades are family to me, Saric. I'm trusting you.' He tugged the cover off one pommel and pointed to the yanstones. 'Worth more than all our lives combined.'

Saric's green-grey eyes lit up. 'Why not just use them like Alere did in the alley yesterday? Bring the lightning.'

'What?' Corin frowned. 'She didn't do that. It was pure luck that lightning struck those men attacking her. There was a storm, remember?'

Saric's jaw hardened. 'You're wrong. I know what I saw.'

Corin hesitated, then shook his head. 'No time to argue. Get them to Kett as fast as you can. He'll know what to do with them. Tell him what's happened and tell him I'll be waiting to hear from him.' Corin gripped Saric's thin shoulder. 'With this rain there'll be a lot of water in that drain soon, so don't stay long. Be safe.'

'I will. You…well, don't get yourself killed, alright? Alere likes you.'

'Wait.' Jarran rummaged in his robe and came up with Alere's bracelets. He handed them to the boy, who gaped in astonished avarice. 'These belong to Alere. She said to give them to Mina.'

Saric nodded, his expression firming into determination.

The dim bulb popped, plunging them darkness. Saric swore inventively. Corin felt his way to the grate and yanked it out. He found Saric's hand and lowered him into the unseen depths below. He let go. There was an almighty splash, some coughing then Saric gave the all-clear and sloshed off westward. Corin replaced the grate. He had to be insane. He'd entrusted a fortune in iron and yanstones to a thieving kid he'd known for a day. Smiling ruefully, he faced the door.

It exploded inward in a shower of wood splinters and men.

Lanterns shone and rain spattered into the room. Swords appeared at their throats, the arms holding them shortened for the thrust. Big, angry mharebi, smelling of sweat and damp leather, blocked the doorway.

'We surrender,' Corin yelled, raising his hands high. 'We surrender.'

CHAPTER TWENTY-SIX

ALERE

For a nerve-wracking hour, Alere paced the luxurious bedchamber, growing more and more anxious and frustrated. The room provided no opportunities for escape. No secret doors, no ceiling airvents, no trapdoors under rugs. The keys were still nestled against her breast, but there was no point going that way. In fact, keeping the keys on her was a bad idea. She hunted for a hiding place, settling finally on the flat top of the square timber pillar holding up the canopy over the bed. People rarely checked high when they searched.

She considered using the yanstones to subdue the guards. A quick sweep of the minds outside showed Hallon had eight posted at her door and several more on the stairs. Her skills with the stones were too limited. One or two, maybe. There was no way she could be sure of overcoming them all, quickly enough. One alarm call would bring every mhareb in the place down on her.

She tested the bronze bars on the window. Firm. A twisted wet towel might bend them, but the wall beneath was sheer and dropped straight into the heavily-guarded front courtyard. Surveying the street provided no new information. The mharebi sent out to search for Jarran now strolled back into the compound, laughing and chatting. Did that mean they'd found him? Had she missed seeing him brought back?

In vain she tried to connect with Mina, Kett, Gavon or Corin through the stones. From Mina and Kett she met only wards that did not drop when she probed. They weren't listening for her and the distance decreased her strength. She couldn't get through their wards. Gavon's mind was an incoherent mess of pain and heat, his thoughts rambling and impossible to decipher. He must be feverish from his injury. After trying to soothe him, Alere withdrew for fear of being pulled into Fusion with the chaos in his head.

From Corin she got only blank nothingness. Not even the flickers of dream-Outers that often seeped through cracks in a sleeping person's wards. Surely, she would feel his death so he must be either deeply unconscious or drugged. She held tight to that hope. He had to be alive. But if Corin was captured, and Jarran with him, they were back to square one.

Once, in sheer desperation, she even tried Rohne, only to find the same absence of consciousness. If he were also drugged, that would explain why he hadn't made his presence felt during the rescue. Which could mean Rohne was not here voluntarily. Maybe, if he knew Mina was safe, he might be persuaded into an alliance to help Alere and Jarran. But there was no way of being sure without speaking to him.

Finally, tired to trying to wrap her head around potential scenarios, Alere sank crosslegged onto the bed's multicoloured silk quilt. Setting her back straight and laying her hands in her lap, she sought for peace in meditation. She'd never been good at it. Kett had long since given up encouraging her to master the skill. Now was as good a time as any. It was that or chewing her fingernails.

She had no sooner settled into a rhythm of slow breaths when the door handle jiggled and a rough male voice warned her to stay clear. She yanked the small knife from her hair and jumped off the bed, standing several steps from the door with the blade behind her back.

The door flew open, hitting the wall with a thud that ensured the space behind was empty. Jarran stumbled into the room. A burly mhareb, with a scornful sneer and a loaded crossbow, pulled the door closed again. The Jun-Heir dropped to his knees, spitting blood onto the expensive silk rug. His orange robe hung loose, bloodstained and torn. Over it he wore Corin's dark green quarn-goat leather jacket.

Alere ran to his side and hauled him to his feet. He swayed, blinking at her, one eye already swelling. A cut spilled more blood onto his cheek and into a mouth reddened and puffy.

'Mina?' His mumbled exclamation was a mix of relief, joy and regret. His shoulders slumped. 'No, you're...'

'Shhh,' she warned. 'The guard may be listening. Lie down and let me help.'

He collapsed onto the bed and rolled onto his back with a groan. Finding a small hand towel, she wet it in the bathroom and wiped the blood from his face. He flinched and grabbed at her wrist.

'Definitely not Mina,' he murmured.

Alere bridled then continued wiping, more gently. 'She has her skills, I have mine. She tends to use hers to patch people up after I've used mine to break them.' She forced a grin, trying to distract him from the pain. 'We make a good team.'

He chuckled and grimaced, clutching at his ribs. 'Don't make me laugh. It hurts.'

'What did they do?' She opened the front of his robe, noting with dismay the darkening bruises on chest and stomach. Hopefully they hadn't ruptured liver or kidneys. She prodded the ribs, noting a soft spot and a sharp gasp from Jarran.

'Couple of fractured ribs,' she said briskly. 'Split lip and cheek.' Taking the cloth away she wrung it out in the bathroom and returned to sit on the bed. She lay the cloth over his eye and cheek. 'Nothing that won't heal in a few days, although you'll have a scar without stitches. Well,' she conceded, 'the ribs may take awhile.'

He groaned faintly and shoved himself into a half-sitting position, peering at her through his one good eye. 'I prefer Mina's bedside manner as well.'

Alere grabbed a dry robe out of a drawer.

'Here. Change so you don't die of a lung infection. Rafi would be annoyed at me if I killed off another Jun First.'

Jarran chuckled and groaned again as he shed the dripping, torn orange silk and dried off. 'Funny, that's exactly what Corin said about you.'

Alere checked the pockets of Corin's jacket but found nothing. She buried her face in it and breathed in his scent, then tossed it aside and moved restlessly to the window again.

'Is Corin alright?' He had to be. Her heart stuttered at the thought of him captured and in pain.

'He was with me. They took him, too.'

Alere leaned her head against the bars and clenched her teeth. He couldn't be dead. She stared blankly out the window. The rain had stopped and the glistening streets were populated only by late night revellers and unveiled jiaoji soliciting trade. Jarran joined her, limping and towelling his hair dry.

'I'm sorry,' he said quietly. 'We wrecked your escape plan and got Corin taken prisoner. But thank you for getting Mina out.'

'Don't thank me, yet,' she warned, not missing the possessive note to his voice when he spoke of Mina. 'I still don't know if she's truly safe. Where did they take Corin? What happened to Saric? Was there a man named Kett with Corin?'

He winced, touching his cheek. 'Corin said Kett had taken Mina back to a warehouse.'

Alere sank into a chair, relief washing some of her fear away and turning her knees soft. So Corin hadn't lied about Kett getting Mina away. She covered her face, needing a moment to get control of herself again. She hadn't realised she was so worried about both of them, until she wasn't any longer. Well, not as much, anyway.

'Saric escaped into a storm drain when we were trapped in a building.' Jarran grimaced. 'Corin was knocked unconscious almost straight away.' He pointed to his bruises. 'This was an attempt to find out who else was helping us.'

She opened her mouth to explain and he cut her off.

'I'd rather not know, if you don't mind. If I don't know, I can't tell.'

'Makes sense. Where did they take Cor?'

Stretching, he sucked a quick breath and pressed at his ribs. His mawei-tie had fallen out and his hair hung in wet tendrils.

'They took us both out to the slave compound, so I guess he's still there. I assume they'll work on him when he wakes.'

A faint touch on her Outer wards brought Alere to her feet, hand out to stop Jarran from speaking. She concentrated, waiting. There, again: someone tried to connect with her. But who? To find out she would need to drop her Outers, as the contact was indistinct. It was either Rohne playing tricks, or someone at a distance or lacking in strength or experience – like Kett or Mina. She'd have to take a risk.

...?

Alere? Kett's mind, loaded concern, relief and affection, flooded into her Outers like an embrace. For a moment she said nothing, too overwhelmed to speak. She sank back into the chair and let the connection with him wrap around her from the inside out. Even though he held her firmly in the shallowest part of his Outers, the solid warmth and closeness of him brought her to the brink of tears, for some strange reason. Kett and Mina were both safe. She could handle anything now.

You're alright? she finally managed, pulling herself together.

Yes, and Mina. What happened? Saric has told us what he can.

She could feel, bubbling below his surface Outers, controlled anger and frustration at not being able to help or protect her.

Wait, she frowned, *how are you doing this?*

Amusement flickered through his worry for her. *Corin gave Saric his blades and your bracelets. I'm using the bracelets.*

You lied to Rafi about having the gene. She'd suspected, at the time, but hadn't been sure. She'd rarely known Kett to lie at all, so she'd dismissed it as her imagination. For a man who'd drummed the virtues of honesty into her, he'd certainly come up with a number of surprises recently.

Anything else I should know about? she asked, acerbically.

There was a pause before he replied. *Nothing that will help you right now. Tell me how you were captured.*

It would be useless to point out he'd not answered the question, so she replayed the evening in her head for him to see. The speed of this form of communication was phenomenal. In less than a minute he was up to date. There followed a long, thoughtful silence. She drummed her fingertips on her thighs, waiting for him to process the information. Jarran watched her in confusion. He opened his mouth. She laid a finger across her lips and tapped a finger to her temple.

If Rohne is drugged, and you'd locked the door and Suggested to the mhareb to forget, Kett said, *how did they find out so quickly that Jarran and Mina were gone?* His mental tone held suspicion and a hint of worry.

Alere stared blankly at Jarran, whose scowl betrayed bafflement and irritation. Kett was right. How had Hallon discovered the prisoners' absence so fast? An unwelcome thought nibbled at her certainty, returning no matter how often she thrust it aside as impossible.

Maybe Shasa succumbed to the brainwashing after all? I don't understand, though. Why would she play along with Liu for so many years only to betray him now?

Perhaps her role was to feed information to Hallon and the stakes weren't high enough to betray Liu, until now. There's more to this than we know: more agendas, more secrets. I think we need to assume the worst.

But why did they let Mina go?

Maybe Hallon wanted...wait...

Sharp tension blanked his Outers as he shifted his concentration to something else. Anger and worry flicked past. His thoughts settled into a cold acceptance, frightening to feel. Then he was back, calm but tightly focussed, restricting her access to his shallowest Outers.

Liu's warehouse is under attack. Hallon's mharebi.

Sick realisation twisted Alere's stomach. Shasa *had* betrayed them.

Kett broke in on her fear. *I need to get Mina and Gavon out. I'll give her the swords – yours and Corin's – and the bracelets and tell her to contact you. Saric will take her and Gavon to a safe-house Shasa doesn't know about. I'll give them and the children a chance to get clear. If you don't hear from me within two hours, then you try to reach me. If you can't, well...it's been fun, Alli.*

No! She shot to her feet and clutched at the window-bars. *Kett?*

His presence vanished, leaving her alone and bereft as never before in her life.

ROHNE

Smiling in satisfaction, Rohne swung his legs off the bed and prepared for his next step. Mina was safe enough and her part would come later. She was, at least, away from Hallon and with people who would bring her to Madina in time. For now, he was better off on his own. He could move a lot faster.

Arranging Mina's rescue had taken great delicacy. Alere's strengths grew daily and, without the yanstones, his ability to direct her thoughts was slight. Every time he connected, the pain in his head spiked, so he had to be careful. Luckily, she wasn't aware of the bond he'd established in their rapport back in Shanzhai. There may still be opportunities in the future to make use of that. Although, if things went as Hallon intended, perhaps not. He smirked.

Whatever happened to her, it didn't much matter. Hallon would keep her out of the way. She would be too preoccupied to interfere in Rohne's plans.

For now, his task here was done. Things were set in motion. Based on what he'd Seen of Alere's actions in the next day or so, it was time to move on. He had one person to see here in Chengdu, then Madina awaited.

Telekinesis opened the lock on his door. He walked, unchallenged, past the eight mharebi stationed outside the rooms. A brief foray took him into Hallon's bedroom to retrieve the bracelets. He picked them out of the box resting on the side table and snarled in disgust. Fakes. They felt wrong. There was no connection, no silver-gilt flare of power, no light into the darkest corners of his mind. Nothing.

The sound of marching feet echoed in the hall outside. Scowling, he dropped the bracelets back into the box. Alere had somehow managed to get the real ones out with Mina. Unexpected and annoyingly resourceful of her. Without the stones he could control a few mharebi, but not more than a dozen or so.

Rohne grimaced. He had no time to find the real ones, now. He could pick up more in Madina, at the Alcazar. Undoubtedly Mina would bring the bracelets with her, eventually. It was a setback, but not an insuperable one.

Moments later, standing on the street outside, he felt eyes on his back. The pale smudge of Alere's face showed in the second-storey window. Grinning, he saluted. Her mouth fell open. Still laughing, he ran into the dark alley opposite, dismissing her, focussed on his destination.

His was the power to change the course of history. To be humanity's guide. Time to make that happen.

ALERE

'Jarran!' Alere beckoned to the man urgently, until he joined her at the window. She pointed at a figure vanishing into the gloom. 'That man. Diyu, he's gone. I'm sure it was Rohne.'

Jarran peered blearily out. He'd fallen asleep and she regretted waking him for he was battered and exhausted. 'I don't see how it could be. He's locked up next door. Didn't you say he was drugged?'

Alere frowned. 'I thought he was. I couldn't reach his mind.'

It was Rohne. He'd looked right at her and saluted. How had he walked free? If he'd been able to get out so easily, why wait until now? Perhaps her guesses about Rohne and Hallon had been wrong. Perhaps they were on friendly terms and he'd never been a prisoner. What was Rohne up to?

She had too many questions and no way of getting answers. There was no point in arguing all this with Jarran. He didn't know, either.

'Nevermind,' she muttered. 'Sorry. Go back to sleep.'

Jarran tried to stifle a yawn and winced. 'What about you? It's been three hours since you spoke with Kett.' He laid a gentle hand on her arm. 'Staying awake won't make him get back in touch. Unless you've thought of a foolproof way to get out of here, you need to sleep or you'll exhaust yourself.'

'I still think I could take out the mharebi, kill Hallon in his sleep and get out the window of his room.' She took up pacing again. She'd tried to sleep, but the tension in her belly coiled around her spine and throat like a quetzal-snake and wouldn't let her rest.

'No,' he said patiently. 'Hallon has eight mharebi posted outside our door and his, now. You wouldn't have a chance to get through them all before they raised the alarm. Besides,' he added, 'that would leave Corin behind and you said you wouldn't do that.'

'Oh, go back to bed,' she snapped. After a moment, he did, leaving her to stew. He was right, she just hated to admit it. Sleeping felt weak, like she was giving up on Kett. She needed to know he was alright. She left her Outer wards down, in case he could reach her. But there was nothing: no sense of his presence, no wards, nothing. Just as with Corin. The lack terrified her.

She continued to stare out of the window, listening to the sounds of late-night revelry, hoping each person who staggered past the house was Kett.

Alere?

Mina? Alere gasped. Silver-gilt warmth swept through her. Iron and smoke. Comfort and wholeness. Unity. She basked in the connection for a moment then withdrew to a shallower level and glanced back over her shoulder. Should she wake Jarran? No. He needed the sleep and would just distract her with pointless questions. *Where are you? Are you alright? Kett? Gavon?*

Mina's thoughts were ragged with exhaustion, her control over the link fitful. *I'm with Liu, Saric and the children. Gavon's here, too. His fever has broken. He's weak and walking aggravated the wound. But I think he'll recover.*

Kett?

There was a long, heavy silence. Alere pressed shaking fingers to her lips and closed her eyes.

I don't know, Mina admitted. *He stayed behind to seal the entrance to our escape tunnel. I'm sorry, Alli. I couldn't convince him to come.*

Alere sucked a long, steadying breath. *No, I know. He's stubborn like that. And I haven't been able to reach him or Corin.* She pushed aside the thought that both Kett and Corin might be dead. It simply wasn't possible. Mina's gut-deep anguish at the shared realisation tempted her to wallow in grief. But that way led to madness and Fusion. Alere shored up her Inner wards and pushed their connection back into her shallowest Outers. The pain eased. She could deal with the heartache later. They couldn't be dead, anyway. For now, Jarran was her priority.

Where are you? she asked Mina.

I...I probably shouldn't say. In a safe house that Shasa woman doesn't know about.

So, Liu believes she's responsible, too?

Mina hesitated. *He and Saric are convinced she didn't betray us. But Kett believed she did. Who else could have told Hallon where to find us?*

It doesn't matter, now, anyway.

What about Rohne? Can he help you?

Rohne left, Alere said flatly. *I saw him go.*

Mina's shock was palpable. Dismay, betrayal and hurt all shuttled through her Outers.

Mina, Alere said, *I think we have to accept that Rohne's got his own agenda. Whatever he's doing, he doesn't really care about you or me. Let him go.*

I thought he loved me. He's like a brother. I can't believe he'd betray us. There must be a reason. Maybe I should try to reach him with the bracelets.

No! Alere re-inforced the order with a swift, subconscious instruction planted in Mina's mind. *We can't take the risk. We can do this without him. Trust me.*

What are you going to do?

I'm not sure, yet. Just make sure you hang onto my swords, those bracelets and my bag. You did get my bag?

Yes, but—

I'll try to keep you updated. But if Hallon finds the yanstones I have, I'll lose contact. If you don't hear from me for twenty-four hours, go straight to Valera, the Shah's Xintou. Tell her what's happened. Get a message to Rafi. Then get Gavon out of Chengdu.

Alere, I can't just leave you and Jarran.

You have to, Mina. You're the next Jun-Heir to Rafi. If Hallon kills me he'll turn the city upside down to find you. Promise you'll go.

There was a long silence and Mina's misery seeped through Alere's wards, sinking her heart into unfathomable darkness.

Very well, Mina replied softly. *I'm sorry, Alli. This is my fault. If I hadn't run from Shanzhai—*

Stop, Mina. Alere was harsher than she meant to be, but the raw depth of their link made controlling her emotions almost impossible. *It's not your fault Hallon abducted you. And I shouldn't have pushed you away. Just be careful, now.*

I will. But, please...

I know. I'll try.

Alere severed the contact.

She reached again for Kett or Corin and came up, again, against nothing. Angry and teetering on the edge of a black chasm of pointless, all-engulfing fear, she snatched up a pillow off the bed and buried her face. The stuffing muffled a scream of utter frustration. Tears, long held at bay by sheer willpower, prickled at her lids and soaked into the pillow. They were tears, not for her own situation, but for the aching absence of her friends and fear for their safety. Curling around the softness, she lay beside Jarran and, eventually, slid into uneasy sleep.

CHAPTER TWENTY-SEVEN

ALERE

Alere awoke with the first greyish tinge of light colouring the sky outside. Foreboding drove her to her feet, tiny jewelled dagger in hand. In the half-lit room, nothing moved. Jarran still slept, snoring, the bruises from last night dark shadows on his face. The feeling of impending trouble grew stronger, wrapping around her throat and driving adrenalin into her blood until her whole body trembled.

She shook Jarran, keeping a palm over his mouth. His fingers locked around her wrist and his one eye fixed on her, wary. When he relaxed, she put a finger to her lips. He struggled out of bed, wincing and holding his ribs. They stood, side by side, watching the door as heavy footsteps measured the hall outside. She tucked the dagger into the back of her robe belt, out of sight.

'I spoke to Mina last night,' she whispered, hurriedly. 'She's alright.'

Jarran's eye lit up. 'Where is she—'

The door clicked and flew open. Two mharebi stepped inside, alert and watchful. A third threw a bundle of clothes at Alere with a terse order to dress. She weighed up her options and shook the clothes out. A heavy, indigo bamboo cloth day-robe with lighter blue trous. Better than what she had on, anyway.

When she headed for the bathroom, one of the men raised his sword to her throat.

'Stay here.' He smirked.

Jarran stepped in front of her; forming a human privacy screen and raising his chin belligerently.

Grateful, Alere swiftly drew on the trous and switched robes. The trous were too big and slipped low on her hips so she tucked them into the yanstone necklace. She also hid the cloth belt from the old robe, and her little knife, inside the front of the robe. Kett had always said anything could be a weapon.

The thought of him brought a lump to her throat. She swallowed hard and buried it deep in her belly.

Stepping out from behind Jarran she lifted her chin with as much dignity as she could muster. 'Now what?'

The man closest jerked his head at the door. 'The master wishes to see you.' He switched his swordpoint to Jarran. 'Not you, just her. You wait here.'

Jarran opened his mouth and Alere held up a hand. 'I'll be fine. You rest.'

Heart thumping uncomfortably, she fell into line behind the first mhareb and followed him through the hall. Shazi! She should have taken the yanstone belt off and hidden it in the room. If Hallon found it… If he happened to have the xintou gene… She had no wish to discover the outcome of that scenario.

Too late, now.

She was marched downstairs, through the back entrance to the house. The rear door gave onto a small, lush garden with a rich variety of plants in all shades of blue and dark purple. Vivid and alive in the mild Chengdu winter, it was complete with fruit trees and a glasshouse containing thick-leafed black plants more suited to somewhere warmer. A fountain gurgled on one side. Cool air brushed her cheek: soft and fresh, washed and scented by the rain. In an aviary in one corner, gold flashed. A dozen gold-furred jin-birds twittered and jumped from branch to branch within, sometimes clinging briefly to the bronze bars and poking their heads between the metal before disappearing again into the shadowed corners.

The wooden back gate opened and she was ushered through, into what appeared to be a training ground. A low stone building wrapped around three sides of a large, packed-earth square. At various points around the square stood timber poles, from which dangled bronze wrist-shackles. On one wall hung racks of wooden, replica weapons. Behind the building towered the compound wall, topped by a patrolled walkway, glass shards and electrified wires. The mharebi walking the wall carried multi-shot crossbows.

The building itself consisted mostly of a series of cells. Around fifty by a quick count of doors. A place to house slaves. Oppression and fear were almost tangible, enhanced by the slam of the garden door closing behind her, cutting her irrevocably off from life.

'Ah. There you are, my dear.' Hallon's voice, full of bluff good cheer, greeted her. He waited, relaxed in the misty dawnlight, on a wooden bench close to one wall of the cellblock.

Faces appeared at every small, barred window in the compound. A mhareb walked around, dragging a tanjo stick along the bars until all the watchers disappeared.

Alere stopped three paces away, waiting for Hallon to say something, waiting for a clue about how to act and what to do next. Had Shasa revealed Alere's existence to Hallon? His words gave no indication. And, without knowing what conversations he'd already had with Mina, it was best to let him lead.

He rose, walked around her, then regarded her for a long moment, sliding his gaze the length of her body in a leering, disquieting way. A deliberate show of dominance to unnerve her. Alere lifted her chin, forcing herself to stay impassive and study him as a weishi would.

A scar ran from above one eyebrow into his salted, receding hairline. Another notched his right ear. The scars, his muscular physique, hard hands and uncompromising mouth spoke of a warrior. This was a man to be watched. He would be ruthless in his application of strength and pain to get what he wanted, but also had the mind to be more than a bully.

Hallon wiped the leer away, his dark eyes thoughtful.

He wagged a finger. 'I wasn't sure until this moment. You look so much like her I thought we'd made a mistake. You really aren't Mina, are you? And this is a little obvious.' He yanked the blonde wig off her head and tossed it aside. 'So, let me welcome *you* to my little world, Alere Koh-Lin. Come, sit.' He sat and patted the seat next to him.

Anger clenched her fists. She should have reacted as any normal, untrained woman would; as Mina would. He hadn't tried to dominate her, he'd tested her. She'd given herself away through sheer pride and stupidity. No. Shasa had given her away. The bitterness of unwanted truth tasted acid in her mouth.

It was pointless to pretend so she sat, keeping her face calm and hands relaxed in her lap.

He smiled, though it held no mirth, only superiority. 'Smart girl. I like that. Come, we have much to discuss.'

'Really, shenshi?' She let scepticism colour her tone, and used the honorific deliberately. Let him think she held him in respect. 'What, exactly? The terms of release for Jarran and myself perhaps?'

'Precisely.' He raised his brows at her.

Alere gaped at him, impossible hope lifting her heart for a moment. Could they have misjudged the whole situation? Was it possible Hallon was not the villain Liu had made out? Diyu! Was nothing as it appeared?

Hallon chuckled. 'Let me explain. First of all, I must compliment and thank you for your disposal of Ven Zah-Hill. The man was a positive blight on your Jundom.'

'Thank you.' She inclined her head. 'But it wasn't for your benefit, believe me.'

He waved a hand. 'I know but you did me a great favour. I had no idea how I was going to gain control of Mamlakah, without going to war against Hanna's junren. Now you've handed it to me on a platter.'

Alere controlled a hot-tongued retort, merely waiting in polite, inquiring silence.

He patted her leg and only the presence of his three mharebi prevented her from impaling his hand with her tiny dagger. 'No, I'm hardly going to go into all the details of how I'll achieve that. That would be foolish. My plans are mine, alone. However, I've had to be flexible lately and, out of courtesy, I will tell you your part in them.'

'Oh?' she said sweetly. 'I play a part in your grand design? I'm flattered.'

'Yes, indeed.' He ignored the sarcasm. 'Quite a large one. You see, when I arranged for Jarran's kidnapping, I was intending to take Rafi and you – well, Lianna, because I didn't realise at the time who you were.' A black frown twitched at his brows for a moment, sending a shiver down Alere's spine. 'Unfortunately, my men failed me. Then Mina fell into my lap. So I simply adapted.'

'Given you no longer have Mina,' Alere said, 'I'm agog to know what you have in mind.'

Truth told, she had a sinking feeling she knew what he intended, but she needed more information. There were too many of her friends' lives at stake to rush into anything.

Hallon relaxed back on the bench and faced her, his knees falling apart in a display of male control. Slowly, one subtle shift of limb at a time, she moved until she was in the mirror position, reflecting back his masculine body language. Then she went one better and opened her arms, hitching her elbows on the back of the bench. The merest hint of unease flickered and he folded one arm defensively across his lap. Alere was careful not to let a smile show.

'Exactly how does Mina's escape fit in?' she asked.

Hallon laughed, the scar on his face more pronounced as the skin pulled oddly. 'She didn't escape, my dear. I let her go. You were the one I wanted.'

Alere couldn't prevent the betraying stillness of her body, or the involuntary clench of her jaw. But she reduced the rest of her shock to a mere lifting of her brows. An ironic twist of his lips said he wasn't fooled.

'And I suppose you let Rohne go as well? Why?' she asked, as coolly as she could.

A faint echo of her surprise slipped across his face. 'Rohne? Who's that?'

She hesitated, thrown offbalance. 'The... the man you caught with Jarran and Mina. The one who sat next to your son at dinner two nights ago. He was imprisoned in your guest room next to Jarran. Rohne Marin-kin. Dark red hair. Amber eyes.'

Hallon scowled. 'You are mistaken, girl. There was no such person in my house. I have let no-one, but Mina, go free.'

She opened her mouth to object; to try and make sense of it. How could he not know Rohne? But his confusion seemed genuine. Forcing confrontation would achieve nothing. She slid into rapport with the stones still around her hips and tested his Outer wards. Solid. So solid she had no hope of drilling or cracking them in the limited time she had. Not surprising. Liu said he'd been raised in the Shah's palace with a senior Xintou Bonded to the family.

But had Rohne somehow penetrated his wards and erased all memory of himself from Hallon's mind? If so, then he was far more skilled than she'd realised.

Sweeping her mind across Hallon's again, just in case she'd missed a chink in his mental armour, she found a thin, silver-gilt strand stretching away from him into infinity. It felt like the same sort of connection that had drawn her to Mina, back on the chuan. Was Hallon a twin? As far as she knew, Hallon was definitely the younger brother to Jahil. Who was at the other end of the thread?

'No.' Hallon made a chopping gesture, all pretence of polite good humour vanishing. 'Enough games. I let Mina go to lure you into taking her place. You'll serve my purpose much better. She was a pawn. You are the…well, let's say the castle. A much more useful piece of Rafi's qi board to hold.'

Letting the question of Hallon's wards go for the moment, Alere refocussed. Her task was to gain her own and Jarran's freedom. And to find out if Corin and Kett lived. That was more important, now that Mina was safe. Rohne could wait.

'Oh yes,' she agreed, pretending to stifle a yawn and glancing around the stark, dusty yard. 'I forgot. You were going to tell me my part in all this. Please do.' She waved a gracious hand for him to continue, keeping her expression blandly polite.

The sun cleared the buildings, filling the cool morning with light and warmth, catching the golden sandstone of the high walls and glittering off the shards of glass along the top.

Hallon glowered, perhaps unsettled by her refusal to be intimidated. Good. She slid one hand slowly into the front of her robe, finding the coiled silk belt. Around her, the three mharebi had relaxed their vigilance. Their attention wandered as time stretched and her conversation with Hallon showed no sign of becoming violent. If she was going to do anything, it needed to be soon. The slaves would probably be brought out shortly to begin their morning routine. That meant more mharebi.

'I think you've seen my son, Feddor?' He leaned back again, once more urbane and cool.

Alere rolled her eyes. 'Really? *That's* your great plan? You're going to, what, force me into the hunli ceremony with your son to gain control over my father's Jundom? Bit unoriginal.'

With a genuine laugh, Hallon patted her thigh. 'How very theatrical, my dear. No. Feddor has no need of a second-rate Jundom in the south. Jahil's only children are slave-get and can't be Shah. So Feddor will inherit the whole of Melcor. I mention him only because he'll be out to join us in a moment and I wanted to warn you. He can be a bit of a hmar, if I'm honest, but he needs to be part of this morning's... activities. After all, he and you are the next generation of rulers. You should get to know each other.'

Offbalance again, Alere could only stare at him. 'What do you want from me, then?'

'You do have something I want.' Hallon waved his hands expansively. 'And I have something you want – well, three things, actually. I believe we're in a position to do business, you and I.' He gave a soft, humourless chuckle. 'Although I think my bargaining position is slightly stronger.'

'If you believe that's true,' Alere said, keeping her calm with an effort and thinking fast, 'you'd best lay your cards down. I'll judge for myself who has the stronger hand.'

She crossed one leg over the other, towards him, and smiled winsomely. Peeping through her lashes, she leaned forward to let the front of her robe fall open a fraction. With her left hand she twirled a curl of hair then stroked her fingertips slowly down the length of her throat. Balled in her right hand, she now had the thin silk belt ready.

Hallon raised his lip in a scornful sneer. 'Oh, stop with the jiaoji performance, girl. I've been bound in the hunli for twenty-five years and I've had my pick of female and male slaves for even longer. I've seen everything you can do, and more. Tempting though it is, I'm not a young man to be controlled by his lusts.' He sent her a dry, knowing look. 'And I'm not Ven.'

Cheeks flaming, Alere sat back and tugged her clothing into place. 'Fine. What do you have and what do you want?'

'Much better. Along with your own life, of course, here's what I have.'

He signalled and two mharebi appeared, each pushing a male prisoner before them. Both prisoners had bags over their heads and wrists tied before them. They stumbled across the dirt courtyard and were forced to their knees before Hallon. Their clothes were torn and an ominous brown-red blotch stained the left side of one man's shirt.

Alere held herself aloof, knowing who she would see when the moment came. She'd already recognised Kett and Corin. When the bags were removed, she swept a bored gaze across her friend's battered forms and returned Hallon's interrogative gaze with a blank one of her own. It was best if she didn't dwell on the bruises on Kett's face, or think about what lay beneath the bloodstain on Corin's shirt. Both men were gagged and stoic. But their tightly clenched teeth and fists revealed a battle with pain. She couldn't watch for long without betraying herself.

There followed a long silence. Hallon's expression slowly changed from expectant to faintly impressed. Alere said nothing, did nothing; simply stared at him as though still waiting for his hand to show.

At last, he let out a snort. 'You know what, girl, I can see why Rafi picked you for his heir over that milk-and-water sister of yours.'

She gathered her feet beneath her in preparation, trying to control the rush of blood and adrenalin. It had to be now, before her temper got the better of her.

The sash slipped through her fingers. She leapt to her feet. She looped the silk around Hallon's throat and flipped backward over the bench. Landing behind him, she dropped low between the wall and the bench. The belt tightened in her left hand. She palmed the tiny dagger in the right and smiled grimly at the choking noises. Her heart pounded loud in her ears.

Hallon clutched at his throat. His face turned dark red as he gasped and gargled for air. A shout went up from his mharebi. Fierce satisfaction curled through her chest. She relaxed the belt's tension a little and brought her lips close to his ear, keeping his body between her and the mharebi high on the walls. Two still stood guard over Kett and Corin. The others approached cautiously, eyes darting between her and their master, strangling beneath her hands.

'Tell your men to back off,' she murmured, 'or I *will* kill you.'

CHAPTER TWENTY-EIGHT

A soft *snick* by her head gave warning. The sound of a single-shot, single-hand crossbow being primed to fire. Alere sliced up and back with the dagger. It met resistance and she heard a gasp of pain. The bolt flew past her ear and embedded in the bench. She swept a leg and hooked the mhareb's ankles. He fell and cracked his skull against the wall close behind.

But the movement allowed too much slack in the belt around Hallon's throat. He snatched his boot-knife out and cut through the cloth. He leapt away to the safety of his men, holding his throat and coughing, his face slowly returning to normal. Alere dropped the silk and sprang onto the bench, trying to get close again so she could regain control. Taking Hallon hostage was her only hope.

She lashed a front kick at the nearest mhareb. His jaw crunched sickeningly and he collapsed, unconscious. Another jumped at her as she leapt for Hallon. The mhareb grabbed at her with empty hands. He must be under orders to take her alive. She spun to one side and jabbed an elbow in his nose. He stumbled, gasping, clutching at his nose, blood streaming through his fingers. A kind of exultant, powerful joy flooded her, gave her strength and determination.

An arm snaked over her shoulder, almost locking a sleeper hold on her neck. She wrapped one hand around the forearm and jammed the daggerblade into muscle with the other. He yelled. She flung him over her hip and wrenched his arm. Tendons crackled as his shoulder dislocated. He screamed and rolled away, the arm limp and useless.

Panting, Alere looked for the next. But dozens more mharebi swarmed from the buildings around, all of them armed and running to help their master. The men standing behind Kett and Corin had their weapons laid across exposed throats.

The chance was gone. The fierce strength drained away like a tide, leaving only muddy remnants of hope.

Hallon rubbed his throat, glaring. He signalled his men, who grabbed her arms and dragged the jewelled dagger from her trembling fingers. Rage and ice-cold fear solidified into a lump in her stomach. Had she just sealed Kett and Corin's deaths? She couldn't bear to look at them, but drew herself upright and lifted her chin.

A younger man, wearing a spurious expression of concern, now stood beside Hallon. Feddor. The image of Hallon, but with vivid blue eyes and a pudgy red face, he bore an air of petulant disgruntlement. Possibly he was annoyed to find his father still alive. He had the soft hands and smooth skin of a man who'd never seen real battle or spent time working. Where his father wore the serviceable, tough leathers and sturdy cloth of a warrior, Feddor wore silks sewn to imitate the same.

'Father.' His tone was condescending. 'Leave her to me. I can get her to do it.'

Alere repressed the urge to kick him out of sheer irritation. It would be a fleeting moment of revenge and would only serve to worsen the situation.

Hallon ignored his son. 'Remove her robe, search her and tie her to the pole.' His voice was hoarse.

Rough hands tore at the blue day-robe and cut off her breast-binder. Clad only in loose trous, she kept her face steady and unafraid. But bile rose in her throat as they pulled her over to a post. Bronze cuffs snapped tight around her wrists. The mharebi dragged the chain until her arms were stretched above her head.

With her cheek against wood worn smooth by the tears of a thousand slaves, Alere clutched at the chains and waited, knowing what must come next. Hands patted her body, pausing at her hips.

Fingers fumbled with the necklace. It fell away, tearing a hole in her mind as the yanstones left her skin. Some of the strength underpinning her defiance vanished. She sagged against the post, holding back a protest by force of will, alone.

Footsteps approached. Hallon's breath brushed her neck.

'I see the rumours about Ven's skill with a whip are true.' He traced the score-marks across her back with his fingertips. 'Although you have healed remarkably fast.'

She suppressed a shiver and ground her teeth.

'I am disappointed you didn't even wait to hear what I wanted in exchange for your lives and the lives of your friends,' he said. 'I don't call that very business-like.'

The yanstones were close by and she ached for their contact. Why hadn't she used them? Why did she always fall back on the way of the weishi instead of using her mind? Shazi! Now it was too late. Yet another opportunity lost.

'Now,' Hallon said conversationally, 'you'll give me what I want and I'll think about whether to let you go or not.'

'Would you stop the feihua and tell me what it is?' Alere growled. 'This would be a lot less messy for everyone if you'd get to the gouri point.'

'Very well,' Hallon replied. 'This.'

The necklace dangled from his fingers.

'You have it already.' She borrowed a leaf from Corin's irreverent book. 'And I don't think it really goes with your outfit. Maybe some rubies?'

'Zift!' He shook it at her. 'Not this trinket.' He stuffed it into a pocket. 'This I'll give to my wife. I want the whole deposit. I want the iron it came from.'

Relief soared through her. He didn't know about the power of the stones and iron combined. And he didn't have the gene, or he would have noticed when he handled the necklace. But did *everyone* know about the gouri iron?

'Look, Hallon.' She kept her tone as reasonable as possible. 'I don't exactly carry tonnes of iron ore around with me, do I? How the diyu am I supposed to give it to you?'

'Easily.' He snapped his fingers. A man wearing the soft indoor shoes and orange robe of an administrator trained by Messenger House, placed a thin sheaf of papers in his hand. Hallon waved them at her. 'You'll sign this trade agreement. When you return to Shanzhai, you'll begin full-scale mining and send the ore to me. That will free you. I'll also commit junren to help Jarran stabilise his Jundom and hold his throne.'

'I don't have the authority to sign that,' she said evenly. 'It would be meaningless.'

Hallon inclined his head. 'But you will by the time you get to Shanzhai. Rafi is about to suffer an unfortunate accident, leaving you as Jun Second.'

'Qusi, you gouri wisix hundan!' She spat at his feet, but cold fear sleeted across her skin. 'You're bluffing. Go ahead and whip me. I won't sign it.'

He paced around her, eyeing her back and caressing his chin with one hand. 'I believe you're right. Clearly flogging you would do no good at all, would it? Fine.' He signalled his men. 'Release her and tie her to the bench instead. Put *them* up in her place.' He smiled thinly. 'I know your type: heroic and arrogant. But you can't stand to see others suffer. You feel you're the only one who deserves it.'

Four mharebi grabbed her arms and legs and hauled her to the bench. Chains and manacles bound her to it. Half-naked and trembling in spite of the quickly-rising sun, she could only watch as the mharebi yanked Kett and Corin to their feet and tied them to the pole in her place. She strained uselessly against the bindings. Her throat closed around a strangled cry and she fought panic.

As the shirt tore from his back, Kett shook his head, the message in his eyes clear.

Steeling herself, Alere set her teeth. The mharebi unwound their whips and drew back. If only she had the yanstones and the emotional detachment they afforded. Important over what she wanted, she reminded herself. Both men were strong. Hallon wouldn't kill them or he'd lose leverage over her. Important over what she wanted.

Hallon was right, though, she didn't know if she could stand to see these two men, whom she loved, in pain because of her.

Leather whistled through the air, snapping across flesh with a *crack* that rent the morning and tore at her resolution. A red weal bloomed across Kett's bare back and his body jerked, muscles writhing beneath the skin. His hands clutched at the bronze chain.

Crack.

The second man wielded his lash and Corin flinched. A blood-line appeared on his skin. His head dropped forward and his chest heaved. The faintest groan escaped the gag. She pressed her lips together, almost-uncontrollable anger welling in her heart.

Crack.

Hallon returned to the bench and crossed his arms over his broad chest. Off to one side, Feddor ignored the flogging. He yawned, inspecting a ring on his finger.

Rage boiled in Alere's stomach. The desire to kill Hallon seared soul-deep.

Crack.

No. Anger wouldn't help. She had to think clearly. Alere drew on the memory of the yanstones' influence and detached herself. She switched off the part of her that felt every touch of the whip; repressed the love that lived every moment with the men.

Important over what she wanted.

Deliberately, she blanked her expression and regarded Hallon, finding him observing her with interest and expectation. She raised one eyebrow and relaxed back against the bench. The chains jangled as she lifted a hand to scratch her nose. Cold logic over love and anger. Recklessness would not save any of them now. Utter and absolute self-control was the key.

Crack.

This time Kett groaned aloud, his fingers releasing the chains and knees sagging. Slowly, he straightened again. The air thickened with anticipation of her reaction. Hallon and Feddor both watched her closely. If she broke now, Kett and Corin's agony would be for nothing. Hallon would know he could get her to do anything he wanted. She had to hold on.

Crack.

They had to hold on.

Fear welled. She was making the wrong choice. Hallon would kill them if he thought they were of no use against her. They would die here, in front of her and she would be responsible. She would lose everything she cared about in one blow.

No. She pushed it firmly aside again, calming her mind and feeling the stones' power, even from within Hallon's pocket, although that might be her imagination.

Important over what she wanted. To save their lives she had to let them suffer. She gave a small yawn.

Crack.

Corin's knees gave way. His head lolled and he slipped into unconsciousness. Alere kept her eyes steadily on Hallon, allowing no hint of her fear to show.

Crack.

Kett shuddered. His feet slid from beneath him. He grabbed at the chain and dragged himself up again. Alere ignored him.

Reluctant admiration flared in Hallon and he raised a hand. 'Enough. Hand them over to the healer. I want them well enough to take part in the Games in two days.'

Alere heard his words with mixed feelings and held them all close to her heart, revealing nothing. Relief now would be as bad as fear or anger. She had won this round, but at great cost and the sound of leather hitting flesh would haunt her sleep.

'Father! A few more and she would have broken.' Feddor's protest was ignored by both. A flicker of contempt crossed Feddor's face. He folded his arms and curled his lip, schooling his face to blankness again when he caught Alere watching.

Kett and Corin were dragged away, into the northern building. Hallon dismissed many of the mharebi, leaving only Feddor, three guards in front of Alere and one she couldn't see, but sensed, behind.

'Very well.' Hallon waved a hand at her. 'I must admit I'm impressed. Not many people could stomach seeing their own companions flogged and not beg me for their salvation. You have the makings of a great Jun, my dear.' He cocked his head. 'What *will* make you sign that agreement?'

'You have nothing I want,' Alere said coolly, amazed when her voice came out steady. 'Even if you kill all four of us, we're not important. Jarran has heirs and I have a sister to take my place.'

'Ah.' Hallon glanced over her head. 'Shasa, have you brought Mina back yet? You led the assault on the warehouse last night. Report.'

Alere stiffened. The mhareb-slave woman emerged from behind the bench and knelt before her master. Shasa kept her eyes averted, not meeting Alere's wrathful gaze. Alere itched to claw at the woman's eyes. She had betrayed Corin and dozens of *children*. How could she do it?

'No, Master, I'm sorry. Mina, Gavon, Liu and most of the children escaped through secret tunnels I didn't know about. I have men searching, but the tunnels link with the stormdrains. They run under most of the city. Liu and the others could be anywhere by now.'

There was a long, ominous pause. A hint of fear shadowed Shasa's face. Alere savoured a small taste of vengeful satisfaction. Let him punish her.

Hallon rose and put a finger under Shasa's chin, lifting it. 'You failed?' The coldness in his tone boded ill.

Shasa swallowed. 'I'm sorry, Master. It's only a matter of time before we find them, though. I swear we'll have them by the Games.'

Hallon inspected her and nodded at last. 'Very well. But we have a bargain, do we not? If you fail to deliver Liu Gray and the Koh-Lin girl then the deal is off.'

'Yes, Master.' Shasa dropped her eyes, fists clenched by her sides.

What was their bargain? Was Hallon offering her freedom, perhaps? Was that why she'd betrayed Liu and Corin? Could she be that mercenary?

Hallon stroked her head once and caressed her cheek with his thumb. 'Report to my room this evening. After Jahil leaves. He's coming later to inspect the latest batch of slaves.' He brought the yanstone necklace out from his pocket. 'And give this and the matching bracelets to Faira as a gift from me. Tell her it's for her new outfit for the Games. Dismissed.'

'Yes, Master,' Shasa repeated, accepting the necklace. Still avoiding Alere's gaze, she strode away.

Alere's heart sank as the stones vanished through the timber gate. With every step Shasa took, the stones' power attenuated. It faded to a faint tingle in the back of her mind; no more than the knowledge they were somewhere near. She was reduced to just Alere once more. The heady, gold-fire extension of her self, into something bigger, better and more powerful, was gone. Adrenalin also faded and reality displaced defiance. Alere wrapped her arms across her bare breasts. The sunwarmed chains pressed into her skin.

The bench beneath her creaked as Hallon sat beside her again. His large, calloused hand fell heavily onto her shoulder. She couldn't help the instinctive elbow strike response. He shifted and easily grabbed her arm. Straightening it effortlessly, he rested his forearm across her elbow and simply watched her.

Fear sleeted cold through her limbs; stealing breath and strength; paralysing in its power. In one simple move, he could break her arm. And he wanted her to know it. That was almost the least frightening thing he could do. The last twenty minutes had all been for show. He wanted her to feel the rush, the hope, the belief she had a chance of outwitting him. He wanted it to drain away when she realised she and her friends were at his mercy. The game was his and his alone.

He wanted her to know she had lost the fight of the mind.

CHAPTER TWENTY-NINE

ALERE

'I will do you the courtesy of two things before you make your final decision.' Hallon's tone was gentle, even as the pressure on her elbow increased. 'I will not take by force what you offered freely before.' His gaze flicked to her breasts and he smiled faintly. 'I know you think your jiaoji training would help. Believe me, it wouldn't. However, we will be fellow rulers soon and I would not like that experience to… colour our working relationship.'

Alere could do no more than stare coldly back at him. She had nothing else in her arsenal.

'And the second thing?' She tried to keep her voice steady.

'You will have today and tomorrow to reconsider.' He released her arm and she flexed her fingers, feeling the ache in the elbow. 'After that, if you still refuse to sign, your friends will participate in the Wushi Games on the thirtieth. The same will happen if you try to escape. You are the only one who can prevent their death. If you haven't signed by the thirtieth, then you will be a guest in my box at the amphitheatre to watch the festivities. When they are brought out to fight, you'll be given one last chance to sign.'

He studied her lifted chin. 'I can see you have faith in them and you think they could win the Games. Should they do that, I shall take great pleasure in tracking them – and you – down in the Seyd-Hunt. You have two days to decide. If you don't sign, then you all die and I'll take Shanzhai by force.'

'And if I did sign,' she said, curling a lip, 'what would stop me from reneging on it the minute I got back to Shanzhai?'

'Nothing, of course,' he said calmly, 'except your word as Jun-Heir. And the fact that I would keep one of your friends as collateral for the first year. As a guest, of course.' He gestured to his mharebi. 'Take her back and bring me the other. I'm sure he'll be willing to sign the agreement I have for him.'

Unshackled from the bench, but with the cuffs still chafing her wrists, Alere was hauled upright. As she stumbled away, between two mharebi, Hallon's laugh followed her.

'I will say this for you, girl,' he said. 'To borrow a term from the slaves: you are *gangzhi*. I respect that.'

The mhareb to her left sucked a quick, quiet breath. His grip tightened spasmodically around her arm.

Alere said nothing and walked blindly back to the house. She had never felt less like steel in her life. Everything she'd thought about herself was untrue. She'd been arrogant. Defeating Hallon could never be a simple matter of manipulating him, as she had with Ven. Why had she thought outwitting a child like Ven made her smarter than a man with over thirty years experience in breaking slaves and controlling a jundom?

At the bedroom door, the mharebi unshackled her and prodded her into the room with the tips of their swords. She didn't resist. She had no spirit with which to fight back. Instead, she stumbled inside, every limb weighted by the knowledge of her conceit and failure; her condemnation of Kett and Corin to death or slavery; her inevitable capitulation and the destruction of everything and everyone she cared about. She had failed Kett, herself, Jarran and her father. Even Mina would never be safe with Hallon aware of her potential as leverage.

Jarran tried to speak with her as the mharebi grabbed at his arms. She sank into a chair, ignoring his demands for information and guidance. Who was she to guide him?

When the door slammed behind him, she flung herself onto the bed and curled around her pain and fear. Numb and overwhelmed, she stared blindly at the blank wall. She refused to let tears fall, though they burned in her chest and stung her eyes. Eventually, exhaustion overcame her, and she slept.

CORIN

Waking was not the most pleasant experience of his life. First, as awareness returned, came the discomfort of lying face-down on a hard surface with his head turned awkwardly to one side. One hand dangled, numb. His body was cold and sluggish. He tried to raise his arms. Agony sleeted across his back and memory came with it. Chains clanked. His wrists were shackled.

With an involuntary gasping grunt, he dropped back into his original position and clenched his teeth, riding out the waves of pain. The sharp scent of healing ointment masked the smell of old blood and his back felt sticky and cold. But someone needed to tell Hallon his healers shorted the mayao in their medicines. Then again, he probably instructed them to. After all, slaves were replaceable and mayao to numb their wounds was expensive.

'Don't move, Cor.' Kett's deep voice brought his eyes open again. 'There's no point. We're not going anywhere in a hurry.'

Corin turned his head the other way. The weishi lay on a wooden pallet of his own, in the same position. He wore only thin, coarse-woven trous. His back was bared, blood-streaked and glistening with medicinal ointment. Only the strain around his eyes showed he was in pain.

Corin raised his head to inspect their prison. They appeared to be alone in a small, dim-lit bare room of sandstone and little else. A tiny, high window on one side showed nothing but shadowed sandstone wall and a sliver of pale peridot sky. A stout timber door was the only exit. The floor was of solid, close-packed stone, scrubbed clean but darkened with old stains.

'Did she break?'

'No,' Kett said. 'Not while we were there. I don't know what happened after we were brought here. You've only been out for about twenty minutes.'

'When she had the garrotte around his throat, I thought she might actually win. Then…I don't know…' He grimaced. 'I'm not sure I could've done what she did – just watch her being flogged.'

Kett gave a low laugh. 'I'm certain I couldn't. She clearly had great faith in us.'

'Is that it?' Corin couldn't help the doubt creeping into his voice. 'Or is it because she believes that feihua of "important over what I want" she keeps spouting. Who put that into her head, anyway?'

There was a long silence and Kett sighed. 'That one is Mistress Li's teaching. You've seen the words inscribed on the front of Xintou House: *clarity, stability, responsibility and compassion.* Sounds good but it's been twisted into "important over what I want". The House mistresses drill it into the girls night and day. Alere rebelled against it for many years. Now, as she's seen a bigger world-view these last weeks, she's taken it to heart. After all, for a Jun or a Xintou there is merit to it.'

Corin snorted. 'If you want to make her into a cold-hearted chouhuo.'

Kett didn't reply. His expression hardened. Corin had the uneasy feeling he'd again crossed some sort of invisible line. But it was truth, even if Kett didn't want to hear it. He closed his eyes and waited awhile, listening to the faint noises drifting in through the window. It sounded like a group of people outside were fight-training. Grunts, the clash of wood and the thud of falling bodies mingled with cries of pain and frustration. Laughter followed – probably from mharebi onlookers. Occasionally, the crack of a whip made him flinch in recollection. Gaisi!

'How did you end up here?' he finally ventured. 'I surrendered to stop Hallon's mharebi from killing Jarran.'

'Yes, I know. Saric made it back to the warehouse with your swords and the bracelets. He told us.'

Corin heaved a sigh of relief. 'I was worried the little hmar might steal everything and disappear.'

'You underrate him.' Kett's reply was tinged with scorn. 'Saric not only returned everything, he also shouldered responsibility for leading you and Jarran into a dead end. And promised to guide Mina and Gavon to safety when Hallon's men attacked the warehouse.'

'Attacked…' Corin clenched his jaw and swore. 'Did they get away alright?'

'Yes,' Kett said shortly. 'But you should probably know that Shasa led the assault. She had her men searching for Mina. The only reason Mina and Gavon escaped was because Liu hadn't told Shasa about a series of tunnels under the building.'

Had Kett punched him in the stomach Corin couldn't have been more stunned. He turned his face away. Guilt and betrayal stole hope and crushed the nascent seeds of trust. He hadn't listened to Alere when she'd warned him. He'd wanted so much to trust Shasa that he'd ignored his own experience and his friends' warnings. Zift! Would he never learn?

'So.' He thrust the betrayal aside, as he had so often before. Shasa was just one more in a long line. That was life. 'What next? Did you hear what Hallon has planned for us?' Finally certain he had himself under control, he turned his head back.

'Yes,' Kett said. 'He wants us patched up and ready for the Wushi Games in two days. I assume he's using our potential deaths as last-ditch leverage against Alere.'

Corin swore.

ALERE

Alere woke to an empty, washed-orange room. She stumbled to the bathroom, her head thick and eyelids puffy. Splashing water on her face did little to ease the ache in her head. A check in the mirror told a sad story. A growl at her reflection served only to worsen the image. Pathetic, that's what she was: falling asleep while her friends were imprisoned and in pain. Enough wasting energy on tears. It was time she did something. She fought against despair. But what?

She drank thirstily from her hand, tasting copper from the pipes. Her stomache ached from more than the barely-contained fire of rage. When had she last eaten? Sometime last night before the rescue attempt.

Jarran! Rushing back into the sleeping room, she stared at the rumpled bed. Where was he? Outside, the day slipped away. Only the last few lingering rays of sunlight glimmered between buildings across the road. The sky deepened from emerald to indigo.

Jarran had been gone since her return that morning. Where was he? Her whole point in being here was to free the Jun First. Had she failed at that, too?

A knock on the bedroom door snapped her head around. Hurriedly, she ran to the drawers and snatched out a garish red robe. There was not enough time to find a weapon and plan an attack, but she could at least be less vulnerable.

The door flew open as she finished tying the belt. A mhareb stepped in.

Short and stocky, with a broad face and angular black eyes, he watched her warily for a moment, checking her empty hands. Someone who knew not to get too close or to give her an opportunity. He placed a tray – holding a bowl and wineglass – on the floor. A second man aimed a crossbow at her stomach. Behind him stood two more, also with weapons at the ready. She grimaced.

'Wait,' she called, as the mhareb grabbed the door handle. 'Where's the man who was here with me?'

The mhareb bowed. 'Master Hallon released him this morning. Sent him back to Madina.' He edged closer. Still too far beyond useful ma-ai, fighting distance. 'The master said to tell you: all it took was one little signature and he got to go home.' He bowed again and hesitated. Before he closed the door, he gave a furtive look over his shoulder and murmured, 'Molian.'

The door shut.

"Molian". Where had she heard that before? Had Hallon really let Jarran go? What was the agreement and what had Hallon threatened him with to make him sign? It wouldn't have taken much to convince Jarran his children were vulnerable, no matter where they were hidden.

Jarran's desire to protect his daughters was laudable, but if he gave in to Hallon once it was only a matter of time before the Slavemaster made more demands. With Hallon's threats hanging over him, Jarran was still a prisoner and his rule of Mamlakah was compromised before it even began.

But what did Jarran have that Hallon wanted? What had bought his freedom? Something that gave Hallon control over Mamlakah. Perhaps renewing the ridiculous trade agreements Ven and Hanna had instigated? No, that wasn't enough. That merely gave Hallon resources he could take by force. He had an army of junren trained and waiting to march on Mamlakah.

Control. That was the key to Hallon. He wanted control and power. He revelled in it. So, what did Mamlakah have that was unique to it? Something that would give him greater control over Melcor and Mamlakah. Something besides Shanzhai's iron deposit.

Alere paced over to the window. Once more revellers, screaming with laughter and already drunk, staggered and danced along the cobbles as the end of year celebrations drew closer to the wildness of Mianshou. Such unruliness must drive someone like Hallon insane. No wonder he went on the Hunt each year at this time. It must give him a release for his frustrations. The hunt represented something over which he had absolute power: a person's life.

Oh. That was it: control over *every* aspect of people's lives. Hallon didn't want what Mamlakah had, he wanted what *Madina* had.

Xintou House.

It must be eating Hallon up that his brother, the Shah, had a Bonded Xintou and he didn't. To him, Xintou must represent power, control, respect. Especially the latter, given the superstitious awe with which Xintou were held in Melcor. Hallon must have offered Jarran his daughters' safety, and military support. Hallon would march on Madina, put Jarran securely on the throne...and take control of the Xintou.

Xintou House had no defences and Rafi, if he still lived, was not in a position to fight off two armies. Hassan's forces could be no more than a week away from Madina. If Hallon attacked from the north, the city would fall and Xintou House with it.

Her House sisters were trained as peacekeepers and diplomats, not warriors. The House spent years indoctrinating the girls to use their mental gifts only for peaceful resolutions. Celia had been an exception. And even she had believed that her choices were justified for the greater good. If Hallon took control of the House, what would he use them for? Alere swallowed, envisioning her sisters in his implacable grip. What *wouldn't* he use them for?

Somehow, he had to be stopped.

Alere paced the room. Hallon had outwitted her, and she could see no way to best him. No weakness she could exploit. No way to even get to him with a weapon, since he'd stripped everything from her.

She sank into a chair and held her head. The tray on the floor caught her eye. Food. The very thought was nauseating, but she had to eat. The meal was nothing special: cold meats, cheese, bread and a jilla fruit. But it helped to clear her mind. She sipped at the wine, screwing up her nose at the thin, sharp flavour. At least it was the wrong sort of wine to hide the flavour of istilqa or sabat, so she wasn't being drugged.

After eating, she leaned forward in the chair, with elbows on knees. She swirled the pale green wine and considered her options. She couldn't agree to handing Hallon the iron. He would use it to make weapons and tighten his grip on Melcor and Mamlakah. She also couldn't underestimate him again. He'd manipulated her from the moment she set foot in Chengdu. With Shasa's help, he'd led her right into a trap and she'd been too blinded by arrogance to see it.

She had to warn Mistress Li and Rafi. But how did she outsmart someone who had thirty years experience in keeping people in? The keys, assuming they were still where she'd left them, would do little beyond opening her own door. Without weapons she couldn't hope to subdue eight mharebi in complete silence. Even if she could, how did she get the others free? Kett and Corin were injured and would be guarded. Shasa had said there was no way of escaping from the slave-compound. But was that true?

If she simply escaped, Hallon would either kill Kett and Corin, or put them into the Hunt. She wasn't prepared to make that sacrifice. Important over what she wanted had limits and that was hers. If she couldn't easily escape this house with Kett and Corin, what about the Games? Was that an opportunity? She didn't know anything about the Games. Gavon had described it as a bloodbath. Could Cor and Kett be in the final twenty survivors, given their injuries? They were both good, but neither was as extraordinary as Gavon, the only slave to survive both Games and the Seyd Hunt.

What were Mina, Gavon, Liu doing? Were they trying to mount some sort of rescue? Had they rallied the Selb?

Alere groaned. She needed to find out what Liu planned, if anything. A successful escape, from either here or the Games, would be easier if she had outside assistance. Even the chance to send a message of warning to Madina would be better than nothing.

On impulse, she imagined dropping her wards, in case Mina was trying to contact her with the bracelets. It was strange not to be able to sense anything. Hard to remember this was how she'd lived most of her life: trapped and alone inside her head. She'd become so used to hearing the low-key thrum of other people's unshielded thoughts that it seemed too quiet without them.

Nothing.

What next? What other options did she have?

'Molian.' She sat upright. That's where she'd heard it: in Jun Fourth Hassan Wen-Gates's house. He'd said that word as an offhand blessing of some sort. It meant something like: "endurance" or "to be tempered". The mhareb who'd said the word was the same man who'd reacted this morning when Hallon had labelled her *gangzhi*. Perhaps a Selb member? Liu had said a quarter of Chengdu's population were slaves and the Selb drew from both slaves and freefolk alike. Could she get a message to Liu through the mhareb? But what if the mhareb was one of the Selb Shasa had planted in Hallon's staff, and Shasa was watching him? Or had that been a lie, too?

She tugged at a stray lock of hair by her ear and took another sip of wine. She had no real concept of who the Selb were, or what their ideology was. Only that Gavon despised them, and they had something to do with the worship of steel and the use of it to cleanse people of evil. Both of those sounded ominous, but that was not enough to understand what they wanted. But she couldn't throw them on Hallon's sword just to facilitate her own escape.

Alere tossed back the last of the wine. It was too complicated to get her head around. She needed Kett's clarity and incisiveness. He had a gift for seeing through to the heart of things. Or she needed Corin's flair for subtlety and downright sneakiness.

The memory of her friends, as she had last seen them, curled her fists into anger and she had to release a long, slow breath to calm herself. There was nothing she could do about their situation, so fretting was pointless.

A soft scratching at the door handle brought her quickly to her feet, wineglass still in hand. A broken glass made an excellent weapon.

CHAPTER THIRTY

ALERE

The door opened wide enough to admit a single person then closed softly again. Alere blinked in astonishment at the plump, gold-clad figure.

'Valera?' Alere kept her voice low. 'How...?'

Hope leapt. Here was an opportunity. Valera, Jahil's Bonded Xintou, would be able to help her get free, or get a message to Rafi and Mistress Li.

The Shah's Xintou raised her veil and glided forward, her plain, round face wreathed in smiles and her hands outstretched. 'Alere, my dear girl. It's been a long time.' She kissed Alere on both cheeks then grasped her hands and held them apart, inspecting her closely. Her pale blue eyes crinkled at the corners. She drew Alere to the chairs. 'We have a few minutes to chat. As soon as Hallon mentioned you were his guest I had to rush right up and see you. I'm sorry I didn't know you were here. I have a gift for you, but you'll have to visit me at the palace to get it.' She studied Alere again and shook her head. 'You've grown so beautiful. Why, last time I saw you, I think you were only fifteen and so very cross with Mistress Li over something or other. What was it again?'

Alere gaped at her. Did Valera think she was a guest in Hallon's house, not a prisoner? It certainly sounded that way. Then Valera looked significantly at the door. Of course. Hallon would post someone to eavesdrop. Valera raised the smallest finger of her left hand, a signal between Xintou when asking for permission to speak mind-to-mind. Alere opened her Outer wards even as her mouth replied to Valera's verbal question.

'I think I'd climbed out a window so I could meet a…um…friend at the tavern.'

Mistress Li sent me a message. Valera's light, gentle voice sounded in her head. *Rafi sought her advice when he arrived in Madina. She said you may need assistance. Jahil agreed to help and brought me here tonight. I planted the thought in Hallon's Outers that he should mention you and give me leave to see you.*

'Oh no,' Valera said aloud, 'I remember now. You'd snuck out. You wanted to watch your friend's weishi grading ceremony and were caught by Weishi HouseMaster, Anh. What a troublesome child you were.'

Valera, this is important. Jarran has signed some sort of agreement. He's been released to return to Madina. You must tell Rafi to send men to find him. It's not safe for him to travel on his own. I'm being held prisoner, along with two of my friends. Hallon's going to put them in the Games and the Hunt. Can you help us get out? Can you seed the thought into Hallon that he should free us?

'Yes.' Alere said uneasily, finding it challenging to keep up a sensible two-level conversation. 'Mistress Li said I was trouble – frequently. But I'm sure you didn't come just to remind me of my shortcomings. Are you here with Shah Jahil?'

Valera drew herself up, her expression haughty, subtly reminding Alere the older woman was both senior Xintou and there to help. Being rude to her was counterproductive. Alere sent a quick apology. Valera inclined her head gracefully and replied.

I can see your fear and anger, child. Be calm. Jarran is safe. He convinced the chuanzhu of the chuan Hallon put him on to turn back and dock, instead, at Jahil's private berth at the palace. He came to beg for help in freeing you and your men. He told us of the agreement to hand over Xintou House Hallon forced him to sign. He has no intention of honouring it, of course.

'Oh yes.' Valera waved an airy hand. 'Jahil is inspecting the new slaves. He wants to pick a Guanjun – a champion – for the Wushi Games. Such a barbaric practice. You'll be there to watch, of course?'

Jiche! Tell Jarran to get himself back to Madina. Rafi needs him. Alere was both relieved and surprised at Jarran's actions and honesty. The fact he'd stayed rather than running back to Madina, spoke well of him. But he needed to get back to Madina to consolidate his seat before Hassan arrived.

He insisted on staying. I must tell you, Alere, that I have no way of getting you free tonight. I'm not Bonded to Hallon so my ability to influence him is very limited. I could do this much only because his wards were lax with his triumph over you. Jahil also received a visit from Liu Gray this afternoon. Liu's spies told him of Hallon's offer to you. So I have a message from Liu.

Message? What message? Why can't Jahil just order Hallon to free us?

Surely you know how things are here? Jahil has little true power. If he stands against Hallon he'll forfeit everything. Including his life, mine, and those of his wife, his jiaoji and her children.

'I mean,' Valera continued, fanning herself, 'the Games will be such a press. And the slaves and people *will* slobber over me as though Xintou were some sort of magical beings. But I'm obliged to be there.'

Alright. Alere resigned herself. *What does Liu want us to do?*

Your men need to win the Games. Then they will be taken for the Hunt and that's where Hallon will be most vulnerable.

Alere's heart contracted. It was true, of course. Outside, away from his protective compound and mharebi, Hallon was far more exposed. But he also had thirty years of experience in Hunting the

Seyd. He knew the terrain. He'd seen all the tricks; killed hundreds of Seyd and survived.

Kett and Corin would go into the Games already wounded. They would be lucky to survive at all. They had no way of co-ordinating with Liu, unless she could catch Mina trying to communicate, and that was a matter of luck and timing. Besides, in another few hours, Mina would take Gavon and leave for Madina. She'd promised.

Alere dropped her head into her hands, frustrated at the lack of action and the lack of information. Everyone involved had another agenda. Jahil most likely wanted his Jundom to be free of his brother's interference. Hallon coveted two entire jundoms. Liu wanted freedom for the slaves. The Selb wanted... She had no idea what they wanted and that worried her. Jarran had probably stayed for Mina and would prioritise his daughters. Even Shasa had some unknown bargain with Hallon. Every single person in this game wanted something, and wanted to use Alere and her friends to achieve it. Did *anyone* care what became of them?

If she signed the agreement with Hallon, would he really release one of the men? Which one did she condemn to a year of slavery? And there was no guarantee Hallon wouldn't simply change the terms and demand more for a release at the end of the year. And the thought of Hallon with the Shanzhai iron in his control as well... Signing the agreement might release one person, but condemn Jahil, Rafi and thousands of their people to death.

She wanted to *do* something that would ensure her, Kett's, and Corin's freedom without destroying Mamlakah and Shanzhai. But she was blocked at every turn. The only thing left was to risk sending her loved ones to death, either in the Games or the Hunt.

She had no other choices.

'Yes,' Alere finally replied, her heart heavy as the words fell, 'I believe Hallon has made arrangements for me to attend. In his box.'

Simple as that, huh? she threw at Valera. *Just win the Wushi Games and survive the Hunt – something that's only been done once in the last two decades. You give them a death-sentence.* She stood, took three paces away then back, glaring at Valera. *Fine, but you need to do something for me. Two things. First: send Jarran back to Madina.*

I can't. He's left the palace and is with Liu, in hiding.

Alere covered her eyes for a moment. The man was impossible. His entire Jundom at stake and he stayed to help a woman he'd known for a little over a week. If that was love then it was a stupid, selfish path that would lead to his death and Mamlakah's destruction. She groaned. Who was she to think that way? She would do the same to save Kett and Corin.

The other thing I need is this: at the Games, Hallon's wife will be wearing a necklace made of iron and yanstones. It belongs to Rafi. I must have it back. I don't care how you do it. Get it.

Valera frowned at her. *Is jewelry really the most important thing right now?*

Just do it. Alere smiled superficially at the Xintou. She hesitated on the verge of asking Valera to tell Mina to contact her in the morning, but that would reveal the yanstones' power and something in her refused to share that knowledge with a Xintou.

Her mind blanked. What had she intended to say? She shook her head. Couldn't have been important.

After a moment's hesitation, Valera rose to her feet. 'Well...' The Xintou brushed fussily at her gold silk robe and took two steps towards the door. Stopping, she frowned up at Alere. 'Well then. I guess I'll see you there.'

Walking with her to the door Alere accepted her air-kiss with an angry intensity the older woman clearly didn't miss, for she became even more flustered, glancing back to twice.

An idea struck and Alere raised her little finger. Valera paused in the act of drawing the gold veil down over her eyes.

One more thing, Valera. Alere drew a deep breath as the idea gelled into a solid, if stupidly-risky and sketchy, plan. *Don't let Jahil select a Guanjun. He'll have one on the day. I know someone who will be perfect.* Alere slammed up her wards for fear the Xintou would Read her too closely.

'But Liu—' Valera hesitated and glanced at the door. 'Very well.' Doubt and worry flickered across her expressive face. She twitched down the veil and knocked on the door. She left with one more backward glance.

Valera's footsteps faded. Alere thumped her head once against the door and turned around to lean on it, staring at the timber-beamed ceiling. Uneasiness gnawed in the pit of her stomach. She had committed Kett and Corin to the Games. Even if they won, they would not come through unscathed. They were good, but so were their opponents. Gavon had said only the best two hundred went into the Games.

Viewed from a Slavemaster's perspective it was a ruthless way of eliminating the most troublesome slaves each year. Liu had said free folk who committed serious crimes were also added to the Games. That meant the day served as a reminder of who was in charge. Of how fine the line was between freedom and slavery.

And now she'd thrown two wounded men into a fight for their lives and two days of being Hunted. All so half a dozen other people could get what they wanted.

But what choice did she have? The fate of Mamlakah, Shanzhai and the Jun First depended on her sacrificing Kett and Corin. Alere swore and thumped her head against the door again. Despair branded her heart with fire and pain.

She slid to the floor and buried her head in her arms.

PART III

CHAPTER THIRTY-ONE

CORIN

The massive bronze doors swung open. The crowd erupted into wild cheering and applause and the wall of noise reverberated through Corin's body. He edged from darkness into brilliant sunshine, along with the rest of the slaves destined to spill blood today. It took a moment for his eyes to adjust and his brain to assimilate the vast, colourful insanity of the Wushi Games arena.

He spun a slow circle and scanned the audience, searching for Alere. The amphitheatre was circular; constructed of rising stone tiers. At least ten thousand people milled, sat, and walked about the venue, all talking and cheering at the top of their voices. By their colourful, holiday garb, he assumed most to be ordinary folk or minor nobility. Mostly men, some women, but also a few children. What sort of parent thought this bloody scene appropriate for a child?

Adrenalin spurted in his blood and his hands trembled by his sides. He sucked a slow breath. A small part of him had hoped Alere would sign the gouri agreement and prevent things from coming to this point. High and mighty principles were all well and good, but surely their lives meant more to her than a lump of iron. When he'd mentioned that hope to Kett, late the night before, the weishi had simply given a short, sardonic laugh and shaken his head.

'Trust her, Cor,' he'd said. 'If she hasn't signed then she has a good reason. She won't abandon us to die, if that's what you're worried about.'

Slightly ashamed of his instinctive mistrust, but finding it impossible to let go, Corin had slept badly. Today he felt thick-headed and sluggish. He stretched the kinks out of his neck as the slaves jostled into the centre of the amphitheatre's sandy floor. He breathed in air far sweeter than the fetid atmosphere of the slavepens beneath the arena, where they'd spent the night in cramped, stinking discomfort.

'Well,' he said, somewhat overwhelmed, though he wouldn't admit it to Kett, 'I always did love an audience.'

Kett chuckled. 'This is probably the biggest one you'll ever have, so now's your chance to give them a good show.' He flexed his shoulders, grimacing. Bare-chested and leanly muscular, with a red sash around his hips to identify him as Hallon's, Kett stood half a head over most of the surrounding men and women. The stripes on his back and the black weishi tattoo on his wrist were livid against his skin. He was, undeniably, intimidating. Corin glanced down. His own appearance was equally barbaric. A little pool of emptiness formed around the two of them and the other slaves looked at them askance.

Up in the stands, more children moved amongst the crowd, bearing trays and selling food and drinks. Corin's mouth watered at the sight. He'd had little to eat beyond bread and thin vegetable soups for the last two days. Jugglers, dancers and musicians gyrated their way up and down the stairs, keeping the crowd entertained. Still more people streamed in, pointing and chattering as they emerged through doors punctuating the stone tiers.

In front of the lowest tier of seats stood a ring of mharebi wearing the Shah's gold-and-white colours, the gold salamander emblazoned on their alzin vests. Some faced inward, towards the Games competitors, some outward to the crowd. All were armed with crossbows and kusarigama.

He still couldn't see Alere.

'She's straight ahead of us.' Kett jerked his head at the arena's northern end. 'About thirty paces away, on the fourth tier. Under the red and white canopy.'

Corin spotted her. Dressed in a clinging, dark-violet robe, she was barely recognisable beneath the veil that hid the lower half of her face. Only the intensity of her stare, and the slight lift of her hand, confirmed her identity.

Seated next to her, Hallon and his wife were resplendent in matching white robes. Around Faira's neck glittered the Koh-Lin necklace. Corin grimaced at the sight of the flickering silver-gilt fire. Even in the shade, the stones caught and magnified the orange sun into eye-aching brilliance. It must kill Alere to be sitting so close and not able to reclaim it.

To Alere's left sat Feddor. His blood-red, much-bejewelled robe clashed horribly with both Alere's dark violet, and with his own ruddy, petulant complexion. He stared at Alere with an expression of covetous smugness that made Corin want to rip his teeth out. Then Feddor turned the same expression on Hallon.

'Did you see that?' Corin elbowed Kett. 'Feddor is up to something.'

'Yes,' Kett murmured. 'I also see a glint in Alere's eye she gets when she's about to do something she knows I won't like. Be ready. Whatever's going to happen it will most likely be fast and bloody. There's an access staircase inside the tunnel beneath their box. Only two mharebi on guard. When things go suilie, get off this killing ground. Get up there and protect her at all costs. I'll have your back. Agreed?'

'Did you really think you needed to say that?'

Kett thumped Corin on the shoulder, avoiding the lash-marks. 'For all I knew you *might* be harbouring some deep shield-mate bond that kept you here, by my side.'

'Hardly, my friend. Everyone knows I look after myself, first.'

'I know you try hard to make sure others believe that,' Kett replied softly. He held out a hand. 'Whatever happens, it's been an honour.'

After a moment's hesitation, Corin grasped the man's calloused hand. He cleared his throat before replying. 'It has but I do wish you'd stop being so gouri noble. It makes it extremely difficult to dislike you and shows up my worst flaws.'

Kett smiled, his grip tightening.

A shrill whistle pierced the din thrice. The crowd's cheering died away to a low murmur and all heads turned to the canopied areas at the northern end. Next to Hallon's red-and-white, stood a gold and white pavilion. Empty, it awaited the arrival of the Shah and his retainers. Beyond that were the blue-white pavilion of Alcona Ebrahim, the green-white set aside for Chan Ling, and the black-white for Bahad Sinclar. Alcona Ebrahim inspected her nails and yawned. Chan Ling languidly picked at food on a small table next to his seat, and Bahad scowled at the field of combat, drumming his fingers on his knee.

An off-key trumpet fanfare made Corin wince and heralded the Shah's arrival. Jahil emerged through a private entrance and took his seat in the pavilion. Tall, thin and greying at the temples, he was the antithesis of his warrior brother. Corin had seen the Shah before. By all counts, he was a sensitive, cultured man with a distaste for crowds. A scholar by inclination. He would make an excellent ruler to bring Melcor out of the dark ages and to rid the country of its dependence on slavery. But Jahil was no more than a puppet. His strings were pulled first by Hallon and second by Laya, his sharp-tongued wife of thirty years.

But Corin suspected Jahil, like many introverted people, could be harried only to a certain point before he dug his heels in and refused to budge. Now that was a thought: could that trait be brought forth to their advantage?

Laya followed her husband into the shade, ignoring Hallon and his family as she passed them by. Hallon's mouth moved and Faira laughed. Laya's cheeks flushed. According to Rafi, she both hated Hallon for his control over her husband and feared his retribution should she goad Jahil to open defiance.

Mallika, Jahil's favourite slave, appeared with her four children. She received no more than a cold glare from Faira, and a supercilious one from Feddor. Hallon ignored them. Alere watched with open curiosity as the family passed. Corin studied them as well. The three teenage daughters moved with the same extraordinary grace of their mother and all had her expressive dark eyes above the veil.

Lan, Jahil's son by Mallika, was as tall as his father, but almost as broad in the shoulder as his uncle. He had a thoughtful brow, intelligent dark eyes and dark hair swept back into a smooth mawei. As he passed Alere, she glanced up and Lan's step faltered. When he took his seat, he spoke into Jahil's ear. His eyes were still on Alere and Corin had no trouble guessing his question.

'What do you think Hallon told Shah Jahil about Alere?' Corin murmured to Kett.

The weishi eyed the Shah narrowly. 'Impossible to say. We have to assume Shasa revealed that she isn't Lianna Koh-Lin. Which puts

Alere in a difficult position. Hallon may also be threatening to reveal her kin-child heritage to destabilise Rafi's rule.'

Anger and hurt boiled again, low in Corin's stomach. He ground his teeth and forced himself to relax. He couldn't let the memory of Shasa's betrayal derail his mind at a crucial moment. He threw his shoulders back and lifted his chin.

'Come, my friend,' he said cheerfully. 'No point in speculating any longer. If we're going to kill people soon, do let's find a few like-minded souls. We may not end up as martyrs after all.'

He blew Alere a kiss. Her fingers whitened on the chair arms and her kohl-rimmed eyes glistened above the veil. She half-rose from her seat, only to sink back when Hallon waved a piece of paper in front of her. With a scornful glance at it and him, she turned away. Hallon shrugged and tucked the paper into his robe.

'It's certainly not my intention to die,' Kett responded, obeying a mhareb-slave who herded them into a group in the arena centre to give them final instructions. 'Frankly, I'd rather not partake in this at all, for I've no taste for killing without reason. However, since we have little choice, we need to take steps to survive.'

Kett gestured him close and pointed at the other slaves milling about the grounds.

'Looks like fifty from each slavemaster. Colour-coded.' He indicated the red-painted wall behind where they currently stood. 'And the arena's divided into four based on colour, too. What do you think? Each team starts in their quarter?'

'Yes. I asked the other slaves last night. While you were busy sleeping.' Corin sent him a wry smile. 'Not exactly a complicated set of rules. Each group gets a cache of weapons. Twenty are left standing at the end.'

'And if there's more than twenty?' Kett shaded his eyes against the rising sun and inspected the grandstands.

'Each Master choses at least five from his group strong enough to be Seyd. The rest are shot by the mharebi,' Corin said grimly.

'Ah.' Kett frowned. 'Then we need backup.'

The contenders muttered and shuffled around the grounds with heads bowed and shoulders hunched, watching each other with suspicion and fear. Many were thin and malnourished, bones jutting and eyes sunken. Here and there amongst Hallon's slaves, some stood with chins lifted defiantly and shoulders thrown back, usually alone. The other slaves avoided them, as though conditioned to distance themselves from troublemakers. Corin made note of them as Kett strolled towards the nearest.

Kett murmured into the man's ear. The slave, after a startled moment, glanced around the arena and nodded. A few more exchanges and the slave moved off and began speaking to another. Kett picked out a new target. Corin did the same.

Within a few minutes, Hallon's fifty combatants shuffled over to Kett. Corin, with a cynical eye, watched them approach. Most were the right sort – defiant, strong-willed, not yet given up hope on life. A few were not, but that was to be expected. With any luck there would be enough to make a stand, anyway.

Had it ever occurred to the competitors to stand together and refuse to fight? Had Kett thought of that? Then Corin scanned the mharebi lining the arena and grimaced. Hallon would order the Shah's men to slaughter everyone on the ground if they refused to fight each other to the death. How ironic.

Kett reappeared by his side. 'Did you see Liu cavorting around up there in his acrobat's outfit?' He indicated the tiers on the western side.

Corin jerked a thumb at the other side of the arena. 'And Saric and a large number of overly-casual children bearing rather thick trays.'

Kett chuckled deep in his chest. 'I don't think we'd have to search far to find Gavon in the crowd either. Probably swathed in one of those white head-wraps the men use to keep the sun from their heads.'

Corin measured the sun. When it rose high enough to sit in the specially designed sun-cradle on the amphitheatre's northeastern rim, the Games would begin. He judged they had maybe half an hour left. Time to move things along.

'If they're all here, why hasn't Mina contacted us to say what they're planning?' Corin searched for Alere's twin. She would most likely be here, but difficult to spot amongst the thousands of veil-wearing women.

With a shrug, Kett swept the audience with a shrewd gaze. 'I suspect it's a matter of timing, more than anything. If we'd been smart, we would have arranged specific times to connect. Since we didn't, we're hoping to drop our wards at the right moment. And since lowering wards takes concentration, we can't do it all the time. So far we've been unlucky.'

'She could've been recaptured.' Corin made the suggestion unwillingly but it had to be said.

'Doubtful,' Kett replied. 'If so, she'd be up there with Hallon's knife to her throat.' He smiled wryly. 'Or free because Alere would sign in an instant if Mina were held to ransom. She knows her sister hasn't the training to hold out, as we do.'

Corin checked on Alere. She was ignoring Hallon, who seemed to enjoy whatever he whispered to her. Now, a mhareb in full fighting gear stood behind Alere. Even wearing a leather helmet, Shasa was instantly recognisable. Anger carried Corin unthinkingly in her direction. Only Kett's heavy hand on his shoulder brought him to his senses. Rage and guilt again bubbled so hot through his entire body it shocked even him.

'Not now, Cor.' Kett eyed the armed mharebi surrounding the arena. 'I know you're angry, but we need to stay focussed or we'll all – and Alere – die here. Revenge can come later.'

Corin shook off his restraining hand. 'Important over what I want again, huh?'

'Yes. It will pay us to be smart and careful. I suspect there's a lot more than our lives and access to the Shanzhai iron riding on the outcome of today's Games. And a few more players. Too many, perhaps.'

'What makes you say that?' Corin noted the furrow on the weishi's brow.

'There are a large number of men sitting in the crowd. On their own. Silent, still and carrying concealed weapons.'

Corin reassessed the audience. Kett was right: the crowd was liberally peppered with men who sat quietly, with hands hidden beneath their voluminous robes.

'The question is,' Kett said, 'who are they working for? Hallon, Jahil, the Selb, Liu? Like I said – too many players and we're the pawns in the middle.'

'Well, do let us brief our fellow pawns on our plan before they start the festivities without us. Hate to miss out.'

As they moved amongst the slaves, Corin and Kett did what they could to bind together a core group. They chose those who seemed to have fighting skills and a will to survive. Given the short time they had with these people, creating a team that would function was a long shot.

Kett found four other weishi: three men and a woman. Plus five men who had trained in Mamlakah as junren before being captured. All leapt at the chance to fight alongside others of the same ilk, recognising their best chance of survival. The rest were nothing special, except for their defiant attitude towards their Slavemasters.

All bore the multiple tattoos showing they'd been bought and sold several times to different, lesser Slavemasters before ending up in the Games.

Kett circulated amongst them, speaking in low tones, introducing people to each other, asking who they were and where they were from. He brought pairs together into small groups. Groups into larger units. Always questioning, listening, nodding, advising. Lightly touching one man on the arm, another on the shoulder. A smile here, a word of encouragement there, a grave acknowledgment of fear for another. It all seemed deliberate and purposeful, but to what end?

Corin listened for a minute then finally understood what the weishi sought to achieve. He was welding them into a community. Finding similarities and using those to create an *us*, which made it easier to turn the other Masters' combatants into *them*. It made a group of strangers, with no reason to kill anyone, into a tribe. Being part of a tribe meant anyone outside that clan was now the enemy. A threat to survival.

The man was an absolute genius. Within a matter of minutes he'd taken a disparate group of frightened, untrusting misfits and created the closest thing to a fighting unit imaginable under these circumstances.

They needed one more thing: a reason for the crowd to cheer for them.

CHAPTER THIRTY-TWO

CORIN

Corin grabbed Kett's arm. 'Give them a name to rally behind and you'll've done it.'

The weishi's mouth twisted into a wry grin. 'We are – the Survivors. Tell the others.'

Corin laughed and continued his work: passing on the name, creating a team with an identity and hope. A buzz went around the assemblage. The Survivors moved as a group to the red-marked, northeastern side of the arena. The sun would be at their backs and shining into their opponents' eyes. Corin squinted at the orange glow. No more than fifteen minutes remaining.

Kett's words now held more urgency. He divided the Survivors into five teams of ten, each with their own Unit number. Corin, he made leader of Unit Two; himself of Unit One. The others followed three of the Mamlakah weishi and each Unit had a junren acting as second in charge.

They were now close to the northeastern wall and the nearest audience could hear some of Kett's instructions. Corin spoke with deliberate clarity to his Unit, repeating their team name several times until someone in the tiers above caught it up and passed it on. The words 'the Survivors' rippled out through the crowd. The excitement became almost tangible as the audience found a connection to their entertainment. A chant swelled and the whole arena reverberated with the word: Sur-viv-ors! Sur-viv-ors!

The Survivors flushed with hope. Tentative smiles displaced fear. Heads lifted and backs straightened.

A stir rippled through the crowd. The chant died away, whispers travelling as people craned to see. Valera's sedate, gold-clad figure emerged into the sunshine. She surveyed the expectant arena with a gold-veiled gaze then continued past Hallon's pavilion, to join Jahil. As she passed before Hallon's family, she touched Alere's bent head. A gasp of shock washed through the onlookers.

Corin chuckled grimly. With that one touch, Valera had effectively hampered Hallon's ability to do anything to Alere today, in front of a mass of people who held the Xintou in awe. By Hallon's thunderous expression, he knew it, too.

The trumpeter blarted his instrument again and an announcer raised a polished brass megaphone.

'*Shenshis, shunus, ladies and gentlemen,*' he yelled, repeating himself when the hubbub didn't immediately die away. '*The Wushi Games are about to commence. Will the Shah's Guanjun step forward and be recognised.*'

Who had Jahil chosen in his tour of Hallon's facilities? Corin and Kett had been kept locked away from view during the visit. Pity. The Guanjun was the only competitor given indemnity from the Seyd-Hunt, if he survived the Games.

There was a short, expectant silence. The slave-combatants shuffled their feet in the sand and looked askance at each other, but no-one stepped forward. Finally, a clear, light voice carried across the amphitheatre, audible to even the most distant seats.

'I claim that honour.' Alere strode to the railing before Hallon's pavilion.

The crowd erupted into a babble of questions and shouts demanding explanations. Jahil turned to Valera, who nodded and raised a hand towards the onlookers. The crowd noise immediately died to whispers.

Kett groaned and wiped a hand over his head. Behind Alere, Hallon rose to his feet, his face purpling. He opened his mouth, but Jahil's calm voice interjected.

'Very we—'

'No! I claim the honour.' A man arose from the masses, not far away in the northwestern tiers.

His head and face were swathed in a white wrap, so only his eyes were visible. But his rough voice was unmistakable: Gavon.

Now it was Corin's time to groan.

'They're both mad,' he growled to Kett.

After a moment's shocked silence, the crowd babbled their confusion in a rising wave of noise. People leapt to their feet, screaming, faces red, fists clenched. Others rose, cheering. Arguments broke out, arms waving, fingers pointing.

Hallon grabbed at Alere's wrist, his angry words impossible to hear. He shook the agreement paper threateningly at her. She twisted free of his grip, tore off the violet veil, and threw it at his feet. She snatched the paper and, with great deliberation, ripped it into eight pieces. Holding Hallon's gaze, she let the agreement scatter on the breeze. She snapped something at Valera, who said nothing, but her mouth thinned beneath the gold veil obscuring her eyes.

With a glare at Hallon and another at Gavon, Alere gathered her skirts and hurried to the door leading to the arena. Her fingers worked at the complicated wrapped silk-robe as she went. Gavon's long, loose robe billowed as he limped down the stairs.

They emerged, side by side, onto the arena floor. Alere clearly argued vociferously with Gavon but he simply pointed up the stairs she'd descended. She shook her head. He threw up his hands in defeat, then removed his robe and dropped it to the sand, revealing his ordinary travelling clothes and bronze-studded leather vest and armguards. He kept the headgear concealing his identity.

The crowd's hum rose in volume until the trumpeter sounded his horn again. Tense silence strangled speculation. Again, Jahil looked to Valera.

The Xintou frowned and gazed, not at Alere, as Corin had expected, but somewhere off into the crowd. Her frown deepened.

She nodded and fixed her attention on Jahil.

Jahil, with a quick glance over his shoulder at Valera, lifted a hand.

'I accept both as Guanjun.' He paused to let the wordswell die away again. 'Let the Games begin.'

ALERE

With shaking fingers, Alere undid the last ornate fastener on her robe, letting the long swatch of material loop over her arm. It was too restrictive and bulky to fight in. She ran across the sand towards Kett and Corin. Gavon limped behind her, muttering imprecations against impetuous, unmanageable women. She ignored him. Applause rippled from the stands. She ignored that, too.

She met Kett and Corin and examined them. They both seemed exhausted already, and frighteningly vulnerable without shirts, armour or weapons. She sidelined fear and frustration and tried only to show joy, kissing each on the cheek.

The crowd catcalled and hollered jeering insults.

'You shouldn't have volunteered, Alli,' Kett said severely. 'Keeping you alive was our job. Now you've made our sacrifice pointless.'

'Sacrifice?' Corin raised a sardonic brow. 'I'm still intending to get out of this alive.'

Kett ignored him.

'I'm sorry,' Alere said, hanging her head. 'I couldn't sign that agreement. If I'd signed yesterday he would have kept one of you as a slave, anyway. If I'd signed today you would both still die. I couldn't think of anything else to do.' She forced a smile. 'At least we'll all die together.'

Corin laughed, a sound she was grateful to hear even if she didn't understand it.

He wrapped an arm around her waist, drew her against his side and kissed her. 'Well, Kett, you did say she wouldn't leave us to die.'

'Not *quite* what I meant,' Kett retorted.

He assigned her and Gavon to Unit Three and gave the weishi unit leader strict instructions to protect both. He murmured into the man's ear. The weishi paled, glancing at his new charges.

'Ye don't need to babysit me,' Gavon growled. 'I'll be—' He encountered an implacable glare from Kett and subsided, folding his arms.

'To succeed,' Kett said aloud, laying a hand on his shoulder, 'we can't afford weakness and you're already injured. Noble and understandable as volunteering was, you endanger Alere and you know it. Now she'll be worrying about protecting you, instead of herself.'

Gavon glared back at him, but a stricken, angry tension about his eyes betrayed his unease. His mouth thinned.

Horrified, Alere protested. 'Kett, that's unfair. He doesn't deserve that. I—'

'Don't, Alli.' Kett pulled her aside, his voice low and harsh. 'Don't challenge me now. I have fifty men and women depending on me to bring them through this bloodbath. As Guanjun you can be a symbol of hope for them.' He swept a hand at his frightened crew. 'But this will only hold together if you support me.'

He held her gaze for a long, tense moment. She kept herself in check, riding the reactive anger and trying to consider his words unemotionally.

The faces of the fifty watching them ran the gamut from mindless panic, through fear, anger, and despair. She smelled terror in their rancid sweat, saw it in their trembling hands and wild eyes. But in the ones looking to Kett, there were glimmers of hope. He was right. If they were to survive, they needed a clear chain of command and a leader. Kett was the logical choice, since the team was his creation. Important over what she wanted. Saving Gavon from hurt feelings was hardly comparable to saving his life.

'Ya-zheng, shifu.' She bowed her head as the full import of what she'd volunteered for broke over her.

No. She needed to give them a visible demonstration of her willingness to follow his lead. She lifted her head and threw back her shoulders.

'Ya-zheng, shifu!' Her shout was loud enough for all the Survivors and half of the audience nearby to hear. She bowed deeply, palms on her chest, weish-style.

A ragged cheer went up from both groups.

Kett returned her bow gravely and pointed at Unit Three.

'The weapons will be brought out shortly. Make sure you both have something.' He studied her critically. 'And get rid of the robe. It will interfere with your movements.'

'Bai, shifu,' she snapped.

A quick skim of the nearest crowdmembers, gawking between the mharebi, showed what she needed: a skinny teenage boy, wearing a thick, coarse shirt and a leather vest. She caught his attention and waved him nearer. He hesitated, then edged closer to the impassive mharebi lining the railing.

Alere stripped off the purple robe and bundled it into a ball of shining silk. A shocked murmur and titters of laughter swept through the audience, followed by lewd comments from several men. She paid no attention to them or to the vulnerability that went with wearing only a pair of loose silk trous and a breast-binder in front of thousands of people.

She held the cloth up so the boy could see it. 'This, for you to sell or give to your girl, in exchange for your shirt and vest.'

'Done,' he shouted, busy with the toggles, his face alight. 'You are *gangzhi*, shunu.'

He shrank in on himself, covering his mouth and glancing fearfully around. No-one said anything, but two hard-eyed men wearing concealing robes and headgear took an interest in him from a tier nearby.

When nothing happened, the boy heaved a shaky sigh. Within seconds he had his shirt and vest off, balled in his fist. He looked doubtfully at the mharebi between them and Alere did the same. Would they allow the exchange?

She raised the cloth questioningly at the mhareb directly above. His gaze flickered to her, the purple silk, then to the men on either side of him. Finally, he glanced at the Shah, who nodded. Hallon snarled something at his brother. Jahil disdained to acknowledge or answer.

Alere drew back her arm and threw the bundle as hard as she could. It opened and fluttered, a brilliant butterfly against the pale green sky, and dropped…too short. It would fall back inside the compound and she had no time to waste on this. Already four mharebi dragged a crate of weapons across the sand towards Kett and his men. She needed a weapon more than she needed clothing.

At the last second, the mhareb stuck out his crossbow and caught the floating material on one limb. A huge roar rose from the crowd behind him. The man flushed and flicked the robe back over his shoulder. The boy caught it and tossed his bundle down. She saluted both and dragged the clothing over her head, wrinkling her nose at the material's unwashed smell and itchy roughness. Applause followed her as she rejoined her Unit.

She found Unit Three of the Survivors as everyone scrambled to claim a weapon. Small disagreements arose, but the Unit leaders and Kett settled them quickly. Her Unit leader was a lean, older weishi named Paol. With a low bow, he presented Alere with a ceramic short sword and a bronze dagger. The sword was badly weighted, with chipped edges. But the dagger was sharp. She bowed ceremoniously, accepting the weapons, knowing it was a show for both the crowd and the others in their Unit. As he straightened, Paol flickered her a grave smile.

Finally, Kett drew the five Unit leaders and their seconds together, beckoning Alere and Gavon over, too.

'Does everyone understand the tactic?'

There were nods, but some seemed dubious. He elaborated. 'We'll come through this if we stick together. When the trumpet sounds, we form up against the eastern wall.' With the tip of his sword, he drew a half-circle in the sand and divided it into five wedges. 'The arc will consist of five close-fighting weapons from each Unit. Behind the arc are those with pikes to jab through the gaps. Behind them, the replacements.'

He stabbed the chipped ceramic blade into the sand. 'No matter what happens, we hold the line. Defend and protect your neighbour. If one man breaks and runs, *let him go*, and Hold. The. Line. If one falls, those behind drag him into the middle and a replacement fills the gap. If you get tired or injured, swap out and rest. Our enemy will be unlikely to attack as a cohesive group. You'll be dealing with individuals scared for themselves and trying to watch their own backs.' He twirled a finger to indicate all of them. 'We will watch each others' backs. That means more of us will make it. Are we clear?' The nods were more decisive this time.

Kett straightened, gathering their attention and holding it close. 'Make sure your Unit understands the importance. If we break trust, we fall. If we hold and protect each other, we survive.'

The task of briefing the Units had barely been completed when the trumpet blew its call to action and the crowd roared its approval. The Survivors took up their position against the wall, their formation ragged and imperfect, but still more structured than the other three teams.

The Games began.

CHAPTER THIRTY-THREE

ALERE

Bile rose into Alere's throat. A huge warrior in Bahad's group – a Jadidan by his shaved head and full beard – laid about with an axe and a sword. Hacking into his own team mates, he split heads and severed limbs with indiscriminate ferocity. Blood soaked the sand around him. A space formed, leaving him as a gore-spattered island in the centre. He screamed his defiance, thumping his chest. His face inhumanly bloody and savage.

Opposite, in the Chan Ling area, two factions faced off. Each appeared reluctant to start hostilities, perhaps held back by the knowledge that the first kill would release the dam and blood would pour. They circled and feinted, shouting insults. The crowd egged them on with boos and derisive comments.

About half of the combatants in Alcona Ebrahim's blue colours marshalled themselves into a rough phalanx and shuffled across the sands towards the Survivors. The rest formed into small groups of three and four. They fought amongst themselves, leaving bodies scattered throughout their area.

Alere struggled to calm herself, to focus and concentrate. Sweat slicked her palms and prickled under her arms. One of Chan Ling's people swung an axe and beheaded a woman in a single blow. Blood sprayed from her neck. Alere swallowed hard as her mouth filled with saliva and her stomach churned. Behind her, someone did throw up. The sound and scent started a minor chain reaction in others. Corin snapped at his Unit's second in command to get people to help the ill and bury the puke to hide the smell. Slowly, the Survivors got themselves under control again. The formation drew into a tighter semicircle.

Somewhere, beyond the pounding of blood in her ears, someone called Alere's name. She shook herself. It had to be a hallucination. No, there it was again. From somewhere behind and above.

The nearest potential enemy was far enough away. She could risk a quick check. She gestured another Unit member forward to take her place in the line.

'Alere?' It was Saric's light, anxious voice.

Alere stood as tall as she could, trying to see between the mharebi and over the high wall. There: she glimpsed a white, scruffy head bouncing in and out of view as the boy searched for her.

'C'mon.' His tone changed to wheedling. 'Let me get closer? I can't see a thing. You can have a free sweet-xun bun.'

One of the mharebi snarled an insult at the boy and told him where he could shove his bun. The man beside him gave a cruel laugh. Instead of pushing Saric away, he dragged the boy closer. He snatched a bun off the tray, took a bite and threw it back in Saric's hopeful face.

'It's disgusting you little haraami!' He grabbed the tray, hauled the straps off Saric's shoulders and flung it over the edge, into the arena. 'Go get it. Then you'll have a real close view.'

Alere shouted a warning and thrust an unwary team member aside. The wooden tray smashed onto the sand and shattered. A high-pitched scream sounded from above, followed by a guttural laugh. The mhareb had Saric balanced over his head. The boy struggled in vain. Alere let go her weapons in preparation. Trepidation weighed down her legs and held fast the breath in her throat.

'Kett!' she yelled over her shoulder. Silhouetted against the sky, Sarics legs thrashed. He squalled like an infant and swore like a yongbing.

'Not now, Alli,' Kett shouted back.

The nearest enemy was only twenty paces away now and gaining ground. Bloodlust rose in their eyes and they closed on the Survivors.

Saric's screamed invectives turned into a shriek. The mhareb hurled him over the edge. Alere held her arms out in desperation, prepared to do what she could to break his fall. A heavy hand shoved her aside. She tripped over the broken tray and curled into a roll. She found her feet as Saric's flailing body landed squarely in Gavon's outstretched arms. The yongbing staggered. His knees buckled under the weight, but he stayed on his feet.

A huge roar erupted from the crowd. Thousands leapt to their feet, clapping wildly. Alere caught a glimpse of Hallon's laughing countenance. Behind him, Shasa's cheeks were death-pale, her eyes wide and horrified. Her hands were clasped over her mouth. Oh, so she cared now, did she? Chouhuo.

Valera, Jahil and his family were all on their feet. Jahil's youngest daughter buried her face in her mother's stomach. The other Slavemasters showed little interest, either busy eating or, in Bahad's case, sleeping.

Saric wriggled free of Gavon's grip and landed on his feet. He made a rude gesture at the mharebi above. The crowd cheered and the boy swept them and Gavon a bow. Gavon snorted, snatched up his sword again and limped back to the line.

Alere crouched before Saric, examining him for injuries. 'You alright? You're mad, you know that. What was the point of provoking them?'

'This.' The boy pointed at the sand.

There, glinting beneath the remains of her tray, a hint of shining metal. She swept the buns and broken wood aside. Her team mates pounced on the breads and stuffed them hungrily into their mouths, sand and all. Reverently, she drew out two steel swords and two daggers. Relief and delight weakened her knees. She yanked the suede covers off her own and ran her hands over the yanstones. Warm security spread into the darkest corners of her mind and the weariest parts of her body.

She grabbed Saric and hauled him into a hug.

'You are mad, but thank you. Here.' She passed over her ceramic blade and bronze knife. 'Keep to the back and try to stay alive. Don't kill anyone if you can help it. But also don't trust anyone except me, Kett, Corin or Gavon, got it? Yell if you need me.'

Saric gave her a jaunty salute. 'Got it. Staying alive is always my aim, anyway. And you're welcome.'

'Corin!' She spotted him, right in the forefront of the arc.

He stood next to Kett, his eyes firmly fixed on the approaching enemy. He didn't respond to her call. She didn't bother to yell again. He probably couldn't hear, anyway. His whole focus was forward. The Ebrahim team were just outside ma'ai, hesitating and shuffling as they worked themselves up enough to attack.

Pushing through Corin's Unit, she thrust his weapons under his nose. He swore at her for distracting him. His anger petered into surprise as he focussed on his blades. He handed off the inferior weapons and grabbed his with a sigh. Then he pulled her close and stole a fleeting kiss. It was sweet in its taste of fear for her and himself, deepened by his touch on the yanstones.

He broke the kiss and stared at her in astonishment. Shaken by the intensity of it, and instinctively needing to put distance between them, Alere pointed over his shoulder. He nodded, but his eyes held hope, now.

She turned to make her way back to her Unit but someone grabbed her wrist. She spun, dagger-drawn in automatic reaction. She stopped the strike. Kett's grip tightened and he studied her with troubled eyes. On impulse, she kissed his cheek, heart full of fear at potential loss.

'Be safe, Kett,' she whispered.

His lips twisted into a small, ironic smile. 'I will if you are.'

She had to chuckle. It was an old exchange between them, reversed. He released her. There was no time for fears, so she swallowed them down. She touched the lingering marks of his fingers. The memory of their warmth lay heavy in her heart.

She found her spot in the line, next to Gavon.

Gavon yanked aside the white cloth over his face. 'Alright, boyo?'

'Yes,' she replied, eyes resolutely on the approaching enemy, only five paces away now. When he turned away, she checked on him. His skin was pale and most of his weight rested on his good leg. His mouth was set in a grim line.

'Gavon, I expect you to still be standing when it's over, hear me?' she growled.

He gave a snort and thumped her shoulder. 'What ye expect and what ye get aren't always the same, boyo. Remember that.'

There was no more time for conversation. Alere locked firmly away the fears threatening to paralyse her. The blood-fever of battle roared. Time slowed. The first attacker stepped into range, a sword raised over her head. Stupid minutiae caught Alere's attention. The bright red colour to the woman's hair. The sharp, hot smell of urine as the slave next to her panicked. Sand, gritty and uncomfortable, that worked its way inside the thin, silk slippers she wore. She should have swapped those, too. She licked her dry lips, salty with sweat.

Somehow, the part of her mind monitoring more important things raised her sword in time to block the first strike. It was a sloppy reaction and the clash jarred her arm. Her blade came through unscathed. The woman's bronze weapon snapped near the hilt. The blade flipped over Alere's head and landed somewhere behind. The redhead stared at the stump, astonishment snapping her out of the blood-thrall.

In that instant she was just a woman: frightened of dying and prepared to take Alere's life if it would save her own. Alere hesitated, reluctant to kill. The woman was hardly her enemy. She was just another victim of the slave trade and its Masters.

They gazed at each other. Neither moved. The sounds of violent, mindless death roiled around them. There was a squelching sound. The redhead's eyes widened and her lips parted. A scarlet-stained ceramic blade protruded through her chest from behind. She sank to her knees, the life already draining from her. The Jadidan giant wrenched his blade free of the dead woman's chest. He stood on the body, leering at Alere, twirling the axe in his other hand.

To Alere's left, one of her Unit fell and the line opened. A man in Sinclar black tried to break through. Alere had to engage to hold the line. She flipped her dagger over, slicing at him backhand as he tried to slide past. Her blade opened a gash in his bicep. He raised his arm instinctively to check the injury. Alere stabbed beneath, straight into his heart. He clutched at his side and fell.

The Jadidan's axe blade arced towards Alere's head. The fug of both fear and doubt vanished. She spun aside and let the axe swing past. The Jadidan had put too much into the strike. The heavy blade carried on. The edge buried itself into the fallen man's body. Alere delivered an overhead swordstroke that cut through the back of the Jadidan's thick neck. His corpse sagged, twitching.

'Boyo!' Gavon's gruff yell caught her ear.

He had retreated from the line and was busy behind, dragging the wounded and dead aside. The pile of corpses was already depressingly-large. He staggered towards her, his face pale, white headdress stained red. The cloth over his injured leg was black with blood and more oozed from a jagged gash across his chest.

He pointed to her right. She saw nothing but Survivor team-members desperately battling to hold the line. Weapons glinted in the bright sunlight and limbs flailed. Screams of agony and triumph intermingled with the horribly organic slicing of flesh, and the crunch of sand beneath bare feet. The smell of blood, offal and vomit hung heavy in the cool air.

Two fighters separated, revealing Kett and Corin standing back to back. They were besieged by eight men in Alcona's blue colours. Kett and Corin held their own, but barely. Blood from a slice on Kett's shoulder washed his left arm bright red. A slash across Corin's back hampered his sword-arm.

She stuffed her sword and dagger into her belt. Snatching a short, bronze dagger from a dead hand, she leapt onto the pile of bodies. The soft footing shifted unpleasantly beneath her feet. She put the thought of what was under her aside. Height was important now.

Saric appeared at her side with four other daggers ready and two more jammed into his belt. He held one out. Alere hefted the one she already held, judging its weight. It was badly balanced and she'd be lucky to even hit someone.

Kett cried out and dropped to one knee, a dagger point-deep in his thigh. Reversing the knife, she threw it at the Alcona man who stood over him. The bronze blade buried itself up to the hilt in the

Alcona slave's tricep. He screamed an oath. Kett used the moment to regain his feet. He jammed a dagger into the man's throat. Shoving the body into another of his assailants, Kett yanked the blade from his thigh. He thrust it into an exposed gullet and sliced across to the liver.

Saric slapped the next into Alere's palm. She threw but her target moved and the blade missed. She flicked the third knife at a large man who swung an axe at Corin's head. It didn't rotate as she expected and hit handle-first. That achieved nothing but to bruise the already-angry Chan-slave. It did distract him long enough for Corin to sweep his leg and follow through with a sword-cut to the throat.

It wasn't enough. Two more slaves stepped into the breach. Swiftly, she flicked another pair of blades. One found its mark in an exposed stomach. The other, unexpectedly blade-heavy, hit flat against a chest and fell to the sand. She watched in growing despair. Corin was driven from Kett's side by a heavy attack. Kett's leg gave beneath him. Alere hurled yet another knife. Her target moved and she missed again.

Desperately, she sought for help. She was too far away and using the wrong knives. Wasn't there anyone in their Units to help? No, each member of Unit One and Two was already hard-pressed to hold the line. Unit Four lay decimated, scattered on the sand. Unit Five had only a few team members left alive. The Survivors were disintegrating.

Saric slapped another dagger into her hand and held up empty palms to indicate it was the last one. Alere hefted it uncertainly, studying Kett and Corin. At least fifteen opponents lay dead at their feet. More came at them. Both were wounded and neither could hold out for long. Corin held two at bay. His footwork slowed and his strokes were less powerful. He shook his head and blood dribbled down his neck. Two men launched themselves at Kett. He turned aside, but his steps were uncertain. His leg dragged. If she threw successfully right now, she could help one of them.

Her choice could mean the survival of one and the death of the other. Who did she save?

Steadying herself, she drew back her arm...and chose.

CHAPTER THIRTY-FOUR

ALERE

The blade found its mark and lodged in the throat of her target. He collapsed, blood bubbling on his lips.

Three sonorous trumpet blasts rang out overhead. The signal to stop fighting. They repeated. Alere gave a sob of relief and covered her mouth with a bloodied hand. She checked to see if the attacking slaves heard the trumpet.

Both Kett and Corin yelled at their opponents, although she couldn't hear the words. Supposedly, anyone delivering a kill-strike after the trumpets forfeited their lives. But if the Slavemasters held hard to that rule they would find themselves with no Seyd to Hunt.

The crowd roared. The trumpets sounded again and the crowd's din faded. Applause and encouragement intermingled with cries of disappointment and the occasional chanted 'sur-vi-vors!'. A child wailed. A woman's shrill laugh cut through the deeper voices of the mostly-male audience.

It took a few seconds for the trumpet notes to filter through the crowd noise, blood-rage and fear, but slowly weapons lowered. The remaining slaves stopped. Armaments fell from fingers made lax by the waning of battle-fever.

The aftermath set in.

In the middle of the Ebrahim area, one man stood alone amidst the bloody consequences of the Games. He screamed and hurled his pike at the Slavemasters, high in the stands. A nearby section of the crowd laughed and the weapon fell short, bouncing off the stone wall to land uselessly on the ground.

A woman in Bahad Sinclar's colours contemplated the short sword in her hand. Blood seeped thickly from a wound in her stomach. She collapsed to the sand, bereft of whatever drive had kept her standing. A blood-spattered man in Hallon's red blinked dazedly then fell to his knees, vomiting and sobbing.

A young man in green, barely more than a child, curled into a ball. His arms wrapped around his head and he rocked back and forth, crooning something incomprehensible. It was a reaction that lurked on the edges of Alere's own Inners. But if she gave in, she and her friends would not survive the next few minutes.

Saric and Gavon lived, so she leapt off the grisly mound and ran to Kett and Corin. Kett knelt in the sand, head bent, arms and torso bloodied, chest heaving. Sliding in beside him, she raised his face. A weary smile lifted his lips. One eye was half-closed from a cut on his brow.

'Kett.' She hooked an elbow under his uninjured arm and tried to haul him upright. 'You have to stand up.' A quick glance over her shoulder showed the four Slavemasters and Jahil rising from their seats, preparing to descend into the arena. 'You have to get up or the mharebi will shoot you when they choose the Twenty. Please?'

He struggled upright, but his lips were white. She ripped three long strips off the shirt of a nearby corpse. One went around Kett's shoulder. Another she folded into a pad and tied onto the deep thigh-wound. He leaned heavily on her, swaying. Gavon appeared at her side and slid under Kett's arm.

'I'll hold him while you see to Corin,' he said.

'You're little better, if at all. Let me...' She shredded more cloth and reached out to tear the material over the re-opened injury on his leg, intending to bind it.

He pushed her hand away. 'See to Corin.'

Something in his weary, pale face made her swallow her instinctive argument. She went to Corin and found Saric already there. He had Corin on his feet, propping him up when he listed to one side. A quick check showed mostly superficial cuts. One to his calf and a shallow slice above his ear that bled a lot but seemed to be only skin-deep. The one on his back looked worse than it was. It bled freely and must be painful. His eyes were vague, which was worrying. Had the headwound concussed him?

Alere slapped his cheeks lightly until he managed to centre on her.

'Alli,' he mumbled. 'You're alive. Am I?'

She smiled weakly, wiping sand and blood from his eyes. 'Yes, but not for long if you don't focus. Hallon and the others are coming to choose Seyd for the Hunt. There are only maybe twenty-six or seven left alive. I need you alert and strong so they don't shoot you. Got it?'

He stretched a bloody hand towards her. The sword was still in his fist. He blinked at it in perplexity and ran a thumb over the yanstone, leaving a smear on the silvery surface. In an instant, his eyes cleared and he straightened.

Surprised, she glanced at the stones and back at him. 'Can you heal yourself, Cor? As I did with mine? Try and I'll see if Kett can do the same.'

She returned to Kett's side. Even half-prepared as she was, when she pushed the stones into Kett's palms the shock of his warmth rippled disturbingly through her body. His hands were on her skin, his mind inside hers.

'Kett?'

He gazed in distant wonder, staring through her at something only he could see.

'Kett?' She tapped his cheek. 'You need to heal yourself.'

p364 *Aiki Flinthart*

'I'll try.' His fingers gripped the pommels.

How much time and energy did he have? Could he even make the stones work? She checked the Slavemasters.

Jahil emerged onto the arena floor, with Lan close behind him. Valera, and Jahil's women and daughters remained up in the pavilion. Hallon, accompanied by Feddor, followed the Shah. Shasa shadowed her master. Behind them, trailed the other three Slavemasters and their entourages. Fifty or more of Jahil's mharebi ran down from the walls and filed into the arena. They herded the remaining slaves into the centre, delivering mercy to those too injured to stand.

'Drop all weapons.' The Games master's voice, amplified by the megaphone, echoed around the grounds. 'Drop all weapons, line up and stand before the Shah.'

Two mharebi appeared next to Kett and yanked the ceramic sword from his hands. Alere protested when hers were taken, but a mhareb prodded her into the sorry lineup of slaves standing before Jahil and the Slavemasters. She ducked under Kett's arm, helping him to stay upright. Gavon limped into place on his other side. Corin, similarly disarmed and still unhealed, joined them. He swayed and held onto Saric's shoulder.

Alere glanced quickly along the line of slaves. Most were injured in some way, though few as badly as Kett and Gavon. She did a swift head-count: Twenty-four, excluding Saric, herself and Gavon. As Guanjun she and Gavon should be left out of the Seyd-count. Surely, even Hallon wouldn't send a child into the Hunt? Saric wasn't meant to be on the arena floor in the first place.

The Slavemasters arrived. Alcona appeared bored, Jahil and Lan uncomfortable, Bahad and Feddor revoltingly-eager. Hellon simply smiled, his expression smug. Each of the four Masters wandered down the line, inspecting slaves marked in their own colours, prodding them. Feddor toed a woman who lay on the ground, nearby. When she groaned and stirred, he produced a dagger and slit her throat himself, wiping his blade fastidiously on her clothing. Alere shuddered.

Jahil stayed ten paces back, avoiding those he would condemn in a few moments. Lan's eyes were fixed on Alere, his expression one of puzzlement and interest. She ignored him.

Hallon moved slowly past Alere. 'The time has come to Choose the Seyd, my brother.'

Jahil returned nothing but a faint glare of contempt. Shasa, close behind her master, gripped her weapons tightly, her ice-blue eyes barely skimming over Alere and Kett. Instead her gaze lingered on Corin and Saric. Beneath superficial coldness lay barely-masked, unmistakable fear. When Corin spat at her feet she turned away, her mouth compressed and eyes downcast.

Her bargain with Hallon also required Shasa to present him with Liu and Mina. They weren't here. Would she face some sort of retribution? Did she now regret her actions? Alere could only hope so. The woman deserved whatever punishment Hallon meted out.

Uneasy with the vindictive trend to her thoughts, Alere brought her attention back to Hallon. There had to be something she could do to prevent her friends being taken as Seyd or deemed unfit and killed – but what? Without yanstones, weapons or an army, she could think of nothing.

A mhareb held Alere and Corin's steel weapons reverently out to Jahil. Hallon crossed over to where his brother stood. He extended a hand towards a hilt. Two mharebi guarding Jahil blocked Hallon's approach.

'Brother.' Hallon spread his hands wide. 'They are the spoils of war. They came from *my* slaves and as such belong to me.'

Jahil picked up Corin's sword, inspecting the blade's line, hefting its weight, holding it up to the sunlight. The yanstone flared and sparkled.

'I think not, brother. These belong to me, now. Besides, I see you already have a steel sword. Be content with what you have.' His mouth twisted into irony and he indicated the weapon strapped to Hallon's hip. Alere ground her teeth. Kett's sword. By her side, Kett stiffened and growled, low in his throat.

'Get on with your games.' Jahil flipped a negligent hand at Hallon. The Slavemaster's face purpled but he held his tongue. Perhaps he was restrained by the presence of so many mharebi wearing Jahil's colours. Or by the ten-thousand strong crowd watching his every move. He bowed stiffly.

Fourteen of the remaining twenty-four wore Hallon's colours, a fact he pointed out loudly to the other Slavemasters. He made a great show of inspecting each one and picked out a few, telling them to step backward three paces. He chose those least injured.

He paused in front of Alere. 'You, step back.'

'You may not Choose the Guanjun, brother.' Jahil's soft, reasonable voice carried clearly in the arena's expectant hush.

Hallon's mouth twisted into a snarl but he stalked past. His eye fell on Saric and Corin and he laughed. He turned to Gavon, tore off the concealing headdress and tossed the stained cloth aside. After studying Gavon's weathered, bloodied face, he laughed again and swaggered over to Bahad. There, he murmured into the man's ear and seemed to take great pleasure in his fellow Slavemaster's outraged reaction. He clamped a hand onto Bahad's shoulder and spoke again, preventing whatever impulsive action the younger man may have been considering. Bahad's expression segued into crafty understanding.

Gavon drew back his shoulders and raised his chin.

The four Slavemasters came together. Their talk erupted into low-voiced argument involving a great deal of arm-waving and indignant pointing. Finally, they seemed to reach some agreement. Alere checked the ragged line of remaining, un-Chosen slaves. Excluding herself, Gavon and Saric, there were seven, which meant there were only three places in the Twenty.

Bahad Sinclar strutted along the line. He stopped in front of Gavon, a broad grin showing uneven teeth.

'You – step back. You are Chosen.' He sneered.

'You may not Choose a Guanjun,' Jahil repeated flatly.

Bahad pointed at the Shah. 'And *you,* my Shah, should not select a Guanjun who has already *been* Chosen. This man is Gavon Abdul-kin, the Seyd who slaughtered my father ten years ago. By the laws of the Hunt, his life is *mine.*'

Jahil hesitated. His gaze brushed over Alere's and held resignation and pity. Ah. So there was no hope. Jahil had no power to defy tradition and free a man already meant to be dead a decade earlier. His mouth pulled down at the corners. He inclined his head, slowly.

Gavon sent Bahad a long, burning glare but said nothing. He simply turned his back on Bahad and limped to join the Twenty. On the bottom tier of the crowd-seats, the nearest eager watchers spread his name. The whispers swept through the audience. A firestorm of excitement rose, swelling into a frenzied chant that coalesced into a wall of sound.

Gavon's name filled the sky.

He flushed dark and raised a hand in acknowledgment. The crowd screamed in response, stamping their feet in thunderous approval.

Bahad shouted abuse and threats, attempting to silence the mob. Finally, he signalled to the trumpeter, who blew six sharp blasts, quelling the sound to a low murmur. A lone voice, high in the stands, screamed out one word: *Gangzhi!* An uneasy silence followed, interspersed with edgy laughter and whispers. Jahil's mharebi turned their crossbows on the audience.

Chan strode forward and pointed imperiously at one of the two remaining men in the line up wearing his green, ordering him back into the Twenty. Alere's heart stopped. That left only one place. One of her friends would die, here, if she couldn't think of a way to prevent it. If she signed Hallon's stupid agreement would that work or had it all gone too far now?

She hadn't thought past joining Kett and Corin on the field of battle. Her focus had been on getting them through the Games alive. She'd thought that might win Hallon's respect and he would back down and let them go or renegotiate his terms. How could she have been so naïve? He hadn't kept his place as the strongest Master for thirty years by being soft or compassionate.

Hallon strolled to where Alere still stood supporting Kett. The Slavemaster stopped in front of her and pointed to her friends.

'Last chance, girl,' he murmured. 'Agree to sign and one will remain as a slave for your bond. You can still save one of them.' He strode two steps to her right and scanned Corin's injuries with amusement. 'And I believe I'll also make a swap. You.' He pointed over Corin's shoulder at one of the men in the Twenty. 'Return to the lineup.'

When the man protested and held his ground, Hallon signalled. Two mharebi cocked their bows and shot him in the chest. He gaped at the protruding bolts and staggered three steps backward. His knees collapsed. Blood sprayed from his mouth as he folded to the sand. The crowd cheered, applauding madly. Lan and Jahil both paled and swallowed.

Hallon fisted Saric's white-blond hair, forcing the boy's face up.

'Let me go you wisix kalb!' Saric yelled, lashing out with a kick at Hallon's knee. Hallon stepped aside.

'You, boy, can join the Twenty.' Hallon thrust the child back, into the arms of one of the mhareb. The man wrapped Saric up and held him firmly as the boy thrashed, swore and kicked.

'No!' 'You can't!' 'Master!' Corin, Alere and Shasa all cried out at once.

Shasa rushed forward, throwing herself to her knees before Hallon. Her hands clutched at his booted foot. Her head bowed in supplication.

'Master, please?' She raised a stricken face to him. 'You promised. Please?'

Hallon raised one brow and kicked his foot free. 'No, my dear. *You* promised. You promised to bring me Liu Gray, *and* the Koh-Lin girl today. That was the condition of saving your brat from slavery and giving him safe passage to Mamlakah. *You* failed. He may not be my son, you chouhuo, but he's your get. So he's *my* slave and I Choose him.'

Alere gaped, mind thick with confusion. Saric was Shasa's *son?* Which meant all of her machinations had been to protect him. And if Saric, who was almost ten, wasn't *Hallon's* child, then... She looked at Corin, who gazed at mother and son with his mouth agape and eyes wide. The resemblance, now Alere was attuned to it, was striking. Saric was Corin's child. Saric had stopped struggling and seemed unfazed but wary. He must be already aware of his parentage – both sides.

Shasa rose to her feet. Fear and desperation warred in her face. She gazed at Saric. He snarled at his captor. Her expression firmed. She drew her sword and stood between Hallon and Saric, chin and weapon raised defiantly.

'Choose me instead, Master. He's a child. I've failed you, I know. Hunt me.'

CHAPTER THIRTY-FIVE

ALERE

Hallon jerked his head at the mhareb, who released Saric. The boy ran to his mother.

'Shasa.' Saric grabbed her arm. 'Don't. I can win the Hunt. You know I can. Then I'll be free.'

Shasa glanced down at him. Pride and love swept fear into beauty for an instant. A small smile played at her mouth and softened the hard angles of her jaw.

'I know, my little one—'

Hallon's dagger plunged into her chest and tore her heart in two. Turning a look of utter astonishment on her Master, she coughed once and collapsed. The sword fell from her fingers. Her eyes drifted towards Saric even as light faded from them.

Alere gasped and covered her mouth.

Saric froze, mouth open, fingers still entwined in hers, staring at his mother's body. Anger bloomed in his young face. A scream of shrill, soul-reaving rage ripped from his throat. He launched himself at Hallon. Alere grabbed the boy around the waist, holding him back. His nails tore at her skin. She held him close, murmuring useless reassurances into his ear. Tears broke forth and streaked the dirt on his cheeks. He turned in Alere's arms and buried his face in her shoulder, sobbing uncontrollably like the child he still was.

Her own tears froze into icy determination.

A collective sigh drifted down from the audience around the arena, as though they had held their breath as mother protected child and released it with Shasa's death.

Corin dropped to his knees beside Shasa's body, his expression dark with guilt and renewed loss. With an unsteady hand, he stroked her cheek. He dipped a fingertip into the blood oozing down his own neck and touched it to her forehead, leaving two red dots. He repeated the gesture, placing a mark beside each eye and on the centre of her lips. The traditional face makeup for the hunli ceremony; the wedding in which he and Shasa had never had a chance to take part. He closed her eyes and bowed his head. Tears dropped onto her golden skin.

His hand slid to hers. He snatched her sword free and rose, slashing at Hallon. Hallon stepped easily aside and struck Corin in the temple with the pommel of Kett's steel sword. Corin's head snapped back. He collapsed bonelessly to the ground, his body draped across Shasa's. Her sword fell to the blood-stained sand. Hallon kicked, his boot sinking deep into Corin's stomach.

The crowd groaned. Alere echoed it, fearing him dead until the faint pulse at his neck throbbed and his chest rose. Relief buckled her knees. The smug, knowing expression on Hallon stiffened them. He signalled to his mharebi. The men wrenched Saric from Alere's arms. She protested. A knife pricked her throat. They forced the boy into the Twenty. Gavon gathered Saric close, putting an arm around his shoulder.

Alere scanned the arena. She took in Corin's unconscious, bleeding figure, Kett's exhaustion and still-dripping wounds, Shasa's lifeless corpse, Gavon's pale, bloody face, and Saric's grief. This devastation was partly her fault. If she had signed that gouri agreement she'd have saved all of them this pain.

She'd thought doing the noble, important, self-sacrificing thing of not signing – for the greater good – was also the right thing. The irony was, when considered from a purely political point of view, her actions were still right. She had saved many thousands of people from the weapons Shanzhai's iron could produce in Hallon's hands.

However, sometimes doing what she wanted *had* to be more important than doing what was right. This was one of those times.

And what she wanted, more than anything, was to slit Hallon's throat.

Alere smiled grimly to herself. If she viewed it from a certain perspective, killing Hallon could also be considered the right thing; the important thing. It would free Jahil to be a Shah in more than just name.

Wait…name… name…why did that remind her of something… what was it? Something she'd read in the Weishi library. Something she'd thought about during training with Gavon, on the boat. Something about the rules governing combat in Melcor…something to do with her name.

Oh yes. *That* would work. Certainty displaced horror and fear. *Now* she knew what to do.

As Hallon approached, smug and arrogant, Alere smiled. Genuinely. Nastily.

His eyes narrowed, assurance faltering.

Before he could threaten her again, Alere checked on Valera in the pavilion. Her attention was fixed on the drama unfolding in the arena, her hands clutching the seat arms. Alere raised a little finger and dropped her wards.

Valera, can you Broadcast? She awaited the xintou's reply anxiously. Not all xintou were strong enough to Broadcast to an audience of this size. If she could, every unwarded mind in the arena would hear the next things that came out of Alere's mouth – and she needed them to hear.

Yes, but—

Just take what I say and do it, Valera. Every thought and nuance, not just the words. I want them to feel me. And, no matter what happens, keep Broadcasting until I tell you to stop.

Done properly everyone should feel what she felt, all without realising the feelings were imposed from the outside. To make this work, she must keep tight control over her Outers and that was likely to be difficult.

You want me to manipulate the audience? What are you intending? Valera's reluctance was obvious. Xintou House training specifically forbade influencing unwarded minds on any scale.

This is the only chance I have to save my friends. Please?

Not unless you tell me what you're doing! I won't be a party to something that will jeopardise my Bonded's life.

Jiche, Valera! Don't you understand? If I don't do this, your Bonded Shah, and his whole gouri Jundom will fall. Hallon won't let Jahil live much longer. And he'll slaughter Jahil's children for good measure. Stop arguing. Mistress Li sent me, remember?

...Very well. Valera didn't bother to hide her anger. *But I will shut the Broadcast down if I think you've lost control or if you're doing something that will harm my people.*

I won't.

Alere threw back her shoulders.

'I invoke the Challenge of Equals.' She projected the words aloud and mentally. Both were coloured with a hint of sarcasm and implied Hallon was decidedly less than her equal.

Valera's transmission swept through the watchers. Astonished whispers became shouts. Questions and answers, bandied from tongue to tongue, were an ocean's roar of insanity.

Trumpets sounded and the noise died away. All heads turned towards Alere.

Lan brushed past the mharebi guarding his father and came to stand before her.

'Who are you to invoke that Challenge?' Though his bearing was haughty, his question was laced more with curiosity than antagonism. 'Are you aware it's a fight to the death?'

Alere inclined her head, choosing her next words carefully. 'I am a Koh-Lin. Daughter and heir to Rafi, Jun Second of Mamlakah.' She allowed scorn into her Outers and raked Hallon with a cool sneer. '*More* than your equal. By that right I Challenge you, Hallon Nasim.' Scorn slid into sarcasm. 'Of course, as the lesser rank, you *can* refuse.'

Hallon's face darkened. He half-raised Kett's sword.

'Equality status accepted,' Lan said loudly. The nearest crowd members gasped. 'State your grievances to establish validity of the Challenge.'

She walked forward, slowly, timing her words to her steps and her emotions to her words. Flash-images of the last few days went with each emotion, directly into the minds all around.

Fear. 'You have kept me and my companions prisoner.'

Anger. 'You kidnapped the new Jun First of Mamlakah.'

Hallon sneered and stared insolently, unperturbed. The crowd began to murmur again.

Pain. 'You threatened and beat my friends.'

Disgust. 'Tried to extort wealth for your own gain. Threw us into this barbaric show for your entertainment.'

Dismay. 'And murdered a mother protecting her son.' She let a sharp stab of guilt through. That elicited stifled gasps from the audience.

Horror. 'Lastly, you have built an army and conspired to cause a war between our Jundoms.'

Hallon stiffened and glanced quickly at his brother, but said nothing.

She remained deliberately outside ma'ai. Too far for him to make any unexpected moves. But close enough that she could see his intent. He took a deep breath, visibly calming himself. The anger-borne blood drained from his face and Kett's sword slickered back into its scabbard.

Jiche. What did it take to rattle this man?

Disdain. 'So, I take it you refuse?'

In the back of Alere's mind, Valera's fear and hesitation niggled. She couldn't lose control of this.

The crowd were deep in thrall with the Broadcast now. She could sway them whatever way she wanted. The Shah's family, including Hallon and Feddor, were clearly warded and unaffected, though. Somehow, she had to get inside Hallon's head. It was, as Kett said, a mind game. What did Hallon want? What buttons could she push to upset him?

Ah…

Valera. The thought went on a tight-focus, only to the xintou. *I need you to use your Bond with Jahil. Get him to goad Hallon into accepting my challenge.*

Alere! That might put Jahil in danger. You know I can't—

If you want your precious Shah to survive, and his son to be the next on the throne, then this is your best hope. I've heard some of Hallon's plans and, believe me, they do not include Jahil being alive.

And what good will it do anyone if Hallon kills Jahil right now?

Jiche, Valera. You have my word. I'll step in front of Hallon's blade, myself, before I let him kill Jahil today. Agreed?

… !

Jahil's body jerked, puppet-like. He stepped up. 'Hallon, am I to understand you're thinking of refusing the Challenge? You cannot.'

Hallon snarled at his brother, hand once more on his hilt. Jahil held his ground but his eyes were wide, his skin waxen. Both Feddor and Lan gaped at the Shah in open astonishment.

'Finally growing a spine, my brother?' Hallon muttered, unaware the entire arena could, through Valera, hear every word he said.

Another gasp washed through the crowd, sounding like a whisper of wind in the forest.

Jahil swallowed hard, but straightened and raised his chin. Valera's doing, or his own?

'By our laws, brother,' he said clearly, 'you may not refuse a lawful Challenge of Equals unless she is not, after all, your equal. But you told me, yourself, that this girl is the Koh-Lin Jun-Heir. If her claims of kidnapping and imprisonment are unjust, brother, surely you will prevail. Unless you think you cannot beat her?' Jahil made a show of surveying first his brother, then Alere, highlighting the difference between them.

Hallon stood a full head taller and his weight was almost twice hers. He was older, yes, but with thirty more years of experience. He carried both sword and kusarigama and wore ceremonial leather and bronze torso armour beneath his outer robe. Alere was unarmed. She wore only purple silk trous and a blood-spattered shirt.

The crowd's babble rose again as acknowledgment of her rank by the Shah filtered through and realisation followed. The Slavemaster had kidnapped and imprisoned a noble of equal rank and higher importance. The significance was impossible to miss. Alere saw the battle inside Hallon's head in the small muscle movements around his eyes and mouth.

If he accepted and lost, then he tacitly admitted her claims were true. When she killed him, his possessions and assets became hers as compensation. If he accepted and won, killing her would visit Rafi's full wrath upon Melcor. And Rafi would be backed by the whole of Mamlakah, since Hallon had also kidnapped and tortured the new Jun First. If he refused the Challenge then he lost face in front of the other Slavemasters. Lost his control over the Shah and the populace of Chengdu. Fear-inspired control depended on strength and brutality. Running from an unarmed woman would hardly bolster that image.

'Very well.' Hallon drew himself up haughtily. His eyes glittered. Rage showed in every corded muscle of his arms as he clenched his fists. 'I accept. Give us space and I will finish this quickly.' He shucked his white robe. Beneath, he wore the chest armour and loose white trousers.

Then he drew the kusarigama from his belt and unwound the chain.

Though she suppressed it, he must have seen the flash of uncertainty in her. A mutter of quick, incomprehensible comments drifted across the arena. Her doubt infected the onlookers as Valera Broadcast it. Alere ground her teeth. She needed to keep stricter control over her emotions. She needed the crowd on her side, not his.

Around her, mharebi moved back. They dragged bodies aside and herded the living slaves out of an expanding circle in the middle of the sandy floor. Alere glanced swiftly over at Kett. Corin was awake again and the pair supported each other. Kett returned a steady, impassive gaze, giving her nothing in the way of hints or ideas. He merely nodded once, slowly. Oddly enough that gave her heart. He had faith in her. Corin's expression was one of frowning uncertainty. She quashed a flicker of anger.

A quick look at Gavon lifted her spirits. He gave a small nod and pointed at his feet, reminding her to watch her opponent's feet for clues to timing. She'd never quite got it right, but this was no time to think about that. Instead she sent Valera a hint of the love she bore for all three men. It filtered, on a sigh, through the audience. A mhareb next to Kett shifted closer and put an arm under his elbow, helping him to stand. Now, should Hallon prevail, someone might champion them.

Hallon trod lightly into the circle's centre, swinging the weighted ball at the chain's end. She inspected it, trying to estimate the length of the chain. Jiche! This weight was spiked. The bronze blade was double-edged and longer than the one she'd trained against. Her empty palms slicked with sweat and her hands shook.

'Shunu.' A soft voice by her side caught her attention.

Lan approached. Sand crunched under his feet. He held out her weapons. Respect and a hint of fear darkened his eyes. What happened next would affect him and his father, so he had every reason to be afraid. The crowd burst into applause as she accepted them with a small bow.

She started to slide her thumbs across the stones for reassurance, but stopped. The stones had a detaching effect on her in times of stress. The last thing she wanted was to disconnect from the audience. They needed to live this with her, and possibly feel her death. If they felt every moment, every fear, every scrap of pain and anxiety, she might have a chance at achieving her aim here: ending more than just Hallon's life.

Alere?

Distracted, she stumbled as she approached Hallon.

Mina? Where are you? She separated their communication to keep it from the Outers accessible to Valera. Hopefully the xintou had been too busy Broadcasting to hear.

Oh, thank goodness. I've been trying to reach you since the Games started but you had your Outers closed. We're here – Liu, Jarran and I. How can we help?

Alere felt the fear Mina held at bay; how hard it was for her to cope with the bloody, horrific scene of death in the arena. How determined Mina was to overcome her revulsion and help. For a fraction of a moment, Alere rested in the comfort of Mina's protective, healing mental embrace.

Have you brought my bag, Mina?

Yes.

Sucking a shaky breath, she refocussed on Hallon. Just before she moved into ma'ai, she sent an instruction to Mina. It was one Valera would never agree to, as it profoundly violated Xintou ethics. Indeed, Broadcasting already troubled Valera deeply. Mina, however, had never had those ethics drilled into her. She was so horrified by Hallon's actions she was willing to do what was needed – for the moment. If it worked, it could shift this battle in Alere's favour. If not, she could be in serious trouble.

Hallon's grin widened and he twirled the kusarigama chain. The bronze glittered in the sunlight. The chain whistled through the cool air.

'Ever fought against one of these, girl?' he taunted. 'I'm betting you haven't. C'mon. Let's see how long you last. I'll enjoy killing you.'

CHAPTER THIRTY-SIX

ALERE

Alere circled left, trying to judge Hallon's intentions by his movements. He swung the chain and circled with her, weight balanced. She narrowed her focus to him. Blocked out the sounds of cheering and scattered applause from the stands; the sun's heat on her head; the smell of blood, vomit and decay rising from the warming sands under her feet.

Hallon's grin turned wolfish. What was the reach of his weapon? He released the chain. The weight flew at her and she danced back. He kept a short loop close to his body, probably hoping she would now misjudge the length. The spikes dug into the sand and scored deep lines when he reeled it in. The chain was longer than the one used by Gavon. Hallon would always see her coming and have time to react.

He shot the chain at her again, letting out less this time, trying to lure her closer. She skipped outside the arc and let it sail harmlessly past. He threw a third time. She misjudged the angle. The tip of one spike caught in her shirtsleeve. It tore into her left arm, ripping the cloth and skin. Not deeply but painfully. Blood trickled down her arm and onto her hand, making her grip on the knife slippery. She couldn't afford to wipe it or bind the injury.

'First blood,' he said, sneering.

Alere ignored the sting. 'You'll have to do better than that.'

'There's still time to sign the agreement before you die, girl. I promise I'll kill your friends quickly if you do.'

'You really think I'd sign an agreement giving you weapons enough to kill your brother and to take over Melcor and Mamlakah outright?' she taunted, circling again.

He didn't seem to hear the stunned murmurs spreading through the surrounding mharebi and up into the stands. With a growl, low in his throat, he shifted two steps closer.

'I think you need to die now. I'll get your sister to sign, instead.'

Whirling the weight faster this time, he shot it straight at her ankles. She jumped and deliberately landed on the chain, intending to grab and pull on it. Hallon was too quick and yanked. Unbalanced, she staggered.

A spike from the ball caught her foot. It ripped the slipper off and tore into the thin flesh and tiny bones. She hit the ground hard and plunged her dagger deep into the sand as an anchor. Hallon tried to drag her closer. She twisted to unhook her foot from the metal. Excruciating pain wiped all other thoughts from her mind as the spike ripped free.

Somewhere in the distance, the audience screamed as her pain entered their minds. Her xintou training made her slam up her wards to protect them. She dropped them again. Having them feel her pain was what she wanted. The stadium reverberated to the sobbing protests and groans of those connected to the Broadcast.

Alere refused to check her foot. She rolled away over one shoulder and scrambled upright. Agony from torn skin almost paralysed the leg but she clenched her teeth. If she didn't check, she wouldn't know how bad the injury was. Instead, she focussed on Hallon, letting the people feel her determination. Weishi techniques helped to sideline pain for later.

She was on the ground only a matter of seconds, but that was long enough for Hallon to close the gap. He was now near enough to use the weight much more effectively. Already it whirled high over his head. A few more steps and she'd be within range of the blade as well.

Dodging quickly was impossible now. Could she wear one strike and engage him at close quarters? No. Her ground-fighting was good, but he had a weight advantage. If he pinned her arms with the chain she'd never be free in time.

She couldn't take too many more blows from the spiked ball, either. Despair and pain threatened to derail her thinking. Her foot throbbed and sand ground into the injury.

There was no way to defeat him.

He was bigger, faster and with the longer reach. She'd never mastered fighting against the kusarigama. She'd been mad to think she could beat someone of his skill and experience.

He flicked the chain. She stumbled aside, but not fast enough. A spike embedded in her thigh and she screamed. The crowd screamed with her, but Alere barely heard them. She yanked the weight free and Hallon laughed as he reeled it back in. He straightened out of his warrior's crouch and twirled the chain idly. A smug smile played on his lips. He knew he'd won. He was just playing with her, now.

Alere caught a breath.

He knew he'd won. Believed. In his mind. A game of the mind.

That's what this was all about. Not his skill with a weapon. His skill with intimidation. To break him, she needed to take away his power; his belief in the power of his weapon; his belief in himself.

She knew what to do now. It was all in the timing and footwork.

His right foot shifted slightly. The weight flew. She dove, rolled, regathered. Gritting her teeth against pain, she ran forward. The weight passed overhead. He pulled back, but too late to regather for another throw. She closed to blade-distance. While he was still balanced for the chain, she struck at his right arm, slicing at the exposed elbow joint. The steel bit deeply.

With a cry of anger, he dropped the chain and thust at her with the curved, sickle-like blade instead. It was an ill-considered move. A sword-thrust with a weapon designed for sweeping strokes. He was either out of practice or had been uninjured in battle for so long he'd forgotten how to deal with the pain. It wouldn't take him long to remember. She had a tiny window of opportunity. But she didn't want to kill him straight away. There was still one thing to get from him.

She twisted aside from the blade. The movement became a circle-step that carried her behind him. A single stroke, with her whole body behind it, brought the edge of her blade across his back. It hacked into the leather and bronze armour, biting deeply into his skin. The armour prevented it from being a kill-stroke, but she'd only intended it to wound. Hallon arched away and she yanked it free. She plunged her dagger deep into his left thigh and he screamed hoarsely. He staggered three steps his expression one of astonished agony.

She pointed at his thigh. 'That was for Gavon.' She indicated his back. 'And that was for Kett and Corin.' She allowed vengeful anger to trickle through into her thoughts. With it she sent images of her friends' injuries and how they came to be.

He swore eloquently. Cursing her, her parentage and her entire Jundom.

She revealed a hint of grim amusement. 'Possibly, but will you yield?' Now she wanted the audience to see her as justice; as the fair and honourable one.

'The Challenge of Equals is to the death, and you know it,' Hallon snarled at her, keeping his voice low. 'I'll see your head on my fence before the day's end, chouhuo. And your father's after that. Followed by anyone in Mamlakah who resists my rule. Including your guisunzi Jun First. Your sister I will chain to my bed and use for my pleasure. Your friends will die in the Hunt tomorrow, painfully. Then I will take my army, march on Shanzhai and slaughter everyone in it.'

The backwash of shock and revulsion reverberated through her mind as his words reached their audience. Alere smiled at him and took pleasure in the confusion flickering across his twisted face.

'Thank you.' She bowed and limped forward. 'It wanted only that. Look around, Hallon. They see you truly now. Even if you win, and kill me, you've lost. Look.'

She held her hands up, indicating she wouldn't attack. He glanced at the mharebi and at the audience. He couldn't miss the anger, disgust and incipient rage on their faces. Jeering insults rained on him. Shouts of derision rose. Emboldened, the crowd heaped years of scorn and retribution on their oppressor. Realisation bloomed and Hallon's face turned ashen.

A game of the mind, as much as the sword.

But Hallon was not the sort to take humiliation lightly. Nor to give up easily. Turning an implacable glare on her, he whirled the chain once more. Alere blanked everything else out and watched his feet and his chest. He was angry and unsettled. He might make a mistake. Or he might over-run her in his rage and kill her before she could strike. Everything would depend on his next throw.

He shifted. She moved. The bronze chain flew past, so close to her head that the spikes caught in her hair and tore a few strands free. Her blade swung at full-force. She struck, not at Hallon, but at the chain. Hardened steel sheared through the bronze like butter. The weight flew free to land somewhere behind her.

Hallon staggered backward, unbalanced. His injured leg gave beneath him and he dropped to one knee. Alere limped closer, ignoring the sand grinding into the torn flesh of her foot. A deft flick of her sword cut the kurisagama from his fingers, sending it skittering across the sand.

She held the steel tip to his throat, arm shortened for the thrust. 'Yield.'

The entire arena held its breath. Not a sound could be heard beyond her own heartbeat and the uneasy shuffling of mharebi feet on sand.

Hallon lifted his face, a cunning glint in his eye. His left hand snatched out a dagger from a boot-sheath. She drove her blade into his neck at the collarbone. Steel severed the artery and windpipe in one precise, measured blow. Blood sprayed onto her arm as she pulled free. She stood over him, waiting until the realisation of death showed in his eyes before she spoke.

'That,' she whispered into his ear, 'was for Shasa.'

He collapsed sideways onto the sand, his eyes blankly reflecting the brilliant sun overhead.

Deliberately, she held back the spark of pity in her deepest heart, but let out the guilt and self-disgust that flared there. It all reflected back at her from the faces of the men and women watching.

Weary, she flicked blood from her blade. She retrieved Kett's sheathed sword and turned away from the body. It wasn't over. There was yet more to do before the day was done.

Lan hurried over, hands out to support her.

'Not now, you hmar.' She glared at him, raising her wards for a moment. 'This is not over, yet. If you want your father and sisters to survive the next few minutes then do *not* make me seem weak!'

He gaped at her, but recovered quickly and thrust his hands behind him. He walked beside her as she limped over to where the Shah and the Slavemasters stood. She relaxed her wards again.

Feddor Nasim, accompanied by two of his father's mharebi, strode over. His expression was a cross between anger and excitement.

'Take her weapons and tie her.' He pointed at Alere.

She stopped where she was, handed Kett's sword to Lan, and tucked her bloody weapons into her belt. She stared at Feddor coldly and folded her arms. His men paused in confusion when she switched her gaze to them.

'You're forgetting something, Feddor,' she said coolly, 'by Challenge Law, as victor *I* now own your father's assets, including these mharebi. They lay hands on me and their own lives *will* be forfeit.'

It was a huge gamble, but it held the mharebi in stasis for a few moments. That might be long enough to sway everything her way once and for all, without further bloodshed.

'She's right, Feddor,' Lan murmured, subsiding when she glared at him.

The idiot would get himself killed at this rate. Jahil voiced his support as well. Alere was hard-put not to groan aloud. Did they have a death-wish? Years of cowardice before Hallon's bullying and *now* they decided to stand up for someone? Honestly. Were they *blind*?

Feddor's uncertainty segued into shrewd anger. He lifted a hand in what was an obvious signal and threw back his shoulders.

'Did you *really* think it would be that simple, girl? I'm not my father.' He sneered. 'I suspected you might do something and I came prepared.' He raked his uncle with a supremely contemptuous look. 'Clearly it's time Melcor was in more capable hands than yours. My father was content to do things in the shadows. I see no need to hide.'

In the stands, a hundred or more men flung off their loose outer robes. They trained crossbows on the Shah's mharebi in the arena floor. Around them, the onlookers shrieked, screamed and shoved one another aside to get away. Not too far, Alere noted. Most only moved out of the firing line, higher into the stands, wanting to see this show through to the end. That suited her purposes, too.

Alere raised her hands to shoulder height, palms out.

'Thank you,' Feddor said, inclining his head with smug graciousness. 'And thank you for doing away with my father. It saved me the effort.' He drew his sword and jabbed it at Jahil and Lan. 'Now tell your men to lay down arms or I'll kill you both here and now.'

Keeping her hands up, Alere interposed herself between Feddor and the Shah. Feddor raised the blade threateningly to her throat.

'Let's consider the situation for a moment,' she said reasonably. 'You've said you're going to take over Melcor and that obviously includes regicide. But don't you think you may have played your hand too soon?' She shrugged. 'If you're going to kill Jahil anyway, how is threatening his life right now going to do you any good?' Alere cocked her head at Feddor. 'You didn't think this through very well, did you?'

Behind her, someone gasped. Behind Feddor, Kett smiled faintly.

Bewilderment passed over Feddor's face. He regrouped and stuck the point of his sword into the hollow of her throat, pricking the skin and drawing blood. Alere clenched her jaw. Cold anger settled in her heart. Like father, like son. She'd thought to spare him. Perhaps not.

'Alright.' Feddor's tone was sarcastic now. 'In that case, Jahil, tell your mharebi to lay down their arms or my men will kill *them*. Better?'

Alere allowed her eyelids to droop. 'Better, but you've overlooked one thing. Several, actually.'

Feddor sighed exaggeratedly. 'Really? What, exactly.'

Alere jerked her head at the stands. 'Them.'

CHAPTER THIRTY-SEVEN

ALERE

Feddor stepped back a few paces. He checked the stands. Alere almost laughed aloud at the expression of confused outrage on his florid face.

At least three hundred audience members also held crossbows. They were aimed squarely at Feddor's men. Around a hundred were carried by children under ten, all focussed and unwaveringly intent.

'Oh,' Alere added sweetly, pointing behind him, 'and don't forget her.'

Feddor followed her finger. His mouth fell open.

'Who?' he croaked, blinking at the three figures approaching across the sands. 'Who?' He glared at the gold and white pavilion, where Valera still sat with Jahil's family, resplendent and mysterious in her gold robes and veil.

'I think you'll find,' Alere said, pointing out the three new players for his benefit and for those listening to her thoughts, 'that is Liu Gray, leader of the resistance here in Chengdu. That is Jarran Zah-Hill, the new Jun-First your father so unwisely kidnapped. And *that* is his Xintou.'

Feddor gaped then swallowed. His fingers flexed on the sword grip and sweat glistened on his brow. He glanced at the stands, to where his men looked to him for guidance. Some lowered their weapons in the face of superior fire-power, intimidated even if the weapons were held by children.

'Xintou…' Feddor murmured.

Alere almost pitied him. Xintou were held in such mystery and esteem here. And they had become so used to Valera's relative helplessness under Jahil's weak rule, they'd forgotten the world contained more than one xintou. All the most extreme stories of their abilities probably now flickered through Feddor's vapid head. It made no difference that Mina wasn't trained. She wore the gold robe and veil. In his eyes, that made her xintou and his fear would do the rest.

A game of the mind.

Alere? Valera's incredulous thought arrived. *Who is that? I don't recognise her mind.*

Not now. Just keep Broadcasting.

What the diyu are you doing, Alere Connor?

Alere Koh-Lin, Valera. Jun-Heir to Rafi Koh-Lin. Don't forget that. And what I'm doing is what needs to be done. Now help me and get out of my head or this could still go against us.

Valera withdrew, but her simmering anger remained.

Mina walked one step behind Jarran, her hands clasped, chin raised in classic xintou haughtiness. Both of them ignored the mharebi, who dropped to one knee. Alere let her conditioned reverence for xintou rise to the surface. Valera Broadcast it and most of the audience fell to their knees. Only Liu's children seemed cynical enough to withstand it. Many of the adults bearing arms for Liu were among the first to bow. Selb, perhaps?

Feddor was unaffected; warded enough to resist the Broadcast. A fierce determination bloomed in his eyes.

'Chouhuo!' He swung his sword backhand at her, with the full force of his heavy body. The blade fell straight at her neck. Alere stepped inside the weapon's arc. She turned and caught the arm, slid closer and jabbed an elbow into his jaw. He reeled back, holding his cheek. Anger flared in his eyes. He rushed at her again, swinging.

His weakness was glaring. He'd probably never been in a real fight. Brought up in second-generation softness. Alere pulled her sword free, regretting what had to be. She spun aside, avoiding his blow. He stumbled past. Her steel caressed his throat. He fell to his knees, then collapsed to the sand, choking. He clutched at his neck. Blood poured through his fingers. Horrified understanding blossomed in him and his mouth fell agape.

High in the stands, Faira shrieked and fainted as her only son died needlessly. Alere flicked blood from her blade, allowing deep regret through to Valera for an instant before hardening herself for the next step.

She addressed the remaining three Slavemasters and drew her dagger, holding both blades ready.

'Anyone else?' She kept her tone conversational, but let them see the absolute certainty in her mind. It was unlikely any of them could ward.

By their shaken, pale visages, they had no intention of attacking her.

Enough! Valera's strident voice cut through her Outers. *I will not be party to this senseless slaughter any longer.*

That's fine, Valera, Alere returned wearily. *Your part is done, anyway. Mine isn't, though, so just shut up and stay out of my way.*

Mistress Li will hear of this, my girl.

Oh, I'm sure she will. And not just from you.

She cut the connection and turned away to greet Jarran and Mina. Alere raised her wards, slid her weapons back into her belt and held up bloodied fingers.

'I'd hug you, but I don't think I should. I am glad to see you, though. Are you both alright?' She peered at her sister, but couldn't see much through the gold silk veil.

Mina's mouth curved into a small, tremulous smile. 'I think so but...' Her hand shook as she indicated the slaughterfield around them. 'This is...'

'I know. But it's not over, yet,' Alere said. Even with Hallon gone, Jahil didn't have the power to stand against the three other Slavemasters. If Alere didn't see this through, nothing would change. Kett and Corin would still be sent to the Hunt, as was their tradition.

She lifted her head and studied the milling crowds. The magnitude of what she was about to propose frightened her. Did she have the right? Just to save herself and her friends from the Hunt? Mistress Li had always supported stability over change. Important over what any one individual wanted. The repercussions would be unforeseeable into the future. She would be destroying a whole Jundom's economy and way of life. Who was she to make that decision?

The breeze changed direction and brought the smell of blood, death and vomit. She glanced back at Kett and Corin and clenched her jaw. Important could go to diyu. Stability could go to diyu. She would *not* sacrifice them to the bloodthirsty mob just to keep the peace.

'We need to disband the slave industry,' she said.

Mina swallowed, wide-eyed. Jarran stepped close to her, protective, frowning.

Jahil and Lan, who had moved close enough to overhear, both spoke up in quiet agreement.

'How?' Lan asked, watching the remaining three Slavemasters.

They'd gathered into a tight group, muttering to each other and eyeing the Shah with a mix of anger and resentment. Bahad appeared to be arguing vehemently with the others, making wild chopping gestures. Their mharebi all had weapons drawn, but they didn't appear particularly enthusiastic. All around the arena, Liu's men and children still had crossbows at the ready. Feddor's mharebi surrendered as it became clear their position was untenable with both their masters dead.

'Liu.' Alere beckoned the xiongshou, who bowed with an ironic obsequiousness that annoyed her for some reason. She chose to ignore it. 'You said the slaves believe a xintou will be responsible for freeing them?'

The man's eyes widened. He glanced at Mina.

'Then let's make that happen,' Alere said. 'Valera won't do it. Mina, link with me and I'll help you.'

She rested her palms on the yanstones, revelling in the silver-gilt darkness of their warmth in private for a moment. She had missed them. Next, she reached out to Mina and showed her how to Broadcast. Somehow she knew Mina had the skill, where she didn't. Or, perhaps together they had the ability. But it needed to be Mina, as Valera would recognise Alere's mind in an instant and the yanstones' secret would be out. Alere wasn't ready for Xintou House to know about them yet.

Understand? She said to Mina, in the privacy of their personal connection.

Mina nodded, worrying at her lower lip. Jarran gave her an encouraging smile. Drawing her shoulders back Mina spoke aloud and in the Broadcast at the same time. The Koh-Lin bracelets on her wrists ensured everyone heard her soft words.

'By the order of Xintou House, the Jun First of Mamlakah, and the Shah of Melcor,' she began. Her mental and physical voices strengthened as she gained confidence. 'From this day, slavery in all its forms shall be illegal in both Jundoms. All slaves are now freedmen and women. The Slavemasters' assets will be sold to provide them with passage home and compensation. The Slavemasters will then be exiled.'

The three Slavemasters raised their voices in immediate protest. A half-hearted dissent arose in the stands. It died beneath louder cheers and the sharp points of crossbows held by hundreds of children with a vested interest in the change.

Mina raised her voice again. 'The Shah appoints Liu Gray as chief liaison in charge of this undertaking. Effective immediately. Anyone who does not wish to support this change may accompany the Slavemasters into exile. This is the will of Xintou House.'

Behind Alere, Bahad Sinclar's voice rose in angry dispute. He shoved aside the restraining hands of his companions. His face reddened, spittle gathering at the side of his mouth as he spewed invectives at Mina.

'You can't do this!' Muscles in the side of his neck stood out and his finger jabbed at her like a sword. 'You can't come in here and destroy our lives like this. This is our jundom. Go back to Mamlakah and stay out of our lives. No *woman* is going to tell me I can't own slaves any more.' Turning, he stalked away, still muttering.

Deeming him more of a mouth than a man of action, Alere took Mina's hand and found her trembling in reaction. 'Are you alright?'

'I think so. It was just...the feedback from all those angry minds. It was like being punched inside my own head.' Mina pressed at her temples.

Alere groaned. 'I'm sorry. I forgot to show you how to ward against that. You'll have a headache but it will go. You did well.' She turned to Jahil. 'Do you think that will do it? Do we need to find another way to reach more people?'

Jahil opened his mouth, but Mina clutched at her arm, her nails digging deeply.

'Alere...Gavon!'

Alere spun in time to see Bahad stride up behind Gavon. The Slavemaster chopped his kusarigama blade through the man's back. Gavon's mouth opened in a soundless scream. His expression twisted in agony as he gaped at the length of bronze protruding from his sternum. Bahad yanked the sword free and smirked as Gavon folded. Blood stained the sand wine-dark beneath Gavon's body. His eyes fixed on Alere and the life slowly faded. His face sagged into slackness and emptied.

'You murdering guisunzi!' Saric snatched at Bahad's weapon, trying to wrench it from the Slavemaster's grip.

Bahad backhanded Saric with casual disdain. The boy tumbled into a pathetic heap on the sand, scarlet blood running down his cheek. Bahad sneered and pointed at Gavon's body.

'That one was *mine* ten years ago. No-one was going to take the pleasure of killing him away from me. Especially not some chouhuo from Mamlakah.'

Most of his words washed over Alere as mere noise. With her hands resting on the yanstones, she harnessed both the blackness in her heart and the stones' power. They embraced her and pushed aside all emotion except cold anger. The stones took away the pain in her arm and foot. They then burned away any compassion she had for the Slavemaster and his ilk. She grinned ferociously. She had never before been so in accord with them. Without regret, she gave herself to them. Their silver-gilt fire consumed her body and mind.

They tempered her into their weapon.

Her blades slithered free. Bahad must have seen the intent in her. He paled and stepped back. He recovered and lifted his chin.

'I'm not calling a Challenge on you.' He sneered. 'By Melcor law you can't—'

She struck. He snatched out his dagger and blocked, his eyes widening. He swung the kusarigama at her. She deflected it contemptuously. The hooked tip sliced a shallow cut into her arm. Irrelevant. Without breaking stride, she thrust her sword-blade deep into his body between the ribs and into his heart. Her momentum carried him backward three steps.

'Yes,' she said softly, 'I can.'

His eyes dimmed. She twisted the steel. Ribs cracked. She withdrew it and turned away before he'd even hit the ground.

Three long strides brought her to Gavon's still form. She dropped the blades and fell to her knees beside him. His limp body lay heavy in her arms as she gathered him close. It was too late, but she wanted desperately to feel life in him. No breath. No heartbeat. No light.

With the stones no longer in her hands, she was released from the cold stone-fire. All the pain and loss welled up from its dark place in her mind and consumed her.

Regathering her weapons again she laid her palms on the stones. She sent to Mina, to Broadcast, all the grief and anger, all the built-up pain and frustration, the fear and hurt of the last months and weeks. From the depths of her being she dredged up the worst of herself and flung it outward. Everyone around the stadium would see and feel as she did at this moment. They would understand, once and for all, the consequences of the Games.

All around her, people fell, clutching at their heads. They shared her loss, her grief, her anger; moaning and crying with her despair.

Valera shot to her feet and shouted Alere's name.

Alere slammed up her wards and heard the gasps of shock as the outpouring of emotion stopped. It was still inside her, though. Still fisted around her heart. Still smouldering in her gut.

Slowly, she lowered Gavon's head to the ground and kissed his cheek.

Someone came to stand beside her. She rose, barely noticing the worst of her injuries were gone. A quick check on Saric showed the boy recovering consciousness and being helped to his feet by Liu. Kett stood nearby, swaying, bleeding. They had done this, to him, too.

Kett spoke, but she simply shook her head at him. Without another word to anyone, she stalked from the arena. Ignoring Mina's tentative call, she found the exit. Outside the arena, she strode towards the riverside blocks of expensive houses where the Slavemasters lived. She was half-aware that thousands of people streamed from the Games. They followed her in silence through the streets of Chengdu. Liu's Selb contingent formed an honour guard of sorts, their weapons at the ready, eyes grim and glittering.

The crowd grew as people demanded an explanation and joined the mob. An excited babble of speculation swirled around them. She ignored it all.

Grief hardened into fury: crimson and implacable. Hands resting again on the yanstones she let their welcoming golden depths protect her; let them take away the grief; let them burn away the pain. She didn't want it anyway. The yanstones absorbed it, and her.

When it was done, all that remained was the purpose for which she'd left the arena.

When that was completed, she could get out of this gouri city.

'Liu!'

The little man would be somewhere near. He appeared at her side, his narrow eyes fixed on her.

'Send runners ahead to the Masters' houses,' she said. 'Free the slaves and take whatever valuables you want that will help your cause.'

'Why?' He ran to keep up with her long, angry strides.

She curled a contemptuous lip. 'Because you won't have a chance once I get there.'

CHAPTER THIRTY-EIGHT

CORIN

Corin hurried to catch up with Alere, shouldering through the crowds that trailed her like the roiling wash behind a shaytan-salamander. He'd had to leave Kett in Mina's hands. She and Jarran would take him to the Shah's palace. The weishi's leg was badly injured and he'd lost a lot of blood. There was no way he could keep up. His last conscious words had been to task Corin with Alere's safety. Corin's head still spun and his calf and back stung more than he cared to admit. But he couldn't let Alere out of sight in this mood. He'd tried to leave Saric behind, but the boy would have none of it. He ran at Corin's side with none of his usual teasing banter. His bloodied face was set and hard; far too old for his age.

He couldn't blame either of them for their feelings. These arrogant hundan Slavemasters had had their own way for far too long. They'd terrorised both Melcor and the northern towns of Mamlakah unchecked for more than two hundred years. Time it stopped. Alere had every justification for her anger. He shared it wholeheartedly.

But the look on her face, when she'd killed Bahad and held Gavon in her arms... That had shocked even Corin. Never had he seen her so angry yet so remorselessly cold. Devoid of humanity. He pitied anyone who got in her way. How the jahim was he supposed to stop her if she turned on an innocent by mistake?

They caught up with her as she stood outside Hallon's house. Already the doors were open. Slaves streamed forth, confused and blinking in the bright afternoon sunlight. Many stopped outside the walls when confronted with what appeared to be an angry mob. Liu and his Selb men weaved amongst them, reassuring, explaining, encouraging.

Several of Liu's older children emerged from the house carrying large, clinking sacks. Liu inspected the contents and waved larger, stronger men, bearing Jahil's colours, forward. They relieved the children of their burdens and vanished towards the palace before anyone in the crowd could protest.

Corin arrived at Alere's side and grabbed her arm, shifting to avoid her ingrained defensive response. She didn't even apologise, simply stared at him with those cold, empty eyes.

'Come with me if you will, Corin, but stay out of my way.'

Something in her tone made him release his grip. She strode into the house.

Saric turned to Corin. 'Shouldn't we go in?'

'I don't think she needs us, kid. I think this is something she needs to do alone.' Corin's head pounded to the beat of his heart and his vision was suspiciously fuzzy. He coughed, tasting blood.

'What if there are mharebi in there?' Saric sounded anxious.

Corin sighed. The kid had just lost his mother, after all, and he admired Alere. Of course he would be worried about losing her. For Corin's part, the wound of Shasa's death – and the guilt for his part in it – was too raw. He didn't particularly want to go back into Hallon's slavepen, where Shasa had lived her last ten years.

He tightened his grip on Saric's shoulder. 'Kid, you saw her expression? Somehow, I don't think anyone is going to take her on at the moment. Even if they did, I don't think they'd stand a chance.'

Saric shook himself free and cast Corin a scathing look. 'Well, I'm going in.' He dashed across the street.

After a moment's hesitation, Corin limped in after him, swearing. Every step jarred pain through his stomach and head. The world swayed alarmingly.

He found them in the slave pen area. They stood in the doorway of the room where he and Kett had been held. Alere gazed at the hard cots and the chain loops embedded in the floor. Saric had his arms wrapped around himself, shivering though the day was warm. He shifted closer to his father. Corin draped an arm around the boy's shoulder and squeezed, his throat too tight to speak.

Alere spoke, her voice low and emotionless. 'You may want to stand back.'

Corin ushered Saric out and they stood in the training grounds together, waiting. Saric surveyed the yard with a troubled expression Corin had no difficulty in interpreting. This was, after all, where his mother had been held.

There was a flash of silver-white light from inside the room, and a detonation that made them both jump. Just as Corin began to worry, Alere appeared at the door, bloodied sword and dagger in her hands. Smoke billowed out behind her. She vanished into another part of the complex and the same light flashed before she reappeared. This time Corin saw a sickened look in her eyes before she closed up again, like a flower when sunlight is taken away.

Without a word, she ran into the main house. Corin and Saric hurried after her. He caught a glimpse of her disappearing into the ballroom and followed. He was fractionally too late, arriving as the light blinded him. Flames nibbled their way up the tapestry hanging behind Hallon's upper table. Alere thrust her way past him, heading for the front door. Corin and Saric trailed after. Shortly thereafter, smoke billowed from upper windows.

A shout went up from the watching crowd. Fingers pointed.

Alere stared expressionlessly at the fire until it had taken hold of the building. Still unspeaking, she stalked up the street towards the next Slavemaster's house, following Liu's directions.

In stunned silence, the crowd followed.

Corin dragged Lan and Jahil aside. 'You need to get your fire squad to get that under control before it jumps to the rest of the houses here.'

Jahil shook his head, bittersweet satisfaction in his eyes. 'Everything on that side of the street belongs to the Slavemasters and their sycophants. If it burns to the ground it will be the best thing for Chengdu. The wind is in the wrong direction for it to jump the street.' He reviewed the enthralled crowd and Alere's retreating back. 'Let her burn it. It's what Melcor needs. We can start again.'

So, it continued. Liu's hordes of children scavenged ahead, gathering as many valuables from the four houses as they could find. The Selb and Jahil's mharebi released slaves and herded them and any of the Slavemasters' mharebi into the street. Alere appeared moments later – a dark, destructive force leaving nothing but fire, smoke and ash in her wake. Within an hour, three massive plumes of smoke spiralled into the sky, hiding the sun and drawing ever more frightened onlookers.

Lan assumed control as the crowd threatened to get out of hand. He ordered his father's mharebi to establish perimeters around each house to keep looters at bay until after the flames abated. He sent for the fire squads, in case the flames did get out of control. But it appeared Jahil's predictions were correct and the blaze was safely contained to the stretch of houses along the riverbank. So, he sent for administrators from the palace, briefed them and assigned them to explaining the new laws and the Slavemasters' exile to everyone who asked.

Corin and Saric arrived at the final complex to find Alere studying its huge, thick walls. The imposing façade screamed money and luxury. Beauty hiding ugliness beneath. This was the Sinclar family holding. Alere's expression became, if possible, even more bleak.

She put a hand against Saric's thin chest when he moved to come with her.

'Not this time.'

'Why not?' The boy frowned at her.

Alere glanced at the house and back at Saric. 'Trust me, Saric, please. I know you've seen a lot, but you don't want to come in this time.'

Saric eyed the house, then her. Finally, he shifted to stand near Liu, for once just a small, lost boy. Corin swallowed hard against a surge of protectiveness, still finding it difficult to accept this boy was his own flesh-and-blood. Saric directed that expectant gaze at him.

Corin sighed. Alere had already disappeared into the house. He limped after her. The pain in his head spiked so sharply as to be almost blinding. Luckily, all the houses followed a similar layout: grand house at the front, slave training grounds walled off in the back. He caught up with her in the compound and she gripped his arm.

She pointed at one of the outbuildings, small and separate from the others. 'Get Liu to send some men into that building.' Pitying disgust flashed across her face. 'Make sure they have strong stomachs.'

Now was not the time to ask how she knew what was in there. He did as she requested, returning to find the other buildings already ablaze. When Liu's two men emerged, their eyes were wild, and they held two wrecks of human beings in their trembling arms. Corin was glad he hadn't gone in with them. He'd seen about as much death and mutilation as he could handle for a day. Or a lifetime.

He followed Alere back into the main house and into the great hall. This time she stood in the middle of the massive room, staring at the ornate decorations and expensive tapestries; the gilded carvings and exquisite parquetry floor.

'I should have saved him,' she murmured. 'I wasn't watching. If I'd been watching Bahad I could've saved Gavon. I should've known what he would do.'

'No, Alli,' Corin said gently. 'It wasn't your fault. Bahad is entirely to blame, not you.'

She sent him a skeptical glare. 'I'll believe that when you believe Shasa's death was not your fault.'

Guilt twisted in his stomach. The truth there was too painful. He'd been ignoring it, but now she'd thrown it in his face. There were so many mistakes he didn't even know where to begin. The memory of Shasa's death would rip at his heart for the rest of his life, coloured by resentment, love, guilt and doubt. And all of those emotions would cloud his relationship with Saric now. And his relationship with Alere.

She walked over to a tapestry and raised her weapons. Corin shielded his face, still wanting to see what she did. A searing flash of light emanated from the swords.

Saric had been right about the lightning in the alley. What the diyu kind of xintou power was that?

The light vanished, and Corin blinked away the red after-image burned onto his retinas. Alere collapsed to the floor, only three paces from the now-blazing tapestry.

He hobbled over, grabbing her ankle and dragging her across the floor, away from the flames. A quick check confirmed she lived and was only unconscious. He stared at her swords and debated a moment. Then he swore, returned and kicked her weapons away from the fire. Coughing as smoke swirled through the room, he jammed her blades into his belt along with his own. Corin gritted his teeth against the pain, heaved Alere off the floor and staggered out the front door.

When he emerged, Lan appeared from nowhere and took Alere from him. All around, Liu's Selb men and women knelt, their heads bowed and hands outstretched, palms upward.

'Gangzhi,' they murmured. 'Molian. Erheyi.'

'Get up!' Lan commanded. 'She's not your saviour. Go back to your homes, all of you. There's nothing more to see here.'

Liu Gray stepped up and repeated the order. The Selb rose and, with murmurs and backward looks, melted away. Liu sent the children off, as well.

'Let's get both of you to a Healer,' Lan said. He led the way to a farmer's huoche on the opposite side of the street. 'Your youngster procured transport for us.'

Corin dragged himself into the back and collapsed onto a pile of sacks. His head was about to explode. He lapsed into unconsciousness before the che-ma moved.

ALERE

Awakening this time held no relief at things past and done, no languid heaviness that spoke of a healing sleep, no joyful anticipation of things to come. This time, on opening her eyelids to see a canopied bed, Alere's heart was ash. For the briefest moment, recollections of the Games flickered in her mind. But something – perhaps an instinct for self-protection – shunted them aside. Instead, she considered the room's white-walled airiness. The crisp, plain sheets under her body. The un-ornamented, heavy timber furniture scattered about the room. The clean scent of plants and past rain that drifted in the window.

It seemed safer to think about these things than to remember.

She lay still for a long time, thinking nothing, breathing and drifting and listening to birds twitter in the trees outside her window. The sun's position said it was morning, but which one?

It didn't matter. She was done caring. Deadlines, marching armies, iron weapons, the fate of Jundoms…none of it mattered. None of it was worth the life of one humble yongbing and one desperate mother.

She shied away from the memory. Life went on. It was time to get up.

Alere rose and walked to the window, heedless of her nudity and the chill morning air on her skin. She barely felt the cold bamboo floor. Numbness clothed her, swaddling her body and heart, protecting her from the world.

A knock sounded at the door.

'Come in,' she said.

The heavy blackwood panel opened and Mina, after one glimpse of her sister, shut it firmly behind her. Lips pursed she snatched up a set of clothing lying across one of the chairs and hurried over.

'Put these on, Alere,' she admonished, 'you'll catch a lung infection in this cold weather.'

Obediently, Alere pulled on underclothing and breast binder. But something in her rebelled at the black weishi apprentice clothing Mina held out. She recoiled, unable to put into words her aversion. Mina said nothing, rummaging through Alere's bag until she produced a set of plain, brown boy's clothing. Reluctantly, Alere drew them on. They were wrong, too, but not as wrong as the other. They would do.

When she finished dressing, she stood still, uncertain what to do next. Mina inspected her closely, a furrow appearing between her brows. She stroked Alere's cheek. Alere barely felt it.

'Are you well, Alli?' Mina's tone was sharp and worried, her eyes heavy with sleeplessness.

'I'm fine,' Alere replied.

'Do you want to see Kett and Corin?' Mina prompted. 'They're in the next room. They…need you.'

'Of course,' Alere said. Why was Mina so tentative? 'How are they?'

Her mouth formed the words, but she didn't want to hear the answer. Yet she had to. All that mattered now were the people she cared about. Why couldn't she feel that?

Worry and doubt flickered across Mina's face. She touched Alere's arm and Alere flinched. Mina's Outers were transparent. Both men were seriously ill. Kett from bloodloss and infection. Corin from internal injuries and head trauma. Mina harboured strong doubts that either would survive.

CHAPTER THIRTY-NINE

ALERE

Wait. How did she know Mina's thoughts? Ah. The Koh-Lin bracelets gleamed on Mina's wrists. Without her own yanstones, not even wards were able to protect Alere from every thought flashing into Mina's head. This must have been what scared Mina so much back in Shanzhai, when she could hear everything Alere thought.

It needed to stop. She did *not* need to hear Mina's fears for Kett and Corin right now. It took everything in her to exist without dissolving into a useless puddle of tears as it was.

Alere searched for a distraction and saw her dagger and sword. She reached for them, only to stop before she touched steel, revulsion sweeping through her. After the Games, how could she use them again? Echoes of yesterday's slaughter resurfaced. She covered her face, clenching her jaw tightly to prevent a whimper of distress.

Mina stroked her hair, her silent concern loud. Alere backed away from her touch.

'Give me a second...' She composed herself, pushing blackness aside. 'Before we go to see them, tell me what's happened. What day is it?' She perched on the edge of the bed and gathered resolution tightly about her like a protective cloak, determined to hold on.

After a moment's hesitation, Mina joined her, folding her hands in her lap. 'It's Er'run. You've slept for almost two days. We're in the Shah's palace. He, Liu and Lan have had their hands full trying to restore order. There have been riots and protests. Many thought it was some sort of elaborate Mianshou prank. I've had to make several appearances as xintou to help Valera reinforce order. Your last Broadcast was heard beyond the arena and out through most of the city. People were terrified and confused.' She gave a wintry smile. 'Apart from that, we've turned the politics and economy of this Jundom on its head and it will take a while for things to settle.'

That was to be expected. If nothing else, it meant Melcor would not be any sort of threat for several years to come, while they rebuilt their economy from the ground up. In all honesty, Alere didn't care, but it helped to prevent her thinking about Kett and Corin. She wasn't ready yet.

'Shah Jahil,' Mina continued, 'is holding a memorial at the arena today. For Shasa…and Gavon. They'll sing the *Song of Passing* and toll the bell. He's expecting the arena to be full. I'll have to go and address the crowd. Jahil wanted to know if you—'

'No!' Alere turned away, swallowing down the lump in her throat. 'No. I can't go back there.'

'That's what I said you'd say.' Mina cleared her throat. 'There's one more thing. Jarran collected a message for you and Corin from the Messenger house, but he can't decipher the code. I took it to Corin but he's unconscious.'

Her fear for her patient flashed into her thoughts again and Alere had to grit her teeth against succumbing to it. Not yet.

First she had to know how things stood. She was dimly aware numbness was part of her grief for Gavon, and her guilt over his death and Shasa's. It would, eventually, ease and the things that had been important before – Kett, Corin, Mamlakah, Rafi and Shanzhai – would all surge back into the forefront. Right now, she could only see what was right in front of her and take tiny steps. Hearing the state of the world from Mina would help her to find the strength and the reason to take thos steps.

She held out a hand. 'Give me the message.'

Mina withdrew a crumpled piece of paper from her robe pocket. Alere opened it and, using the code key Corin had written on the previous message, translated it.

By the time she finished her hand shook and the fears she had locked away in the darkest corner of her mind threatened to overtake her once again. Closing her eyes, she pressed her lips together and fought for control.

'Alli?' Mina's soft, worried voice brought her back from the edge.

'I'm fine.' She stuffed the message into her pocket. 'Take me to them now.'

Mina, after one narrow glance beneath her lashes, kept silent. She led the way to the room, through an adjoining door. It was as austere and functional as Alere's room. A dramatic contrast to the luxury of Hallon's house, and an insight into Jahil's character.

Alere stood for a long moment between the two beds, studying the men. Even to her untrained eye, both appeared deathly ill, their faces grey and slack. Kett's twisted and he mumbled something as she approached, his hands knotting the sheets. Corin's breathing was shallow and faint, the bandage around his head stained red.

'How long?' Alere Read the prevarication in her sister's mind. 'Don't lie to me, Mina, I can Read the truth in your Outers.'

'I...' Mina's eyes filled with tears. 'I'm not sure.' She gestured helplessly. 'Kett might pull through if he can fight off the infection. I've given him the strongest antibiotics I can, but he's lost so much blood. Corin...' She chewed on her bottom lip as the tears spilled onto her cheeks. 'His brain is swollen from the blow to the head and I think one of his kidneys is ruptured. He's bleeding internally. Healer House here hasn't the same surgical skill as the one in Madina. They can't repair or safely remove the kidney and they have no bedspace with all the injuries from the riots and Mianshou celebrations. The most I can do is make him comfortable.'

'He's going to die,' Alere stated. 'Kett as well.'

After a long, uncomfortable silence, Mina agreed brokenly, tears sliding unchecked down her cheeks. Alere shoved Mina's distress aside. There was no space in her for it. Looking from one man to the other she accepted the knowledge. She had a choice to make. She was responsible for this, as she'd been responsible for Gavon's death. And, through arrogance, Shasa's. Celia's death. Ven's death. Radan's death. Too many at her hands. No more.

She turned to her sister. Mina shrank away, eyes wide. She didn't resist when Alere took first one, then the other, bracelet off her wrists and fastened them to her own. They felt strange now. Alien; tainted with Mina's mind. Not familiar like the stones in her sword or the necklace.

'Go to Valera,' she ordered. 'Tell her to bring me the necklace. I know she got it from Faira when she fainted at the Games.'

'But—'

Alere glared. 'Go. Now.'

Mina fled, closing the door hard behind her. Alere snicked the lock and then locked the other door as well. Time was limited. Sending Mina away had been an excuse. Alere knelt between the two beds and touched lightly each beloved face.

In the grand scheme of things, neither man was vital. Kalima, Mamlakah and Shanzhai would all go on without them. A few people would mourn their passing, but the world would continue to turn. If she viewed it dispassionately, Corin was probably more useful in his role as spy and advisor to Rafi. Plus, he now had a son to care for. Kett had given up his right to the Jun First throne and seemed content for it to be so.

However, when Alere faced the abyss of a world without either one of them, the darkness threatened to engulf her. She had to step back, both figuratively and literally, to gain perspective. Their injuries were too extensive for her to save both and to survive long enough to still heal herself. She wasn't even sure what the limitations of the stones' powers were. What if she got halfway through healing them and it failed? She couldn't risk it. She had to save at least one of them. So how did she choose?

The answer appeared in her mind from outside: a third choice. Almost-relieved, she nodded.

CORIN

Corin awoke to the sound of someone sobbing quietly. He squinted at the canopy overhead, not recognising either the place or the context. Where was he? Who wept and why?

His last memory was of falling into the back of the huoche with his body afire in every joint and muscle and his brain aching. Now his thinking seemed remarkably clear and nothing hurt. That, in itself, astonished him, given the abuse his body had suffered. How long had he slept?

The crying continued. Perhaps he should do something. He dragged himself off the unfamiliar bed and grabbed at a bedpost when the room swayed around him. He wore only loose silk trous and what felt like a hat. No, a touch to his brow showed it to be a bandage. He tugged it off, feeling for the cut over his ear. He touched the other side of his head. Nothing. How was that possible? A sword had cut into his head. The pain had been overwhelming, the blood blinding. Come to think of it, he twitched his shoulders, his back felt remarkably undamaged. What the jahim was going on?

He homed in on the source of the noise. A blonde woman knelt on the floor next to what, at first, appeared to be a young boy. The woman raised her face, her stricken expression shifting into astonishment. It was Mina. She looked swiftly back at the body in front of her, then at the other bed in the room. Her hand flew to her mouth.

'Corin?' A rough, male voice drew his attention to the other bed, where Kett sat upright, frowning. 'What's going on?'

Corin shrugged his non-comprehension. Mina moved, struggling to tie a bandage around the head of the person lying before her. Alere. Her eyes were closed, her skin waxen. A trickle of blood ran down her neck, dripping onto the polished bamboo floor. More blood stained the leg of her coarse brown trous; the sleeve of her shirt. When Mina withdrew her hands from beneath her sister, they were red.

Kett threw the bedcovers aside and rose, staggering and paling at the sight of Alere's inert form.

'What happened?'

Mina shook her head. 'I don't know. She asked me to go to Valera and get this.' She held the Koh-Lin necklace in one bloodstained hand. 'When I got back I found her lying here.' She glanced wildly around the room. 'But the doors were locked. A servant opened it for me. There was no-one else here so how did it happen?' Her eyes widened. 'You're... you're both awake and...your wounds...that's not possible! Show me your head and your back Corin.'

He turned.

'You're healed.' She touched the blood on Alere's neck and held her finger up, inspecting it with blank confusion in her eyes. She rolled Alere to one side and ripped her shirt open.

Corin's knees sagged. Kett clutched at the bed.

'She's taken our injuries onto herself, as she did for Mina.' Kett crouched beside her. 'But she's taken them from *both* of us at once.' He checked her pulse, his expression grim. 'She's alive. Corin, help me get her onto the bed. There may still be time.'

'What are you talking about?' Mina demanded, hovering as they lifted Alere's limp body onto the bed Kett had vacated. 'What do you mean "taken our injuries"? Is that what she did for me, on the slave-chuan? She can't! I mean, you are…were both near to death. She can't possibly survive.'

Ignoring Mina's protestations, Kett lifted Alere's hand in his. Light sparkled off the yanstones around each wrist.

'But if she has those, she should be able to heal herself,' Corin objected. 'Why hasn't she?'

Kett stroked her unruly hair and said quietly, 'I'm not sure. Maybe she can't. Or doesn't want to.'

'Don't be ridiculous,' Corin growled, angry at him for even suggesting it. 'Why wouldn't she?'

'Gavon's the first person she's ever lost,' Kett said. 'Surely *you* understand? She'll blame herself for his death, for what happened to us and, I'm willing to bet, Shasa as well.'

Corin swallowed, eyeing her pale face and still form. 'But she's so tough. Why would she give up?'

Straightening, Kett waved him closer. 'I agree, she wouldn't, normally. Either something's wrong and she can't use the stones…or maybe she needs someone to give her more incentive to stay. Someone to show her there's more here than grief.'

He hesitated for a long minute before turning away. Running both hands over his head he gazed at the ceiling for a moment then folded his arms across his chest.

'She needs you, Cor. Bring her back. Take the necklace and get into her head.'

Mina, who had vanished, returned bearing Alere's sword and dagger. She laid them on the bed beside her sister, tucking them under Alere's hands. She wrapped the necklace around Alere's arm and shrugged as she stepped back.

'I thought more stones might help. Valera gave me these, too.' She held up two more bracelets, almost identical to the ones on Alere's wrist. 'But they're fakes.'

Kett put them aside. 'A good thought. Now we need to let Corin do what he can.'

Mina laid her fingers on Alere's neck and chewed on her lip. Her eyes unfocussed. 'I can't reach her mind, either. She's too far away.' She raised frightened eyes to Corin's. 'Whatever you're going to do, do it now. She's fading. Her pulse is very weak. Please?'

Corin groaned. 'Gaisi.'

He committed Alere's beauty to memory, recalling every moment of their time together and savouring it. Then gritted his teeth and sighed. Tears pricked behind his eyes but there was no time for sentiment now.

'It's you who needs to help her, Kett, not me.' He held the man's gaze and grimaced. 'We both know it. We've been tiptoeing around it for the last week or so.'

Letting her go would not break his heart, but it would certainly put a dent in it. She would always hold a place there, for she had awoken him to the possibility of love again when he'd thought it long dead. Now it was time to repay the favour.

Mina's brows twitched into a frown. 'What are you talking about?'

Corin squared his shoulders. He walked around the bed and put a hand on Mina's waist, holding Kett's focus as he drew her away.

'No,' Kett said flatly. 'You're wrong. It's you she loves. This isn't the time to joke, Cor.'

'She chose you, Kett. On the Games field.' Corin jerked his head at the stadium, visible through the window. 'I saw her. She had one knife left to throw and both of us were hard-pressed. Much as it hurts to say, she chose to save you.'

Something like fear flashed across Kett's face and he shook his head. 'No,' he whispered. 'I can't risk her—'

'Don't be a shazi, man,' Corin snapped. 'You're the one she needs. You've protected her for half her life. Don't let her down, now. We'll wait outside.'

His heart was lead in his chest as he tugged a protesting Mina out and firmly closed the door. Giving her up hurt like jahim, but it was her best chance of survival. He studied Mina as she laid a hand on the door panel and closed her eyes. He may have just broken her heart, too.

'You alright?' He gave her a squeeze.

She sniffed. 'He and I talked, back in Shanzhai. He tried to let me down gently. But I knew then he wasn't in love with me, and never would be.' Fresh tears seeped from under her closed lids. 'That was partly why I agreed to leave with Rohne when he offered to take me home.' She smiled painfully. 'It still hurts, though.'

'Tell me about it,' Corin said acerbically, fighting the desire to fling the door open and claim Alere as his own. 'I just hope he can bring her back.'

She paled. 'Oh, Corin, he has to.' She wiped at her cheeks with the heel of her hand, childlike. 'I can't do this alone. I trusted Rohne and he…he abandoned me. I thought I loved Kett and he rejected me.' She buried her face in her hands. 'I can't lose Alere, too. I don't think I could cope.' Her hand curled into a fist and she pressed it against her heart, her eyes wide and dark. 'It's like there's a rope connecting us. And if she died it would break.' She swiped her palms down her thighs and stared at the door. 'And I think I might die, too.'

Corin frowned.

She gave a broken half-laugh and turned her face away. 'I know, it sounds ridiculous. But the only thing that got me through this last week with Rohne and being kidnapped by Hallon…the only thing that I was sure of was Alere and me. Our bond. The strength I get from just being around her.' Mina shook her head. 'It's hard to explain.'

'What about Jarran?' Corin ventured.

Her expression softened. 'He's wonderful, of course. And what I feel for him is so much more…true than the hero worship I had for Kett. I see that, now. But Alere…' She grimaced and sighed. 'I don't know. I just know I'm frightened.'

'Of losing her?' Corin said. 'I don't blame you. I am, too.'

'Yes,' Mina said quietly. 'But also… I don't know. I see things.' She pressed white fingers to her temples. 'In my dreams. Awful things. The fires here. And a horrible black nothingness that sucks me into it like a whirlpool.' Her eyes lifted, frightened. 'What if that's her death? What if Kett can't save her? I'll go mad. That's what I'm seeing, I think. My own insanity if she dies.'

Corin took her into his arms, wishing she didn't look so much like Alere. 'All we can do is wait and see. I'll be here for you, no matter what.'

She clung to him, trembling.

CHAPTER FORTY

ALERE

There was nothing but pain. It invaded every cell of her body and obliterated any kind of rational thought. Each breath drew daggers into her lungs. Each thought burned fire into her brain. Each feeble movement tore muscle from skin and flesh from bone.

She tried to link with the yanstones, but it proved far too difficult. Not worth the effort. After all, she'd saved Kett and Corin and that was what she wanted, wasn't it? She'd saved them, even if she'd failed Gavon.

Forever-darkness beckoned. She floated towards it, willing to let go if it meant the end of this agony.

Yes. A distant, gilded thread of thought echoed the idea. *Let go. They don't need you any more. You can let go.* It seduced her into the shadows.

Another silver-gilt thread tightened, halting her drift. Vaguely annoyed, she shook it, trying to free herself. There were three of them. Three life-connections held her, preventing her from moving on. One tugged her into the gold-fire of pain and life. She resisted. It hurt too much to go back. There was no point. But the thread was relentless, pulling her back, into blistering awareness.

Then the fire wasn't so much pain as warmth, the light welcoming and soothing, rather than burning. It seemed familiar, like the warm arms of someone she knew, someone who cared for her. Who? Mina? Corin?

No. Kett.

Alere?

Kett, what are you doing here? Leave me be. Let me go.

No. His Outers were rich with fear, worry and…something else. *I need you, Alli. Don't leave now. Heal yourself.*

You…need me. Was that enough? Perhaps…No. *You have Mina. I don't have the strength, Kett. It hurts too much. I made too many mistakes. Let me go. Please.*

Yes, you do. You have all the stones and… He dropped all his Outer wards and drew her into his mind. *You have me. I'll help. Come back to me. It was never Mina. I told her in Shanzhai. She left because I couldn't love her. Don't let go, Alli. We're here because of what I said to Mina and…*He buried the remainder of the thought, but she understood. He blamed himself for Mina's capture. *Don't leave me, Alli.*

For a fleeting moment he relaxed his Inners and encompassed her in the deepest, most protected sanctum of his thoughts. Into the deepest intimacy – unwarded, mind to mind. She was loved, treasured, adored, admired. Alere hesitated, afraid. He waited. She lowered her Inners as well. They were as one, entwined, closer than lovers could ever be, part of each other's breath and life-force. Suspended for an untouchable moment, away from the pain of loss, wrapped in each other.

Then, as though he couldn't bear to be so exposed and vulnerable – or perhaps because he feared an inseparable Fusion – he gently closed his Inner wards and drew her towards her own body and life.

She connected with the yanstones and their power surged, golden-bright, through her; repairing, healing, burning away pain, renewing.

Alere drew a shuddering breath, relieved to find it possible and painless. Strong arms cradled her close and she recognised the smell of Kett's skin where her cheek rested against his collarbone. She curled into him and raised a heavy arm, slipping her fingers around the back of his neck and sweeping her thumb along his jaw. His lips brushed her temple and he pulled her closer against his body.

They stayed that way: silent, content, separated from the world's turmoil, reluctant to rejoin it. It was a moment of bliss undisturbed by pressure and responsibility, expectation or fear.

Finally, unable to avoid reality any longer, Alere raised her eyes. Kett's expression was softer than she'd ever seen it. He smiled faintly and tucked a curl behind her ear, stroking her cheek with his fingertips. He lifted her face and kissed her. Still lightly in rapport through the stones, she tasted profound relief, exultant wonder and desire in him, underlain by a deep-hidden dark fear she had no hope of comprehending. The depth of his feelings for her were overwhelming. How had she never seen it?

He broke the kiss and smiled lovingly at her again. 'I'm glad you came back.'

All she'd wanted to escape – all the reasons she hadn't wanted to return – flooded into her mind at his words. Along with them came a faint echo of the voice that had enumerated them and encouraged her to let go, insisted she wasn't needed.

Rohne's voice in her head. How?

Troubled, she sat up, stripping the bracelets and necklace off her wrists and disengaging from Kett's embrace. Her torn, blood-stained shirt clung unpleasantly to her skin, so she shucked it with a shudder of distaste. She needed a bath. Kett yanked a sheet from the bed and cleaned off the worst of the blood. He found one of his shirts and she tugged it on.

Folding her arms around her waist she stared out the window, into the enclosed, formal garden below. Kett wrapped both arms around her, holding her close against his bare chest. She rested her head on him and entwined her fingers in his.

'What troubles you?' Kett's question interrupted her dark thoughts. 'Mina, Corin, Rohne, us, Rafi?'

Alere laughed brokenly. 'Pick one, or all of them.'

'Well, Mina and Corin I can reassure you about. They'll both be fine. Rafi, I don't know. As for us...' His thumb stroked the back of her hand and his arm tightened around her waist. 'I've waited a long time, Alli. It may not always be easy, for we know each other's faults, but you were worth waiting for.'

She said nothing.

He turned her around, held her face between his hands and studied her. A frown knitted his brow. 'Is...Am I assuming too much? Did I misunderstand what I felt when you let your wards down?' He glanced at the door. 'Corin...'

Alere turned his face back and read the self-doubt in his grey eyes. 'No, I'm sorry. Corin's wonderful, but...'

His expression hardened into distant calm. He shifted slightly away, leaving her cold. She suddenly understood. Everyone Kett had loved as a child had rejected or abandoned him: his mother had died, his stepmother had created an entire set of murderous laws because of him; his father had let her. Part of his calm was self-protection, hiding self-doubt.

'Don't, Kett. I think I've loved you since I was ten. I just didn't realise until I thought it was too late.' She laid a hand on his cheek and put all the truth she could muster into her next words. 'I love you, Kett. Don't doubt that. Not ever.'

He gave a broken half-laugh and pressed his forehead to hers.

'Alli...' He lifted her chin and kissed her with a skill and passion that left her shaking. Then he tucked her head against his chest and held her tightly. She listened to his racing heart and smiled.

She stayed that way until their heartbeats slowed and the tension ebbed from Kett's shoulders.

Finally, she leaned back. 'I suppose we can't stay here forever.'

'No.' He ran a hand over his head and gazed out the window. 'The world won't let us. We still have to get Jarran back to Madina.' He kissed her again and rummaged through his bag until he found a shirt.

Alere hugged herself. 'When you were trying to bring me back…Rohne was…' she shivered '…in my head, too. Telling me to let go.'

'How?' Kett dragged the shirt on and frowned.

She shrugged as the details slipped away like a dream. One that, at the moment, she wasn't inclined to try and remember.

'It didn't feel like normal telepathy, Outer to Outer. It felt more like he was in my mind with me. Like he *was* me…no…I don't know how to describe it.'

Before she could elaborate, the door opened, admitting Corin and Mina. Alere left Kett's side, alive to the badly-hidden hurt in Corin. Before she could say anything, Mina ran to her, checking her over and scolding her in a mixture of relieved anxiety and genuine fear. Alere bore it as patiently as she could for a few seconds then stopped her.

'Enough, Mina. I couldn't think of any other way to save them. Acquit me of deliberately trying to frighten you. I'm well, now.'

'Just don't do it again!' Mina wiped away a tear and sniffed. 'I felt so helpless and I couldn't bear to lose you, Alli.' She pressed her cheek to Alere's. 'Not now.'

'I second that.' Corin's cheerful tone ran at counterpoint to the lingering ache in his eyes.

Alere regarded Kett and Mina. 'Would you mind giving us a moment?'

They exchanged glances and left through the adjoining door.

Corin tucked his hands under his arms, scuffing the floor with his bare feet like a child about to be scolded.

'Corin,' she began, not sure what to say.

'No apologies.' He gripped her shoulders and kissed her forehead lightly. Searching her face for something, he released her and grimaced. 'I went into this knowing you didn't feel as I did, and I suspected you loved him. I was hoping time would change that.'

'I'm sorry,' she murmured. 'I do love you, too. Just not...I'm so sorry.'

He smiled, though it was forced. 'Don't be, you zift. We had fun, didn't we?' He touched her hair, hesitated and dropped his hand back to his side. 'You taught me I can love again. It might take me some time to, well, get over you and Shasa.'

Guilt flickered over his handsome face. Unable to stand seeing him hurting, Alere wrapped her arms around him, murmuring more apologies. After a moment's hesitation, his arms encircled her waist. He buried his face in her neck. His shoulders shook and his tears warmed her skin. She held him, for nothing she could say would ease his guilt.

Eventually, they moved apart, but she held onto his hand, afraid to let him go, worried he needed someone to help him cope with Shasa's death. He thumbed away his tears and chuckled ruefully.

'I'm a shazi.' He disengaged. 'I lost her years ago and you were never mine, anyway. I'm not sure why it hurts.'

Alere kissed his cheek. 'Because underneath that care-less mask you wear, you're a loving, wonderful man.'

Corin smiled wryly. 'Keep that to yourself.' He lapsed into troubled silence.

'What will you do now?' She was half-afraid of his answer. She didn't want him to leave, but how he could stay and watch her be with Kett?

He chuckled, but a bitter edge to it cut into her fragile happiness. 'You're not getting rid of me that easily. We still have to get Jarran safely back to Madina. We've got another war to stop, remember?' He shrugged and smiled more naturally. 'Plus, there's Saric. I'm definitely going to need help with that kid or he'll drive me insane. Assuming he wants to come with us, that is. Who knows?'

'Have you seen him? How's he coping. With Shasa's death, I mean?' She pushed aside the image of Shasa's face; of Gavon's face; of Saric's tears. Not yet. She wasn't ready to deal with it, either.

Corin's amusement fell away and all the pain he hid shadowed his expression again. She caught his fingers. He stroked a thumb over the back of her hand and gave a twisted smile.

'He's not here.' He gazed out the window. 'He's off helping Liu find homes for all the child-thieves who want to stay. Mina says he hasn't been to visit at all. Even when she sent a message to Liu that I might be dying.' He shrugged. 'Guess that speaks volumes.'

'Oh, Corin.' Alere laid her head on his shoulder. 'He's just lost his mother. You can't expect him to face losing a father as well. You have to help him deal with Shasa's death. That's what will bring you together.'

He folded his arms. 'Diyu! *I* don't even know how to deal with it. The first time I lost her, I shut everyone out for the next decade. I'm hardly a role model in this.'

Alere captured his face between her hands and kissed him. He groaned and pulled her close, then broke the kiss and leaned his forehead against hers.

'Gaisi, Alli,' he said roughly. 'You'll have to stop doing that or I won't be able to let you go at all.'

'Sorry,' she said. 'I don't want you to be hurt. Give Saric time. And yourself time as well. If I could, I'd send you both away on some grand adventure so you could bond and be away from me.' She looked gravely at him. 'But, as you said, we're not done, yet.'

His smile flickered again. 'I know. Apparently Mamlakah can't cope without us. We'll just have to go save it again.'

Alere stepped back and nodded.

'Alere!'

She halted at Valera's call, waiting until the xintou joined her at her bedroom door before replying. 'Valera. What can I do for you?'

It was the morning of Ahad, the First of Yiyue, the beginning of the New Year, and they were due to leave in a few minutes. The rest of Er'run had been spent in explanations, hurried advice and contingency planning for the next few weeks. For both Jundoms. Alere had developed a greater respect for Liu, Jahil, Lan and even Laya in their brief time together. While Liu was devious and often saw both sides of an argument with impressive clarity and utter ruthlessness, Jahil and Lan were highly intelligent, thoughtful. Lan, especially, would make a great leader. Laya, with the threat of her brother-in-law gone and with something to focus on, revealed a sharp economic brain, full of excellent ideas for how to improve the lot of a people left without a cheap workforce. It would take some time to get the Jundom economically stable again, but it could be done.

Vast numbers of refugees were already moving; slaves leaving Chengdu, mostly, but also citizens fleeing the possibility of retribution by their ex-slaves. And, according to Liu, huge numbers of the Selb fanatics had also left without warning. Citizens and slaves, alike. He had no idea why, or where they were headed, apart from south.

The strain on towns between Chengdu and Madina would be telling, especially in the last weeks of winter when food was scarce.

Alere had, possibly recklessly, pledged Shanzhai's assistance and agreed to come back to put more specific, trade agreements in place. In return Jahil had pledged to send junren to Madina's aid, should they be needed.

Having re-read Rafi's note from the day she saved Kett and Corin, she had a sinking feeling the junren would be needed. She hadn't shown the note to anyone yet, uncertain as to how to move forward and wanting to think about it more before she sought advice.

The note was dated three days before. At that time, Hassan was less than five days from the city, while the Madina troops were still more than a sevenday away, with the roads to the southwest yet blocked by the heavy winter snows. Rafi had been unable to gather the full support of the Jun families. Many of them had now snuck out of Madina and retreated to their country estates to safely await the outcome of Hassan's assault. Madina was in chaos as frightened citizens fled the city, some east to Ma-Safra lands, but more north into Zah-Hill territory, putting strain on the resources of smaller towns and villages unprepared to house and feed so many.

Unless they got Jarran back to Madina quickly, and unified the Jun families, it would be too late. All this death would have been for nothing. If Hassan prevailed, Madina would be once more under the control of a madman and there was no telling what would happen next.

Putting her worries for Madina and Rafi aside, Alere turned her attention to Valera. Luckily the easy-going Xintou had quickly forgiven Alere's behaviour in the Games when she saw the result. Ever since, Valera had been a staunch supporter of anything Alere,

Kett, or Corin proposed in the meetings with Jahil. So much so that even Jahil had been moved to frown at his Xintou and remind her where her loyalties lay.

Now, puffing slightly from her run down the hall, Valera caught her breath and pushed the gold veil up onto her forehead. Tucked under one arm was a slim, silk-wrapped parcel. Apparently satisfied by whatever she saw in Alere's face, she offered it. Alere accepted. It felt like a book of some sort.

'This is the gift I mentioned at Hallon's house.' Valera touched it. 'Mallika found this about six months ago, when she and the girls cleared out some old trunks in one of the storage attics. Since it was bound in gold silk, she thought it must be xintou-related. So, she gave it to me.'

Alere peeled off the wrapping to reveal a thin book. The gold silk cover was dark and brittle with age, the page edges crumbling and nibbled by insects. Afraid to open it lest it disintegrate, Alere glanced a question at Valera, who shrugged.

'Open the cover.'

She did, studying the faded, angular writing. 'Lei Koh-Lin? That's the male honorific symbol in front of the name. What year? Oh…One-sixty-seven. Wasai! This is over five hundred years old! What is it?'

'I don't know,' Valera said. 'It's written in old Mandrin and I can't read it. I didn't want to give it to anyone here to translate for I don't know what it says. I thought it should go to you, since he must have been one of your family.'

'Wait.' Alere caressed the yellowed pages. 'Wasn't it a Lei Koh-Lin who founded Xintou House in something like One-sixty? I always thought that was a woman. That's what the House teaches.'

'Yes.' Valera inclined her head, frowning. 'It is taught that a woman named Lei Koh-Lin, together with the Edwards sisters, founded the Xintou order and built the Madina House in One-sixty-one.' She raised anxious eyes to Alere. 'But it's only known to a few senior Xintou that Lei was a man and that he and Kya Edwards were married. About five years after the House was built, all three of them vanished for several months. Kya and Bree returned alone and would never say what happened to Lei.' She touched the book. 'These writings begin just after the three of them left the House. It's too much to be a co-incidence.'

'So, this could be the lost journal?' Alere said, awed. 'This could be where the Teachings of Lei came from? Could this tell us more about male xintou and why they are forbidden?'

'Perhaps,' Valera said. She put a hand to her cheek. 'I wasn't sure what to do with it. Even the Orange of Messenger House is not safe from attack these days so I couldn't risk sending it to Mistress Li. She's still very ill. I'm not sure who is running the House with Renna gone.'

'Mistress Li is *still* unwell?' Alere shivered, unable to imagine the House without its Mistress.

Valera sighed. 'She *is* over a hundred. It's just very bad timing in terms of what's happening in Madina. I've had no messages at all for several days. Prior to that – apart from the one about you – they were signed by any one of five seniors. The House needs a strong leader in these times and we haven't one.'

Valera sent Alere a shrewd look. 'I know there's something else going on you haven't told me. I know your sister is not a true xintou. And I know you're withholding knowledge of what she, and you, can do. But I won't press you and I won't say anything to the House. You've done me and Melcor a great service. And Mistress Li trusts you.'

Alere made a hasty gesture but held back an acerbic comment.

Valera pressed her lips together and glanced both directions along the corridor. Finally, she spoke again, a whisper in the vast hallway.

'Alere, I'm worried. There's something strange going on at the House. I never agreed with Mistress Li's direction for Melcor. She always advised me to keep the status quo. That I leave Hallon unchallenged and let the misery here continue, while still protecting Jahil. I never understood why. Then she sent me that message advising me to help you overturn everything. Why?'

'Maybe, now she's ill, she's realised she made mistakes?'

Valera's frown deepened. 'I suppose. But it seems very unlike her. She's always been so adamant that things should be as they always have been. The House has worked hard, over the last five hundred years, to keep Kalima stable and peaceful. Why would she deliberately allow you to cause such deep rifts and upset? The unrest is rapidly spreading throughout Melcor. It must, eventually, impact the other Jundoms. It will take years to achieve steady calm again.'

'What are you saying?'

'I'm not sure. I'm wondering if, maybe, Mistress Li didn't send me that message. Just promise me something?'

Shaken, Alere waited without agreeing to anything.

The Xintou's cheeks flushed. 'I have, in a very limited way, the gift of precognitive Seeing. I've Seen something horrific coming to Madina.' She made a frustrated sound, waving her hands vaguely. 'I can't tell you what, exactly, just that something – or someone – will be in Madina soon. Someone we should all fear. With powers greater than any xintou known previously. Someone who can destroy everything we care about. And the very stability on which our whole society is built: Xintou House. So, promise me you'll protect Mistress Li and our House?'

'I…I'll try.' Alere turned the book over and over without seeing it. Troubled, awed by the prospect of owning such a precious item, Alere embraced Valera with genuine feeling. The woman was fussy, but she had risked her life, and that of her Bonded Family, to help Alere and her friends.

'Thank you, Valera,' Alere said, stroking the book gently. 'You've given me a treasure. I hope I can keep it safe until I can get it back to Shanzhai. I'll let you know if it contains anything of importance to the House.'

She let herself into her room and leaned against the door panel. She stayed there a long time, thinking, working out what to do.

Someone who will destroy everything we care about. Rohne. It had to be. He had manipulated Hallon's thoughts, escaped Chengdu, and was now on his way to Madina. Once there, what would he do? Seek the throne for himself? Take revenge on Xintou House for their policy of killing male xintou at birth? What did he want?

Protecting the House was only one of her tasks. Whatever was coming, she needed first to safeguard the people she loved: Kett, Corin and Mina. Rafi and Saric as well, if she could. The grief of losing Gavon was still fresh, gnawing at her heart. A gaping hole in her life even Kett's love couldn't quite fill. She couldn't bear to lose anyone else. Couldn't even stand to think about it. Couldn't be placed again in the situation where she had to choose between those she loved and the greater cause.

Alone for the first time since yesterday morning, Alere curled up on a window seat, hugging her knees. She contemplated the bed, still rumpled and soft with memories of last night. She had only begun to taste the depth of her feelings for Kett, and his for her. They'd had one bittersweet night together, full of hesitancy, laughter, tears. And the discovery of more joyous physical and mental intimacy than she'd known was possible. How could she lose that? How could she risk losing him if they went to Madina and had to confront Rohne?

She groaned and hid her face in her knees, unable to cope with the extremes of emotion. How could she stay sane after such loss and such love at the same time? Her heart was being ripped asunder. If she was to help Rafi at all, she needed to regain control.

Nothing in her weishi, xintou or jiaoji training helped. The ache wouldn't go and she couldn't *think* through the pain and the ecstasy. This *had* to stop or she would be useless when the time came to confront whatever challenges lay ahead.

But how? How did she govern emotions that had a will of their own? Grief wrenched at her at the most unexpected times, derailing her thinking. Love for Kett filled her to the exclusion of rational thought. Either one could be fatal at the wrong moment. Both were too much right now. She needed distance and time to centre herself again.

She stared out the window, into the garden below. The sun, rising over the building, glinted off a window like the yanstones' silver-gilt fire. Alere blinked and certainty held her still. Ah. Now she knew.

In the garden, the Shah's younger daughters chased each other, giggling, around a tree, carefree and unaware. The youngest halted abruptly. With a cry of despair, she sank to her knees and gathered the small, limp body of a jin-bird into her hands. Her older sister soothed her and, together, the girls dug a small hole in a garden bed and buried the tiny golden form.

Twenty minutes later Alere opened the door to admit Corin, Mina, and Kett. As they chose seats around a low table in the room's centre, she poured a dark purplish wine into beaten-copper goblets and passed one to each.

'Er…' Corin examined the contents of his cup and cocked his head quizzically at her. 'Don't get me wrong, I'm all for drinking a decent wine that's not green, even at this hour of the morning. But aren't we meant to be riding to Madina about now?'

Alere smiled at him, glad to see his buoyant humour reasserting itself. He would be alright.

'Of course.' She raised her goblet. 'I just wanted a minute with you all to say thank you and to remember.'

She burned each of their images into her mind. Mina, her mirror and the soft yin to her own firey yang. Corin, alive and joyous. Kett, loving, protective and strong.

'To friends loved and lost: to Gavon and Shasa.' She drank deeply from her glass to ease the tightness in her chest and throat.

Sitting, she waited until they followed suit and drained their own glasses. Refilling them, she lifted hers to each one in turn.

'Mina, you are possibly the bravest person I know. You were dragged into this unprepared and you have been through horrors you never imagined would be part of your life as a village healer. You're strong, kind and I'm lucky to have you as a sister. You certainly deserve better. And I promise, when this is all over, you'll have it. Thank you.'

'Oh, Alli,' Mina said, brokenly. She rose and hugged Alere hard, kissing her cheek and stroking back her hair. 'I'm lucky, too. I love you.' She sat back down and sipped her wine, wiping at tears.

Alere cleared her throat and turned to Corin.

'You, my friend,' she said, 'have the enviable gift of seeing the best in the world even when it's obscured by the worst. You've endured so much, but you've come through brilliant, untarnished, and worthy of love, whether you believe it or not. Don't let that go, Corin. It makes you wonderful beyond words.'

Corin stared at her for a long time, serious for once. He raised his glass in salute and took a deep draft. She spoke to Kett.

'I have no words, Kett...' She took a sip to relax her throat. 'For how much you mean to me. You're the rock my life is built on, my strength, my compass, my love. You deserve someone more than me. But hopefully I won't disappoint you too often.' She laughed and sniffed.

He took her hand and kissed the palm, but there was wariness in his expression as well as love. He knew her too well.

She put down her glass, checked theirs were all empty and stood, brushing her hands off.

'Now I have an apology to make. I'm sorry. I had to do it. Forgive me.'

Kett was the first to catch on. He tilted his cup, studied the dregs, then back at her. Slow anger flared in his eyes.

Corin was next. He groaned and placed his goblet on the table with careful concentration. 'You zift. You *can't* do this.' Even as he spoke he listed to one side, lids closing over green eyes afire with frustration as he slipped into unconsciousness.

Mina, her expression one of bewilderment, simply collapsed sideways onto the couch-cushions.

'Jiangui, Alli.' Kett's slurred words were barely audible as he fought the effects of the istilqa. 'Why?'

Alere crouched beside him and kissed him softly, smiling through tears. 'Because I love you too much to risk losing you.'

He groaned and his eyes drifted shut. His fingers around her wrist lost their grip and dropped to his lap. His head sagged onto his chest.

Kissing him again, she whispered into his ear a Suggestion to stay in Melcor, then quickly did the same to Mina and Corin. She tucked the Lei Koh-Lin book under Mina's hand, complete with a note of explanation. It was too precious a piece of history to take with her to Madina. Her sister would be able to give it to Yasmin or Rafi when this was over.

In Corin's pocket she found the list of towns and contacts along the route back to Madina. He'd already arranged and paid for Dalor's boat back across the river, plus horses on the other side. It made sense to use them. After a moment's hesitation, she also took one of three leather purses he had tucked into his jacket.

Finally, she shouldered her bag and strapped on her swordbelt and bow. Then she stood over her friends, studying their peaceful countenances one last time. Without them to tug on her emotions and divide her focus, she had a much better chance of being what she needed to be.

Taking the bracelets from Mina's wrists, she clasped them around her own and the first rush of gold-fire surged through her mind. Next, she picked up the necklace and, after a moment's hesitation, clipped it around her hips. Resting her palms on the stones in her weapons she opened herself to their influence and allowed all of their silver-gilt purity to sweep through her.

They burned away fear, grief, love and anger, smoothing out the rough-beaten iron of her soul, tempering her, leaving her sharp and clean like burnished steel. They forged her into a weapon with which to purge the malignancy threatening Madina.

The silver-gilt in her mind flared in the eyes of her reflection, mirrored over the fireplace. Alere smiled and the face in the mirror smiled back.

'I am gangzhi.'

THE END

If you enjoyed this book, please leave a review on Goodreads and wherever you purchased your copy. It helps other people to find good books, and helps the author to not quit!

Other books by Aiki Flinthart
Discover other titles by Aiki Flinthart at: **www.aikiflinthart.com**
Or
The 80AD series (YA Adventure/Fantasy)
80AD Book 1: *The Jewel of Asgard*
80AD Book 2: *The Hammer of Thor*
80AD Book 3: *The Tekhen of Anuket*
80AD Book 4: *The Sudarshana*
80AD Book 5: *The Yu Dragon*

The Kalima Chronicles (YA Adventure/Fantasy)
IRON (#1)
FIRE (#2)
STEEL (#3)

Other books
Sold! (Contemporary Romance/Adventure)

Short Story Anthologies
Return
Like a Woman

Connect with me on Facebook
Twitter: @aikiflinthart
Instagram: Aikiflinthart

APPENDIX

Story facts and background

Kalima means 'World' in Arabic. The planet was settled by idealists from Earth seeking a world without conflict. The planet's sun is a K-type orange star in the Gliese 167 system. Rayleigh scattering of light combined with atmospheric dust high in copper oxide, gives Kalima a pale teal-green sky. The sun's orange colour led to dark blue and black-leafed plantlife. Kalima is third planet from this sun. Gliese 167 is a cooler sun than Sol, but Kalima is closer to their sun than Earth is to Sol. Kalima's. 14 month year and its axial tilt and elliptical orbit means the southern hemisphere (the location of the colony cities) has a long spring-summer-autumn cycle and a short, 2-month winter. The northern hemisphere has larger extremes of weather and is, as yet, uninhabited.

Kalima has an active geologic past, which formed continents, volcanoes, oceans and rivers. But, until the terraforming teams arrived, Kalima was bare of life. The rocks created by the presence of life on Earth—such as marble, oils, methane, coal, chalk, limestone, or banded ironstone—do not exist on Kalima. The few iron deposits in existence are iron-sand beaches created by volcanic activity, and meteoric iron. The planet has high levels of copper and a vast desert of copper-rich soil on one of the other continents has contributed to the levels of copper oxide dust in the atmosphere, which causes the green sky.

The colonists chose a lifeless planet and paid to have it Terraformed and seeded with life and complex ecological webs.

Initial terraform teams were sent to Kalima on faster-than-light ships, while colonists took slower, jumplight sleep-ships to allow the teams sufficient time to complete the infrastructure. Five hundred years after departing Earth, the first of three ships arrived, carrying twenty thousand carefully selected colonists.

Mainly of Chinese, Arabic and European descent, colonists were chosen and screened for their desire to live a peaceful, agrarian existence. Kalima's twenty-one Jun families descend from the original twenty-one Funding families who financed the expedition.

Two hundred years after settlement, supply ships from old Earth ceased and colonists were obliged to be self-sufficient. Lack of iron prevented the colonists from creating a high-tech society, forcing them to live in semi-medieval conditions, although many old ideas and skills have been retained. Electricity generation through wind or water power exists in limited form. The ability to make telescopes, lenses and microscopes has not been lost and, although medical understanding of surgery, physiology and healing exists, it is limited by the lack of modern technology. Many books on old technologies have been preserved and, some colonists retained information regarding warfare and weaponry—the basis of knowledge in the Weishi House.

Kalima society is substantially feudal, the Jundom of Mamlakah being ruled by 21 Juns, under the leadership of the Jun First and two Jun Seconds. Melcor, to the north, and Jadid, to the south, are also feudal societies but Melcor's society and economy is built on slavery. Shemal is a democracy.

Languages are mixed. A version of English, borrowing many words from Arabic and Mandrin, is the dominant language in Mamlakah, the first colony site. Similarly, cultural crossovers are normal. Women and men wear robes or high-collared shirts and trous (loose trousers tied at the waist). Robes are worn indoors or while employed in non-active trades and management positions. Otherwise it is common for trous and shirts with jackets or cloaks to be worn. Women wear their hair long and loose or, if of a higher caste, long and up in elaborate hairstyles. Men in Mamlakah wear their hair long and tied back in a mawei (low ponytail or plait). Although now less fashionable, women may wear a transparent veil that covers the eyes and nose only. The veil is symbolic of mystery and high ranking rather than an indication of women's inferiority.

In Mamlakahn society, women are, basically, equal in standing to men. They may be Juns or Trade Masters in any House and are free to undertake any training and job. In any colony, however, women are more valuable than men. Built into the psyche of the colony is the need to protect women that has continued into today's thinking. Weishi House came into being primarily as protection for women of childbearing age from natural hazards, though its scope expanded as the colony grew. Women are the bearers of the next generation and the survival of a colony depends on how quickly women can give birth and outstrip death rates.

The need for high birth rates, and genetic diversity, led to the practice of kin-children. In the early days of the colony, a couple unable to have children was a wasted pairing. Women needed to have children by several fathers in order to keep the gene-pool as diverse as possible. After seven hundred years, the population is approximately half a million.

People/Places/Things

Adeghal – capital of Shemal

Ahmar – Red (Ahmar Mountains run down the Eastern boundary of the kingdom)

Alzin – an aluminium-zinc alloy.

Asalam – northerly seat of the Zah-Hill family.

Aswad – Black (Aswad ranges run down the centre of the kingdom)

Ceramic Swords are made of zirconium dioxide

Chengdu- capital of Melcor

Days are: Ahad (one), Ithnan (two), Thalatha (three), Arba'a (four), Khamsa (five), Sitta (six)

Ghadeb – 'angry' (Ghadeb sea to the northeast)

Gharb – west (Gharb ranges run down the Western boundary of the jundom)

Gunpowder = saltpetre + sulphur + charcoal

Jiali – 'home' – Capital city of the Ma-Safra family lands

Jadid (New) Jundom – south.

Kabir – big (the Kabir river runs through the middle of the kingdom and empties into Melcor's port 700 gongli away to the east)

Kalima – World. Earth-sized planet. Kalima has a 6-day week and a 5-week month. 30 days per month. 14 months in a year and 422 days in a year – two days at the end of the year are not part of any month and are called yirun and er'run. Axial tilt and slightly elliptical orbit means northern hemisphere has extreme seasons but southern is mild with short winters and long growing seasons.

Kuaisu River – 'fast/rapid' river (wraps around the eastern side of Shanzhai)

Luna-Yi – red moon

Luna-Er – blue-white moon

Madina – capital city of Mamlakah. Palace - The Alkazar.

Magnal – magnesium aluminium alloy – light and strong

Melcor – second kingdom to be settled – to the northeast of Madina and on the Ghadeb sea. Reached by trade on the Kabir river.

Metsa – the river running through the western section of the Ma-Safra Jundom, near Newmec. It eventually joins with the Kabir just north of Madina

Mianshou – end of year 2 day celebration during Yirun & Er-run.

Plants are dark blue-black-leafed (absorbing different, greater range of spectra and reflecting less green)

Seryeh River – 'quick' river (wraps around the western side of Shanzhai). The two rivers join and become the Kabir, just north of Madina

Shanzhai – seat of Jun Second Koh-Lin.

Sulcrete – concrete where the binding agent is sulphur rather than lime (limestone does not exist on a planet without an organic geologic history)

Yan – 'flame' = yanstones

Yirun & Er'run – extra two days at the end of the year. Mianshou = End of year celebrations last for these two days and anything done on these days (apart from violence) is unpunishable.

Zalam – slums within Madina

.....

Trade Houses

Artist House (purple veil/purple hat)

Healer House (white veil/hat, grey robe)

Jiaoji (Courtesan) House (red veil)

Merchant House (green veil/green hat/robe)

Messenger House (orange)

Miner House (grey hat)

Trades House (brown hat/veil)

Weishi House (black veil/black hat)

Xintou (telepath) House (gold veil, gold robe) Mistress Li

.....

Jun Families

Jun First Radan Zah-Hill (deceased) (Wife Hanna; Son Ven (deceased)) – Silver and Black.

Jun second Petar Ma-Safra (wife Leah) - silver and purple. No children.

Jun second Rafi Koh-Lin (wife Yasmin;) - silver and green.

Jun third Kennor Han-Asad (daughter Farima) - gold and black (controls Madina city guards. Vassal to Zah-Hill)

Jun Third Yu-Smith - gold and green (vassal to Koh-Lin)

Jun Third Dal Lee-Hay - gold and purple (vassal to Ma-Safra)

Jun Fourth Hassan Wen-Gates - copper and purple. Kin-brother to Jun First. (vassal to Ma-Safra)

Jun Fourth Bren Gray-Saud - copper and black (vassal to Zah-Hill)

Jun Fourth Qin-Turner - copper and grey (vassal to Zah-Hill)

Jun Fourth Knight-Hun - copper and green (vassal to Koh-Lin)

Jun Fifth Jaber-Lun - red and purple (vassal to Ma-Safra)

Jun Fifth Seif-Li - red and green (vassal to Koh-Lin)

Jun Fifth Zhou-Issa - red and teal (vassal to Koh-Lin)

Jun Fifth Easton-Green - red and black (vassal to Zah-Hill)

Jun Fifth Amoudi-Mann - red and grey (vassal to Zah-Hill)

Jun Sixth Ortega-Miller - blue and black (Zah-Hill)

Jun Sixth Quing-Mai - blue and grey (Zah-Hill)

Jun Sixth Price-Khan - blue and green (Koh-Lin)

Jun Sixth Yasif-Do - blue and teal (Koh-Lin)

Jun Sixth Khoury-Ban - blue and purple (Ma-Safra)

Jun Sixth Blake-Swift - blue and indigo (Ma-Safra)

Johnston house - blue & green tartan

.....

Mandrin

Numbers and distances and times

Yi – one (Luna-Yi = first moon – reddish)

Er – two (Luna-Er = second moon – silver)

San – three   Si – four   wu - five

Liu – six   Qi – seven   Ba - eight

…..

Chi – approx 33.33cm

Zhang – approx 3.33m

Gongli – kilometre

…..

Months:

Yiyue – first month of the lunar year (1st month of spring)

Eryue – second (spring 2)   Sanyue – 3rd (spring 3)

Siyue – 4th (summer 1)   Wuyue – 5th (summer 2)

Liuyue – 6th (summer 3   Qiyue – 7th (summer 4)

Bayue – 8th (summer 5)   Jiuyue – 9th (summer 6)

Shiyue – 10th (autumn)   Shiyiyue – 11th (autumn)

Shi'eryue – 12th (autumn)   Shisanyue – 13th (winter1)

Shisiyue – 14th (winter2)

…..

Words:

ading – antiseptic/disinfectant

Bai - to pay respect / worship / visit / salute

Bei – flower bud

Bi – coin

Che-ma – cart horse

Chuizi – a hammer-strike

Erheyi – two-in-one

Feihua – nonsense, rubbish.

Gangzhi – made of steel

Gongren - worker

Gu – archaic - legendary venomous insect / to poison / to bewitch / to drive to insanity / to harm by witchcraft / intestinal parasite

Hepan – river plains

hunli - wedding

Huoche – wagon/truck/van

Jiali - Home (name of Ma-Safra city)

Nari – double-edged sword

Jiaoji – courtesan

Jin - gold

Jinbi – gold coin

jiu – rice wine/liquor/alcohol

Jun - monarch/lord/gentleman/ruler

Junren – soldier/serviceman/military personnel

Kuaisu – fast/rapid

Kuai long – fast dragon

Kui - Chief/head/outstanding/stalwart/exceptional

Lanhua - orchid

Lanse – blue (lancha tea)

Lu – deer

Luotuo – camel

Manxing – slow poison

Mawei – ponytail

mayao – anaesthetic

Mianshou - - to avoid suffering / to prevent (sth bad) / to protect against (damage) / immunity (from prosecution) / freedom (from pain, damage etc) / exempt from punishment

Molian – to temper oneself/ to steel oneself/ self-discipline/ endurance

Nai – mother

Quan - dog

Rong – salamander

Runiu – dairy cattle

Shangwei – captain (military rank)

Shanzhai – fortified hill village/mountain stronghold

Shenshi – my lord

Shi - is / are / am / yes / to be

Shifu – teacher

Shunu – my lady

Song – sponge (cake)

Tiebi – iron coin

Tongbi – copper coin

Watu – poison frog toxin

Weishi - guardian/defender

xiao – similar to/resembling (ie: xiao-cat)

xiang - elephant

Xintou – thoughts/heart/mind

Xiongshou – assassin

Xue – blood

xun – herb

ya-zheng - correct (literary) / upright / (hon.) Please point out my shortcomings. / I await your esteemed corrections.

Yan – flame

Yinbi – silver coin

Yongbing – mercenary/hired gun

Zhi – to stop/prohibit

Zitan – red sandalwood

Zuoce – left side

.....

Insults/swearing

diyu – hell/underworld

Feihua – nonsense / rubbish / superfluous words / You don't say! / No kidding!

gaisi – damn it!

gouri - lit. fucked or spawned by a dog / contemptible / lousy, fucking

hundan – scoundrel/bastard/hoodlum/wretch

huo-zui – living hell/suffering/hardship

jian-gui – curse it/to hell with it

Jiba – penis (vulgar)

Jiche – pain in the ass/damn!/crap!

qusi – go to hell/drop dead

salai – make a scene/raise hell

shazi – idiot/fool

Wasai – exclamation to express amazement/wow!

zhen-shide - Really! (interj. of annoyance or frustration)

…..

Rabic

…..

Days: Ahad (one), Ithnan (two), Thalatha (three), Arba'a (four), Khamsa (five), Sitta (six)

Ahad (one), Ithnan (two), thalatha (three), Arba'a (four), Khamsa (five), Sitta (six)

Ahmar – Red (Ahmar Mountains run down the Eastern boundary of the kingdom)

Al Mamlakah – the kingdom

Alcazar – from Al-qasr – fort, castle, palace

alem'erekh – fight

Aswad – Black (Aswad ranges run down the centre of the kingdom)

Badiya – desert

Dafdae - frog

Gharb – west (Gharb ranges run down the Western boundary of the jundom)

Herq – burn

Heryeq - fire

Iblis - Devil

Istilqa – sleep

Jabal – Mountain

Jadid – New (name for the southern jundom)

Jiyl – generation.

Kabir – big (the Kabir river runs through the middle of the kingdom and empties into Melcor's port 700 gongli away to the northeast)

Kalima – World

Khiba – tent

Madina – City

Malik – King

Mamlakah – the kingdom

Menzel - home

Mhareb – warrior/fighter

Mumit – deadly

Nasir – vulture (nasiri = plural)

Sabat – coma, lethargy, torpor

Shaytan – demon, fiend, serpent

Selb – Steel, betterment, loin, crucifixion

sery'eh – Quick (Seryeh River to northwest of Shanzhai)

Tabib – doctor

Zalam – Darkness

Zanbur – hornet, wasp

Zibal - scavenger

Zinzana – cell/prison

…..

Insults/swearing

Hamagi (hamag = plural) – uncivilised, barbaric

Haraami – thief

Hmar – jackass

Jahim - hell

Kaddaab – liar

Kalb – dog

Kalet – filthy street bastard

Khara – shit! (frustration)

Saafil – base;loathsome

Waa faqri – damn!

Wisix – dirty/filthy (morally)

Zift – Idiot

STEEL

Aiki Flinthart 2019

CHAPTER ONE

If change was inevitable, and freedom so desirable, why did people resist both?

Alere emerged from the huoche and hesitated, taken aback by the crowd massed between her and the dock's edge. Shading her eyes against the aching glitter of sun on water, she studied the shifting, surly mass of ex-slaves and frightened citizens. It was late in the morning of Ahad, the First of Yiyue: the first day of the New Year. Just three days after the liberation of slaves in Melcor. Chaos still reigned in the capital, Chengdu, as citizens and slaves alike tried to deal with their abrupt change in status.

Hundreds of refugees pushed and shoved along the water's edge, desperate to secure places aboard chuans leaving the city. The stench of close-packed, unwashed humanity caught in Alere's nose: the sharpness of urine and fear; the gagging sweetness of rotting food. By the looks of the debris lying around, some people had been here at least a couple of days. The crowd's noisy uncertainty pressed against her ears and mind, almost overwhelming both. Babies squalled and children cried their lack of understanding as parents hushed them, argued with each other and yelled abuse at the chuans waiting, unreachable, offshore.

The crowd divided itself, almost by habit, into two groups: former slaves and free citizens. They eyed each other with growing hostility. A weak orange winter-sun rose in the pale, teal-green sky, warming the air and their ire. The situation was exacerbated by the chuanzhus' demands to be paid for shipping passengers instead of cargo. They naturally took the free citizens over the penniless ex-slaves, leaving the slaves bitter and vocal in their resentment.

Nothing had yet happened, but that was probably due to a fear of retribution amongst those long-habituated to punishment.

Change in mindset took a lot longer than overturning mere laws on paper.

Alere understood the ex-slaves' desire to escape the city and return to their families, but why did free citizens of Melcor abandon their lives? Curious, she edged closer to a knot of men and women, who huddled together and regarded their ex-slaves with a strange mixture of fear and pitying superiority.

It took only a few snippets of their conversation and a slight brush against their chaotic, unwarded minds to understand. They were afraid to lose the luxurious lifestyle supported by slave labour. Afraid of being murdered in their beds by angry, freed slaves. Afraid they might have to work and do the menial jobs formerly assigned to slaves.

Alere wasn't sure whether to pity them, laugh at them, or slap sense into them. She'd fought for their freedom from Hallon's despotic rule. Lost a valued friend. Now she'd left behind people she loved, in order to keep fighting for them. And what were they worried about? Their fat, lazy backsides and already-bulging purses.

They didn't understand the value of freedom and their ex slaves were afraid of it. How ironic.

Had all her pain and loss even been worth it?

Disgusted, she returned to the huoche. The driver passed down her bag, Jarran's and Mina's. Settling her bow across her back and weapons on her hips, she hefted all three bags and hunted for a path to the water's edge so she could signal Dalor Khan to bring his liferaft closer.

Jarran emerged from the huoche, grunting as he repositioned Mina's limp body in his arms. Mina's long, white hair trailed in the dust on the cobbles, the pale ends turning almost as dark as the regrowth near her scalp. They needed to find some white-weed and re-colour her hair.

Alere tugged at her own shoulder-length, dark hair, tied into a man's mawei. What a ridiculous thing to be thinking. Colouring her twin sister's hair hardly ranked as important at the moment. Getting out of Chengdu. Getting Jarran to Madina. They were important. Carting Mina's unconscious body around classed as sheer stupidity.

'We can still send her back to the palace.' She made one last attempt to convince Jarran to leave Mina behind. 'I really think it's the best place for her. Kett and Corin will be with her. We've got less than a week to get you back to Madina before Jun Fourth Hassan Wen-Gates overruns the city and takes your throne. She can't handle a trip like this, Jarran. You know that, don't you?'

He gave her a contemptuous stare down the length of his aquiline nose. 'I know you think she's can't, but you're underestimating her. Agreed, she's not you, but she's a lot tougher than you give her credit for.'

'But she—'

The Jun-Heir glared at her with all the weight of his forceful personality and scorn in his gold-brown eyes. 'Let it go. She's coming and that's final. I promised her I wouldn't let you leave her behind. If you want to drug your friends to sleep and abandon them, that's up to you. I won't leave Mina.'

Alere sighed. Jarran Zah-Hill, new Heir to the Jun First throne, promised to be a difficult travelling companion. His strength of character – impressive at first – now irritated her. He seemed to feel obliged to disagree with almost everything she proposed.

He'd refused to leave the Shah's palace without Mina. He'd simply gathered her into his arms and marched out the door. Alere barely had time to transfer the precious Lei Koh-Lin journal and explanatory note to Corin's slack hands and kiss Kett's sleeping face, before Jarran disappeared down the corridor.

Now they faced the challenge of getting Mina safely onto Dalor's chuan, which bobbed out in the Kabir River's muddy waters. Dalor had probably anchored several zhang offshore to stop boarders from swamping his vessel. At least he hadn't taken the ready money on offer. He could have simply filled to the gunwales with people and left Alere and her party behind. His loyalty surprised her. Now she just needed to get his attention and get her sister, and Jarran, aboard.

Eyeing the amorphous, edgy crowd, Alere decided on a direct course of action. First step was to contact Dalor. She focussed her thoughts on the iron-yanstone chain fastened around her hips. The silver-gilt warmth of their power oozed through her body, tingling beneath her skin. The faint taste of iron and smoke teased her tongue. Gilded strength expunged doubt, worry, and the raw grief still eating at her heart; lifting and empowering, both heady and frightening. It was too tempting to stay in this state of cool, logical detachment. The emotional fallout of Gavon's death and the Wushi Games tortured her every waking moment. Only the yanstones' distancing effect helped her cope.

Alere sought Dalor's Outers and found him on the chuan. His mind was as disciplined and organised as his vessel. It was simple to insert a thought into his surface Outers without calling attention to her intrusion. Dalor believed the idea to be his own. It wasn't exactly in line with the Xintou House ethics on which she'd been raised, but she was in a hurry.

A creaking and clacking signalled the lowering of a liferaft onto the turbid waters. The crowd on the waterfront stirred in response. Alere grimaced. This could get messy.

She made for the ragged demarcation between the two groups. Using a combination of polite requests and hands resting pointedly on weapons, she managed to open a path to the wharf's edge. The ex-slaves shuffled aside with half-apprehensive, half-resentful sidelong glances. The free citizens stood their ground and muttered imprecations and rude comments about upstart peasants. Alere didn't bother to enlighten them.

What good would come from pointing out she was Jun-Heir to the second largest Jundom in Mamlakah and Jarran was Jun to the First? After all, they were in Melcor, not Mamlakah, and she was responsible for the predicament in which these displaced people found themselves. The last thing she wanted was to call attention to her identity.

All the titles in the world wouldn't protect her from their wrath.

'Gangzhi!' A youth in the free citizens cried, pointing at Alere.

She groaned. Of all the people to encounter. She'd swapped her silk robe for his rough shirt only three days before, at the Wushi Games.

'Shunu!' He pushed through the crowd, hesitated and dropped to one knee. From a sheath at his hip he drew a bronze dagger and held it ceremoniously in outstretched hands. 'My blade is yours, shunu. You are gangzhi.'

The word rustled through both groups of onlookers, uttered in tones of excitement, anger, awe and frustration. The boil of emotions fomenting just below the surface found a release.

'You!' An overweight, florid man wearing brilliant blue silks and a pompous expression pushed forward. He thrust the boy to one side.

Behind him, his thin wife tugged at his robe and begged him to come away. Her quick breaths fluttered the pink veil that covered her nose and mouth. She whispered something and pointed towards the rows of slaves, who pushed closer. The man jabbed a thick finger at Alere, his wine-scented breath tainting the air.

'This is *your* fault!' He swept an arm around the dock, managing to imply the ex-slaves were less than human and the free citizens above reproach.

His bulbous lips twisted into a sneer. 'You destroyed our society. You wrecked my business. I'm now forced to live as a peasant, with nothing but the clothes on my back.' He plucked at the silk. 'Me! Ballan Hagan. It's outrageous.'

Behind him stood his bejewelled wife and three daughters, eight heavily-armed mharebi, and five servants lugging heavy sacks, chests, and a golden jin-bird fluttering and squawking in a cage. Alere said nothing. Angry mutterings swelled all around.

'No.' The youth from the Games leapt to her defence, burning with adoring fervour. 'She freed us from the oppression of Slavemaster Hallon Nasim and his kind. She's opened our eyes to how wrong it is to enslave others and gave us the chance to be better than we were. You weren't there. You didn't feel it. Here.' He thumped his chest. 'When Gavon Abdul-kin died in the arena.'

A stab of pain at the memory stole Alere's breath. She drew on the stones to calm her guilt.

'Shut up.' Ballan pushed the boy away. 'Filthy little Selb. Slave-lover. If you love them so much, why don't you stay here and mix with them. Pretend they're equals.'

He gestured and two mharebi flanked him, hands on their kusarigama and swords. Massive and stoic, they were well-paid, unquestioning muscle who would unhesitatingly carry out their master's orders.

Alere peered over the dock's edge. Dalor's liferaft floated just below. She dropped the luggage down to the waiting crew.

She spoke to Jarran. 'Take Mina and get into the liferaft. Stay there. I'll be along in a moment.'

He sent her an ironic look. She glared back.

'Stop being so gaisi noble, Jarran,' she growled. 'On this trip I'm weishi to you. My job is to protect you and get you back to Madina safely. I've trained half my life at this. You're a baker. I *don't* need your help. Get in the raft.'

But they'd taken too long.

Ballan nodded to his men. 'Secure that liferaft. It will take me, not this chouhuo.' Two of the mharebi shuffled to the edge of the wharf and peered over.

Jarran waved the boat offshore. The crewman rowed a few boatlengths away and stayed, watching.

Jarran laid Mina carefully down behind a pile of crates lining the wharf's edge. He returned to stand at Alere's side. Unarmed, but broad-shouldered and tall, his imposing presence was enough to make the mharebi facing him draw his sword.

'Fine. But stay close to Mina,' Alere muttered. 'This could go suilie very fast.'

'Time to practice your Jun Second diplomacy skills?' Jarran murmured.

'They're a bit rusty.'

'Oh, I don't know,' he said, nodding at the steel sword sheathed at her hip. 'They look pretty sharp to me.'

'Young woman...' Ballan trundled forward again, invading her personal space, his tone condescending. 'Order that boat to return immediately. You've obviously no idea what you've done. Clearly you don't understand our ways.' He sniffed. 'It's not decent to be walking around in mens clothing and without a veil. Given you aren't from here, I'm sure you didn't understand us when you freed the slaves.' He waved a dismissive, pompous hand. 'In fact, I'm sure the Shah has come to his senses by now. Those ridiculous laws will be revoked and all you slaves will be back in your rightful places. Come, come.' He sneered. 'We—'

'Do you have a deathwish?' Alere shut her gaping mouth and found her voice. The crowd's temper crowd shifted towards ugly as the arrogant merchant's words passed from person to person.

'My dear girl.' He puffed out his rotund stomach.

'I'm not your dear anything, you zift,' she snarled, losing her temper. 'Nor am I stupid, as you apparently are.' She pointed to the former slaves, poised like a pride of hungry xiao-cats waiting for the command to kill. 'These people are *free*. Melcor is free. There will be no revoking the law. And, for all you're a complete hmar and don't deserve it, *you* are free as well – which you wouldn't be if Hallon took over as he intended. Trust me. I know what he planned for the city. Unless you've always wanted to join an army as a junren, you would *not* have liked it. Now, I suggest you use that freedom and get out of here before these people take whatever you have left as compensation for two hundred years of abuse.'

He drew himself up, his face suffusing dark red. 'How dare you speak to me that way. Do you know who I *am?*'

His ridiculous posturing disarmed anger and Alere relaxed. She surveyed the crowd. They still teetered on the edge of explosion. The situation needed to be diffused. She was wrong to let it get even this far. Kett would be disappointed she'd forgotten her training enough to let things get this out of control. She raised her hands, palms out.

'Look, shenshi, I apologise.' She moderated her tone, trying to drop the level of antagonism. 'You're right. I don't belong here and I don't want to get into anything unpleasant. I'm just going to get into this chuan and go, if that's alright with you.'

Ballan lifted his flabby chin. 'No, it is most certainly *not* alright. I've been waiting almost five hours. You have no right to get passage before me.' He sniffed. 'I am third cousin to the Shah. He relies on me and he'll hear of this, I assure you.'

Uncertain, derisive laughter rippled. It might have all settled and dissipated into nothing, but some shazi in the crowd called a jeering insult at Ballan.

Ballan threw out his chest. 'Get her out of my way,' he snapped at his mharebi. Then he stepped back, smiling smugly as his men advanced and drew weapons.

End of Chapter 1

STEEL will be released mid 2019

www.aikiflinthart.com